Thief

S. MASSERY

Cover Design by Qamber Designs

Editing by Studio ENP

Proofreading by Paige Sayer Proofreading

INTRODUCTION

Dear reader,

Thank you for joining me! If you are unfamiliar with my work, fair warning: my stories run dark (violence, explicit content, etc.). Sterling Falls is no different.
Reader discretion is advised.

This special edition of *Thief* also includes the short prequel story, *Thrill*.

xoxo, Sara

#1: THIEF
#2: FIGHTER
#3: REBEL
#4: QUEEN

THRILL

THE INVITATION

Elora Whitlock,

You are cordially invited to participate in the grand opening of Olympus.

A night of mischief and mayhem—and bloodshed.
One-on-one, no-holds-barred fights.
The winners will receive more than they bargained for.

Festivities begin at 8 o'clock. Please arrive one hour early to:
1 Falls Drive
Sterling Falls

Masks are required.

Sincerely,
Your hosts for the evening
Apollo, Ares, and Hades

P.S. Join us for a special after-party game.

CHAPTER 1

7:05PM

I tie on my mask and stride into the huge marble structure. No one stops me—the place is still quiet at this time of the evening. The real party will start later, according to the invitations sent around town, and on the fliers that seemed magically stuck to any and all surfaces.

Overnight, Sterling Falls was papered with gilded invitations. But a personalized one was dropped into my mailbox earlier the same day.

"You're late." A girl waves, drawing my eye. "This way."

I follow her past the giant staircase, through a darkened archway. She has a quick step, even though she's shorter than me by a few inches, and I increase my speed to catch up. Her dark hair swings in a braid down her back. She leads me through a huge room with balconies looking down into the center. A raised platform sits in the middle.

I can't tear my eyes off it, knowing that tonight, I'll be center stage. Something I've actively avoided for most of my life. But the mask helps. The promise of anonymity eases the worry tightening my muscles.

The girl pays no mind to it, though, and we exit into another shadowy hallway. A few sconces on the walls provide the only light.

“Nice mask,” she comments. “Very...”

“I went with plain and boring on purpose,” I inform her.

It’s not a *total* lie. It was on purpose—but because of my wallet, not my style preference. The little costume shop downtown had a decent selection of masks, ranging from simple to elaborate. The black satin matches my outfit.

It was with a bit of incredulity—paired with a *why am I doing this?*—that led me here. And an insane desire to experience something more than the life I’ve been living.

Sad, right?

She nods once. “Well, it matches your hair.”

The raven color gets me in trouble. It’s so dark it’s nearly blue in the right lighting—and isn’t in my family genetics. My parents are light-haired, and so are my grandparents.

It’s braided into a crown around my head, the ends tucked in at the base of my neck. I didn’t want any opportunity for it to be used against me.

“I’m Tem.” She offers her hand.

I shake it. Her cool, calloused palm slides against mine, and her fingers squeeze twice before I’m released.

We step outside, and the wind whips at my hair.

“And you?”

I fucking hesitate.

There’s a rumor that here, names will be shed. Everything can be left at the door—including our identities. That’s why they require the masks.

She nods like she understands. “You only get one chance. May as well think it over.”

We hike up the hill and reach a small group of masked people. From what I can tell, they're all around my age or older. I'll be nineteen next month. In another lifetime, I'd be considering starting at Sterling Falls University, or perhaps somewhere farther away.

I used to dream of leaving this town. Of going to New York City or somewhere equally giant. Here, everyone knows everyone else. Especially in the summers in West Falls, when there aren't tourists or college students to dilute the population. Being anonymous seemed... far-fetched.

We stop at the back of the pack. We're at the high point, and ten feet forward is a cliff. It drops straight down to the ocean, which batters and roars from here.

One man stands with his back to the cliff. He wears a blood-red mask and red leather jacket. His hands are tucked in the pockets of his black pants. The jacket is open over his bare chest, exposing his abs. He's tall and lean, and his dark-brown hair is pushed back from his face. I try not to gawk, because the mask can only hide so much. His full lips quirk. He eyes us, then briefly shakes his head at Tem.

"Welcome to opening night of Olympus," he says. "My brothers and I have recently acquired this land, and we're eager to put our mark on Sterling Falls. This is why you're here—we sought out thrill-seekers. And some underdogs."

His gaze finds mine.

I ignore the insult, even if it's true. I *look* like an underdog. I feel like one, too.

"The draw of Olympus is desire. What do you desire?" He holds up his hand. "Don't answer me now. Just think about it. Think about anything you want but can't have, and then consider the possibility that *we* can procure it for you."

He's offering us a dose of magic. The sort of thing that doesn't exist. There's no such thing as magic, only illusion and tricks. And the power to make someone believe your version of reality.

"How?" someone calls.

The red-masked man grins. "A favor from the gods, of course."

Goosebumps rise on my arms.

"You know the Titans. The Hell Hounds."

The two gangs have ruled Sterling Falls from the shadows, grappling for power and holding us all hostage.

I'm familiar. And judging from the rustling of movement from the men and women around me, they are familiar, too.

I avoid the gangs at all costs.

I live in Titan territory. My ex-best friend's brother is a Titan. For some, it's a way of life. But it definitely isn't *my* way of living. They don't just live in the shadows—they spread it. Drugs, guns, human trafficking. On the surface, they run ordinary businesses. Clubs and bars, casinos on the fringes of town, a freaking laundromat. Most of the cops and politicians are in the pocket of one gang or another.

"They're nothing compared to us." He straightens his jacket. "I'm Ares. One of the three hosts of Olympus. And tonight, you have the chance to fight. For glory, for a favor, or perhaps just for the bloodlust."

"And if we don't want to fight?" someone asks.

Ares shrugs, unbothered. "Then don't. Leave. Come back when we open and pay admission with the rest."

"How did you pick us?" I have to voice the question.

"You were all specifically chosen," someone says behind me.

I whirl around. A tall boy with a skull mask smirks, his blue eyes on me.

"You're a desperate girl, Elora Whitlock." His voice is low enough that only I can hear him—I hope, anyway. "You're willing to do anything it takes, and that makes you a prime candidate. Underdog or not."

I nod once and try not to let the fear in again. Fear has a way of paralyzing me—consequences of my past—and I've spent a long time harnessing it into something else.

How did they see that when my own parents have been so blind? It isn't that my folks don't care, more like they don't know a solution. Their whole lives are here. Graduate high school and go into full-time employment. Work and marry and have kids. Eventually retire. Die. And the generations will continue the pattern. We'll be lucky if no Whitlocks become entangled in Titan business.

The skull-masked man's gaze lifts to the rest of the group. "We know who you are. We picked you for a reason. And if you put on a show… the afterparty surely won't suck."

"With me," Ares says.

He leads us back into the building, newly dubbed Olympus. And now I see it: the way it resembles a pantheon from ancient Greece. Something straight out of mythology. The marble columns, the carvings in the walls. The feeling of something much more impressive than myself emanates from the place.

"Think of something to call yourselves," Ares suggests. We stop in a large training room. "Something apart from yourself. Be who you want to be tonight. A god—or goddess—amongst men."

I nod to myself.

Be who I want.

But who is that?

When I was a child, my grandmother used to say I had darkness in me. She was the superstitious type. She'd cross herself when she saw a black cat, toss salt over her left shoulder. Kept a horseshoe hung open-side-up above her front door. A random collection of old wives' tales seemed to have taken over her life.

She was old and weathered when I was young and untamed. As such, my visits with her had to be supervised by a parent, or at least someone willing to attempt to keep up with me. It didn't help when I vanished for two days in high school. She, along with everyone else, thought it wasn't sinister—just my own wildness getting the best of me.

But now her oddities come back to me. How she would laugh and cup my cheek when we were alone. *Oh, sweet girl. Your name means light, but I see unfettered darkness behind your eyes. Who made you this way?*

I don't recall seeing her much after that.

But I focus on that dark spot she must've sensed. The secret hunger for violence I've kept under lock and key.

What's the opposite of light? In this weird, twisted world Ares and his brothers have created?

Tem follows me to a shelf of bandages. She watches me wrap my knuckles, then grins. "You know what you're doing."

I shrug. I've been hanging out at the local fighting gym for ages, sneaking in lessons with the owner when he has no-shows. It hasn't been a lot, but what I do have is a lot of time under my belt. Usually with pads on my hands, absorbing punches from the taller, older boxers.

Guys with a lot more potential than *me*.

"Which one are you?" I finally ask her. Since she seems to not be going away. "Which god did you choose?"

"Artemis," she says. "Goddess of the hunt."

I hum.

"It's my real name," she confesses, stepping closer. She helps me tuck the tail of the wrap into itself, keeping it tight. "My parents must've named me this for a reason, you know?

So I may as well make the most of it. I go by Tem to seem more normal."

"Sure."

"And you? Did you decide?"

"I did." But I'm not ready to reveal my choice.

I think back to the invitation I received. One-on-one fights with no rules. Debauchery. Bloodshed.

Part of me hopes that I don't have to go against Tem. She seems nice.

She must sense my hesitation, because she glances away. "Let's warm up."

CHAPTER 2

8:20PM

The crowd is loud. The noise began almost fifteen minutes ago. The skull-masked man was Hades. Which left the third host, Apollo. He went out and made a speech on the front staircase and introduced his brothers. Hades. Ares. Him. Three powerful gods amongst men.

Well, that's the vibe, anyway.

Ares lines us up and has us pick numbers from a cup. It determines who we're fighting and when. There are eight of us here, which means four fights. Besides Tem and me, there are two other women, but they aren't separating us by gender.

This is going to be chaos.

I question my sanity when I draw a number. My fingers curl around the paper, and Ares glares down at me until I show him.

Number four.

The last fight.

"Better make it a good finale," he tells me.

I glance down the line. Tem and one other woman have drawn already. The last chooses and shows him, but I catch the two scrawled on her paper.

I swallow.

The last man to pull is a hulk. Easily double my weight, and he towers over Ares. If you put us together, I am probably eye-level with his armpit.

My stomach flips.

"Four," he declares. He grins at me. "Don't worry, sweetheart. After we give them a show, I'll put you out of your misery."

My apprehension grows. He wants to toy with his food before eating it.

Ares clears his throat. "First pair, come with me. Everyone else… behave."

Tem pats my shoulder and disappears with Ares. A man follows. The crowd cheers, and I go back to the jump rope. My mind filters through the random collection of lessons I've received over the years, but it all seems insignificant.

I wanted to be strong to protect myself on the street and so I wouldn't be a victim again.

But here, I am so totally out of my element.

Yet… I don't leave. There's still time to bail, and I don't do that. I eye my opponent across the room and try to find a weakness. He doesn't give anything away, not behind that mask, and not in his movements.

A favor.

A chance to do something with my life instead of slink home.

I enter a zone. My mind clears. The next few fights seem to fly by, and then it's just me and my opponent.

Ares enters. "Name?" he barks at the man.

He straightens and leers. "Hercules."

Ares rolls his eyes. “Great. And you?”

I throw my shoulders back. “Nyx.”

Ares gives me a wolf grin. “Nyx. Good choice. Let’s go, then.”

Down the hall, toward the large second room Tem and I went through. The one with the balconies and raised platform, and the one now packed with bodies. Masked men and women dressed in lavish finery. Their masks are outlandish, some with giant feathers, others with sequins or jewels.

I can imagine over time how they might reshape Olympus into exactly the thing they want it to be. How people will fall in line to mimic the Greek mythology theme.

I pause in the entrance as Ares joins Apollo on the platform and cast a more critical glance around the room. My skin prickles, like I have eyes on me even from the shadows. I lock on to a man up on one of the balconies. He’s still and silent, unlike everyone around him. And his gaze seems to be on me.

They announce Hercules, and the brutish man hits my shoulder on his way past. The crowd parts for him. And then my name is being announced, the booming voice of Apollo carrying over the noise.

I raise my eyebrows at the man, then break contact and stride forward.

Apollo stands beside Hercules, both eyes and the left side of his face are entirely covered by a mask that resembles tree bark. His suit jacket is open, no shirt in sight. It automatically sets him apart from the people around him.

Interesting.

He’s still speaking, his lips moving, but I can’t hear it. I’ve tunneled in on the path I need to walk and the man I’ll be fighting. I shake out my limbs.

I need this more than him.

I need this more than any of them.

A desperate girl. Hades was right about that.

"Rules?" I ask Apollo once I'm on the platform. I already know the answer, but I want the reassurance a groin shot isn't going to get me kicked out. If it comes to that.

The footing has a little give to it. I test it out, shifting my weight, and wait for his answer.

"None."

A dirty fight.

My blood sings under my skin.

Apollo hops down, and Hercules leers at me. Again.

I ball my fists and step to the side, circling him. He mirrors my movements, but it isn't long before he darts forward and tests the waters—or maybe intimidation is just his chosen strategy.

I'd go that route, too, if my opponent was a hundred pounds lighter than me. Or if I had more courage.

His reach is long—longer than I anticipated initially. I jerk back, avoiding the jaw-shattering hit, but he still catches my chin with his knuckles. My head snaps to the side, and I let the pain flow through me.

Nothing I haven't dealt with before.

He grunts and rushes me. I duck, weaving close to him and managing a quick jab to his side before I'm around him and clear.

Giant and slow.

Good.

His fall will be a thunderclap.

The platform is suddenly superimposed with a dark forest and the feel of dread. I slap my own cheek to snap myself back into it.

Gritting my teeth, I realize it's my turn to attack. I have to before he figures out he can just keep rushing me and probably get lucky. I fake a punch, then again, and whip my foot out. I catch him in the stomach.

His fingers dig into my ankle, and he meets my eyes a second before he yanks. I fall onto my back, the wind knocked out of me, and I gag on nothing. He throws himself forward.

I have just a split second to roll to the side, or else he would've crushed me.

Fucker.

I kick his thigh while we're both on the floor, then scramble to my feet. His fist catches me in the mouth. I go down to my knee again, then drive forward. My shoulder goes into his stomach, and I rapid-fire pummel his back with my fists. Kidney shots.

And then I bring my knee up, slamming it between his legs.

He lets out a hoarse *oof*. His grip on me slides away, and he falls to his knees.

I step away and watch him for a moment, then shake myself out of it. This isn't the time for chivalry. This is when I need to press it.

He gets one foot under him when I return, forcing him to lift his arms and protect his face from my hits. On his knee, he's more my height. I box him on the ear, then smash my fist into his nose. The *crunch* is satisfying, and only a moment later, blood pours down his face.

I don't stop.

I *won't* stop.

That dark thing my grandmother saw in me roars up and out. I see red.

His fist connects, but I ignore the sharp punch of pain to my side. A solid kick to his head knocks him onto his ass. I climb over him and pin his arms with my legs, straddling his chest. A grown man *should* be able to throw me off, but he can't seem to get his body to move the way it needs to. I keep punching his face until he goes limp, and only stop when someone hauls me backward.

My feet catch under me, my legs solid, and someone rips my arm into the air.

Apollo's hand holds my balled fist up.

It's only then that I realize the crowd is screaming—but not out of fear. They're wild with excitement.

"Nyx, our goddess of the night," Apollo yells.

Two men come forward and drag Hercules away. They tap his cheeks on the edge of the platform until he sits up and wipes across his mouth.

I meet his gaze and incline my chin.

He grins a pink-toothed smile at me, then lumbers to his feet. The men help him down and away, while Apollo parades me in a slow circle. He eventually releases my arm, and I take a moment to touch my own bloodied nose. My adrenaline has created a buzzing through my body, blocking out the pain that will surely hit me soon.

"You're owed a favor," he says to me.

Ares and Hades climb the steps and stop in front of me.

I lick my lips and glance around.

In that moment, I want to go again. To fight someone else.

It might've been pure luck that I succeeded against Hercules. It might be insanity to want a repeat.

Hades grabs my wrist and pushes a wad of cash into my hand. He curls my fingers around it, then lets go.

I glance down at the stack of hundred dollar bills.

Too many of them.

My favor… I might've asked for money. They could've easily *let* me ask for money.

"Well?" Ares asks. "Now or never."

"I want more."

Hades' eyes light up. As nonspecific as that is, he understands. He smiles—a true one this time. Maybe he likes being surprised. "Done."

CHAPTER 3

9:10PM

I've lost Artemis—and anyone familiar, actually.

The party spreads out from Olympus, groups of people clustered all the way up toward the cliffs. There are fairy lights staked into the ground. A bar, a keg. Two bonfires, one up close and the other a fair distance away, near the tree line. A DJ blasts music on a stage lit up with neon lights.

The huge doors into Olympus are thrown open wide, spilling more light across the wide steps.

Even though it's been a while since I'd seen a familiar face, I've been surrounded. I'm getting sick of saying thank you to the endless congratulations. From the wonder in their eyes to the hesitancy. After all, if I could drop Hercules, what else could I do?

Their trepidation doesn't make me feel any better, though.

I take another gulp of my mixed drink and drain the cup. I crush it in my hand.

"It was just so brave," a guy says to me. "I mean, I train professionally and even I would've been wetting my pants against that guy."

I force a smile. "Charming."

"I think our fighter tires of your conversation." Hades steps up beside me. "Right, Nyx?"

The guy holds up his hands in surrender. "If the lord of the underworld commands it..." He backs away before Hades can reply, and we watch him hightail it out of our sight.

"You have an effect on people," I comment.

He grins, but it doesn't touch his eyes. His mask is chilling, and his cold gaze only makes him more mysterious. He, like Apollo and Ares, isn't totally dressed up. His white collared shirt is unbuttoned at the top and tucked into his black slacks. Business casual, I suppose. Plus a skull mask.

He offers his arm, and I take it. I'm not sure why—he isn't my type. Tall, dark, and mysterious? No thanks. Besides, my hormones turned off the second the hosts claimed they were worse than the gangs.

I've avoided the Titans and the Hell Hounds for almost nineteen years—I don't need one stupid night at Olympus to become entangled in something far worse.

"I wondered if wanting more referred to your life in general, or simply this evening."

I glance up at him. We slip through the people, making our way toward the cliff.

My heart skips a beat.

"All of it," I answer slowly. "I just... Part of me wants to get out of this town and never come back. But a bigger part just wants Sterling Falls to feel like home."

Because even though my parents are never leaving this place, I've always felt like an outsider. Maybe it was trauma.

Or the dark stain on my soul that my grandmother always saw. Or...

"Judging tonight's fights, I know two things for certain. One, these events will continue. The fights, the illusions. And two, you will fight again." Hades dips his head.

"It might've just been luck."

He smiles like he has a secret. "Perhaps it was luck. Or adrenaline. Or your desperation to prove something to yourself—and everyone else."

There's that word again—*desperation*.

He could be right.

"Besides, I think you might take that cash and invest it back into yourself. Don't you think?" He stops us at the edge of the cliff.

I failed to notice how close to the drop-off we were getting. But now, I scuff my feet, and pebbles shower down the rock face. They disappear into the darkness before they hit the water. The rushing sound is louder now, the *shush* of waves rolling forward and the *crack* of them pounding the pointed cliffside. The larger waves are more spread out, leaving gaps in the break. To the left, the cliff curves back toward Olympus. It creates a little pocket of calmer water down below, protected from most of the waves coming up from the south.

"Here's a piece of your *more*, Nyx." Hades turns me.

A man comes forward. His mask is black and simple, like mine. I can't see any more of his face in the shadows. Just a strong, lean body. White shirt, the cuffs rolled back to expose his forearms. Dark pants.

"What do you—?"

"Enjoy your evening," Hades says in my ear.

He drops my arm and takes a step to the side. Then another. He watches me for a moment, then strides away.

What?

"You fought beautifully," the man says. He seems familiar, but I can't place him with most of his face covered.

I scoff at the compliment. Beautiful might be a stretch.

"Like a savage."

I step forward. "And what do you know of savagery?"

He smiles. "I know I dream of it sometimes, but it's always out of reach."

Ah. That hits too close to home. He's put a new name to that wild, off-center feeling in my chest. Not just darkness, but *savagery*, as he says. I can't decide if that's better or worse.

"You got there easily." He comes into my space. He's taller than I first thought. Taller than the three Olympus hosts.

I have to tip my head back to meet his gaze. And once he's close enough to touch, I can *see* how he's looking at me.

It's a way I don't think I've ever been looked at before, except tonight.

"How do you find it?" There's a weird pulse in my chest, separate from my heartbeat. I shouldn't have this automatic reaction to him. I've never felt that for anyone, let alone a masked man on the edge of a cliff.

He inches closer. "I do crazy things."

I understand that. *This* was my crazy thing. Sneaking out at night, breaking the law, going against my parents—none of that did it.

But the surge of blood in my veins? And the electricity I felt flood through me when Hercules bled?

"Will you do something crazy with me?" he whispers.

"Okay." No hesitation.

I've barely spoken the word when he threads his hand

with mine. His thumb brushes over mine. He pulls me around so we face the same direction, and my breath catches. I know what's going to happen a split second before we do it.

Call it intuition, or a lucky guess.

Whatever it is, there's no stopping us.

He has a tight grip on my hand, and he draws me forward. I clutch his fingers and run with him—it's do or die with the way the waves crash against the rocks—and then we jump. We travel farther than I would've by myself, and the wind shrieks past my ears. Or maybe it's my own scream pouring out of me. My hair rips loose from the crown of braids and whips my face.

I only have a second to inhale sharply and hold it, then I'm engulfed by icy water. I panic and thrash, fighting gravity, until I can regain control over myself.

His hand never releases mine, but he doesn't let me shoot back up. He squeezes twice.

Under the water, I open my eyes and look over at him. The saltwater stings my eyes, and he's rather blurry. We're pushed backward as a wave rolls over us, then out to sea with its withdrawal. At least we're momentarily safe from being slammed against the rock.

My heartbeat is the only thing I can hear.

He grins in the dark water. The faintest illumination of the moon finds us and reflects off his teeth. And then he nods—at least, I think he does.

We kick to the surface, moving farther out into the ocean. Cool air hits my face, and I gulp in a lungful of air. My body quakes with leftover adrenaline and a wicked chill. My mask is soaked, plastered to my face, and I rip it down. It hangs around my neck, loose, and I wipe the water from my eyes.

He mirrors my movement with one hand, dropping his mask and shaking his head. Water droplets fly everywhere.

I splash at him. "What the fuck was that?"

He grins, unfazed. "Elora Whitlock. This is a surprise."

I kick to remain above the water and eye him. The recognition comes quickly, as fast as the knowledge that he was going to drag me over the edge.

"Saint Hart," I answer. I tug my hand from his grip and put more space between us.

My face heats.

Of course we went to school together. Sterling Falls Academy. Of course he had been one of those mysterious, loner artistic kids from East Falls, the sort that every girl secretly has a crush on. I was no exception to that.

I just got fixated on him, and not in a healthy way.

He's from the wrong side of the tracks—literally, in my case. West and East never mingled. We have our forests, and they have their cliffs. Like the one we just took a plunge off of.

It occurs to me that this might've been another test from Hades. A way to poke and prod at my mettle or to hunt for weaknesses. It could also be a message. *We know you.* I don't like that, either.

We all have secrets, and Hades just informed me that he knows mine.

Saint swims closer to me. "What are you afraid of? Me?"

I shove at his shoulder. "The only reason I'm not more pissed at you is because I left my phone in my car." With the cash Hades gave me. The car keys are stashed behind one of the tires. Not my finest trick, but better than carrying everything all night.

Besides, it's false bravado.

I'm not afraid but alarmed.

"You weren't one of the fighters." I'm guessing, because I don't really know.

"I wasn't." He grips my waist and hauls me against him.

My hands automatically find his shoulders, and our legs tangle. Another wave looms, and he presses his lips to mine just as it breaks over our heads. My lungs immediately ache.

For a moment, I feel nothing but the heat at my lips and the way we're being carried swiftly sideways. We surge up, breaking the surface, and Saint's kiss turns rougher. I inhale sharply, and his tongue slides along the seam of my lips. I open for him. He tastes like saltwater. When his teeth tug at my lower lip, I groan.

The water doesn't feel so cold now. My blood is practically boiling.

He releases me. "Let's go."

I raise my eyebrows. "Huh?"

He swims away.

It takes me a second to process, then I follow after him. I'm not the fastest swimmer, and it seems to take ages to fight the current. We go around the point of the cliff and into that little inlet. It's darker here, and I resist the urge to squeak in fear.

I breathe through it instead.

Saint glances back at me and treads water.

I catch up eventually, the calmer water easier to navigate, and he points.

There's a metal ladder bolted to the cliff face. Glow sticks are strung to the bottom of it, and then every few feet onward. It goes... all the way to the top.

Fucking hell.

"You've got to be kidding me."

He smirks. "I thought you liked this sort of thing."

Adrenaline is the only thing keeping me from backing

away. The fight took a lot of energy, and I'm riding a high right now. The alcohol helped a little, too. Later, I'm sure I'll crash and burn. But now isn't the time for that.

I eye Saint. He seems... different. In high school, I wouldn't have pegged him as an adrenaline junkie—if I can even define this as *that*. I wouldn't have thought I'd end up here, either. I let myself drift closer to him and try to picture how the hell this is going to work.

We're lifted by another smaller wave, and the water against the rock rises, as well. It doesn't matter. The ladder keeps going down, into the dark depths beneath us.

"Ready?"

I make a face. "Not really."

He shrugs. "It's either this or swim three miles north..."

Great.

"I wish I knew that before we jumped," I mutter. But I get into position anyway, lining myself up with the ladder. There's no chance in hell I'm letting Saint abandon me here.

"Go," he urges.

The swell picks me up. The sound of rushing water surrounds me. Four feet away, then two. My feet touch the rock, and I stretch up, gripping the metal. White-capped water tugs at me, but I drag myself up a few rungs.

I glance back at Saint, who's barely visible bobbing in the shadows.

He comes in as soon as I'm secure, grabbing a rung and hauling himself up. The foamy water sprays my legs again, and I shiver. We're soaking wet, and the night air is frigid.

He climbs up beside me. "That was fun."

I shake my head and ascend ahead of him. It wasn't *fun*—it was reckless. And each step I take pulls at my already sore body.

I make it to the top and roll over the ledge, flopping on

my back. My chest heaves, and my muscles tremble. Saint falls to the grass beside me a moment later, and we both stare at the clear sky.

"Was that enough of a thrill?" I ask him eventually.

He lets out a loud exhale. "Jumping wasn't nearly as much as kissing you." He twists onto his side and rises on an elbow so he can see my face. "Or seeing you fight."

I glance away.

He reaches out carefully and touches my lower lip. It hurts from being split open earlier. He shows me the red on the pad of his finger. "Tasted a bit of that. I want to taste it again."

I run my finger up his arm. "Do it, then."

Saint doesn't need more prompting. His hand comes up behind my neck and lifts me toward him. Our lips meet.

I taste the blood now, too, and my body tingles. His thumb rubs a circle just under my ear. I nip his lower lip, sharp enough to elicit a groan from his throat. Hard enough to make him bleed, too.

He presses harder into the kiss, lowering me back to the grass. His tongue prods the split in my lip. The metallic taste is on both our lips, mixed with saltwater.

We shouldn't be doing this.

I shouldn't be kissing a stranger—even if I think I know him.

I push him back slightly, and he easily flops onto his back beside me again. Our breathing is ragged.

He exhales. "Let's find clothes, shall we?"

He doesn't wait for my answer. Instead, he hops up. He grips my hands and pulls me to my feet, eyeing me with a weird expression. He doesn't release one of my hands, either.

I'm freaked out by his casualness. By his willingness to stay with me.

We slip back into Olympus unseen and go into the training room. There isn't much here, though, and I turn back to face him.

Just in time for his wet shirt to smack me in the face.

I grab it and gape. Who knew Saint Hart was hiding washboard abs all these years? I mean, *damn*. And, even more shocking, he's covered in tattoos. His chest, all the way down into the waistband of his pants. The inked sleeves stop mid-forearm.

"You might not've been such a loner if you took your shirt off more," I breathe.

He laughs. He tears the mask from his neck and drops it to the floor, then kicks off his shoes. His hands go to the button of his pants. "Trick or treat?"

I roll my eyes, but on the inside? Slightly dying of mortification. "Just because it's Halloween doesn't mean you have to be corny."

He grins. "Take off your clothes, Elora."

"Nyx," I automatically correct.

"Goddess of the night." His gaze sweeps up and down me. "Why did you pick that?"

I shrug, unwilling to get into the details. "Maybe I'll tell you one day."

He pushes his jeans down and steps out of them. His black boxers are stuck to his legs. My cheeks heat, but I don't look away from him. We're out of reach of each other, but I feel like his gaze is a touch all its own.

"What do you want, *Nyx*?" Saint circles around me.

I shiver.

What do I want?

I told Hades I wanted *more*.

But more… what?

The lights go out, plunging us into darkness.

And, inexplicably, here is where I find my courage. But it feels right, too. Everything is clicking into place. The fight, the bruises that pulse with pain, the water droplets on my skin. The cold night air and the darkness and all my fear and hope… it all binds together.

"I want you."

CHAPTER 4

9:45PM

Rebirth.

That's what I imagine is happening to me.

Saint is a lucky coin toss. A shot in the dark from Hades, a *more* he might not have even known I needed. A favor from the gods, as they said. I didn't know what I was going to get when I asked for more.

Maybe I would've said, if pressed, *more nights like this*.

I strip off my shirt and sports bra. My boldness might be my undoing, but I toss the wet fabric away from me and smile at the *smack* of it hitting the tile. I shove my leggings off and kick them away, too, then spin toward where Saint last was.

I reach out and step forward, my fingers leading the way.

They touch cool, wet skin. I shiver. The darkness seems to heighten my other senses. Our breathing, my pounding heart. The chill in the air.

A hand runs along my forearm, tracing up to my shoulder. It moves farther back, curling around my neck.

We don't speak, but his ragged breathing belies his excitement. Mine mirrors his, I'm sure. He pulls me closer to him, and my arm folds in. My bare chest brushes his, and he inhales sharply. I lean forward and kiss his chest, then up. His collarbone. His throat. His pulse hammers just under the surface, and I dart my tongue out to taste the mix of salt-water and sweat. I explore him with my touch, trying to get a better sense of him.

His hand remains curled at the back of my neck, and his other glides down my side. I reach his jaw. He lets out a quiet groan when I suck his earlobe into my mouth and bite. He shifts his hips forward, and his hard length presses into my hip.

He grips my hair suddenly and pulls, directing my mouth to his.

Our lips touch again, and I'm a goner.

There's an ache in my chest that hasn't been there all day. It's akin to the anxiety I would feel walking into school every morning, but now I long for something that's right in front of me.

He nips my lower lip, reopening the cut, but the taste of blood only spurs him on. We clash frantically. He lowers me down until my back hits the mat. I have an out-of-body experience where I swear I can see us, like a bird's-eye view, before I snap back into myself. I never would've guessed I'd be here tonight, with Saint, experiencing... *this*.

I have a confession to make.

I've lusted over Saint for too many years. All through school. I haven't seen him since we graduated. Haven't seen... anyone, really. Elora Whitlock likes it that way.

But Nyx has a different opinion.

Saint shifts again and nudges my legs open. His lips leave mine, and he moves down my body. He presses reverent kisses to my skin. He cups my breast, and I arch off the floor. He brushes his thumb over my nipple. I huff, trying to hold on to my composure. And then his mouth... his tongue. His *teeth*. Lightning strikes in my mind, obliterating everything else.

He travels farther down, pausing at my panties. I'd forgotten about them.

I stare up, unable to see even an inch in front of my face.

The *rip* startles me.

His breath against my core is another surprise.

Then it isn't just his breath but his tongue, and I jolt. My thighs tense, and he grips my hips to keep me in place. I'm not allowed to retreat, although every move has me fighting the urge to say something.

Whether to beg him to continue or stop, I haven't decided.

He latches on to my clit and sucks.

I buck against his face and tip my head back. My mouth opens in a silent moan, and I lose it when he thrusts two fingers inside me. I groan through my orgasm, clenching around him.

Fuck. I'd give anything to see his face right now.

And then he's shifting, climbing back up my body, and he whispers, "You taste fucking amazing."

Well, damn, if that's not the hottest thing to come out of his mouth.

And then he nudges my legs wider and aligns himself. I grasp his biceps.

He pauses, waiting. His muscles tremble slightly.

Oh. He's bare. I might be insane, but I don't give a shit. This thing between us is raw, so why can't the sex be raw, too? And perhaps in the most heroic move, he's waiting for permission.

"Saint," I say as evenly as possible. Still, my voice is breathy. "If you don't fuck me right now..."

"Thank fuck." He slams into me.

He fills me completely, larger than I anticipated, and I dig my nails into his arms. With the spike of pleasure is a bite of pain. He stills for a moment, then slowly withdraws. He thrusts back into me just as hard. My body slides up the mat.

I find his face and pull him down to kiss him again.

He fucks me like he wants to torture me. Slow and steady. I rise to meet him. Lock my ankles behind his ass. His tongue sweeps into my mouth, tasting me. I taste... *myself*. I'm on his lips and tongue.

I bite his lip hard enough to draw blood.

Fair is fair.

It unlocks something in him.

Some of that savagery he was talking about earlier.

It's okay—on another level, I know I want this however he gives it to me. It's exhilarating to be all-in without knowing the destination. To be so utterly lost without a care.

He slips his hand between us and rubs my clit. The combination is too much, and I gasp when another climax hits me. He hisses a groan in my ear, his face beside mine, until my limbs relax.

And then he pulls out of me abruptly and sits back. He pulls me with him. It takes a moment to orient myself again in the darkness, and I curl my legs.

"Tap if you've had enough," he warns. He sounds higher than me now.

"What—"

The head of his cock touches my lips.

Ah.

Another pulse hits my core, and I open my mouth. He's

still tracing my lips, taking his time. I dart my tongue out, tasting him. Fuck, he's huge.

"You're going to swallow every last drop," he groans.

I raise my hands and tentatively hold on to his thighs just as he pushes into my mouth. I open wide and let him infiltrate me, suppressing my gag reflex. He pulls out slowly, then back in. So deep he hits the back of my throat.

I suck around him, my tongue swirling. He hisses out a breath. I don't know why that sound undoes me, but it unleashes something wilder in me. I reach up and cup his balls.

His fingers slide into my wet hair, holding my head still.

"My control is gone."

I squeeze his leg with my free hand. *Just do it*, I'd say, if my mouth wasn't full of him.

I'm too turned on by this to care that before today, we haven't spoken more than a handful of words. And even today, we haven't said anything all that meaningful.

Does it matter?

It's a night.

It's a thrill.

He fucks my mouth until I can't breathe, and tears stream down my cheeks. I hold his legs and refuse to tap out, high on the adrenaline rush. I suck blindly and focus on not gagging, and then he stills. His fingers tighten in my hair. His cock jerks, and his seed spills down my throat. I swallow around him, and when he retreats, I lick my lips.

This is probably one of the wildest things I've done.

The whole night, but this tops it.

"Is your phone in here?" His voice is low.

"No."

He grunts.

The lights above us buzz, then slowly flicker back on.

Weird freaking timing, if you ask me, but I don't comment on it. It could be... I don't know. Faulty wiring in this old building? The grand opening of Olympus is bound to have some kinks that need to be worked out.

I stand and rub the back of my hand across my mouth. Saint climbs to his feet, too, and my gaze automatically drops to his cock.

Yep, about as big as my imagination warranted. My cheeks heat.

He smirks and saunters forward, brushing a lock of my hair away from my face. It's still wet, half-contained in the slipping braids, but he tucks the piece behind my ear anyway.

"Was this..." I clear my throat and glance away. "Was this orchestrated?"

He frowns. "No, Elora."

I nod slowly, unsure if I believe him. I *want* to think this was happy circumstance, fate that Hades told me to enjoy my night as Saint approached. But the cynical side of me knows better.

"Clothes," I mutter. "I really need something other than a wet sports bra."

He nods and glances around. My eyes keep going back to him and the tattoos all across his skin. I want to comment on it, question it, but I keep my lips sealed.

And then he flinches.

I follow his gaze to the door.

It's closed, although I can't remember if we had left it that way, and someone's scrawled a message in dripping red paint. I venture closer, stopping just in front of it.

"Was this here? Did we miss it?" I touch the paint, and my fingers come away red. I jerk back.

Saint grabs my hand and guides me away.

They wrote *my name* on the door. Elora—Nyx. Not this person I've been trying to turn into tonight.

I'm yanked right back into my old self, and there's nothing I can do about it.

The message, as short as it is, feels threatening.

You're done, Elora.

"You've always been a fighter," Saint says in my ear. "That? That's someone trying to fuck with you. Don't let them succeed."

Unbelievable.

"I live with my mom." My voice is wooden. "I've been working, trying to crawl out of the debt her boyfriend put us in before he ditched us. Credit card interest is a real bitch. I have no plans on going to college or getting out of this shit town. This is the first thing that I've—"

"Stop." It comes out strangled. "Jesus, Elora. You've been carrying that alone?"

I nod and brush my fingers off on my thigh, then step away. I can't look at it anymore. And I need fucking clothes.

And, miraculously, we find some. A duffle bag left in one of the corners, presumably by one of the fighters. Saint digs through and hands me a black hoodie. It's huge on me, hitting mid-thigh, so it'll do.

He finds a pair of black briefs and tosses those to me, too.

I frown. "Are these clean?"

He chuckles. "They were folded, so... probably?"

I shake my head and pull them on. It's a better option than wandering around in just a t-shirt.

Saint pulls a t-shirt over his head and gray joggers. I eye him and ignore the awkwardness. It's probably just me, right? I don't know why I admitted those things to him. And

I have to resist the urge to turn around and look at the door again.

"Saint..." I bite the inside of my cheek.

He glances at me.

"Was someone in here with us? Did they write that while we...?"

"I don't know." He straightens, alarm flashing in his eyes. He takes a harder look around the room, but nothing seems amiss to me. "Maybe."

A shiver racks up my spine. "We should get out of here."

CHAPTER 5

10:50PM

We searched Olympus for any sign of red paint, or someone who might have any type of grudge against me, but there's nothing. No other messages, either. Nothing strange at all—well, if you don't take into account the fact that we're approaching midnight on Halloween.

"Did you get the additional invite?" Saint asks me.

We leave the building and head across the lawn, toward the forest. There's a huge bonfire burning near the tree line like a homing beacon.

"The one that said there would be a game after the party? It was just a handwritten P.S. on my invitation." I'm no longer cold, and the aches and pains have temporarily receded. The bruises and split lip that throbbed earlier have faded into the background, too.

"What do you think it is?"

That's a great question. "I don't know."

He takes my hand and squeezes it. "Whatever it is, maybe we should stick together."

I eye him. "Why?"

"What if there's a prize?" Saint winks. "We could split it."

We reach the fire, and I'm saved from answering him when someone approaches us. Hercules. He's taller even than Saint, and that truly puts it into perspective.

"Good fight, Nyx." He offers his hand.

I release Saint to shake it, and the huge man pulls me forward.

"Don't think you'll be so lucky next time."

I frown. "What makes you think there will be a next time? Who would want to see me beat you twice?"

Hercules lets go of me like my skin burns, giving me an annoyed look before stalking away. I watch him head back to a group of girls who seem happy he's returning. At least someone wants to talk to him.

Saint chuckles. "You know how to offend."

I shrug. "I don't like being manhandled."

"Hmm. Seemed you liked it just fine a little while ago..."

I glance away, my face on fire. It just makes him laugh louder.

Tem stands near Apollo, their masks still in place, and the night snaps back into my thick skull. I touch my bare cheeks. *Damn it.* So much for anonymity. This is a small town. Any of them could recognize me and bring it back to my family—or worse, the Titans.

What would they do if they knew a fighter had been sitting under their noses this whole time?

Saint's face is revealed, too.

I curse under my breath and turn back for Olympus. "Saint. I need my mask. Right now, before someone sees me—"

"Hey." He grabs my hand and tugs me to a halt. "Slow down."

I shove at him. "I can't just walk around and let everyone know who I am. Do you know what that would do to my mother if it got back to her? Let me go." I don't mention my father—or worse, Mom's boyfriend who would love another opportunity to use us for money.

"Elora—"

I jerk away from him and run back to Olympus.

This fear is new. It rises over my head, quickly spiraling out of my control. The worst part is, I *know* I'm being irrational. That there's probably a slim chance of anyone caring that I'm here. But I care. Isn't that enough?

We left our masks and wet clothes in the training room.

I race down the now-familiar halls and step inside. I snatch my mask off the floor and grab Saint's after a moment of hesitation.

The door I just came through slams shut.

I flinch, but I'm alone.

The lights flicker.

I rush to the door and yank on it, but it doesn't budge.

A chill sweeps through me. I pull on it again, but the knob doesn't even turn. The door rattles in place.

Trapped. Shit.

"Hello?" I bang on the door. "Is someone out there?"

Nothing.

The lights flicker again, then go out.

I press my hands to wood. It's still tacky with wet paint, but I ignore that to pound on it. "Let me out!"

A low laugh comes from somewhere behind me.

My throat closes.

I'm not alone.

It could be whoever painted the threatening message. Someone who never left Olympus and evaded Saint and me.

The lights come back on, and I blink at the two people in front of me. A girl and a guy. They're in the center of the room, looking just as confused as me.

No one I know, though.

I tie my mask back on and straighten. "What are you doing in here?"

The girl flinches. "We just did as we were told," she says. "We were told to find you."

I narrow my eyes. "How did you get in, though? I've been in front of the door the whole time."

The guy steps in front of her. "Let's go easy on the accusations, huh? How about you? Why are you here?"

I scoff. "I came to get my damn mask—not that it's any of your business."

An alarm goes off. Not a loud one, but all of us jump nonetheless.

There's a phone between the guy and girl and me, on the floor, and it's ringing.

"Are you going to answer that?" the girl asks.

I squint, then leave my position at the door and swipe to accept the call from a blocked number. I put it on speaker.

"Hello?"

"*Someone close to you is missing,*" an automated voice says. "*You have until midnight to find them, or you might never find them again.*"

A hissing sound comes from above us.

White smoke descends.

I lift the front of my hoodie, covering my nose and mouth. I don't know what it is—maybe just dramatic effect or a drug of some sort—and I really don't need to find out. I take a deep breath and hold it before the smoke reaches us.

The girl immediately screams, and she runs past me for the door. The room fills with the white smoke—it's more like fog, curling around us. My lungs ache with holding my breath, but I refuse to breathe it in.

"It's just meant to scare us," the guy says faintly. "It's okay, Claire."

The door swings open, and the girl practically falls out into the hall.

I follow, stashing the phone and ducking out into the fresh air. I hurry well away before I inhale.

The guy is slower, and his steps thunder on the marble. He reaches toward the wall, staggering forward.

"What the hell is this?" the girl screams.

She grabs the guy's hand and tries to drag him forward, but he's struggling. His balance seems shot. She swats at something in the air. He falls face forward and hits the floor like a felled tree.

Well, fuck.

"Come on!" I pull her with me through the main room. None of it feels safe, so I keep going until we're outside.

She immediately jerks away from me. "Why did you do that?"

I wince. "Because you were being an idiot."

"I didn't want to leave him—"

"Then you'd be in the same condition." I cross my arms. "I mean, sure, if you don't care about the game? Or whoever *close* to you is missing?"

"Get fucked," she hisses. "God, it was probably part of it. You don't have to be such a spoilsport." She glances around, seems to pick a direction, and rushes away from me.

You know what?

Good riddance.

I take a look around, myself. The bonfire near the forest is still burning, but now there isn't anyone around it.

Someone close to me is missing.

I almost laugh. No one is close to me.

But then Saint fills my head, and I grit my teeth. Was that Hades' intention? Not part of my favor—just setting me up for this game? What's the point of participating if I'm not close to anyone? If I can't have a little fear with my pleasure?

Or you'll never see them again.

Fucking hell.

Olympus is deserted. The music has stopped, and only the faint whistling of the wind registers. No one's yelling or searching. Not even that girl who left my side.

It's just me.

CHAPTER 6

11:15PM

It's like everyone just... vanished. I circle the huge building, then pick my way back to the fire. Empty cups litter the grass.

"Fucking creepy." I kick one of the cups and send it flying toward the fire. "Some game. No rules. No direction. Just send us off—"

"Are you talking to yourself?"

I whirl around.

Artemis comes up beside me and stares into the fire. "I don't blame you. Those fucking geniuses have created a hell of a puzzle."

"Are you playing?"

She laughs softly. "Everyone is playing, Nyx. But time is running out."

I stare.

"Have you thought about the forest?"

My gaze moves past her, to the giant wall of shadows. In truth? Nope, it didn't cross my mind. But now that she says that... of course they're in the forest. A creepy, dark place on Halloween night.

"How the hell am I supposed to find him in there?"

She grins. "I don't know, but I'm curious to see."

My stomach flips.

"Okay." I've just got to do it. I'm not *afraid*, exactly. More... averse to darkness. Except when Saint was touching me only an hour ago. "Where is everyone else?"

"Some went north, along the cliffs."

"And the rest?"

She motions to the trees.

Right.

"Come on. I'm looking for my brother—so we can search together. Maybe one of us will get lucky." She nudges me.

I nod along. I don't really know her, but some sort of friend to lean on might make it easier. We head to the tree line, and the farther we get from the fire, the colder I get. My hair is still damp from the swim, and my bare legs aren't cutting it anymore. Not to mention my wet shoes.

Ignore it, I tell myself.

There's a narrow trail that disappears into the woods. She goes first, and I take a deep breath before letting the shadows swallow me whole.

Immediately, I'm assaulted by the smell of smoke. I cover my nose and mouth with my sleeve, fighting a cough. Tem seems unaffected, continuing forward like nothing is wrong.

My imagination.

No—worse. Memories.

My heart races, and my body instantly goes clammy.

I fall to my knees and put my head down, trying to regain control over myself.

This is ridiculous. He's *gone*. Banished from my mind.

Why does the smell of smoke, walking through a forest, drag everything back up?

Those days were at the forefront of my mind earlier, too. When I was fighting Hercules.

No one will find you, he whispers. *It's okay. It'll just be you and me.*

I fought. I wasn't successful.

I was a kid. A teenager, but still a child in society's eyes.

My mouth opens and closes, but no sound comes out. A silent scream echoes in my head.

I was taken from school by my classmate's father. A classmate who was a friend… until I was found in the woods two days after I went missing. My accusation was apparently unfounded, because the person who took me dosed me with a hallucinogenic.

My testimony was unreliable.

The person I accused had an alibi.

"Get up," I mumble to myself.

I'm stronger than my past. I just beat a man who calls himself fucking *Hercules* and jumped off a cliff with an almost-stranger. I am *Nyx*. Not Elora. Not the broken girl who's been trying to escape.

This is a life I can take hold of once and for all.

I rub my eyes through the holes in the mask, my fingers coming away wet with tears, and push myself to my feet.

When I regain my composure and look around, I'm alone.

Artemis is gone—but maybe she was never there to begin with. I sway as the trees seem to move.

Maybe the smoke did affect me belatedly.

Maybe I *am* hallucinating.

I follow the path onward, determined to at least find *someone*. Saint, if I'm lucky. Another fighter or player in this game would do, too. Another human so I know I'm not totally insane.

There are strung lights in the trees. They lend a little illumination, and I stumble along. The aches in my muscles have returned sharply, and I pause to catch my breath. There's more light up ahead.

Butterflies float over my head, landing on my shoulders and arms. I brush them off, out of my hair. This path is never-ending.

"Nyx," someone calls.

I spin, but there's no one there. The ground tilts, then rights.

The light guides me to an old cabin. It seems deserted out here in the middle of nowhere, but I don't trust my eyes. The porch is dark—the light I saw comes from the two side windows. There are curtains across the glass, though, that mask what's inside.

I climb the steps and go for the door. The knob turns easily, the door swinging inward. I step inside, raising my hand to block the light bulb's harsh glare. The walls shake. There's a hole in the middle of the floor that widens. The floorboards crumble, the yawning pit races toward me.

But there, against the far wall, is Saint.

He wears a different mask. This one is white, and it covers most of his face. Just his strong jawline on one side is visible, and half his mouth.

"What are you doing?" I grab on to the doorframe and pitch myself backward to avoid falling.

The corner of Saint's lip tilts up. "What are *you* doing, Elora?"

It isn't Saint's voice.

My body quakes against my will, and I lose my hold on

the door. I fall backward. He strides across the dark hole in the floor and crouches beside me.

"I've been waiting for you," he says. "Didn't think you'd make it."

I scramble backward and roll off the porch. I hit the ground hard, my breath forced out for a moment. Panic constricts my throat.

The voice is too familiar. A thing straight from my nightmares.

"What are you doing here?" I choke out.

He follows me slowly, even as I scoot farther away. I should just get up and *run*, but my brain isn't connecting to my muscles anymore. It's like I'm on autopilot trying to get away from him, but escape isn't registering.

Fighting isn't, either.

"I saw you fight. I didn't realize how skilled you were."

I say nothing. I can't think of a single clever thing.

His mouth pulls down. "And then I saw you with *him*."

Saint.

"Reckless girl. You're *mine*, and you let him do unspeakable things to you."

"So..." I wet my lips and ignore the possessiveness. "You drugged me."

Again.

"I like playing games with you." He steps lightly on my ankle, and I freeze. "The smoke, the hallucinations."

I shudder and close my eyes. The smoke was him. The paint was him, too. "I don't want to hear any more."

"It wasn't part of their game. But we're not in their area anymore—we're in Hell Hound domain. They won't come looking for you."

Part of me hopes that none of this is real.

That the hosts of Olympus have concocted a night made up of our worst fears.

Maybe Saint is experiencing the worst trauma of his life, too, in another part of the forest. Not what I should be wishing for—but the alternative is that the man who kidnapped me when I was fourteen is now standing above me.

"What was the smoke?" I ask.

"A water-soluble drug in a fog machine." The bastard is smug. His foot lifts off my ankle, and he crouches beside me. "What do you see?"

Not as much as you'd like.

"Butterflies," I lie.

He pauses, then nods. "Always were a romantic, Elora."

I reach out quickly and knock his mask off. It hits the ground and reveals the *face* from my nightmares. The paralyzing fear comes roaring back.

"You shouldn't have done that," he scolds.

He's right—I shouldn't have. Because now I can't move. My muscles have frozen.

"Why did you come to Olympus?"

He tilts his head. "Luck. And it only took a little while to get my hands on what I needed. I missed some of the party, but what could I do? I haven't seen you in years, and it brought back memories." He traces the scar on my leg. "Did this hurt?"

A broken leg in eighth grade.

"Yes," I whisper.

He nods to himself. "It has to be done again, I'm afraid. To keep you from running."

"I won't—"

"You ran before," he snaps. "I won't let you get away."

I shudder. His obsession is mad.

His hands on my leg, though, makes me want to scream. One above the scar, the other below. He's going to break my leg.

But I'm not the broken girl he knew. I've become someone else.

Tonight is not the night to mess with me.

Rebirth.

Hadn't I thought that already? Before Saint buried himself between my legs? More than that, though: the whole damn night has altered me.

It took me from one version of myself right up to the edge of a new beginning.

This is my trial by fire. Maybe not the intended path, but the necessary one. Nothing deadly was ever created without pain.

CHAPTER 7

SAINT

12:00AM

Time is running out.

I run through the woods, my phone's flashlight glancing off trees. There are smears of red paint on the bark that guide me along. Fucking Halloween. Everything seemed like a macabre illusion until Hades shattered it.

It took us too long to realize Elora was missing.

Hades announced the rules to his game shortly after she left to get our masks. The night was meant to be a scavenger hunt. There were tokens to collect around the sprawling property. Locked doors were to remain locked.

But then the couple was found near the training room. The girl had Elora's mask in her hand and babbled nonsense about smoke-filled rooms and giant snakes. Her pupils were blown out, the girl high out of her mind. And the guy beside her was unconscious.

I think about what I know of Elora. She was a pretty, quiet girl with few friends at school. Kept to herself. Rarely spoke. I saw a likeness in her that immediately drew me to her. But my family…

Stupid.

My younger brother joined the Hell Hounds just before I graduated, and I would've joined him if my elder brother hadn't put me to work in his tattoo shop. *Idle hands* and all that. He was able to get through to me in a way neither of us could reach my younger sibling.

Elora lived in Titan territory. Even crossing through the neutral college district to get to school gave my mother more gray hair than any gang dispute in our neighborhood. Going further into what the Hell Hounds would call enemy territory would have risked everything for them.

When I saw her fight, though… damn.

Somehow, even with the mask and the name, I knew it was her.

She still had that magnetic force about her.

But now she's gone, leaving a trail of red paint in her wake, and my desperation to find her is unfamiliar. Tonight is the first night we've spoken outside of school—and both of us graduated last year. I shouldn't be so attached.

I am, though.

It's undeniable.

This is our moment. Like fate just plucked us both from the sea and put us together.

A scream shatters the forest's quiet, and I swear under my breath.

I run faster, pushing my body to my limits. It took too long to make it to this point.

Now, a light through a window glows between the trees. Someone chases after me, but I'm too fast. Adrenaline and fear urge me on, and I crash through the brush. There's no path, and then I'm suddenly back on one. Only a few long strides farther, I burst out into a small clearing surrounding a cabin.

I skid to a halt.

Elora's on top of a man, pummeling him. She's screaming incoherently.

Listen, I'm all for a fight—but the guy's face is pulp. And somehow, I don't think she wants murder on her conscience.

I rush forward and grab her under her armpits, locking my arms around her chest and yanking up and back. Similar to the move Apollo used to get her off Hercules.

Then, it was easy to tell that she had blown past her limit. She wasn't fighting an opponent, she was fighting a nightmare.

And something tells me that nightmare is on the ground in front of us.

"Shh," I say in her ear. "It's okay, I've got you. You're safe."

"S-Saint?" She goes limp in my grip, and I drag her farther away from whoever the fuck that is. "How'd you find me?"

I shake my head and bite my tongue. She probably doesn't want to hear that it was pure luck.

The lump of flesh on the ground groans.

"Can you stand?" I ask her.

She puts her feet under her, and I slowly release her. She stays where she is, a vacant look in her eyes. I step forward and peer down. The man makes another low noise. Elora did a number on him. His nose is crooked. Cheekbone could be broken, at an angle and already swelling under the layer of blood. His eyes are swollen into slits.

I nudge him with my foot.

"He was the one who abducted me," she says. "When I was fourteen."

Anger surges through me. If she hadn't beat me to it, I would've put him in a similar state. I ball my fists and take a deep breath. We can't... we can't leave him here.

"He drugged me." Her voice is fainter. "I don't know what's real."

I go back to her.

"Stupid bitch," the man moans. He comes back to life, pushing himself up into a sitting position. "You're not getting away with this."

Another person steps into the clearing.

Hades.

His mask is off, and I jolt with recognition. He meets my gaze, and I press my lips together. This is probably a rare occurrence, to catch him like this.

"You violated Olympus." His voice is ice. "Drugged my guests." His gaze flicks to Elora, now under my arm again, and back to the man. "Hurt my fighter."

"You can't do anything." He chuckles and stands. It takes him forever to regain his feet. The man should be unconscious after what she did, but he... he doesn't seem fazed. I spot the white mask a few feet away.

He was at the fight.

Watching her, no doubt.

How deep does his obsession run?

"I'll be taking the girl." He leers. Even his teeth are stained with blood. "This is Hell Hound territory, boys. So you can kiss my—"

Crack.

Elora doesn't flinch, but I do. Hades pauses with his gun extended and smirks at me. Then he tucks it away, and the man falls backward. The hole in his head matches the rest of him.

"Hades—" Elora starts.

"Save it." He stops in front of us and touches under her chin, lifting her face. She meets his eyes. "The big bad wolf of your nightmares is dead."

She winces.

"When you've recovered from whatever he dosed you with, come back to Olympus. I have a proposition."

"Okay," she breathes.

"Until then... I expect Saint will take it from here?"

I straighten and nod. My protective instincts rear up again, and I sweep Elora into my arms. Her red-stained, bruised hands curl in her lap. Hands that save her from whatever he had planned.

"I'm taking you home," I say in her ear. "Okay?"

CHAPTER 8

3:00AM

The witching hour. My eyes stay on the digital clock next to my head.

Apollo had shined a small penlight into my eyes and declared me lucky. The two who were in the room with me ended up at the hospital—I just inhaled a small amount, and my trip should be a short one.

For the last three hours, I've willed myself to return to normal while Saint tended to my split knuckles and lip. The bruises all over my body aren't just from the fight, but...

A tear slips out, rushing down my temple and into my hair.

"He's gone," Saint repeats. "Permanently."

It's been a mantra.

I squeeze my eyes shut. "No one believed me."

"I believe you."

I know. It's on the tip of my tongue, but the words won't come out. A lump forms in my throat. Saint had carried me out of the woods and put me in the passenger seat of his car.

It's hard to explain the hallucinations I was having. Just little changes to my peripherals. Men in white masks glaring at me. Spiders scurrying across the grass. Shadows where there shouldn't be any.

But at least Saint is real.

"A fog machine. He dissolved LSD in the water mixture and..."

I shudder, and Saint gathers me in his arms. He lifts me on his lap, guiding my head to his shoulder. I lean forward, resting my forehead in the crook of his neck.

"Some days I feel too broken to exist," I admit.

He scoffs. "Not to discount that feeling, but you're doing a damn fine job of existing. Even if Hades and I hadn't shown up, you were going to survive."

"He wanted to break my legs."

He doesn't say anything to that. What can he say? The asshole is dead. Shot straight through the head—*that* isn't an illusion. Hades did that for us. For me, I think.

"But I stopped him." I reach the same conclusion I came to three hours ago. It was my trial to go through, and I defeated my demons.

I trace one of the tattoos on his chest. The dragon blinks at me, and I smile.

CHAPTER 9

9:00AM

Saint is curled around me when I wake up. He's breathing deeply, his lips parted, and I take a moment to watch his face. He's still here, even in the light of day. Halloween night at Olympus wasn't entirely a deception.

"You're staring, Elora," he whispers.

I start. "Sorry."

His arm around my waist tightens. "How do you feel?"

I wet my lips. "Parched."

He releases me, and I stand. Surprisingly, I don't feel terrible. My body aches, but it isn't that much worse than training days. My muscles are strong. And the drugs seem to have worked their way out of my system.

We're in his bedroom. The blinds do a crappy job blocking out the sun, the curtains left open. It's surprisingly neat, though. Unlike my own room. I'm the tornado that sweeps through and upends drawers full of clothing to find the perfect shirt.

Framed drawings on the wall next to the door catch my eye, and I ignore my thirst to study them.

In turn, I feel his gaze on me.

The pencil sketches are amazing. Flowers and animals, geometric shapes. Something that looks similar to Apollo's mask, that rough bark texture. And next to them, a human skull with horns protruding from the top. Another type of animal skull with a long nose bone. They've been lightly colored in, golds and pale creams. The animal skull one has leather and feathers hanging down off of it.

"You're talented." I clear my throat and gesture to the bark one. "This one is familiar."

"They'll all be familiar soon enough."

I glance back at him.

"They're using my designs. I haven't finished Ares' yet."

"Hmm. And these?" I slide down a little to the flowers.

"Some of my first tattoos." He smiles. "Do you like them?"

I don't want to admit that his dragon tattoo, the grayscale beast that's curled on his pec, featured heavily in my acid trip after they found me.

"They're beautiful," I acknowledge.

And then I can't take it anymore, and I duck out of the room.

His apartment is small and modest. The short hallway opens into a kitchen on the left, with a cutout above the sink to give a view out into the living and dining area. The far wall is mostly glass, sliding doors that open onto a little balcony.

We're not too high up, just a few floors, but I can appreciate being able to step outside without going to street level.

I find two bottles of water in his fridge, then duck into the bathroom. I resist the urge to peek in his medicine cabinet and squirt a line of toothpaste onto my finger. It'll have to do until I can get home, and I need the sour taste in my mouth to go away.

Once I've cleaned myself up a bit, including taking the elastics out of my hair and finger-combing out the last remnants of braids, I return to the bedroom.

He's in the same spot, gaze on the ceiling. I circle to his side and hand him one of the bottles. He takes it and sits up, twisting the cap off and bringing it to his mouth. He doesn't look away from me as he tips it back and swallows. My attention flicks to his throat, then back up.

When he lowers it, he smirks.

I turn away.

"Is your hair naturally curly?"

I drink most of the bottle of water before I answer. "It's just the braids making it that way."

"Elora."

I flinch.

"Do you... want to talk about it?"

Not really. But I heave a sigh and face him again. "What do you want to know?"

He pats the space beside him.

And I hesitate.

"Get your ass over here," he demands. "We're not talking about this with you across the room."

My eyes widen, and heat unfurls in my abdomen. I don't like taking orders, but his voice just got deeper. And now my body is reacting some sort of way.

I sit beside him, pulling my legs up and resting back against his headboard.

"When we were freshmen at the academy, I was abducted by my friend's dad. He kept me for two days in the woods." I focus on my knees. "He got off on my fear, you know? He forced me to take hallucinogenic drugs and then..."

His arm slides around my shoulders, and he holds me tightly into his side.

"One chase led me to a group of hunters, and they took me back to civilization. Because of the drugs, no one believed I was being hunted—just that my trip made me think it. They thought I got high and wandered off on my own."

My throat closes.

"You didn't deserve that," he says.

I glance up at him. "He was at the fight, and... he said he recognized me. And he wanted to make me afraid again." Quieter, "I was only with him for a short time but I felt myself shrinking again. After being Nyx had opened me up."

"You said he was going to break your legs." Saint's voice is steady, but I hear the barely suppressed anger behind it. "He didn't want to chase you anymore."

"No." He didn't.

Maybe it wasn't about the chase, after all. Just the capture.

"If it were up to me, I'd have kept him alive." Saint's fingers pinch my chin, turning my head so I have to meet his eyes. "I'd keep him alive because death is too easy. I'd flay him apart for touching you."

"We don't know each other."

His harsh laugh comes out hollow. "Bullshit."

"Saint."

"You and I are meant to be." He presses his hand to his chest. "I feel it. I don't know why. I've been thinking about you since we graduated. It's crazy. Fucked up. I've been twisted up about it since we first started going to school together."

Wow.

"That's why you kissed me in the water."

He nods slowly.

"I… I've had a crush on you forever. It's just…"

"We were divided." He nods once. "I know."

I lean forward and press my lips to his. He doesn't move for a moment, and I count to three in my head before I withdraw. But then he catches my face and drags me back.

This kiss is stronger, and he tastes like mint. I'm not sure when he snuck away to brush his teeth, but I'm not mad about it. I lean into him and let my mind go blessedly blank as he explores my mouth. Our tongues tangle, and I fight my urge to climb onto his lap.

My phone vibrates once, then again.

And again.

I pull away, wincing, and reach for it. It only has a ten percent battery left, but it's enough for now. I swipe to answer the call from my mother.

"Good morning," I say cheerfully.

She pauses. Then, "*Good morning?* Elora Jane Whitlock, where are you?"

"I, um, didn't I text you?" I glance at Saint.

His eyebrows are hiked up.

This is my mother, I want to say. Instead, I put the call on speaker.

"Oh, so you did."

"And I told you I was staying with a friend?" Because if she knew I fought, she might combust. "Then going to work."

Silence.

"Sorry, honey, I just saw your empty room and was

worried. It was Halloween, after all. Crazies are out that time of year."

She was one of the only ones to believe me when I was fourteen. Mom's boyfriend was definitely in the *she's a drug addict and liar* camp—which was the beginning of the end of their relationship.

Several maxed-out credit cards later, he bounced.

And that was the end of that.

"I'll be home later today." Except, it doesn't really matter. She usually works a three-to-eleven shift at the hospital. She's had that shift for as long as I can remember, which means she was almost never there to see me home from school, and later, work.

We've lived in different worlds for a while.

Saint places a kiss on my shoulder.

"I made a casserole," she says. "It's in the fridge. I'll see you when I get home, if you're still awake."

He works his way up my throat, and I angle my head to give him better access.

"Love you," she says to me.

His lips touch my ear, and I shiver.

"Love you, too."

I hang up and toss the phone aside. He's moved back down again, sucking a spot on my neck that gives me goosebumps.

"That feels good," I breathe.

He nips the spot, then soothes it with his tongue.

Fuck it.

I climb on his lap, swinging my leg over to straddle him. His hands immediately land on my thighs, pushing the hoodie higher. He releases my neck long enough to pull the sweatshirt over my head. My hands are still in the sleeves, though, and he gives me a wicked grin. He pins my wrists behind my back for a moment and peruses my naked chest.

My nipples harden.

"You're gorgeous," he says. "Absolutely fucking stunning."

I wriggle against him. "Saint, you're killing me."

He gives me a look. "People are going to worship you as Nyx. Let me worship you as Elora."

I stop fighting him. He pulls me back a bit and dips down, taking my nipple in his mouth. I blow out a breath that's half moan. It feels too good.

He finally strips the sleeves off my wrists, freeing my arms. With his mouth on me, I don't bother taking his shirt off the easy way. I rip it off.

He jerks, then huffs a laugh against my breast. I peel the fabric off him and run my fingertips over the intricate tattoos on his shoulders.

"I want one," I declare.

Saint nips my flesh, and my abs tighten. "From me?"

"Yes."

He meets my gaze. "I don't think I can bear it if someone else touches you. Even for a tattoo."

I smile. "Good, because I don't want anyone else."

His lips slam back on mine. My lip splits open again, and the sharp taste of blood mixes on our tongues. He tears my stolen underwear off and lifts his hips. His hard cock rubs my cunt.

I groan into his mouth.

I shove his boxers down enough for his cock to spring free, then guide it to my entrance. He slides in slightly, then out. Again.

"Saint, stop messing with me."

He smirks. "I'm bare. You—"

"IUD," I tell him. "I'm good. Please."

He thrusts in deeper, but still not enough when he withdraws. "Please, huh?"

He holds my hips with an iron grip, keeping me from moving against him, and I grit my teeth to stop a whine from escaping.

"I like it when you beg," he says in my ear.

He rolls us, and my head hits the pillows. He sits up straight and parts my legs, watching his length slide into me. He flicks my clit.

I moan and fist the sheets at my sides.

"Well?" He does it again, smirking when I clench around him.

I stare at him and feel my self-control waver.

He pushes in slowly, deeper, until he's fully seated inside me. I roll my hips, desperate for the friction, and he tsks. "Elora."

"You want me to beg?" My voice is breathless, but it catches at his nod. "Please, Saint, fuck me until I can't remember my own name. I need to feel you inside me."

He moves a fraction, and I release a frustrated exhale.

"Saint," I snap.

He hums. "All right, goddess."

Everything clicks into place. His cock stroking me, his fingers on my clit. His lips on mine. For the first time, everything settles around me.

It took Halloween at Olympus to bring us together—*in more ways than one.*

And I'm never letting this go.

Not if I can help it.

CHAPTER 10

12:00PM

Saint parks his truck next to my car on the lawn at Olympus, then trails me up to the building. Hades had said I should come back when the drugs wore off. Well, I've been thoroughly examined by the man behind me and deemed okay to leave his bed.

My cheeks heat if I think about it, so I push that aside.

Hades, Ares, and Apollo are maskless today. They sit up near the cliff edge on Adirondack chairs, mugs of coffee in their hands. An insulated travel jug sits on the ground between Hades and Apollo.

"Hi," I call.

Hades smiles faintly.

They don't appear how I imagined. Younger. They're only a few years older than me. Handsome.

Intimidating.

His gaze moves past me to Saint, and the two share a look I can't decipher.

Ares motions to the two extra chairs, set up beside them like they anticipated our arrival. "Sit, if you want."

We do. I take the one next to Ares, and Saint sits beside Apollo. I glance at the three hosts of Olympus. They said they were worse than the gangs, but they don't seem that way. They seem…

"Don't underestimate us," Ares says quietly. "Everything we said last night is true."

I realize I don't know their real names—and with sudden surety, I decide I don't want to know. Some things are better off a mystery.

"So, Elora Whitlock. You had an interesting night." Hades appraises me.

"As did you, I'm sure." The bonfire is still burning in the distance, a smoldering pit with white smoke pouring into the sky. "After…"

"After," he agrees.

I cross my arms over my chest. "What did you want to discuss?"

Apollo leans forward. "You."

Great. "What about me?"

"The crowd liked you. Nyx. Goddess of the night. Your mythological counterpart predates even me," Hades says mildly. "Did you know that when you chose her?"

I shrug. In truth, no. I hadn't given it much thought. But my name means *light*, and I was desperate to have something the complete opposite of that. Now, it seems silly. My name isn't my defining feature.

"Here's our proposition." Hades drains the last of his coffee and sets it aside. His blue eyes meet mine. "Be one of our Chosen. Fight for us. Say, once a month. More, if you want, or less."

My eyebrows raise. "That…"

"In return, we'll pay you. Whether you win or lose." Apollo grins. "What, don't you think you're worth that?"

I scoff.

"Think about it," Saint says. His gaze on me is steadying. "They probably pay better than the part-time job you're holding down now."

"How—"

He smirks.

Damn him.

I stand. "Was this whole thing a setup? Some way to... I don't know. Get me to comply? Give me *him* and expect me to do whatever you say? I'm nothing special. The sooner you get that through your thick skulls—"

"Sit down," Hades orders.

I shake my head and head back to the car. This is ridiculous. I should've known when I saw the mask drawings on Saint's wall that he was involved with them somehow.

"Stop," Saint yells. He chases after me and grabs my arm.

I can't do this.

I twist, breaking his grip in a smooth motion, then shove him as hard as I can. He stumbles back and grimaces.

"*You* stop." I grimace. "I can't just be jerked around by the four of you."

"It isn't like that." He comes closer, holding up his hands. "Please, just listen to them. How I feel about you isn't an illusion. It's the one part of the night that was *real*."

Tears fill my eyes.

"If you're lying..."

"If I'm lying, you can kick my ass." He gives me a soft smile. "I haven't felt this way about anyone else, and I feel like I'm about to ruin it before we've had a chance to even begin."

I hate that I want to believe him. No—I do believe him.

Fuck.

I hold out my hand.

He studies me for a moment, then takes it and walks with me back up the hill. I step back toward my chair, but Saint doesn't release my hand. Instead, he sits and pulls me down on his lap.

"Be straight with me." I glare around at them. "Or I'm out."

There's enough cash in my car... I could probably leave. I could at least attempt it.

"Your mother's debt will be wiped," Hades says. "And you'll be given a condo in East Falls. You're a scrappy fighter, but let's face it. Last night was luck. Samson underestimated you and made sloppy mistakes. You exploited them."

I stiffen. "You're wiping her debt?"

"And giving you a place to live." He rolls his eyes. "And you're going into training. Actual training, to stand a chance against the bigger fighters. Or anyone who isn't a complete idiot."

"Why?" It's the only question I can ask at the moment.

Hades smiles. "Because we are worse than the gangs—but this town means something to us. And Olympus is the first step. But first steps are just that... it's a beginning of a new era. And we can't do it *all* on our own, as much as we want to. We need loyalty."

"Loyalty from me," I clarify.

Apollo grins. "You, Elora Whitlock, are valuable. Don't doubt that."

"Plus, it's personal for us," Ares adds. "Sterling Falls needs new leadership."

Saint's grip on my waist tightens. "They're going to take over everything."

So... it's better to be with them. That's what I'm picking up on. But at the same time, I don't feel cornered. Not like striking a deal with a Titan or Hell Hound. If I walk away from this, I could take my wad of cash from the fight and slip back into my regular life.

But I have a feeling Saint wouldn't be coming with me.

"Define everything?" I ask.

Hades' gaze stays on me. "We're going to run the gangs into the fucking ground. Sterling Falls will be ours... soon enough."

Shit. I imagine they don't mean just whatever pots the gangs have their fingers in. They mean *all* of it. Cops, government, businesses. I try to picture one of them as mayor, but the image doesn't quite stick. No, they'd rather be the master pulling the puppet's strings. Big picture thinking.

Or maybe they'd just rather destroy the system entirely.

Anarchy.

That could be an interesting twist of events.

"Okay," I say. "Can't say I'd love to see Sterling Falls without the Titans looming over my neighborhood."

It was them that kept Saint and me away from each other. The fear they've instilled in Sterling Falls.

I have a million more questions, but they all seem to clog in my throat before I can voice them. These three men are strangers to me. But they're offering a lot. Not just freedom but a continued adrenaline rush.

More fights. Enough money to support myself. And Mom, without her debt, can rest easy.

"Fine. I'm in with whatever scheme you're concocting—on one condition."

Hades raises his eyebrow.

I hook my thumb back at Saint. "He stays with me. Package deal."

"You mean that?" Saint asks me under his breath. He holds me like he can't believe I'm real—and, hell, this isn't the first time today I wonder if I'm still hallucinating.

"He's in this, too. I saw his drawings. He's working with you on Olympus, and that means you must trust him—at least a little. And I do, too." I twist around and loop my arms around his neck. "I absolutely mean that."

Nothing worth fighting for comes without a fight.

Hades inclines his head and reaches toward me. I shake his offered hand and smile.

"Welcome aboard, Nyx."

EPILOGUE

A Few Years Later

The girl with the flower mask seems lost.

I glance toward Saint in the shadows, waiting for me, and shake my head once. And then my gaze moves past him, to Hades. He should be preparing for his fight. But instead, he watches her from the entrance to the fighters' chambers.

Curious.

Things at Olympus are never as they seem, and this girl *seems* innocent. And yet, she comes here wearing a flower mask.

Tempting fate, maybe.

She slips through the crowd, away from the fighting platform.

"She one of yours?" I ask Apollo.

He still grips my hand, keeping it raised in the air as we rotate for the crowd. Neither of us smile—but then again, it's part of the personas we've created. Separate from our real selves. We didn't know the price Olympus would exact from us until it was too late.

They say the prize is a favor—but the real prize is walking away before Olympus drags you in... and you realize it isn't the city of the gods but the damned underworld.

He tilts his head, then catches my meaning. He nods sharply.

Interesting.

"Have you broken the news to your brothers that she's yours?"

"Nyx. Leave it alone."

Now a smile does break out across my face. I want to know more.

"I've never seen you be so..." There is no *so*. Apollo is a blank slate behind the deer-skull mask Saint designed for him. Purposefully trying to keep me from prying. Especially in front of a crowd.

Apollo drops my hand and kneels at my opponent's side. He scoops her up and shoots me a scalding look, then hops off the platform and strides away.

That's one way to end a conversation.

They've always been close. Hades, Apollo, and Ares, that is. I've never met a tighter-knit group—and I've never seen a woman come between them, either. Not in the years since Olympus opened and Saint and I became friends with them.

I stop in front of Saint and grin. He wraps his hand around the back of my neck and pulls me into him. Our lips touch. I press up and deepen the kiss. Our tongues tangle, and heat flashes through me. He doesn't mind the taste of blood between us. We both crave each other as much as that first night.

"Are you going to tell me why you look so devious?" Saint finally asks in my ear.

Three men.

One innocent, oblivious girl.

I can't get it out of my head. Of all of them, I think I'm going to root for the underdog. The girl. If anyone can slip into their trio without destroying everything, it could be her. With a little push in the right direction, though… everyone could get a happy ending.

I wink at Saint. "I guess we'll have to wait and see."

Thief

KORA

"You're late." A man with a boar mask flicks his cigarette. The flash of embers falling draws my gaze, but the grotesque mask keeps it. He leans against one of the huge marble columns that make up the front side of the building. I've never seen a place like this before.

It feels like it was transported directly out of ancient Greece.

The door I stand in front of doesn't have a knob, which is peculiar. And it's at least twelve feet tall and carved in intricate patterns that all seem to interlock. I can barely make it out in the darkness.

I wring my hands. "Look, I know. I—"

"I don't need your excuses. You'll have to come back next time. And be punctual."

I scowl at him. "I'm five minutes—"

"Five minutes is a lifetime. You know what an average person can do in five minutes?" He stubs out the cigarette and straightens. He saunters forward, revealing himself in the moonlight. Behind the holes of his mask, his eyes drill into mine. "You want to beat the system? Sneak in?"

This feels like a test. Or a trap.

I try to hold his gaze, but I'd rather do anything but. My skin crawls. And I'm suddenly aware that we're alone out here—this strange man and me. Anything could happen.

"No."

He inclines his chin. "Okay, then."

Okay, then...

He chuckles to himself and turns, disappearing around the side of the building.

I take the marble steps down to the grass and sigh. So much for my grand plan of seeing what Olympus is all about. I'd heard rumors of it—well, not really *rumors*. More like gossip. The girls who live in the apartment next to mine were talking about it.

When I tentatively asked them, they mentioned the masks. And the way everyone dresses up to attend. But they didn't say much more, and I got the sense that it was supposed to be a secret.

And now I'm alone, in an ill-fitting black dress and uncomfortable gold mask, surrounded by parked cars. Meanwhile, the people inside get to enjoy... whatever it is that happens in there.

I sigh and pull out my phone. My clutch is just large enough to accommodate it, my ID, and some cash. Enough to have got me into Olympus and then the cab fare back to my apartment. But it looks like I'll just be calling another cab.

Except, I have no service.

How did I miss that?

I face Olympus again. To the left is an incline, and I can't tell what's beyond it. I head that way, glancing at my phone every few steps. My only other option would be going back down the long driveway to the main road and hoping I eventually get service.

Either way is a gamble.

So I adjust my mask and pull off my heels. I angle away from the driveway beside the building and step onto the grass. It's cool under my bare feet. I make it past the corner of Olympus and climb the slight hill. A noise catches my attention to my left. Here, the moon is brighter. It sits low in the starless sky, huge and yellow, and gives everything an eerie feel.

And then I spot them: six people in a little circle. They're off to the side, away from where people would be able to see them if they were entering or exiting Olympus.

I step forward, about to call out, when one lunges toward one of the others.

No one yells. No one says anything. They don't even seem surprised by the sudden move. But the man the first one went at hunches forward, clutching his stomach, then falls. He faceplants, and the men stare down at him for a moment. One of them kicks him, and he rolls over onto his back. Something sticks out of his abdomen.

The handle of a knife?

I cover my mouth to bite back my scream. He was just *stabbed*—and the five others seem unperturbed. Horror fills me—but even more so when one stoops down and grabs his arms. Another one walks up and pulls the knife out, and there's a glint of wetness on the metal. It catches the moonlight.

My stomach turns, and I fight the bile surging up my throat.

The stabbed one is dragged away, around the other side of the building. They all watch them go, too, until he rounds the corner and disappears from sight.

Then there were four.

I need… I need to report this to the police. Or *someone*. I creep closer, keeping my body low. I probably stand out like a beacon, but I can't stop myself from trying to see more. How would the police catch them if I can't give them any true details?

I keep close to the grass, one hand pressed into the earth to stabilize myself, and stop only twenty feet away. Enough to see them clearer.

Three of them wear masks, like they came out of Olympus. The fourth is older, tall and lean with a trim goatee. He's maskless but seems unbothered by it.

"You sure about this, Hades?" The maskless man shakes his head. "He was in my circle."

Two wear skull masks with horns—but they're markedly different. The first is an animal skull, a deer or something with a long nose bone that extends past the man's own nose. Even in the moonlight, I can see the streaks of gold on his bare chest. And the second seems like the Devil himself. The pale skull looks human, minus the lower jaw, and black horns curl out of the temples.

The human-skull one grunts. Is he Hades? "We don't get things wrong."

"Of course." The man pulls something from his pocket and tosses it.

The third, with a red mask and red jacket, catches it. He thumbs through the roll of cash, then jerks a nod. "Pleasure doing business with you."

The maskless man follows behind the other two.

"Apollo," someone calls from behind them. Warm light spills out from inside Olympus. "They're ready."

The one with the animal mask turns back to the doorway—one I had missed, set into a dark alcove in the side of the marble—and waves at the new person. The door clicks shut.

And then he turns back, and his gaze finds me.

Shit.

"We have an audience," he informs the other two.

I straighten, ignoring the ice pouring down my spine. Because... yeah. I'm screwed. But I may as well look them in the eye, right? I've learned to take punishments like that. I've learned that men hate when you keep looking at them, even after they try to beat you down.

I found out the hard way.

Hades saunters toward me. His long stride eats the distance. Behind his mask, his eyes are shadowed. His full lips press together, revealing his displeasure.

Snakes writhe in my belly.

"I'm sorry—"

He stops in front of me, and my breathing halts along with it. His open shirt reveals perfect abs. My eyes fall to his shoes, then back up to his face. Even with the terrifying mask, he's gorgeous. And very clearly deadly.

A smirk lifts the corners of his lips, like he knows the effect he has on women. There's a cruel edge to it, though. And soon we're joined by the other two, the red-masked man and Apollo.

After the Greek god of sun and light. I'm not sure if he's supposed to be portraying that god exactly, though, because there's a darker side to this man.

And the last... red. Blood drips down his chest, although it seems more like it was painted on. I don't know who he is, but he seems soaked in violence. I can feel it in my bones.

And that brings me back to Hades. The king of the underworld. I came to experience Olympus, and now I'm standing before the gods who rule it.

Curiosity tugs at me, until Hades raises his hand and touches my cheek.

No, not touching.

He curls his fingers around the edge of my mask and *rips*. The ties break easily, the gold falling away from my face. My lips part, and I automatically lift my hand to my face. My cheeks are hot. Embarrassment and fear wind under my skin, grappling to be the primary emotion.

He drops the mask and crushes it under his foot, then leans forward. "Do you know who we are?"

I shiver at the roughness in his tone. "I can guess."

He smiles. It's not a happy one—it's a *tempt me to do worse* smile. The kind you give to your adversaries, not your friends. "What did you see?"

"N-nothing." I step back.

He comes forward, staying right in front of me. "Why don't I believe you?"

"Please," I whisper. "I won't say anything."

"About nothing?" He tilts his head. "What would you say if you didn't see anything?"

"I'm sorry." My throat constricts, and I keep backing away. I drop my heels but keep my clutch close. I shouldn't have come here. I should've stayed in my apartment and made friends in daylight. Or waited until I started work next week, befriended a coworker.

Stupid.

"She's going to run," the third says.

I glance over Hades' shoulder at the red-masked man.

"Let her." This from Apollo. There's a knife in his hand, and blood on his skin. He was the one to stab the other man. To kill him.

Their stares are too intense—and they're right. I want to

run. I want to sprint as far away from here as possible. I tremble and hold firm.

Until Hades breaks his stare and glances back at Olympus.

My self-control snaps, and I spin away from them. I sprint back down the hill. But instead of angling for the road, I dodge between cars and head for the woods.

Not the best decision to go barefoot, but I can't stay in the open. I'm not in the best shape, and I'm breathing heavily by the time I make it past the last row of cars.

For a moment, I wonder if they're going to let me go. Then a howl breaks open the night. It's very clearly a human voice. One of the three declaring the hunt? Full-body chills break out down my spine, and I push myself faster.

In my head, I can hear them running after me. Their laughter and pounding footsteps. It might be my imagination, though, because the only thing I can *really* hear is my ragged breathing.

I'm the prey they're after.

There's an opening in the tree line. A trail that becomes clearer the closer I get. I run for it while my heart threatens to explode out of my chest.

The forest swallows me in darkness. The trail is almost impossible to see. The trees block out all of the moonlight, and rocks dig into the bottoms of my feet. I wince when something sharp jabs the soft arch.

I fumble for my phone's flashlight, turning it on just as another howl sounds. I flinch.

My phone falls from my grip, the bright light arcing through the air. It lands light-down on the path, and I scramble on my hands and knees to find it. Panic rises in me, constricting my throat, and I brush away fallen leaves and pine needles frantically. My fingers land on the smooth glass screen, and I check it quickly. Undamaged.

I climb to my feet. The woods have fallen silent. No more howls, no footsteps. The silence is almost worse, because I have no idea where they are. If they're still coming after me, or if they have me right where they want me. I struggle to catch my breath, to calm my heartbeat and ease the tightness in my lungs.

But I need to keep moving. I shine it down the path and scream.

Hades strides toward me.

I backpedal and trip over something, falling hard on my ass. I ignore the spike of pain up my spine and crawl backward. "Please don't—"

I hit legs.

Hands grab my upper arms and hoist me up, and my courage flees. The pain in my foot is overshadowed by fear and adrenaline. My phone's flashlight shines up, illuminating the trees that seem to tip toward us.

Hades stops just in front of it. It gives him a sinister look with his mask firmly in place. And I feel strangely vulnerable without mine.

He tilts his head, then crouches and lifts my forgotten clutch.

I risk a glance over my shoulder. The red-masked man holds me close. He grins, leaning in and running his nose up the shell of my ear. Goosebumps break out all over.

"Kora Sinclair."

I flinch against my captor's grip.

Hades flashes my ID at me, then resumes scanning it. "Why are you here?"

"I came to see—"

"Why are you in my city, Kora Sinclair?" His eyes narrow,

and his lips press into a thin line. He stalks forward and appraises me under a more critical eye. "Dressed as you are. In a hand-me-down dress and plastic mask. Did you know what you were walking into?"

I get the impression that he usually only has to ask a question once, and people snap to obey him. And with the red-masked man right at my back—and Apollo god only knows where—I *should* be one of those people.

But my weakness has always been that I don't give up when I should, so I stay silent. Besides, the dress wasn't *that* cheap. I set my jaw.

The red-masked man chuckles. "I like her. Maybe we should keep her."

Keep me?

Hades shakes his head once and comes closer. He tugs on a lock of my dark hair. "Tell me."

I stare past him. I've never been so glad to have changed my appearance before I left home. Because if he's memorizing what I look like... this isn't the real version of me. It's just another layer I've created to protect myself.

But then he pulls harder, and I wince.

"A scholarship to SFU." I hate that I admit it to him, caving just because he's touching me. Or maybe I give in for another reason. Survival instinct finally, *finally* kicking in. "A full ride for next year."

"Listen to me very closely." He twists my hair around his fingers, forcing my head to tilt. The pressure on my scalp is on the verge of painful. "You made a mistake by coming here. And we don't give second chances. So you're going to leave Sterling Falls, because there's nothing left for you here."

He releases me and slides my ID into his front pocket. The ID that has my name, my parents' home address. The parts of my identity that I can't change overnight: height, weight. Birthday. Eye color.

My stomach rolls again, and I bite my tongue. The copper taste of blood fills my mouth, and my nausea worsens.

"I'm going to hold on to this." Hades smirks. "Just in case you decide to tell anyone about what you saw. Either way... no one will believe you. As of this moment, Kora Sinclair doesn't exist."

The red-masked man at my back releases me. Hades steps past me, and my knees give out. I hit the ground and stare at the light on my phone. Their footsteps recede, until it's just me in the woods.

His ominous words ring in my ears.

Kora Sinclair doesn't exist.

Part of me wants to believe it's a joke. That their reach can't possibly be that long. But they killed a man without flinching. He has my ID. My name. He knows I'm here for school.

The light on my phone flickers, then dies.

And I'm left in the dark.

CHAPTER 1

Three Months Later

The dive bar is dark and crowded. It gives off a bad sort of energy that I only picked up on after I'd been there a few times. Every time I leave, it feels like the negativity clings to my skin.

Still, no one reaches out to grab me as I wind my way through the tables. The guys lounging at their tables ignore me. The waitresses and bartender turn a blind eye.

I'm invisible—my new profession.

The man standing guard at the back room holds out his hand.

Now I do pause, pursing my lips. "He asked to see me."

"He's busy."

"Fucking a girl? Nothing I haven't seen before." Indifference.

That's the only way I've survived the last three months. *Uncaring.* Stamping down every single emotion until there's nothing left.

I've done my best to channel that moment. The one

where Hades declared I didn't exist. I didn't believe him, but I'll give him credit: he worked fast.

My escape plan was solid. Move to Sterling Falls, work over the summer, get to know the town and the campus, then start school in the fall. But when I arrived at my new job...

They acted like I hadn't interviewed.

Hadn't come into their office *twice*.

I was shown the door and asked not to return, like it was my fault they didn't know me.

If I hadn't sunk all of my savings into the apartment I rented, I might've just called it quits and went back home for the summer. But my rental lease was ironclad, and that meant I'd be out thousands of dollars if I turned tail.

And then summer orientation rolled around, and I was called to the financial aid office on the first day.

There was an issue.

My scholarship disappeared. An error in the system, maybe, because apparently they didn't know I accepted it. My lack of response prompted them to offer it to another student, so there was no more money for me.

No job.

No scholarship.

I knew the point—*he* wanted me gone.

But too bad for him, because I wasn't going anywhere. I couldn't. Not when I had someone even worse waiting for me in Emerald Cove. Call me foolhardy, but by June I was pissed as hell. The first month was the hardest. I applied for jobs *everywhere*, but no one called me back.

I should've withdrawn from SFU. Because of the eleventh-hour mix up, I had no financial aid to speak of, except for the last-ditch effort loan I was able to procure. It covered my first semester's tuition and rent, because the only thing that would be shittier than this predicament is homelessness. I pulled five hundred dollars out in cash to use for food, but it went too quickly.

But now I'm here to try and beg for more time from my lender.

I know, I know, it sounds bad. What sort of lender conducts business in a bar?

But listen.

No bank in their right mind would give a jobless, creditless girl a loan. My first mistake was trying to find creative workarounds. My second mistake was telling the bartender of Descend all about it while spending my last few dollars on vodka instead of... I don't know, a burger. Or a train ticket out of here.

It should've been a sign when the bartender didn't card me.

And I was certainly not going to cry to my parents about this. Not when I fought so hard to get here. To them, everything is fine and has been fine. I just started classes last week, and being at a real university is everything I've wanted. It can help me land a decent job—in another city, to be sure—and I'll actually go somewhere with my life.

My dreams are so close I can touch them... if I can figure this out. Reapply for the scholarship for next year, maybe. *Something.*

"He's not fucking a girl," the guard sneers. "He's on a call."

I cross my arms, snapped back from my depressing thoughts. It can be a bit of a downward spiral—but isn't that what I've been doing for the last three months? Spiraling?

"A call," I echo. "*He* asked to see *me*."

He raises an eyebrow. "And *you* took your sweet time getting here."

That's true. But nerves delayed me, because being unable to pay means...

Well, I'm not sure. I managed to pay the first two months. Barely. But the third was due a week ago, and the price is too high. I don't have the money. *Any* money.

I swallow. I've hit the bottom and somehow, I keep digging myself deeper.

I half-expected him to break down my door and cut off my hand when I told him I didn't have any money left. I'd lost ten pounds in the last month, I felt tired all the time, but could I quit school? Admit defeat?

Absolutely not.

I borrow my school books from the library. Occasionally, I sneak into the dining hall so I won't pass out from hunger. It might be slightly more than *occasionally* at this point, though.

"He has something for you." The guard jerks his head toward the bar. "Sit. Eat something before you fall over. He'll be out soon."

I grunt, but my stomach cramps. I can't even deny that I'm starving, so I slide onto a barstool and motion to the bartender. He comes over and takes my short order, returning fairly quickly with a basket of fries and a soda.

"You eat that crap?"

I glance over my shoulder at the guard. "You give a shit?"

"Just wondering how you stay skinny."

I roll my eyes. "Eating on a budget, jackass."

The fries are lukewarm and have a slightly stale taste, but it doesn't stop me from eating as fast as I can. I feel a bit feral. No one gives a shit, though.

"Your turn," the guard calls.

The door behind him cracks open, and I shove three more fries in my mouth before standing. I take my drink with me. The guard lets out a sigh as I pass. Am I that unsavory?

Three months in this town, and I don't know how I ever thought it was normal. It's ruled by two gangs, whose focuses range from war to money. But in the end, those two things both translate into one: power.

"My invisible girl," the lender calls when I enter. He's smug behind his huge metal desk. "How's the food?"

"Could be better." I shrug and sit, crossing my legs. I've made myself bold recently to hide my fear. He only gave me the loan when I demanded it. Said, at first, that he didn't deal with *little girls*. I made him change his mind, and I wholeheartedly regret it.

He snickers. "Sure."

"You needed me for something?"

His eyes light up, roaming up and down my body. My curves are hidden under a baggy t-shirt, but he doesn't seem to give a shit.

"Do you know who declared you the invisible girl? Who wiped you off the map?"

I grit my teeth and don't answer.

I've avoided Olympus like the plague since that night. It hasn't stopped me from trying to sleuth out who they are. I've come up with nothing, though. And I can't figure out where they fit in. Two feuding gangs have the power in Sterling Falls, but so do they.

Clearly, because one minute, my life was together. The next... *poof*. But I never learned his name. Just Hades. Their masked faces are burned into the back of my mind. Hades, Apollo, and the third with the blood-red mask. Hades was the one who decided I had to disappear. The one who pulled the strings and made it happen. I know it in my bones. *He's* the one I have a grudge against.

"Well, at least you still have some fire in you." He leans forward, bracing his elbows on the desk. "You do this for me, and I wipe your debt."

I straighten in my seat. "Completely?"

"Yep." He pops the word and raises his eyebrows. "You have thirty seconds to decide."

I freeze. "Wait. You're not going to tell me what it is? What I have to do?"

The room presses in on me with the weight of decision. Of the risk that's going to be involved in saying yes—or no. I desperately want revenge... but it's the desperation that gives me pause. It's a weakness. An exploitation.

And I'm already here because he exploited a need.

He winks, ignoring the indecision on my face. "I can't ruin the fun."

I narrow my eyes. "Then, no."

"Great." He beckons me forward. "Give me your hand."

"Why?"

He glares. "You ask too many questions."

Abruptly, he rises and circles around the desk. I hesitate when he stops beside me. He's just an inch taller than me and built like a bulldog. Squat and packed with muscle. His hair is dark with streaks of gray. And more than that, he gives me a creepy feeling—like all the negative energy of the bar emanates from him.

Our similar height doesn't factor when he towers over my chair.

"Here's the deal, invisible girl. You owe me money. And unfortunately for you, I can't just let you walk away from that without penalty. How would that look?"

I swallow.

"Every day, your debt grows bigger. Interest, you know. I

have a business to run." He squints at me. "Give me your arm."

My stomach twists. I suddenly wish I hadn't eaten the fries before I came in, because the nausea is at the forefront of my thoughts. And not losing what little I ate on his shoes.

The gleam in his eye is a test.

At the end of the day, I choose nonviolence, so I do as he asks and give him my arm. It's a weak attempt to placate him.

He takes my left wrist, running his finger across the underside of it, then stands and pulls my arm flat across his desk. I tug back, sudden fear strangling me, but he holds firm.

He moves to his side again and locks a cuff on me before I can get free. It's attached to his side of the desk, the chain coming up and barely allowing any wiggle room. My arm is stretched out across the surface, my body halfway out of the chair. I shove against the desk with my other hand, but he comes to the other side and snatches that one, too.

"What are you doing?" I promised myself to never show fear around men like him—and here I am, trembling against his desk. I can't even keep my voice from wobbling, like I'm on the verge of tears.

You've survived worse.

He ignores my question and goes to the fireplace.

I yank at my wrists again, but the metal cuffs don't budge. What sort of sadistic bastard *is* he?

He grabs a metal rod and frees it from the flames, then circles back around to his chair.

"Such pretty skin." He traces my left wrist with his free hand. "This is the consequence for being unable to pay me."

"A brand?" I can't take my eyes off the glowing white-orange end of the rod. Loathing and fear turn my stomach, and I press my lips together to keep from gagging. "You can't be serious. I will get your money—"

"You might think I'm the scourge of the earth." He's turning this into a damn conversation. "And you'd be right."

He shows me the hot end, so I can see it clearly: an hourglass.

Chills sweep down my back.

"Kronos is the Titan of time and the ages. We choose our names when we enter into this life. It's a rebirth, of sorts, or an awakening. I've always been obsessed with time. How it slips through our fingers."

A Titan—I knew he was in one of the gangs, but I have a sudden feeling that it's more than that. I'm going to be sick. And on top of that, I'm ashamed of myself.

"Please don't." I pull again, although it's pointless. I know I can't get free.

Eyes are the windows to the soul, aren't they? That's what everyone always says. But my pleading doesn't soften his—if anything, his expression deadens. "I did you a favor. And you repay me with insolence and trying to escape your debt—what, without lifting a finger?"

I shudder. "I didn't try to escape it. I needed an extension—"

He reaches out and pinches my cheek. He stares into my eyes and lets me see behind the curtain. Just a peek. And what I see scares the shit out of me. There's nothing but depravity in his expression. "I hope you scream."

Every bad thing that's ever happened to me comes roaring back—but this time, fear takes a back seat to fury. If he was so serious about not doing business with me, he should've kept refusing.

I spit at him. "Fuck you, old man."

He smirks. He doesn't even wipe away the saliva that

drips down his cheek. He just steadies my left hand, palm up, and lifts the rod. I can't look away as he flips it around, until the glowing white hourglass hovers above my skin. The heat burns into me, even inches away.

"Stop, stop, I'll do whatever you want." I'm reduced to begging, but I can't seem to stop the words from slipping out of my mouth. "I'll do it—"

"Your thirty seconds passed. And I'd be remiss if I didn't say that I'm going to enjoy this."

He meets my gaze for a moment, before his attention returns to my wrist. The same wrist that has held more bruises in the shape of fingerprints than I can count. The same wrist that's been broken more than once. There's a thin scar farther up my forearm where the bone went through my skin.

My arms have endured a lot of trauma at the hands of others.

So when he holds down my arm and presses the hot metal to my skin, I don't feel it for a moment.

Just a moment, though.

And then the smell of burning flesh hits me, and agony rips through me. I clench my teeth so hard, I catch the edge of my tongue. Hot blood fills my mouth, but it helps me suppress the scream the bastard wants.

He pulls the metal away, and my body flashes hot. God, it's like my skin is on fire.

I fall forward onto the desk. My forehead rests on my forearms for a moment. I have to push aside the throbbing pain and rein in my desperation to get out. My panic rides up, closing my throat. I've got a weight on my chest that makes it impossible to breathe.

I don't do well being trapped and hurt.

He laughs and shoves the brand back into the fire, probably to prepare it for the next unsuspecting victim.

He sits in his chair and tips back, crossing his legs, and ignores the way I'm hunched over his desk. He scoots forward, until my curled fingers are inches from his chest. And he watches me with far too much amusement.

This is his position of power.

With people stretched out across his desk. Defeated.

"I warned you," he eventually says. "I warned you that we didn't do business with little girls like you. But I will enjoy our next meeting, if it's anything like this one."

I shudder. "You're a fucking sadist. Let me go."

"You should put a salve on that when you get home." He flashes me a key, then unlocks the cuffs. First my uninjured arm, then the other.

I stumble backward, cradling my wrist to my stomach. I can't even look at it.

He eyes me and my quick shuffle to the door.

"Invisible girl," he calls. "If you don't pay next month, expect a repeat. Or..."

It's enough to give me pause, and he knows it. He's dangling that job in front of me. Job or favor, I'm not sure what to classify it. It could be a suicide mission, for all I know. But I'm expendable.

We both know it.

He raises his eyebrows when I stop moving.

"Fine," I grit out. "Is it going to get me killed?"

He laughs. "Only if you get caught."

I swallow. "If I'm successful, we're clear. No more debt. No more favors."

"And if you're unsuccessful, then payments continue... with double the interest." He opens a drawer and removes an envelope, tossing it across the desk. "You have until the end of the month. That's the only grace period I'm going to extend to you."

I dart forward and grab the envelope. When I'm halfway to the door, he makes another noise. I slow to a stop, grinding my teeth.

"Yes, one last thing." He strides across the room and steps into my space. Our height difference isn't so great now, but he feels larger than life. A small smirk curls his lips. "If you even *think* of leaving Sterling Falls, all bets are off. I won't just go for you, though. I'll find your family. The accountant mother, the dear father who works at the newspaper in Emerald Cove... Or maybe that charming best friend of yours. Marley. She'd look good pinned to my desk, as you were. Maybe I'll work my way down the line and see whose scream is the sweetest. I'll take what's due to me from their flesh... then I'll take the rest from you."

He pats my cheek again, then holds up a photo. It's of Marley and me on the Sterling Falls University campus. I jerk back.

"Yes, invisible girl. I do my research. Whatever little plan you concoct to escape, know that I've already thought it. And moved to prevent it. Run along, now."

I hightail it out of there with the envelope crumpled in my fist.

He knows my family. My best friend. That's how all the villains operate, isn't it? They find leverage and they'll exploit it however they can.

Tears fill my eyes once I'm on the sidewalk and rushing away from Descend. I'm the worst sort of idiot. The kind who doesn't even know she's in over her head until she hits the bottom of the freaking ocean.

It takes me half the walk to realize that I could've skipped the brand if I had agreed to Kronos' blind deal. My arm throbs, from my wrist all the way up my shoulder. I pull it away from my shirt and immediately put it back. My skin is angry red and blistered.

Downtown has changed with the rest of the city. Everything is at an angle, like the skyscrapers have buckled under expectation. In the daytime, the shops beckon passersby to enter. It was built to entice tourists and college students—people who don't really understand Sterling Falls. It's all a trap, though. A well-thought-out illusion. Behind every shop, every restaurant, is a darker scheme. And that became clear when the curtain was ripped aside.

My eyes were opened, and there's no going back.

When I first moved here, I had no idea. Sterling Falls was my shining beacon of hope. The argument I had with my parents to even let me come here... I risked my relationship with them to make it work.

They're reasonable people. Mom's an accountant at a small, family-owned firm. She worked her way through school. Dad started as a writer for the Emerald Cove—the town I grew up in—newspaper, and since climbed up the ranks to editor without a degree.

But reasonable can only stretch so far to accommodate dreams.

And now... nightmares. Funnily enough, I moved here to *escape* my nightmares. Somehow, I waltzed right into another one.

I hurry through West Falls until I reach SFU's campus. West Falls is Titans' territory, something I didn't know until after I accepted the loan from the man who calls himself Kronos, and I'm eager to leave it behind. He's their leader. He must be. Kronos never said as much, but after today, I'm fairly certain.

The Titans and Hell Hounds are the two gangs in power.

I want to know how Hades fits into it. Where Olympus sits in relation to the gangs. And I don't want to know to satiate my curiosity—I need a plan.

Today's conversation with Kronos solidifies my theory that the trio isn't part of the Titans. Which leaves the Hell Hounds... or they're something else entirely.

I slip into the student center, taking a seat off to the side until the attendant for the dining hall is distracted. Then I enter. No one bats an eye, and I load up a plate with food. Once that's done, I fill a cup with ice, another with water, and find a chair at an empty table. I glance out the window at the darkening sky and let out a sigh.

I only allow myself a moment, though, before I shake out some of the ice into a napkin and cover my burned skin. I let out a hiss of pain and squeeze my eyes shut. *One, two, three, four*. The pain's still there, but I'm not in that room.

My panic ebbs.

I finagle my setup so I don't have to hold the ice, then dig into the food. I shovel it in like they're going to kick me out at any moment—and at this rate, they might. I see some pitying glances every now and then.

Maybe that's just my paranoia talking.

I need to come during busier times. To blend in even more.

The pasta sits heavily in my stomach, but I'm too hungry to stop. Too nervous about when my next meal will be to enjoy it properly, either. Every bite is bland.

Once the plate is empty, I push it away and guzzle the water. The ice in the napkin is melting into a puddle, and my wrist throbs, but I ignore those for the envelope. I pull it from my hoodie pocket and carefully rip it open.

Just a single piece of paper. That's... it.

No instructions or guidance—just two words. *Hades' Mask.*

My stomach flips, and I roll my shoulders back. He wants me to steal it? I can close my eyes and envision the white-bone skull mask. The twist of the cruel lips under it.

At that, I shift. There was nothing in my agreement with Kronos about protection. If I *don't* do it, I'm destined for another brand on my arm, and paying with *double* interest—because I highly doubt I can come up with the money for payment by the end of the month. And I can only imagine how much my debt will rise the longer I'm unable to pay. If I can't pay, he'll take it out on my family. Or my best friend.

If I do it... Getting caught might get me killed.

I close my eyes and remember the man they gutted. They got away with that. I know they did, because there wasn't even a blip of mention in the newspaper.

If I learned anything from my dad, it's that people love macabre. A dead body—especially one with a knife wound in his abdomen—would make a great headline. But there was nothing. Just like there was nothing left of me.

I rotate my arm and stare down at the underside of my wrist. The skin is red, the hourglass bright and raised. The outer lines are thin and curved like two bells.

It's delicate, but it isn't pretty.

My skin crawls. Just having been in Descend for less than an hour is enough to give me a grimy feeling. I fill my pockets with transportable food and the paper from the envelope, then hurry out of the dining hall.

My apartment is a short trek away, and I've never been so grateful to lock the door behind me.

I unload my pockets and drop the keys on the counter, slinking into the bathroom. Once my shower is complete, I smear antiseptic on my wrist and wrap it in gauze. I can't look at it for more than a few seconds without that skin-crawling sensation returning.

I was taken advantage of—again. But I let it happen this time. My past wasn't my fault, but Kronos? It was my own stubbornness that put me in that room.

So… I have the rest of the month to get the mask. I'll do my research. See if he leaves it somewhere when he isn't wearing it… if he doesn't sleep in it. The asshole might have welded it to his face if it would give him more of an edge. At that thought, I snicker.

I've already decided that I'm going to do it, and my success will depend on preparation. I've been living in my own version of hell all summer because of *him*, and I need to remember that. I need to let it fuel me for just a little longer.

It's been three months… and don't they say revenge is best served cold?

I can only hope that they don't see me coming.

CHAPTER 2

My door opens, and my best friend enters without knocking. "Guess what?"

I shake my head from my position on the couch. It's Friday night at the beginning of the semester, so I suppose anything is possible. She found a new boyfriend? She discovered a new bar for us to try? Not on my budget. "No idea."

"You don't even want to guess?" Marley shoots me a dramatic frown and stops in front of me. We've been friends forever, and her antics don't faze me in the slightest.

"No." My mood has been foul for the last week while I put off the inevitable. I took that piece of paper from Kronos and threw it away. I don't need the constant reminder. I should be scheming, but instead I've thrown myself into school. I kept envisioning Kronos carving into *her* skin, and the nightmares were enough to make me wish I could skip sleep altogether.

Homework, however, has proven a noble adversary. I love school, but even I'm getting sick of how much reading I'm doing to stay ahead.

At least my semester is paid for. I don't have to worry about *that* until December. Then I'll either have figured something out, or I'll be on my way back to Emerald Cove with my tail between my legs. Or will I?

I guess it depends on my debt. And what Kronos decides to do with me.

Just steal the freaking mask, Kora, and get home.

My parents might forgive me for the sudden abandonment of my education, but I know I won't forgive myself.

December is a far way off, at any rate.

Marley clears her throat.

I close my book and give her my full attention, ignoring her stink eye. She wears a bold, dark-pink halter-top dress that accentuates her curves, dark eye makeup, and light-pink lip gloss. Her blonde hair is loose and falling around her shoulders in waves.

Bombshell status, basically.

She keeps her hands behind her back, which is a bit strange. But I'm distracted by the freaking *dress*. It's so out of the ordinary—she's a blouse and leggings kind of girl most of the time—that I can only gawk for a minute.

"You look stunning. Why?"

She rolls her eyes. "Seriously?"

"Why are you hiding your hands behind your back?"

She frowns. "You've been here for three months, Kora. Have you had *any* fun?"

I glance down at my arm. I found wide, light tan leather bracelets on a street vendor's cart that cover the bandage. My skin still carries an echo of pain if I think about it, or if I roll my wrist wrong. But I've managed to avoid questions—and seeing my mutilated flesh—altogether.

"Are you saying you think I'm boring?" I force my voice to be teasing, but she's right: I've been a stick-in-the-mud. It's hard to be *fun* when you're worried to death. I can't let her be hurt by Kronos.

And I have no idea how I'm going to steal Hades' mask.

Kronos said it was going to get back at Hades, but I have no idea how stealing his mask will accomplish that. Add it to the list of things I'm freaking clueless about.

"Yes." She laughs, then reveals what she was hiding: two masks.

I jerk back, suppressing the hollow sensation in my gut. "What are those?"

She glances down. "Masks." The *duh* is evident.

Shit. *Shit*. I never told her about my first trip to Olympus. It didn't exactly end so well… and besides, she wasn't even in Sterling Falls. She's a year ahead of me, even though we're the same age. I spent a year at community college. And up until I got the scholarship to SFU, I thought I'd remain there, getting an associate's degree in business.

Now it seems I might end up right back there if I can get out of Sterling Falls.

Marley ignores my hesitation and holds the seashell mask up. It covers the top half of her face. Silk straps hang down, meant to tie it on in two places.

It fits her easygoing vibe.

"And, um, this one is mine?" I gesture to the second one.

It's a striking mask, one side covered in pink and white pressed flowers and the other in lace and silvery beads. I take it from her and run my finger over one, and I'm almost disappointed that they're made of cloth and glue. It's a lot prettier than the cheap gold one.

"So, is that a yes?"

"Where are we wearing these?" I ask because she expects it, but I can already see the outside of Olympus. The boar masked man smoking against the column. Hades. Apollo. The red-masked man.

She bounces up and down. "It's a surprise. Let's find you an outfit!"

An hour later, my dark-red hair is curled, my lips are painted in a similar color, and I've managed to find a white, flowing dress that stops mid-thigh. After Hades took my ID, I decided I was letting my past control me. So I switched back to my natural hair color—which was a brighter red when I was a kid, and since darkened into a deep auburn over time. Once it was back to normal, it made me feel better.

I had already lost so many pieces of myself, at least I could recognize myself in the mirror. Oh—and I pierced my nose. The silver ring sits snugly in my septum. It was on a whim. I was passing the shop and just walked in. Marley freaked out when she saw it, then demanded to know why I didn't take her with me.

The whole time I do my makeup, Marley just smiles to herself. She thinks she's doing me some good, ducking in and out of the bathroom to mark my progress. While I'm preoccupied, she finds the strappy gold heels—the same ones I wore three months ago.

A lump forms in my throat. It took me forever to find my way out of the woods and locate my heels, and longer still to get home. I threw them in my closet and haven't touched them since.

"Ready?" Marley straightens my dress and flips my hair forward. She analyzes my expression and tilts her head. "What aren't you telling me?"

I swallow. Here's the part where I could unload everything—but how could I do that to her? And tonight, when we're supposed to be having *fun*, of all nights?

But then I remember that Kronos threatened not only me—but *her*. How can I do that to her? I won't.

So I lie. "I'm fine. Just a little nervous for this *surprise*."

She nods, accepting the lie, and loops her arm through mine on our way down the block. She brought her car with her, and we pile into it. It's an old, beat-up Subaru that has probably seen four different owners before her. Still, it runs, and that's good enough for us.

She takes us past SFU's campus, through the downtown section that marks a neutral territory for the gangs, and up into the hills. The road narrows, but she seems unbothered. This road seemed a lot less treacherous when I was stuck in the backseat of the old cab. In Marley's little car, going at the speed of light... I slip my hand around the door handle and squeeze the life out of it.

"Have you been where we're going?" I almost say *Olympus* and ruin my own lie.

"Last year," she admits. "Janet asked if I wanted to go with her a few times... I'm sorry. It was kind of shitty being here and making new friends on my own."

I can't expect my best friend to only hang out with me. Besides, we never thought I'd be able to join her. Attending the same university together was a dream we let go of long before high school even rolled around.

She got back to Sterling Falls a few weeks ago to find me... well, drowning.

Things got better when she showed up, but there was no way I was dumping everything on her. How I had managed to make so many mistakes within three months of arriving, I don't know.

And then something occurs to me. "Do we need to pay for tickets?"

She glances over and immediately picks up on my worry.

She knows money is tight, at least. "Oh my god, I'm so sorry. I should've told you. I can spot you this time."

I let out a sigh. Financial struggles aren't new to me. But calculating every last move I make, down to the penny, has taken some getting used to. It's made worse by offers from Marley to cover me for certain things.

Things I should've been able to afford if I had that job, and that scholarship, and that *life* that got whisked away from me.

I'm holding things together by threads.

The hills suddenly even out, and she slows. There's a line of cars ahead of us, all heading for the same place: the sprawling marble building called Olympus. It's a silver-and-shadow beast that sits on the slight rise. The marble columns in front are as impressive as I remember. This time, though, the front doors are open. A golden glow emanates from within, and light leaks out onto the main yard.

The effect is rather magical.

We turn onto the property and find a parking space. I take a deep breath and stare at Olympus.

This time is going to be different.

I'll actually get to go inside, for one. And I have Marley.

Even if I do see them—which, I suppose I need to see them in order to steal Hades' mask—I look different. The red hair, the septum ring. I've lost weight, on top of that. My curves have disappeared.

Marley gestures to the flower mask in my lap.

I tie it on and flip down the mirror. The mask goes, in an odd, bold sort of way, with my dark lipstick, hair, and the white dress. It's a statement—although I'm not sure what sort of statement I want to be making.

Marley hasn't pointed out the out-of-place cuff on my wrist, either.

The weather is warm for early September, but something about the atmosphere elicits a shiver up my spine. I glance over my shoulder toward the woods, then quickly straighten. I never found out what actually happens in Olympus. Besides the attire. I didn't ask after my first, terrible attempt.

We join the crowd that's heading up to the mansion. A man in a black raven mask stands at the door, collecting cash. A raven mask, I note. Last time it was a boar. I wonder if they're different employees or just... different masks.

Marley elbows me. "I got you, remember?"

I nod and bite my cheek. Having someone else pay for me just stacks guilt on my shoulders, but I try not to let it dampen my already iffy mood. "I'll pay you back."

The line inches forward. I crane my neck to see inside, but the angle is wrong. All I can see is one of the doors swung inward. The carvings are more apparent, and I want to get up close to run my fingers over them.

I had missed the crowd before. This time, we're surrounded by similarly styled people.

Everyone wears masks, and they're in various degrees of fancy. Some men and women are in formal wear—long dresses and tuxedos—and others just have open-collared shirts, skirts, and cropped shirts. I can't get a handle on how we're *supposed* to be dressed.

Marley and I have landed somewhere in the middle.

We finally get up to the front, and the raven-masked man stares at us for a beat.

My best friend opens her purse and pulls out two bills, but oddly, the man's dark eyes bore into mine. I squint at him, trying to see if I recognize him as the smoker who stopped me three months ago.

That's ridiculous, though. I can't tell if it's him any more than he would recognize me.

I've noticed that the unimportant details of that day have smudged in my mind. Like how many minutes I was late, or which column the man leaned against. The vivid things, I can't get rid of. And oh, how I wish I could.

"No charge." His voice is rasping and unassuming.

Yet, the chills return.

Marley has no such trepidation. She calls a cheery thanks to him and drags me inside.

I cast a quick glance at the door and make out a curving wreath of leaves at eye level. And then we're in.

I should've suspected something grand from the size of the door. But I had no idea this awaited us. We stride through a large atrium. There is a staircase directly ahead of us that goes up to a landing then splits in two. The second floor, high above our heads, has open railings to overlook the atrium and staircase.

Marble pillars line the sides of the atrium, hiding shadowed alcoves. It continues on either side of the staircase, and arched doorways lead farther in.

It feels a bit like choosing between Heaven and Hell.

Built into the wall over the staircase landing is a statue. It might've at one point been marble, too, but it now drips with black and gold. The immobile man has a distinctly ethereal appearance, and his golden crown sparks off the light.

"Drink," Marley says, shoving a flask into my hand. "It'll help you stop twitching so much."

I still. The *last* thing I need is to go into this with dulled senses. But I can't deny that every brush of another body has me flinching. It's a combination of Kronos and my past, balled up into one. Men who seemed kind at first but quickly proved my instincts wrong.

My judgement is off.

But I do trust my best friend, so I twist off the cap and take a big swallow. The gin, her drink of choice since we were teenagers, leaves a distinctly *pine* taste in my mouth. I grimace and shove it back at her.

She chuckles under her breath.

"I don't understand the point of this." It seems no one is leaving this room, and some people are acting like no one else is around them. A few stand in clusters, chatting with who I have to assume are friends, and others stand alone. We're all so close, though, that it doesn't really matter.

I have the urge to climb the staircase and explore every inch of this place. The building could've come from ancient Greece. The marble, the carvings, the gold accents. We've been transported to another world.

And that's further accentuated by the masks. They, like the people and their outfits, range from unassuming to ostentatious. A woman passes us with a rich purple mask that covers most of her face, and giant purple plumbs create a crown effect.

"I've never had them let me in for free," Marley says in my ear. "I think you're my good luck charm. But just wait—they'll be starting soon."

"Starting *what*?"

She winks. "Watching you figure it out is going to be the best part of the night."

I sigh.

But then something catches my attention. Not something—*someone*. He comes down the staircase and stops on the landing.

At the same time, the giant doors behind us close with a *boom*.

I suppress my flinch.

It's Apollo.

He's gorgeous in the light. Gorgeous and scary, although I think I'm just transferring my fear from the last time we met onto him now.

You know what he's capable of.

His bare chest is painted in streaks of gold handprints dragged down his skin, disappearing into his brown leather pants. His mask is the same gold animal skull. Golden horns spring out of the temples and twist up and back, and leather strands with feathers and beads hang off the sides, brushing the tops of his shoulders.

I'd guess him to be some sort of warrior, directly out of a myth.

He waits for the crowd to notice him. Quiet falls over us all, our rapt attention snared on him. The way he would want it, I can't help but think.

His dark eyes sweep over the crowd, and I take the slightest step back. The skin around his eyes is painted black, adding to the allusion of his mask. When we're silent, he raises his arms out to either side.

The crowd can't help but lean forward slightly in anticipation.

I want to run.

"Welcome." His voice isn't loud, but it carries across the room. It's deep and goes straight through my chest. He gives us a feral grin. "Welcome to Olympus."

The people around me stamp their feet. Marley included.

I glance around, my brow crinkling, and that *otherness* feeling in the pit of my stomach increases. I've carried it around since I became the invisible girl, but here, it seems magnified.

"I'm Apollo. Your host for the evening." He takes a step down, closer to us. "Last week, we found our Chosen. *This* week, they fight. But who will succeed? Who will walk out of our halls with their dignity—and other things—intact? Who will have to be scraped off the floor?"

The crowd cheers. They're incited by the violence. The noise bursts out of them like a flock of birds taking off, sudden and chaotic. I suppress my wince. I don't know why I feel so betrayed by Marley. I don't like blood. Want nothing to do with it, having seen my fair share of it. I watch her for a moment, but she seems as rapt as the rest of them. I'm just along for the ride. So, I turn my attention back to Apollo.

Shockingly, his gaze seems to be on *me*. Shivers like ice race down my back. I wouldn't be surprised to have just been doused in cold water. I'm different, I remind myself. The hair, the septum ring, the outfit. At the same time, my face heats behind the mask and makeup. He can't be looking at me—but my body is certainly reacting like he is.

He holds my stare for a long moment, but then his eyes do move when he continues, "The doors are open, my friends. See you soon."

His hand twitches, and a sharp *pop* echoes in the room. Smoke bursts from the marble at his feet, billowing upward and obscuring him. When it clears, moments later, he's gone.

Marley grabs my hand. "Wasn't that epic? Come on, we need a good view."

Already, the crowd is pushing up the stairs. Some stay on the same level and wind around the staircase, going through the other archways.

"A fight?" I clarify. "Really?"

"It's more than that." She squeezes. "It's not... It's cathartic. And these people do crazy things to be chosen. It's an honor."

"How many times have you been here?" I shouldn't be mad, but she never mentioned it.

And I guess I never mentioned it, either. So we're both liars.

She winces. "Janet and I went a few times. Maybe four or five?"

I sigh and squeeze her hand back. "I'm sorry. I shouldn't judge—and I've been a terrible friend. You coming to get me out of my funk is very nice."

She adjusts her seashell mask and smiles. "Well, good. Thank you. And I wouldn't bring you here if I didn't think you'd like it. Plus, we can just ogle the man-candy."

Well, that's not the worst thing in the world. "Okay, fine."

She leads the way up the stairs, throwing elbows and cutting her way through the bodies. We take the left staircase. At the top, the option to turn left is blocked off by rope. We go right. If we were to take another immediate right, it would connect to the side of the atrium where the other staircase meets.

"This place is wild," I say under my breath.

She nods. "Definitely. It's part of the magic."

Isn't that how I had thought of it earlier? Magical. Yet, I'd reckon that this sort of magic exacts its own sort of price on someone.

I'm reminded again of the instructions Kronos left for me, and the time allowance he gave me slipping down the drain.

Greek mythology has always been of interest to me. Hades is the ruler of the underworld. A dangerous man, one of three brothers—Zeus, Poseidon, and him. We have

Apollo, and the red-masked man might have taken a god's name. I wonder if there are more Greek gods floating around Olympus.

The wide hallway has arched openings every few yards on the right side. People mill around, stopping at the small bar closest to us. Farther down, another one. Raven-masked men pour the drinks. But it isn't just drinks—they're taking bets, too. Handing out gilded cards in exchange for cash.

We ignore the bar and keep going, then through one of the openings. We're on a balcony much like an old theater box. Some are larger than others, but most hold seven to ten people at the rails. There are no seats—I guess because they don't want people getting *too* comfortable? Or maybe because no one bothers to sit down in this sort of atmosphere.

I look down to a clear view of the ring. Below, bodies pack together and inch closer to the fighting ring. The room is filling up, as well as the balconies. The chatter in the air is loud, and the energy palpable. It doesn't smell like a fighting ring. There's no trace of sour sweat and fear. No blood. Just the sweet fragrance of women's perfume and something spiced.

"How often do they do this?" I glance at her.

Apollo steps up onto the raised platform. He kicks at the floor, which I now notice is made of sand, and claps.

"Every other Friday," she says.

I calculate in my head. There are four Fridays in September, and this is the second. So if I can return in fourteen days and manage to steal Hades' mask... If I fail, I'll have just under a week to figure out a different plan.

I take everything in with a much more critical eye. Not as Kora Sinclair, suddenly, but something else entirely. A criminal.

"Introductions for those who are new." Apollo grins. He's one of the Greek gods, of course. The god of sun and light. All that's missing from his outfit is a bow and arrows.

I get the feeling that his gaze is on me again, but I don't dare check to see. My attention flickers around the room, and I grip the rail tightly.

"Three fights for Chosen tonight. Three winners who will walk away with..." His lips curl up again in a sneer. "Favors from the gods."

It seems sacrilegious to even consider it, but I suppose that's just my parents' Catholic upbringing.

"And as always, my fellow hosts." Apollo points up to our level, but to one of the smaller boxes—one that actually has two ornate seats. They're more like thrones than chairs.

My breath gets caught in my throat.

One stands *on* the chair. He wears all red, too much like blood. His mask is made of black and red feathers, covering the upper half of his face. His red leather jacket is open, exposing his bare chest—and *abs*, like Apollo's, glistening in the low light. His pants look like black suede.

He's the one whose name was a mystery.

"Ares," Marley whispers in my ear.

Ares. I test it out on my lips, silently mouthing his name. God of war. The violence—the *blood*—makes sense.

Someone shuffles on my other side. "Hades is a beast when he chooses to fight."

I glance at the man beside me. His mask is purple and black, with little lightning streaks across it. Bold, if he's attempting to be something akin to Zeus.

But then I register what he says, and I turn back to the gods on their thrones.

The second man... my stomach drops.

His mask is bone-white, like a skull without the lower

jaw. The familiar twisting black metal horns rise from the forehead. I've seen those horns in my nightmares, looming out at me from the darkness.

His black suit jacket is open, similarly exposing his bare chest. Like Apollo's gold streaks, his chest and neck are smeared with charcoal. A dark tattoo peeks out on his chest. There are no adornments on his mask. No jewels, just… a weird feeling under my ribs.

"Rumors are that Hades' mask is a real human skull," the Zeus man comments.

Marley nods, leaning back to talk around me. "I heard that, too."

My stomach swoops. "He fights?"

"He hasn't in a while. But maybe we'll get lucky in the coming weeks. It's always a show." The man nudges me. "You okay?"

"Peachy," I manage.

Maybe.

"Well?" Apollo calls to the audience. Ramping us up. Again, his voice isn't loud. But it carries. "Are we ready?"

The crowd around him yells and stomps their feet. I grip the polished brass handrail in front of me, trying to shove away the sick feeling. He continues talking, introducing the fighters—the *Chosen*—but I block it out. I don't care who fights.

Instead, I study Hades as subtly as possible. He lounges back on his chair now, his legs spread and chin resting on his fist. He gives off a disinterested energy, which seems at odds with the atmosphere in the room.

There's a tattoo on his hand, disappearing down his forearm and into his sleeve.

How am I going to steal his mask? Rip it from his face like he tore mine away and hope to disappear?

Another roar from the crowd, and Marley's elbow jabs into my side. I return my focus to the fighters, who have both stepped up on the raised platform. Their masks are much more practical: just fabric tied around their heads. The two men are bare-chested, slick with oil. Their black shorts don't hide much, either.

Apollo doesn't say anything, he just steps away.

And the fight begins without a word.

The first crunch of fist and cartilage has me staggering backward. I can feel the pain in my own nose. Their blood drips onto the sand, quickly swallowed by it. I keep moving backward, and although it doesn't erase the noise, I can manage not seeing.

I can pretend the grunts are something else entirely.

I move into the hallway and close my eyes.

"Do you regret coming?"

I spin around, instantly on guard.

Ares stands in front of me. His red mask is even more grotesque up close. It seems like liquid sprayed across his mask really is blood staining the feathers.

The god of war.

I picture his hands on my arms, holding me while Hades declared me... *invisible*. Nothing. He sees me now, though, and maybe it's because of the mask. Maybe I'm only valuable when I don't have a name attached to me.

A bitter taste fills my mouth.

"I..."

I do regret coming with Marley. My best friend's thirst for violence is much stronger than mine. She thought I'd like it because of what happened with my ex, but it's that very thing that drives the nausea. And this place is a very real reminder of what happened three months ago.

"I don't think I understand the fanfare." I force my shoulders to raise in a slight shrug.

"We can do something about that." He holds out his arm. "Come with me."

I meet his gaze, and my heart skips a beat. His *eyes* are red. And unlike Apollo, there's no makeup darkening the skin visible through the holes in his mask. It's like he wants people to know he's both human and monster at the same time.

That wasn't apparent in the dark, the last time we met.

Something must happen with the fight, because the crowd erupts into wild cheers.

His chin lifts ever so slightly, and I take it as a challenge. Maybe he's not used to resistance or people being squeamish about the fights. It's ironic that the god of war has noticed when no one else even looked back.

I take his arm. My fingers curl around the warm leather of his jacket, in the crook of his elbow, and I let him guide me down the hallway. The raven-masked men at their stations eye us. Everyone else is on their balconies, focused on the fight below. It's like we're both invisible.

Truly, this time.

We round the corner and come to a stop at a black curtain. Ares sweeps it aside and reveals those two chairs he and Hades occupied earlier.

Hades is gone. Which is fine—I don't need him to potentially recognize me. Ares might, too, but I'll cross that bridge when I come to it. I should be scoping out the area. Figuring out how—and when—to take Hades' mask.

Ares leads me around to his chair, then sits... and takes me with him.

I let out a little squeak as I fall into his lap, and his hands grip my hips.

"What are you doing?" My voice shakes—sue me.

"It's more enjoyable if you know what's going on." This way, his lips are right at my ear. "The big guy has been coming to Olympus for months. Sometimes he loses, sometimes he wins. He's a Titan, but no one knows that here."

I find myself nodding along. The Titan looks rough below. They're circling each other, both breathing heavily, but the bigger man favors his left leg. And then Ares' words register, and my chest tightens. A Titan like Kronos. The burn on my wrist aches all over again, and I'm glad Marley didn't point out my bracelet.

Ares, though, runs his finger over my forearm. He pauses on the cuff, then sweeps back up. He might mean it to be soothing, but goosebumps rise on the backs of my arms.

"And the other one?" I don't know if I hope he's better or worse.

His hand flexes on my hip. "A college student with balls."

I analyze the smaller man with renewed interest.

"Do you find him intriguing?" His voice is bitter.

But didn't he just want me to watch?

I glance away when the two fighters meet in the center again, trading quick blows. My gaze travels the balconies, absorbing the costumes and finery, but then two fingers on my chin directs my attention back to the face of the man whose lap I sit on.

My skin heats under his touch—and his stare. It seems he doesn't really care about the fight below, either. His gaze moves all over my face, down the exposed column of my throat, to the white dress. Then back up. It doesn't feel degrading—just curious. His attention pauses on my lips.

"You're a curious thing, aren't you?" His voice is almost too low for me to hear. "Too innocent for the likes of Hell."

I stiffen. "Trust me, I've been to Hell. This is nothing."

He hums. The sound isn't audible so much as it vibrates in his chest. And I can feel it, and my heart pounds in response.

Something happens down below, because the noise level skyrockets.

We're locked in our own sort of fight, though. I won't be the one to look away from his red eyes. I can tell myself all the lies in the world: that he doesn't scare me. That he doesn't recognize me. That this place doesn't terrify me. That I'm not completely out of my depth with the Titans.

He smiles and runs his finger down my jaw. "I look forward to discovering your version of Hell."

I push off his lap, and he lets me go. He does seem quite like how I always pictured the Greek gods. Arrogant, exquisite. Uncaring on the surface—but it's like he has embers burning behind his eyes. And he doesn't match up with the nightmare version of him that I've kindled in my memories.

All of this is too alluring for my own good.

"See you soon," he calls after me.

Somehow, I can still hear him. Even as the crowd shrieks and cheers around me.

CHAPTER 3

"You want to go back?" Marley gapes at me. She presses the back of her hand to my forehead. "Are you sick?"

I crumple my failed chemistry test in my bag, ignoring her hand. "It was interesting."

I haven't been able to get Ares out of my head. His burning red eyes, the way his hands gripped my hips. Maybe I'm cursed, because my nightmares revolve around that place. But it's better than other nightmares. And the past few days, dream Ares has been less scary and more seductive.

When I'm awake, all I can think about is how the hell I'm going to sneak away with Hades' mask. And my debt. And my hunger.

It's caused a major distraction in my schoolwork. So much so that I completely forgot about one of my first tests and blanked on at least half of the questions. The only *good* thing is that there's no scholarship hovering over my head to be yanked away if I flunk out of school.

Everyone—including my best friend—is in the dark.

She doesn't think it's odd that I ask her to swipe me into the dining hall when we eat together. And I think she's been chalking up my weight loss as a *good* thing. The opposite of the freshman fifteen that she put on when she got to campus last year.

I just haven't corrected her.

She narrows her eyes. "You were green under that mask the whole time."

"And you're the one who thought I'd like it," I counter.

"Fair point." She swipes us into the dining hall. She doesn't even bat an eye to do it. "I did think you'd like it because it's like being in a different world. But then I clearly saw you *not* enjoying it, and I felt bad."

I nod once. If she looked across the space and saw me on Ares' lap, she certainly didn't mention it. And upon my arrival back at her side, I made up some lie about finding a bathroom. I don't like keeping secrets, but I suddenly find myself holding on to a lot of them.

We've been friends since first grade, when her parents divorced and she ended up moving with her mother to Emerald Cove. Originally, she's from Sterling Falls, and she always talked about wanting to return here. Her father still lives in town, I guess, although I haven't met him yet. I don't know if she's seen him more than a handful of times in the last year. They're not on the best terms.

While she came straight to SFU after high school, I worked and took a few classes at a community college. I was already a year older than my high school class, thanks to having to repeat kindergarten. The community college was going to be it for me… until I got the scholarship.

Marley and I celebrated together. She had already committed to live on-campus with her freshman roommate again but promised she and I could find a place next year.

The world of possibilities that opened up with the scholarship seemed daunting and exciting in equal measure. But in one night, the rug was ripped out from under me.

And I can't even tell my best friend that I don't know what I'm going to do past December. If I leave without settling my debt, Kronos will use Marley and my parents against me. Hell, he might even kill them.

My resolve strengthens. The only way out is to steal that damn mask.

"Now that I know what to expect, I want to go back." I shift. "I mean, if you want to."

She hesitates. It's my fault—I've been a shitty friend. Haven't I been saying that all along? I came to her college and immediately turned into a scared little hermit. She had a life already. Other friends. And while we're best friends, it's never been more clear that we're on different playing fields. Socially, anyway.

"It's okay," I tell her. And really, it is. I've been working up the nerve for the last week and a half to even consider it. Now, it's Thursday, and my allowed time to steal the mask is running out.

I still haven't figured out *how* I'm going to do it. But the when seems reasonable.

What better time than during a fight? Or after, once he's taken it off? I could follow him and see where he puts it. A simple snatch and grab.

Well, simple is relative.

She nods to herself. "A few of us were talking about going, so you should just come along with us. It'll be more fun in a group."

I mask my nerves with a smile. I don't think her friends like me very much. Blame it on my hermit status, or maybe they're just threatened by me. My first meeting with them was disastrous... a spilled drink, an accidental insult, and you'd think I killed their cat.

"Awesome, thanks. And I've got my own ticket this time." Because the thought of her offering to pay again doesn't sit right. I can probably scrape together the cash.

We eat, and I head back to my apartment. I'm halfway home when the hair on the back of my neck stands up. I glance over my shoulder.

Act normal.

A man trails me by about half a block. He just *seems* menacing. Like everyone else should move away from him —or better yet, run away. Bald head, black leather jacket that could very easily hide weapons. My imagination runs away from me.

I can't help the worry, though, even if it might just be coincidence. I take a few unnecessary turns, then check to see if I've lost him.

I breathe out a sigh of relief. The street behind me is empty.

But then I step up onto the stoop of my apartment building and stick the key in the lock, and the man seems to come straight out of thin air. I catch a glimpse of him out of the corner of my eye, but it's too late. He grasps my wrist, twisting it harshly until I drop my keys. His other hand grabs my hair.

I squeal and kick at him, struggling to get free, but his blank expression doesn't falter. He doesn't so much as flinch when my foot connects with his knee, but he does shove me face-first into the door. My cheek hits the glass. His grip on my hair tightens, cranking my head back until I wince. My neck is exposed, and pain runs from my scalp down into my back. My eyes fill with tears.

"Time's running out, invisible girl." He leans in. His

breath stinks of garlic and cigarette smoke. "You have six days."

I glare at him with one eye, although the effect is probably lost. Half of my face is smooshed into the glass panel of the door. He doesn't react, just lets his gaze drop down my body and back up.

"Kronos sends his regards." He releases me and strides away, hands in his pockets.

I push off the door, panting and trembling. *They want me afraid*. Or to pay. Every day, my debt grows bigger, and my small stockpile of cash grows smaller. I gather my keys and finish unlocking the door, then hurry to my apartment. I flip the deadbolt and stand in the center of my mostly empty apartment.

I should feel ashamed of how few possessions I have. There was a point when I thought I'd be able to make this place more... homey. There's a secondhand couch, side table, lamp. Enough utensils in the kitchen for one person, *maybe* two, depending on the meal. A mattress on the floor in the bedroom.

It's just... sad.

I hate it. I have the urge to smash the lamp and bring the whole building down around me with my anger.

My bank account wouldn't allow such a thing. Right now, it has the meager remnants of the loan, and that's it. Money that I loathe to touch, knowing every penny I spend on food or electricity is another cent I don't have to repay Kronos.

So, no, I can't destroy my apartment and all my belongings.

But I can do *something...*

Scope out Olympus.

If nothing is happening there tonight, it should be empty. Right?

Or I can tell whoever I find that I forgot something behind… from two weeks ago.

Great idea.

I text Marley and ask to borrow her car, then check my closet for my most inconspicuous outfit. Black hoodie and pants screams *thief*, doesn't it? So I slip on a pair of jean shorts and a white blouse.

The weather has remained steadily warm. Home is the same way: nice for nine months of the year, and volatile for three, or two if we're lucky.

My nerves are shredded by the time I pick up Marley's car. She's running late to her last class of her day, so she smacks a kiss on my cheek and drops the keys in my palm without any questions.

On the way, I consider how to get Hades away from his mask. This is realistically my last chance, unless I want to stalk the man *under* the mask and figure out where he puts it when he isn't Lord of the Underworld. Or face another brand on my wrist.

I shudder. *No thanks*.

Something tells me Kronos will be even less pleasant… or perhaps more gleeful. He seems to be the sort of man who enjoys collecting his pound of flesh from unsuspecting people.

That was me—naive and *stupid*.

I reach the long driveway that leads up to Olympus and slow the car to a stop. Details I had missed the last two times I was here jump out at me. Namely, the cliffs just behind the mammoth marble building. In the daylight, the drop-off, with the ocean extending below, is quite noticeable.

It doesn't seem so magical in the gray light, either. More

like a forgotten remnant of ancient Greece, unearthed and planted... *here*. Of all places.

Someone wanted to resurrect the feeling of a pantheon. A temple for the three gods who inhabit its halls. A pantheon and a cathedral smashed into one. It makes me feel small, driving toward it.

I automatically shiver, and I almost turn around. But instead, I park and get out, ignoring my budding trepidation. Instead, I approach the cliffs. I'm not sure why they draw my attention more than Olympus, but I'm mesmerized. The climb is familiar, and I have to fight my instinct to run.

Memories pop across my eyes like camera flashes.

Here is where I spotted them and stopped, and *here* is where I removed my heels. And *there* is where the man was stabbed. I avoid that stretch of grass at the corner of Olympus and continue up the hill. This is where I didn't quite make it, to the level ground at the top of the rise.

It's grass up until the edge, and I creep closer. The drop-off plummets twenty, thirty feet down into the ocean. Waves crash against rough stone, the noise like thunder.

I can almost imagine the spray reaching all the way up here. I stare down, craning as far over as I dare. The sight of such forceful water is hypnotic. And only two miles north of here begins a long stretch of beaches. To the south, forests. Sterling Falls is in its own little bubble with trees and water on all sides.

Wind whips up the cliff face, pushing me back a few feet. The last thing I need is an unwanted swim... and no way back to shore.

A tendril of fear winds through me. They could've easily driven me *this* way. Shoved me off the side and went back to their lives.

"You're wasting your time," a woman calls.

I spin around. She stands maybe ten feet away, her arms folded across her stomach. Her dark hair whips around her face, and the more of me she sees, the harder she scowls. She's probably close to my age, maybe a little older. Her face is all sharp angles.

"Sorry, what?" I step closer to her—and away from the edge.

"They're not here."

I cast a glance back at Olympus.

Is Olympus the event or the location? I never found that out.

"The guys," she says impatiently. "If you jump, it'll be for nothing. No one will see you."

"Except you," I point out.

That gets her to smile. "Yeah, but I'm not going to jump in after you."

I shove my hands in my pockets. "I wasn't going to jump."

She shrugs. "Could've fooled me."

"And I certainly wouldn't do it to get the attention of *the guys*. Whoever they are." Whoever they are when they aren't pretending. And I have to wonder how many desperate girls she's stopped from pitching themselves over the cliff's edge. Or how many she's sat back and watched beg for their attention.

"Hmm," she responds. "Well, if you're not here for their special brand of currency, or to see if they'd save you from the waves, why are you here?"

"I was curious. And I wanted to get a scope of the place before tomorrow night." A half-truth. I stop in front of her and lift my chin, willing her to believe it.

Her lips quirk for a moment. Then her face goes smooth

again, and she nods with understanding. "Ah. Before the glamour takes hold."

"Exactly."

She motions for me to walk with her. There's no other car on the expansive lawn besides mine. I can't quite figure out where she's come from, or why she even bothered to come over. Although, if she was worried about a jumper...

"Fight nights always bring out the bloodthirst in people. It's stoked by the masks. There's nothing strictly *magical* about it, but they work hard to give that illusion to people. In a way, the masks allow our Sterling Falls citizens to be the freest version of themselves."

I find myself nodding along to her words. I can see how that would happen. No repercussions. Anonymity. It could translate to a certain sort of freedom... or recklessness.

"Do you attend?"

She grins, but it's more like her teeth are bared. "Sometimes. But only if I can fight. I don't like to just observe."

I appraise her again. She's taller than me, and leaner. She does have a certain cutthroat edge to her, so, yes. I can easily picture her on the platform, beating someone twice her size.

"And tomorrow?"

"Yes. And Hades, too. A real treat." Bitterness.

We pass the entrance of Olympus, one of the massive doors cracked. I guess I won't be getting another peek inside.

"Is he a main attraction or something?"

She stares at me, then laughs. "Oh, I like your innocence. You were here the last fight night, right?" She snorts. "Oh, don't give me that look. I know a new addict when I see one. Well, expect double the crowd. I'm sure rumors have spread that Hades threw his hat in the ring. Or, threw his *mask* in, as it is."

I tilt my head. "He doesn't fight in it?" The other fighters all had black fabric ones. Why would Hades be any different? But it isn't bad to keep playing dumb. Not all the time, anyway.

"No. It'll be safe and sound in his rooms until after." She rolls her eyes. "Don't fall for his act, okay? For me. Since you seem like a decent human."

I chuckle. "Don't worry. I doubt I'll even be sticking around in Sterling Falls long enough for that to happen." I'm still holding on to the hope that I'm successful and that I can erase my debt and leave this damn town.

She narrows her eyes. "You're not staying?"

"Eh, I don't know. I haven't made up my mind. I'm a student for now."

"Sterling Falls is like no other."

That, I can agree with.

I force myself to shrug. "Yeah, well. Some things are out of my control."

Everything hinges on tomorrow night. I can tell a little lie to my parents that school didn't work out. That SFU isn't for me. Move back into my room in their house… get a job in Emerald Cove.

Life will go on, but it seems a lot bleaker right now.

Even if I manage to wipe out my debt with the Titans, I don't know if I even want to see if I can afford to keep attending. I could reapply for more financial aid… maybe start again next fall. It's such a massive headache that I don't want to consider it.

"You seem a bit chaotic." She lifts her brow, silently daring me to disagree.

I can't, though. I *am* chaotic.

We stop at Marley's car, and she faces me. It's a subtle hint to leave, but I appreciate her kindness. I extend my hand. "Thank you for... all of that."

She takes it and gives me another big smile. "You ever want someone to talk to, just ask for Artemis. Until we meet again."

I nod. I don't bother to ask her *who* I would ask for her, but I suppose I can figure that out if I decide to take her up on it.

Hers is another Greek goddess name. If I wasn't at all familiar with this town, I'd think it's coincidence. But she must have some affiliation with *the guys*, as she called them.

I start Marley's car, and she strides back toward Olympus. I watch her for a moment, then shake myself out of it.

Even if I wasn't able to go inside, she's given me valuable information.

Hades is fighting.

And when he fights, he'll take off his mask in favor of the fabric ones all the Chosen wore last time. All I need to do is find his room to make it happen—and not get caught with it.

I chuckle to myself, if only to keep from crying. I've never stolen anything in my life, and here I am trying to play criminal mastermind.

Something tells me this isn't going to go smoothly... at all.

CHAPTER 4

I tie the same floral-and-lace mask over my face. I'm buzzing with nerves, and I haven't been able to sit still all day. The plus side: my apartment is spotless. The downside: I've talked myself out of this more times than I can count, but I'm still here.

Marley meets my eyes in the rearview mirror. When they'd picked me up, her friend, Janet, had already claimed the front seat. And another two sit to my right. I don't really care to know their names, and so I didn't ask. I'm not part of this friend group. Although, I have a sneaking suspicion I *should* know their names.

"It was so nice of you to go with Lee since we were busy last fight night," Janet says to me. In other words: Marley never would've taken me if they hadn't had *plans*.

I force a smile. Marley asked me to play nice. She might've asked the same of them, and this little jab is under her bullshit threshold. Janet has a red mask that reminds me of Ares. Ruby-red jewels crusted over her brow and cheekbones. Her lips are stained red, too.

"Nemesis," she says when she catches me staring.

I cock my head. "Excuse me?"

"Oh, sorry, did you not know? The masks and costumes are fashioned after more Greek gods. Of course, there are some off-limits ones." She taps her chin. "What is yours supposed to be?"

I shrug. Punching her would not be playing nice—and I don't like violence. But Janet certainly does love trying to get a rise out of me. I speak through my teeth when I answer, "No idea."

Janet turns back around in her seat. We're almost there, at any rate. We crest the hill, and Olympus awaits. We park farther back than last time. We seem to be later to arrive. There's already a long line at the door.

"What is yours?" I whisper to Marley on our way to the back of the line.

She stashes her keys in her little clutch. "Aphrodite. Legend says she was born into the sea and arose fully formed on a shell."

Interesting. I'm glad the mask and the darkness hide my hot cheeks. Marley could've told me that all the masks had a Greek god or goddess inspiration.

"Janet likes Nemesis because she's supposed to embody righteous anger." My best friend slips her arm through mine. "Anything for her anger to be justified, right?"

I chuckle at that. "True."

"You'll notice a lot of repeats. Different forms of the same ones. Some go for bold choices, like Zeus or Poseidon. It makes me wonder if those people are trying to catch Hades' eye. Another way besides fighting."

"Come on, Lee," Janet calls from ahead of us. Her mask matches her red skin-tight dress.

I wrinkle my nose. "I can't believe you let them call you that."

She snorts. "It caught on before I could stop it. But it's not totally bad. And you look nice tonight."

"In my mystery-goddess outfit?" I glance down at the same dress I wore last time. I didn't have any others besides that ill-fitting black one. There was no way in hell I was going to risk Hades *recognizing* it after he insulted it. And besides, this one matches.

I switched up my hairstyle, curling it into loose waves around my shoulders, but that was as far as my effort to be different extended. I considered changing my septum ring for something I could flip up into my nose and hide but decided against it.

I tap the mask. "Seriously, where did you find this thing?"

"I just bought it when I bought mine. It's innocent. It fits you."

I elbow her. "I'm not innocent."

"No, you're not. But sometimes you seem like you could be." She stops us and squeezes my hands. "I just want you to be happy, Kora. We've been on weird footing since school started, and I'm sorry if I've made you feel like you're an outsider."

My eyes burn, and I blink rapidly so tears don't fall. "I... Thank you. It means a lot that you care. I've been... I don't know, honestly. But we'll get back to normal. I promise."

The line moves quickly. Janet and the other two end up behind Marley and me. We step up to the door, and a man with a raven mask extends his hand. And then he blinks at me, his gaze quickly sweeping up and down my body.

Marley scowls at him. "She's not your eye candy."

He grins and leans toward her. "No, she's definitely not mine."

Her glare doesn't lighten, and she stiffly holds out the

cash. He takes it, running his finger along her wrist. She gasps and pulls away quickly.

My gaze bounces between them, my eyebrows up, but he just keeps her eye contact and waves her through. She moves past him slowly.

You're late. I can hear the man's voice in my head again. I try to do the same—to quickly pay and get it over with—but he holds his hand up. "I won't accept your money."

I huff. "Why not?"

Free entry last time... I thought it had to be a one-off.

"What's the holdup?" Janet calls. "You short on cash, Kora?"

The man's raven mask is quite peculiar. The purplish black feathers are so tiny around his eyes, the detail perfect. They get bigger the farther out they get, winging backward and giving the man a windswept look. The feathers blend with his black hair. And the glistening black beak extends forward, curling down and narrowing into a sharp point. It can't be just a regular mask.

"Go ahead," he says, tilting his head to the door.

I fold the bill in half and shove it into my bra, hoping he can read my own glare through the lace and flowers. It's hard to look tough—or mad—when I'm covered in floral. Ignoring that and the blustering behind me, I scoot past him. I find Marley close to the staircase after a few minutes.

True to Artemis's word, the place is *packed*, with more coming in every minute.

Marley bounces up and down in excitement, a wide grin on her face. Tonight, her seashell Aphrodite mask is paired with a baby-blue dress. She and I are quite the pair in a sea of dark colors.

Unfortunately, Janet and her two cronies find us too

soon. She marches up to me and pokes my shoulder. "What the fuck was that?"

I stagger back. "Excuse me?"

"Why did he let you in for free?" she demands. "They never do that."

I cross my arms. "Maybe not for *you*." *And your snotty attitude.*

Marley shoots her a look. "They do it on occasion," she says. "It isn't like you don't have the money for it, Janet. Daddy's trust fund supplies your addiction."

And I don't have two dimes to rub together if I want to keep food in my belly. That, blessedly, remains unspoken.

"Did you hear Hades is fighting?" One of the cronies nudges Janet. Her name might be Erica, but I honestly can't recall it. "It's going to be a good night."

Marley pulls out her flask, and shockingly, the other three girls mirror her with their own little flasks. Low security events, I guess, allow this sort of thing to happen. *Or*, Olympus isn't exactly legal—and therefore, they don't give a shit.

Soon enough, the huge atrium can hold no more people. Marley is close on one side, and strangers all around. When I take a deep breath, I inhale anticipation and the slightest odor of sweat. Everyone seems to be restless tonight.

The outer doors boom shut, and Apollo appears, same as the previous time. His attire is the same, bare chest and gold paint, the animal skull mask.

"Welcome to Olympus," he says. "Tonight is a special night, with special fighters."

We let out a cheer. Well, everyone around me does. As soon as he appeared, my chest tightened. I open my mouth and mimic the excitement filling the room.

But dread… dread has taken its place. It runs through my veins like ice water.

Because I won't just be attending. I can't just sit back and watch the fights and pretend everything is okay.

I have to do something I've never attempted before.

"We have five fights tonight," Apollo announces. "Our eight Chosen… one of whom will fight my dear sister, Artemis."

My jaw drops, but the crowd yells and hollers. Even Marley and her friends scream and clap, and I doubt they've met the girl. But *I* met her—and of course she's Apollo's sister. It's right out of the myth, after all. Twins.

Are they twins?

"And the last has bravely challenged Hades." Apollo's tone is grave.

Boos and hisses fill the room. I glance around, surprised. Hades is beloved?

"Our thoughts exactly." He sneers. "For those who don't know, my name is Apollo. I'm your host for the evening." He scans the room, then gestures wide. "The doors are open, my friends. See you soon."

Instead of the fanfare of two weeks ago, this time he goes to the banister and leaps over the edge. He lands much lighter on the marble floor than I would've thought possible, then strides quickly through the dark archways.

Marley grips my hand. "Let's go."

I start to fight it—after all, I should be downstairs to find Hades' rooms—but then go with the flow. There's nothing I can do right off the bat, and I'd bet that Hades will be fighting last. *Then*, I can steal it.

We go up and into one of the boxes, claiming our place. I keep my fists at my sides. My nerves take the form of snakes in my belly, and I glance around for an escape. Just in case I'm actually going to puke.

A short time later, Apollo hops up onto the platform. Bodies press in on all sides. A sense of claustrophobia hits me. Marley was beside me, but Janet managed to slip seamlessly between us, and I'm swept away. More people are close behind us, peering between bodies for any sort of glimpse.

The bottom level is worse. The crowd down there is rougher, jostling for positions. They press so close to the platform, they'd practically be in it if it wasn't a different height. Rich people and ordinary ones are all tossed in the same lot in Olympus. We're all the same, hiding behind our masks and suppressing our fear.

Bloodlust is what rules this night.

Someone bumps me, and suddenly I'm towed backward.

The hand on my elbow doesn't release me until I'm free of the double layer of bodies, and I can breathe again. My spot at the rail is immediately claimed by someone else, like the sea swallowing a trail of footprints.

I whirl around and then jerk back.

Ares grins at me.

His mask and red eyes are the only thing the same about him. I take in his new costume in belated shock. He wears an open white collared shirt, but it's covered in—hopefully fake—blood. Like he violently murdered someone before strolling in here. It seems dark in the dim light, and there are even smears of it on his chest and over his abs.

That wouldn't be unusual, right? I saw them do it once. They can do it again.

Before I can stop myself, I reach out and touch one of the dark spots on the fabric. I half expect my fingers to come away red, but it's dry.

"I thought I might see you again." His smile is quick.

I glance around. "You're going to miss your introduction."

His eyes gleam, and he leans down until our faces are level. "No, I won't."

I bite my lip. I don't know what it is about him, but he has me curious. It's a pull from just behind my ribcage, a desperation to uncover all his secrets.

Mysterious Ares.

Above it all, I want to know the men I'm stealing from. It's clear that stealing the mask isn't just an act against Hades—it's against all of them. And I want to know who's behind *this* mask.

"Did you come back to watch Hades?"

"No." I tip my head to the side. "Is that what you really wanted to ask me?"

He straightens to his full height. He's quite a bit taller than me, but I'm not intimidated by that. Even though his hands on my arms in the forest sit fresh in my mind, and their howls sometimes ring in my ears, I'm not scared.

What I *should* be is wary.

Wary of pretty boys with masks and ill intentions.

Of dark rooms and violence.

Ares is the God of *War*. Of bloodthirsty rage.

He takes my hand without asking and pulls me into him. His lips touch my ear. "Come with me again, little flower. Your friends haven't noticed your disappearance. And didn't you have more fun with me last time?"

Goosebumps race down my arms. His voice is husky and low, its own form of seduction. I find myself stepping closer to him.

The mask.

"I want to see more." My cheeks immediately heat at his intrigue. "Of this place, I mean."

He smirks. "Of course." He maneuvers my hand, still in his clutches, to once again wrap around the crook of his arm. When he leads, the people lingering in the hall spring out of the way. They don't really give a shit about me, but *him*?

Ares doesn't take me downstairs like I imagined. We pass the split staircase that descends into the atrium, and he steps on the rope that blocks the other hall. He helps me over it, and then we're on the forbidden side.

Once past, a coldness descends on me. *This* feels like the point of no return.

I let him take me farther into Olympus. We pass closed doors, but he makes no move to explain or show me. My heels click on the marble floor, loud now that we're away from the crowd. His footsteps are nearly silent.

We reach another, infinitely more modest set of stairs. They curve down and out of sight. But before we go, he tugs me to the side and presses me against the wall.

I know, *I know* he wants to kiss me. Or something. There's a friction between us that moves under my skin, and this is proof that he feels the same. There are a million reasons why I should push him away right now. His body leans into mine, and his face is so close.

If I were myself, the dominant movement would scare me.

And even though I'm playing a part, I can't erase my past. My whole body stiffens, my fears lingering on my skin like scars. I press my hands against Ares' bloodstained shirt and try to play it off.

He immediately drops his hands from the wall on either

side of my head and retreats. Not far, but far enough that I can breathe.

His red eyes sear into mine. "Someone hurt you, little flower?"

I force a smile and edge to the side, to the stairs. "I don't really want to talk about that."

He makes a noise in the back of his throat.

"I'd say it was a long time ago, but..."

Six months. I've been away from Parker for *six months*, and I only enjoyed my freedom for a handful of days. I made the mistake of trying to get into Olympus.

Then *they* found me—and I disappeared.

He studies me.

I throw my shoulders back, my line of thinking scaring me. I can't show all my cards. In fact, I'd be better off revealing nothing. "I'm not that person tonight. Isn't that the big appeal of this place? To be someone else?"

Ares nods carefully and offers his arm again.

I seem to like touching him, so I take it. He guides me downstairs, and the marble hallways transform from light and golden to charcoal-streaked silvery marble. We pass darkened alcoves every once in a while, and a few times I swear I see movement. Blackened candelabras stand at the edges of the hall, holding lit candles at eye level. Sconces on the wall add little illumination. The candles throw shadows and flickering light across the walls and floors.

I inhale. The hall smells like the spice I detected the first time I arrived. My nerves are fraying. And my damn heels tap the marble with every step. We're not sneaking, I know that. But I *will* be sneaking... eventually. I should've planned for this.

"Where are we going?" Even though my voice is low, it seems to travel far out in front of me. There are long, narrow windowpanes in the marble on one side of the hall. The moon is visible through one, and I steel myself.

He doesn't answer.

I glance up at him, but his face is in shadows.

Who did I decide to trust in the dark?

"Ares."

His gaze snaps to mine.

"Where—"

"You don't like surprises," he states.

I grimace.

Unsurprisingly, he smiles. He flips between the God of War and a smiling man too quickly for me to keep track. It's jarring, and I'm left unsettled. It's a good thing. I *shouldn't* trust him or be calm around him. My guard needs to be up as sure as my mask tied around my face.

"You want to know what made me pull you from the crowd?" His voice matches my low pitch. He's a storyteller captivating his audience. "It was the desperation in your eyes when you looked over at us last time."

I jolt.

"I know," he continues. "Masks are supposed to hide everything. But, can't you see? It makes people show their true colors. Your desperation—for whatever reason, I'm not judging. Others long for what they don't have, either the will to fight or the courage, or the extravagance of Olympus.

"And every damn part of that is fascinating to me. I see it all. I take it all. *That* is the price of admission, more than the cash we collect at the door."

Damn.

We pause at another alcove, and he drops my hand. He faces me and brings his hand up, hovering just above my cheek.

"Why are you so captivating, mystery girl?"

I huff a laugh. "I'm not."

He traces a finger up my arm, ghosting over my skin. Both hands so close, but so far away. "I want to touch you."

I fight an internal battle. My brain loses when I challenge, "Do it, then."

His stare burns my skin, as if trying to see under the mask. It's a heady feeling, brazen mixed with fear of discovery. His attention on me. I've been the invisible girl for too long—I've almost started to get used to it. To feel my worth squashed beneath *their* shoes.

Am I using him right now? To get close to Hades' mask?

The red eyes are just part of his costume.

I need that mask.

But whatever happens next isn't going to let me walk out the door with it. That'll be a task I can't flirt my way out of. And even though I close my eyes and picture Hades' glare when he ripped my mask from my face, I don't think Ares will do the same.

As he said—a mask is revealing in its own way.

Restlessness sweeps through me. Then his lips touch mine so softly, with a hesitancy I wouldn't have paired with Ares. The masks should make us bolder, not more vulnerable. Not softer.

I inhale, surprised, and his wild scent fills my nose.

He retreats.

No. I grab his wrist and move it so his hand cups the side of my neck. The contact is more electric than I could've imagined, and I suck in a sharp breath. My other hand curls in his shirt, and I use it to guide him toward me. At the same time, I press up onto my toes.

My lips meet his harder than the first time. He groans and complies, immediately stepping farther into my space. My back bumps the wall. We crash together, our mouths opening. He tastes like whiskey and the flavor I imagine when I think of destruction.

His hand doesn't move from my neck. His fingers hardly even twitch on my skin, except his thumb. His thumb rubs a spot under my jaw, back and forth.

Butterflies detonate in my chest.

His thumb keeps moving even when he pulls away. We breathe heavily, inches apart in the dark, and reason slowly seeps back into me.

Reason—then *shame*. I'm here to deceive them, and that kiss just made it a hundred times worse. I need to find Hades' room. I need to steal his mask and get the hell out of dodge. This flimsy lace-and-flowers mask is the *only* thing that hides my identity.

My dark-red hair does me no favors if they come looking for me.

Neither do the girls I came with.

This is all wrong. I'm too… trackable.

I move to the side, and he lets me go. As soon as I'm free of him, the ache in my chest hits. Why, though? For a man I've only just met three times, who scares me more than he should. Why do I have the urge to step back into his embrace, even if it's wrong?

"This way," he says briskly, stepping past me. The moment shatters.

He heads down the corridor, and I follow.

We don't touch again.

CHAPTER 5

I catch a glimpse of fighters through open doors, each waiting in their own private room. Apollo comes into the hallway from the opposite side, leading the way for two raven-masked men dragging a limp fighter between them. Her feet slide on the marble.

"Hey! Chaos!" a female voice calls.

I automatically turn, and I'm not sure why.

A fighter steps into the hall. Her long dark hair is swept back in two braids that frame her face, and the rest is loose curls down her back. She wears a tan sports bra and matching shorts, just a few shades lighter than her bronze skin. Her dark-brown fabric mask hangs loose around her neck.

"Artemis," I greet her. *Apollo's sister.* So strange. I can't see it—but then again, I've only ever seen him in the mask.

She grins. "Knew it. That red hair will get you in trouble. Couldn't stay away, huh?"

I shrug, although she just confirmed what I already feared. If someone wants to find me after this, it won't be difficult.

"And in the fighter pit, no less." She whistles. "You work fast."

I peek ahead at Ares, who has stopped to talk to Apollo farther up the hall. The two seem deep in conversation, so I return my attention to Artemis. She seems full of restless energy, even though she's still. I can't explain it, but... I get it. Trying to contain that power and unleash it when she needs it. Not waste it.

"When do you fight?" I ask. "And who?"

"I can show you. Want a tour? Since your guide seems occupied."

"Sure."

And off we go, slipping past Ares and Apollo. The roar of the crowd is louder this way, so we must be nearing the entrance to the main room.

Artemis points at a closed door. "Hades is in there. *Preparing*."

I raise my eyebrow. "What does that mean?"

"I don't know. Probably meditating or something equally atrocious."

I laugh. Yeah, from the few glimpses I'd seen of Hades, I can't picture the man going full yogi. There's something intriguing about him doing some sort of deep-breathing exercises, though.

"Samson," she says suddenly, pointing into another doorway. The large man is idly punching a bag, his knuckles already wrapped. "He's fighting Hades as *Hercules*."

I grimace. "He's huge."

She smirks. "Yep." Farther down, her footsteps slow. The double doors are open at the end of the hall, letting in the sound and light from the main room. She gestures at the last door, which is closed. "Nyx. My opponent." Artemis's voice is barely audible. "She's one scary motherfucker when she fights."

I elbow her. "You can take her."

Her chin lifts. "I know. But she didn't get to be one of the crowd favorites by being weak."

Only the strong survive.

"There you are." Ares stops beside me and narrows his red eyes at Artemis. "You know the rules, Tem."

She makes a face at him, then nudges me. "See ya around, Chaos."

My lips quirk, but she doesn't explain her nickname to me or Ares. And then there's no more time to ask, because two fighters stride past us, led by Apollo.

Ares takes my arm—I guess we're back to touching—and guides me along behind them. One fighter pauses as the other goes first and is introduced by Apollo, and then the second is called out. We stride in behind him, the crowd filling in at our backs. In a matter of seconds, the path back to the fighter's corridor is blocked.

Ares moves to the side, giving me a clear view of the fighting ring. The steps rise just a foot in front of me. But no one crowds me, and I have the sense I can thank Ares for that.

I look up and meet Apollo's gaze. He holds it for a moment, and nervous energy pours through me. His dark eyes flick to my lips, or maybe my nose ring, then back over my mask. He tears his attention away and announces the fight, then hops down next to Ares.

The two are almost the same height, although Apollo's animal skull mask, with the tall horns, gives him the illusion of being taller. He's bulkier, too. Barely. I try not to gawk, but his muscles are huge. The gold paint glitters under the lights, and there's a faint sheen of sweat on his skin.

I force myself to watch the fight. It feels like eyes are on me, but I know that's just paranoia talking.

Two men are up on the platform. From here, I can make out the grimaces after every hit. The reverberation of skin and muscle with the impact. I can't breathe when one of the fighters takes a massive hit, and blood sprays out of his mouth. He falls to his hands and knees and spits out blood.

The crowd goes nuts.

The still-standing fighter leaps forward and kicks his opponent. I force myself to keep my eyes open and watch it.

This is a lesson in patience. In how to swallow my horror. In how to wear a true mask and believe my own lies.

I glance at Ares, only to find him watching *me*.

"You hate this."

I don't bother answering him.

He hums under his breath. "Curious."

I suffer through this fight, then another. Artemis is the fourth fight to go, and the people lose their minds when they see her. And then the noise rises to a deafening level when Nyx stalks out.

She's the polar opposite of Artemis in almost every way. Where Artemis has muscles packed on her lean frame, Nyx is willowy. She's tall and thin. Her blue-black hair is braided and hangs down the center of her back. Her mesh long-sleeve top reveals her black sports bra under it, plus her tattoos. She's covered in them, peeking out from her black shorts and even on her hands.

That gives her a bit of an edge, appearance-wise. And her name, Nyx—it makes sense when you see her. The goddess of the night seems like she could swallow darkness whole and it wouldn't even affect her.

The two prowl around each other. Artemis kicks sand at

Nyx, but the latter doesn't even flinch. Then Nyx darts forward and attacks. She's *fast.*

If I thought the last fight was bad, it has nothing on this one. The tension crests, and for a moment the whole place is silent. And then Nyx lands the first blow to Artemis' jaw, and the silence shatters. I'm jostled into Ares.

He glares at whoever hit me, and then a bubble forms.

My stomach is in my throat. They trade blows and blocks, staying locked together for moments at a time. Artemis's elbow catches Nyx in the throat, and she doesn't give Nyx a chance to recover, or take a break, before she's smashing her face in.

The latter falls, her arms up to protect her face. Her forearms get battered, and Artemis releases a wild sound. But somehow, impossibly, Nyx flips her off. Artemis hits the sand flat on her back. For a millisecond, Artemis stares at the sky. Then she scrambles up and lurches away.

Blood streams down Nyx's face, and she spits out a mouthful of red. Her teeth are stained with it. She grins at Artemis, who circles warily. It's too gruesome.

I sneak a glance at Apollo and Ares again. That's Apollo's sister up there, but both watch with cold expressions.

I search the crowd. My gaze trips over Marley on one of the balconies. Janet is beside her, whispering something in her ear. The other two girls are clapping and cheering at the railing.

I take a step backward. And another.

Ares doesn't notice—or if he does, he doesn't care. Someone fills in my spot, because *this* is the first of two fights no one wants to miss.

I just need to be invisible again.

For a moment.

I press my hand to my chest and stare at the back of the

head now directly in front of me. I count my breaths. Five seconds to inhale, one to hold, four to let it out. It isn't a foolproof system by any means, but a weight lifts.

Well, sort of.

The danger of what I'm *about* to do still hangs over my head like a guillotine.

Something happens, and the people around me jump up and down. I fight another urge to cover my ears and further back up. I bump into someone—multiple someones —but they don't care. I catch a glimpse of Apollo leaping up onto the platform and raising a tattooed hand in the air.

Nyx, then.

Bummer.

Instead of one of their crew grabbing Artemis, Apollo carries her out in his arms. I'm crammed sideways, packed into bodies, as Nyx follows them out. We stay like this, riding an edge of anticipation, until Apollo returns.

"A worthy opponent," he says. "Nyx is one of our best fighters. She graces us with a show every time she competes. But now... the main event of the evening. Are you ready?"

They roar their approval, stamping their feet.

"Then let's get on with it," Apollo yells. "Introducing our challenger, the Chosen crazy enough to dare take on the king, *Hercules!*"

I snort. But then the man I saw punching the bag earlier strides out, and he has to *duck* so he doesn't hit his head on the doorframe. In the larger space, he seems monstrous. He isn't Hercules, but one of the monsters the legendary Hercules had to fight. Not to mention, I'm pretty sure Hercules is from Roman mythology...

Ah, well. No one seems to care.

"And the legend himself," Apollo continues.

The crowd immediately hushes.

"Born right here in Sterling Falls. He survived against the odds. And now he's here to fight for you sorry lot." Apollo smiles, lessening the blow of his insult. "Our staff has already informed you that betting *on* Hades is forbidden. Because the bastard of this town never fucking loses. But who knows, maybe Hercules will get lucky."

There's clearly a favorite here.

But before I can do anything, the lights go out.

I push backward as people jostle, uneasy with the darkness. I can't see anything, and I feel blindly behind me until I touch cool marble.

Before, the whole place was dim lighting and dark atmosphere—but it's like they're showing us how truly lost we would be without any light.

A single spotlight flickers back to life, illuminating the fighting platform.

And there he stands. An illusion meant to mess with our minds, like Apollo's smoke trick. Chills break out through my body, and I know I'm not the only one.

Hades stands tall, but there's no fabric mask wrapped around his eyes. No, he wears an elaborately painted skull on his skin. I only catch a glimpse as he moves around the ring. The black under his jaw is streaked down his neck, much in the same style as Ares' and Apollo's paint. His chest is deliciously bare, and his black joggers hang low on his hips. There's an undeniable V leading... well, past the waistband.

I gulp.

He has an animalistic stride. That of a predator. Even though Hercules is much larger than Hades, he's lesser.

Easily.

There are no more announcements. Apollo is off to the side, with Ares, and I almost, *almost* forget I'm here to steal the mask Hades usually wears. This is my stroke of luck. To get out of here while everyone is distracted.

I glance around and catch sight of Artemis. She leans against the wall with an ice pack pressed to her face, but she's still standing—that's got to mean something, right? Nyx got the upper hand tonight. It happens. But nothing irreparable.

I slide my finger under the leather bracelet and press down on the brand. Loathing for my own skin crawls through me, so I quickly drop it. Instead, I slip toward the door, then into the hallway.

"Hey," a guy calls.

I jump.

One of the fighters from earlier comes toward me. "You're going to miss it."

I force myself to scowl. "Ares needed something, and you know how he gets."

The man laughs. "Bummer. Hurry up, Hades likes to toy with them a bit."

He strides past me, and I scurry away. I stick close to the wall, although that won't save me if I'm caught again. One flimsy lie won't hold up for very long. I stop in front of a closed door that I'm pretty sure is Hades' room, and I try the door handle.

Miraculously, it opens smoothly.

I tiptoe just past the threshold and glance around. There's not much in here that might separate it from another fighter's room. The marble block walls, glowing sconces on the wall, a lounge chair that appears to be black velvet and a three-cushioned black leather couch. A table and chairs off to the side. There are two windows of frosted glass, too.

No mask, though.

I close the door gently behind me and venture farther in. I've got no choice in the matter. There's another door, farther back, and I head for that. It opens into a large bathroom.

And there, on the counter, is the skull mask. The black metal horns curve up, but they're shorter than they looked the other night. And sharper. The whole thing is lighter than I thought. The bone is smooth, drilled holes allowing for black ribbons to be threaded through the edges and secured onto his face. I glance around, checking that the room is empty still, and lift the edge of my dress.

I tie it to my thigh, the skull facing out to the side, and drop the fabric again. It covers it... barely. The horns curl back and press against my skin, but that's manageable. My skirt is flowy enough that it isn't noticeable, but I fear it'll be noticed nonetheless. I suppress my fear and hurry to the door, then slip into the hallway.

No one sees me.

I let out a shaky breath and continue down the hall, toward the staircase Ares and I came down. Except... there's no staircase. I get all the way to the end and turn around slowly. Did I miss it? I go back, slower, my heart steadily picking up speed. This section is dark, the sconces unlit, and shadows cling to the walls. But there *was* a staircase here. And now it's gone. My other option is to go back through the main room, but pushing through bodies feels like another sort of trap.

I don't know how a whole stairwell could just vanish.

I open some doors for good measure, but the fighters' rooms are empty.

Fuck.

With hesitancy, I make my way back into the main room. The crowd is still in the dark, a spotlight on Hades and his opponent, but very clearly nearing the end of the fight. Hercules sways on his feet, and his jabs have become sloppy.

Someone said Hades likes to toy with them—and I see that clearly now. He circles Hercules, barely sweating. Not a scratch on him. I begin my journey through the crowd, gently maneuvering people out of the way.

But then something bigger happens, and I'm caught in the surge forward.

On the platform, the giant man has fallen.

Hades glares down at him, and then his gaze swings out across the screaming crowd.

I step behind a tall woman. I just need the doorway.

Desperation holds my lungs hostage.

Surely they'll start to move in that direction now that the fight is done. I make it, finally, bursting into the arched, dark hallway and gulping in a deep breath. Nerves thrum along my skin, and I shouldn't feel hope—not yet. Not until I'm far away from this place.

Or better yet, not until I can hand over the mask to Kronos and my debt is wiped away.

The atrium is empty. No raven-masked man stands guard, no guests linger. I nearly trip over my feet in my hurry, and I yank on the door. It's giant, but I expect it to... I don't know. *Move*.

It doesn't.

I shove at it with all my strength, lean my full weight back, but nothing happens. I step back and stare at the curved Greek-style wreath of leaves.

You're late. I have a weird moment where I can see through the door, to the me of almost four months ago. And the man in the boar mask warning me that I was too late.

A low howl cuts through the air, and my blood turns to ice. The hairs on the back of my neck rise, and I spin around to face Apollo. He comes out of the entrance beside the staircase—the same one I just exited.

His dark eyes land on me, bore *through* me, and I might disintegrate under his stare.

"Leaving so soon?"

I throw my shoulders back and try to act calm. I've had months to work on my indifference with Kronos, but now *everything* rests on my acting. "Family emergency."

He cocks his head. "Is it? What sort?"

"The bloody sort, probably." Ares comes from above, slowly striding down toward us.

I had last left him on the ground floor—how did he get up there?

"No, they—"

"They, who?" A third voice joins us. Hades emerges from the shadows.

I briefly debate closing my eyes. It's the final nail in the coffin, I think, to be caught so close to the exit—and by all three of them, no less.

In Sterling Falls, Kora Sinclair doesn't exist anymore.

He stops in front of me. His makeup runs from sweat, and his lip is split. I had missed that part, I guess, and missed it when I reemerged. It's surprising that Hercules was able to land a blow on him at all, given the hype around Hades and his fighting skills.

Blown out of proportion, maybe.

But up close, he's the same man who destroyed my future, even with a different mask. Same height, same voice. Same glower.

I shift back, and my shoulder blades hit the carved door.

Hades glances at Ares. Three gods and *me*. Who am I to them? Hades jerks his head, and Ares disappears. Of the three of them, I would've counted Ares to be... I don't know.

Kind, at the very least. He had no problem treating me gently earlier.

That's laughable of me to think that he would be *nice*.

"What's this about?" My demand is a false bravado I wear like armor.

Hades chuckles. He puts his hand on my collarbone and pushes gently, keeping me against the door. Not that I need any more incentive to be afraid, but his touch floods new fear through me. I squirm in the silence and mentally prepare for something horrible to happen.

But then Ares returns, dragging the fighter who caught me in the corridor. He has the fighter by the back of the neck, and he tosses him to the floor at our feet.

"This her?" Hades drawls.

The fighter jerks, scrambling up. "Y-yes."

"And?"

"Said she had to get something for Ares. Seemed fishy, seeing as how she's dressed like that in the fighter's section." He gestures to my dress.

Now I do close my eyes, because *fuck*, how many times has a lie come back to bite me in the ass? No worse than this one, I'm sure.

Hades laughs. It's cold and exactly like Kronos. I should've known this terrible plan was going to get me caught. There's nothing I can do about it now, though, right? Except face the punishment and hope it doesn't kill me.

"You wanted to rob us in our own house?"

I open my eyes. Part of me needs to know what's coming. But I refuse to answer. I doubt they prescribe to *innocent until proven guilty*. Nothing I can say will help me.

Especially if they lift the skirt of my dress.

True curiosity fills his gaze, and his eyes flick up and down my body. "What was it?"

I press my lips together.

He chuckles and shakes his head, then turns to Apollo. "Hold her."

A squeak leaves my lips when Apollo steps forward.

Ares blocks him.

My heart pounds louder, thundering in my ears.

"Just tell him." Ares stares at me, trying to convey something. Like, *if you don't comply, I won't be responsible for what they do next.*

He saw through me in seconds and backed away when I was afraid. But... my gut tells me Hades will lean into my terror.

I finger the hem of my dress and slowly lift it. I hate to do it—part of me wants to keep playing dumb.

That's naive—these guys would never let me walk out of here without at the *very* least searching me.

His mask is revealed on my thigh.

As soon as it is, Hades' hand wraps around my throat and squeezes. My air is cut off abruptly, and he pins me against the wall.

Panic consumes me.

I scratch at his wrist and forearm. He might not be trying to kill me, but I can't breathe. It's suddenly not Hades, but my ex staring down at me. Crushing my throat and willing me to lose consciousness. I stare at him, ignoring the mask pressing on my face and the paint on his. His eyes are ice blue. They remind me of cold water and drowning.

Wait for the laugh.

Ares steps forward. "She's—"

I can't breathe. I try to say it, to warn the stranger wearing my ex's face, but no sound comes out. He doesn't know his own strength, and I'm no stranger to passing out. It comes toward me as the ocean rushes toward the sand. The sound fills my ears, until I can't concentrate on anything except the pressure around my throat.

My mouth opens and closes, over and over.

The room spins, and then, like a candle being blown out, my vision extinguishes.

CHAPTER 6

Before I'm even fully awake, I consider the worst-case scenarios.

I can't help it—this is how I operate. Contemplating the worst brings a certain level of preparation, and an overall realistic-leaning-toward-optimistic outlook. I know, I know, how can someone only think the worst but *also* be optimistic? I figure, even if it's bad, there's still a good chance I'll come out on the other side.

Option one: I'm still in Olympus. They make me fight for my freedom.

That would suck. I'm not a fighter. At all.

Option two: I'm *not* in Olympus, and they've discovered the brand, put everything together, and plan on laughing in my face while dropping me off on the Titans' doorstep.

That would be the easiest form of punishment.

Option three... Maybe I won't wake up, because Hades dragged me into Hell.

But option three is definitely out, because I crack my eyes open.

I struggle to place myself. I'm on a bed. The fluffy

comforter and blankets under me *feel* expensive, just from the twitching of my fingers at my sides. Soft and cloud-like. My mattress on the floor of my apartment's got nothing on this.

Furthermore, I'm alone.

I sit up suddenly and blink heavily. The room tilts.

How hard did I hit my head? Did they just let me fall after Hades...

I shudder and shove that memory out of my thoughts. I need to be cool and figure out an escape route.

The room has dark-blue walls, a white rug placed diagonally over hardwood floors, a black lamp. A gray dresser, all the drawers closed. It's too neat. A man's room, clearly, but one with expensive taste. The white comforter just seems dangerous.

I smooth my hands over my dress, tugging the skirt down my thighs, and a flash of gratitude that I'm still *in* my dress washes over me. It dissipates rather quickly, though, when I realize my heels are gone, and so is my mask.

My hair has come partially undone, and chunks fall in waves over my shoulders. I run my fingers through it, then touch my nose ring. My throat. Taking slow inventory. I swallow easily. It isn't even sore.

Okay.

Focus, Kora.

The door swings open, and dark eyes crash into mine.

Apollo—without the mask. I'm not sure how I know it's him—maybe it's his dark-brown eyes. Or his warm skin tone that looks so good with gold streaked across it. Call it intuition.

I don't know the face I was expecting under the mask, but he isn't it. Because he's *beautiful*. Short black hair. High cheekbones. Full lips. Dark scruff on his jaw that the mask had hidden.

I suck in a breath and scoot backward, until my shoulders bump the headboard. Because I don't know how to react to seeing him. And how it suddenly conflicts in my mind with the deer-skull mask.

He holds out a bowl. "Soup?"

"What?"

He comes in and toes the door shut. "My mother always used to bring us soup in bed when something bad happened. It became a comfort food." He nudges my leg aside and sits on the edge of the bed, then practically forces the warm bowl into my hands.

I grasp it to keep from spilling but stare at him. "Apollo."

He inclines his chin. "You guessed it."

"Is that your real name?"

He smiles. "Yes."

"And Artemis is your sister. Her real name, too." I frown. "And I'm where, exactly?"

"So many questions." He has a way of looking through me. I felt it when he found me in the crowd at Olympus, then again when they caught me with Hades' mask. It's unsettling.

I lift my chin and ignore the fact that he's peeling me apart with his gaze.

His mood shifts, and the seriousness is evaporating.

He smirks. "Let's make a deal. If you finish that soup, I'll answer three questions."

"Six," I counter.

And then I risk a glance at the bowl, because shit, what if he gave me pea soup? It's the bane of my existence—although I'd probably still eat it to get some answers. And because my stomach cramps at the thought of food. It's not pea soup, luckily, but tomato. One of my favorites. Not such an awful bargain, but worth negotiating.

"Three."

"Five," I try.

"How about none?" He raises a thick eyebrow.

I glare at him. I'm not in a position to be glaring, I suppose, but they kidnapped me. Right? I'm allowed to be annoyed. I do want *some* answers, so...

"Fine," I grit out.

He waits, pointedly staring at the bowl, until I raise it to my mouth. He didn't give me a spoon, and I'm not about to transform into a savage and use my fingers. The flavor explodes on my tongue, and I have to stop myself from moaning.

The last time I had a full meal was in the SFU dining hall with Marley. And that seems like ages ago instead of yesterday afternoon.

As I gulp it down, Apollo watches me. He doesn't touch me, but I can practically feel his fascination. I'm the curiosity. The one who stole Hades' mask for no damn reason.

Suddenly, my stomach flips.

I failed.

I set the bowl down in my lap and wipe my mouth to hide my shaking. I'm so... *so* screwed. Worse than I was three months ago, when they turned my life drastically upside down.

Kronos is going to take the debt from my flesh—I can almost guarantee it.

He pulls the bowl toward him to see what's left, then tsks. "You can do better than that."

I take a deep breath and gulp the last two swallows. Then I show him and lean my head back. I don't trust him, but somehow, the idea of running nauseates me further.

"Where am I?"

He smiles. "Our house."

"What's going to happen to me?"

"You're going to your judgement day."

I laugh. *Fuck me*, this day is just going stellar. "This isn't one of my three questions," I warn, "but can you *not* talk in riddles?"

His smile widens into a full-blown grin. "We don't forget faces, Kora Sinclair. Even if they try to change them." He rises from the bed and takes the bowl. "And you don't get to decide what counts or not. I enjoy riddles. And I enjoy your confused scowl when something doesn't *immediately* make sense."

My expression drops. He knows my name.

Of course he does.

My red hair didn't hide a damn thing—in fact, it might've made it worse. It's not like I can tell him that *this* is my natural color. Close to it, anyway, since the box dye did some damage. Protesting that isn't worth it in the scheme of things.

"Come with me." He tips his head toward the door.

I climb out of bed carefully. It takes me a moment to regain my balance, and he watches me with an even expression. My knees knock together, and heat rushes into my face.

When I'm steady, I go with him. What else am I supposed to do?

"Was that your bedroom?"

He wears a gray t-shirt, and his dark hair is wet. I should've noticed that when he first came in. But now I have an unobstructed view of his back as he leads me down a wide hallway, and I spot some gold paint he missed behind his ear.

I smile at the absurdity of it.

"Nope," he replies.

I bite my tongue. I still don't know Hades' real name. Or Ares', my red-eyed demon.

We come to a wide staircase and head down. A cream runner softens our footsteps. The stairs also continue up to a third level, but I don't get a chance to ask. We descend into the front hall. There's a double-door front entrance, and I spot a front sitting room before we head in the opposite direction.

My eyes are drinking in this huge, sprawling house. It's too big—bigger than it should be if the three of them live here alone. We pass by the kitchen. The backside of the house seems to be made entirely of windows. Finally, we reach another room down a longer hall.

Apollo stops just inside the room, and I hesitate beside him.

One stands when he sees me. The other reclines in that chair, his legs up on a cushioned ottoman. The lounging one glances over, and my shoulders automatically hitch up in self-defense. His eyes are the giveaway—ice blue and freezing cold.

Hades, whatever his real name is, has cleaned the skull paint from his face. He seems the same as I remembered him in my nightmares—his energy, anyway. Domineering. Brutal. I imagine he'll give an order, this so-called judgement day of mine, and whatever he says will be law. His hair is light brown, and without the skull mask, he has a heartbreakingly gorgeous face. And body.

Not fair. Someone as evil as him shouldn't be as handsome.

Ares, then, stands in front of me. He's stopped a few feet away, his gaze hard as he sweeps me from head to toe. When his eyes flick to mine, they soften for the briefest moment. It's too fast to latch on to, though, and a cold man stands before me again. His eyes aren't red anymore—they're bright green.

I kissed *him?* He's out of my league. By miles. I should've known from the abs, but his freaking face confirms it.

I tear my gaze away and take in the large room. It feels lived-in, unlike the others.

The walls are black, with one wall of windows—and glass-paned French doors. There's a freaking spiral staircase that goes up to a bookcase-lined hallway that circles the room. Bookshelves everywhere, although they're not filled with books. It's staged, like they bought the house as is from a realtor. Or they hired an interior designer and didn't care what they stuck on the shelves.

In the center of the room is a cream rug, with an L-shaped couch framing it. Another chair is next to it, facing a huge television hung on the wall next to Apollo and me. Through another opening, on the right, is an office.

"Well?" This from Hades, who drops his feet to the floor.

"Well, what?" I should just keep biting my tongue.

They know me, and I'm still in the dark about all of this. All of *them*. It's starting to feel like this town has secrets I've been ignorant about for the last three and a half months, and I'm only just now pulling back the curtain. Revealing nothing good.

Hades inclines his chin. "You survived."

I shrug. What can I say to that? I've survived a lot.

"Tell me, Kora Sinclair, why did you want this so badly?" He lifts the skull mask from the arm of the chair and casts a glance at it. He tosses it to me.

I catch it, although it puts me off-balance. "I..."

As far as I know, my true purpose with the Titans is still

a secret. The leather cuff is secure on my wrist—not that there's any guarantee they would know what the brand means if they saw it.

I can lie, and maybe they'll let me go.

"It was a dare." Which isn't strictly a lie...

His eyebrow tics. "What was? Be specific."

My throat is dry. Apollo and Ares shift. They're somewhere behind me, and I hate that, too. The trapped, suffocating feeling comes roaring back. I tap my finger on my thigh and count my inhales.

It doesn't work.

I edge to the side again, putting both of them in my sight, and focus on the mask in my hand.

"Steal something from Olympus," I make up. "The most creative—the most impressive—wins."

Hades rises and saunters toward me.

I backpedal until I bump into the wall.

He doesn't touch me, though. He just takes the mask and holds it up to his face. His blue eyes meet mine through it. It doesn't have quite the same effect, but my breath catches nonetheless.

"No one steals from us." His voice is deadly quiet. He drops the mask onto one of the shelves behind me. "Do you know what it's worth?"

I press my lips together and shake my head. Whatever it is, I can't pay.

"You," he says.

Someone jerks at the edge of my peripheral.

"What do you mean, *me*?" My bravado isn't strong enough for this. But somehow, I stay steady. "It's a *mask*."

He sneers. I can imagine what he's thinking: *poor little girl just doesn't understand*. And I don't. I don't know why a mask is worth wiping my debt. I don't *really* know what it symbolizes, or who this guy is in front of me. I only know he watched a man be stabbed. He chased me through the woods without remorse. And then erased me from Sterling Falls.

"When fighters win, they are granted favors. But *we* won this round, sunshine. And that means you owe us."

"A favor," I clarify. "From me."

"For now." His gaze lifts again. "Get her out of here."

I don't wait for them to manhandle me again. I pivot and retreat back the way we came. I stop just shy of the front doors.

"The garage is this way."

I glance back at Ares. Whoever the fuck he is.

His gaze goes soft again—*not* my imagination earlier, then—and he sighs. "Let me drive you home, Kora. It would be a long walk."

"Just take me to the SFU campus." My feet hurt already imagining the walk back to my apartment, but my pride won't accept anything else.

He nods once and leads the way to the garage door. There's a long row of cars—another thing that shouldn't be surprising but is. The whole house has a modern feel to it, but some of these cars are ancient. Collectors' items, maybe. They're tucked against the far wall.

I eye the motorcycles, then a black Mercedes that Ares stops beside.

He opens the passenger door and braces his forearms along the top. "It won't bite."

"And you?"

He smirks. "Only if you're into that kind of thing."

I hesitate. "What's your name?"

"Apollo didn't tell you?"

I shake my head.

"Wolfe James." He holds out his hand, and I watch it for a moment. Then I take it, and his cool palm slides against my hot one. His fingers grip my hand, steady and sure, and he squeezes lightly. Then he releases me, and my arm falls back to my side.

"I'm..."

"I'm aware of who you are. Get in the car, Kora." He tips his head to the waiting seat.

I grimace and slide in. The interior is black leather and high-tech electronics. It's way, *way* fancier than the rust-bucket I drove in high school. And if it hadn't died at the beginning of summer, I would still probably be rumbling around in that thing.

The Mercedes purrs to life, Wolfe behind the wheel. The garage door opens, and he pulls out. I crane around to get a view of the house.

My jaw drops.

It isn't a house. I knew that walking through it. But seeing it on the inside and seeing *this* from the outside... two different ballgames.

"Impressive, right?"

I think Apollo only led me through a fraction of it. Sure, it's a house in the sense that someone lives there. Or, maybe three someones, but it's also a giant fucking mansion. It's larger than any I've ever seen. Maybe it's the biggest in the whole city. I can see hints of Olympus in it, too, in the four pillars out front. The color scheme inside, all silver and charcoal gray, white, and gilded accents.

We're on part of the driveway that leads straight to the garage off to the side. The main driveway, though, splits off and curves around to the front and ends in a circle. It's all framed in by trimmed hedges.

"How...? Did Olympus pay for that?"

I can just picture the horrified look on my mother's face if she knew I was talking about how these guys afforded a huge house. But, come on. There's no way you get *this* in Sterling Falls without pulling some serious strings.

"We have connections." Proving me right and leaving me hanging. He hits a button, and a gate inches into the hedges. Once it's open, he turns onto the main road.

I'm supposed to draw my own conclusions. And the longer I think about it, the more my stomach drops.

How the hell did I forget?

How did I let the glamour of Olympus, and the masks, and their pseudonyms, hide everything they've done to me? Of *course* they're powerful. Or at least, *he* is. Hades. He practically snapped his fingers and I was out of a scholarship—and my future.

Stubborn Kora.

I should've gone home when I had the chance.

I glance over at Wolfe. He's not innocent, either.

Damn it.

My cheeks burn when our kiss comes back to me. I kissed him *knowing* he was one of them, and I did it anyway. An ache fills my chest. I dig my fingernails into my bare thighs and try not to lose it completely.

"What are you studying?"

I glance at him sharply.

He eyes me, then refocuses on the road. "Such a strange question? Indulge my curiosity."

"Well, *I'm* curious why the hell you three erased my life, but I doubt either of us is walking away from this exchange satisfied." I cross my arms over my chest. The air-conditioning is on full blast, chilling my skin.

"I'd love nothing more than to satisfy you." His voice is

too damn alluring. Low and husky like this, in the darkness. “But you’re right—that’s something I won’t answer.”

I nod once. We reach SFU in record time, and I hop out as soon as the car rolls to a stop. The window lowers behind me, and I stiffen at the whirring sound.

“Kora,” Wolfe calls. “Don’t think you’re getting away so easily. This is just a temporary reprieve.”

Reprieve from what?

I bite my lip and hurry away from him. I guess I’ll find out what he means whenever the fuck he wants me to… but until then? Left in the dark, as usual.

CHAPTER 7

I don't see anyone I shouldn't for four days. No Titans, no Wolfe or Apollo or *him*. Not that I really expect to see them, but Kronos has to know I failed his task. He has to know that I've got no chance of stealing the mask.

Maybe he's counting down the days like I am, although I can guarantee he's looking forward to it more than me.

Guys like him revel in pain.

I've been attending classes and pretending everything is normal. Interacting with classmates. Sneaking into the dining hall to have dinner with Marley. But there's no denying my days are numbered, and it hangs over my head. I've taken drastic measures to avoid anyone who *might* be watching. I go home at different hours. I've begged Marley to drive me when she can, or clung on to another group of students heading in the same direction.

The hourglass brand is shiny and pink. It's a new scar that I will have to just... live with. Or get used to, at the very least. It's a constant reminder of my fuck-up.

I brush my finger over it and exhale. Part of me regrets

coming to Sterling Falls at all—and another small part just regrets venturing to Olympus in the first place.

Today, Marley and her friends—plus me, the tagalong—are headed to the beach on the north side of the town. It's up the coast from the cliffs Olympus sits on, the waters friendlier there. It's where the tourists go. There's a boardwalk and little restaurants, an open-air arcade, and even a rickety old roller coaster.

I visited it a few times over the summer, but it got too expensive without a car. And too crowded. But now that it's October, with the temperatures cooling off, there should be fewer people visiting.

Rumor has it that the North Falls is another neutral territory for the gangs. No one has claim over the ritzy area that feels more like a beach town than whatever the hell Sterling Falls *actually* is.

I fasten a few bracelets on my wrist. I have to change up that tan cuff, or Marley will be suspicious. Once the brand is hidden, I grab my canvas bag. I've got a towel, water, and a mostly empty bottle of sunscreen. My loose sundress hides my bikini, and my flip-flops are worn out. I feel... tired.

That might be because I'm surviving on one meal a day.

My stomach spasms at the thought of food, and I'm just about to go hunt around my barren cabinets again when my phone buzzes.

Marley: *We're downstairs!*

I abandon the kitchen to check myself in the mirror one last time. I found a large straw hat that should protect my face and shoulders from the sun, and I stuff it into my bag on my way out.

Marley's car idles at the curb, all the windows rolled down. So it's easy to hear her when she says, "Jan, you mind if Kora sits up front?"

Janet pauses a moment, then throws open the door and slides into the back with her two cronies. I really should learn their names... but now I don't have to even talk them. I'm ninety percent sure one of them is Erica, which is good enough odds for me.

I climb in and shoot Marley a thankful look.

She grins. She's dressed like me: a sundress with a bikini underneath, sandals. Her carefree attitude isn't totally forced, though.

"We're stopping at Marsha's, right?" Janet asks.

"Who's that?" I stop myself from turning around to ask her directly. No need for *that* sort of negative energy.

"It's a deli on the boardwalk." Marley glances into the rearview mirror and nods. "And yes, that's the plan. They have amazing sandwiches."

You never realize how many interactions revolve around food until you can't afford to participate. I open my mouth to say so, then snap it closed. My bank account is running on fumes, but I could probably buy a bag of chips or something. There's a handful of loose change in my otherwise-bare wallet.

Besides, I'd rather die than admit how much I'm struggling.

From my apartment on the east side of SFU, it's about a twenty-minute drive north to get to the beach. There seems to be a bubble around the university that's gang-free, too. I haven't been able to deduce if that's just coincidence or by design—and if it's on purpose, what the line is.

Surrounding the university is the so-called college district. A ton of apartments, shops, restaurants. A thriving downtown area, populated by students and young professionals. We pass through the financial district next, a quick blip on the map, then the city falls away and we descend into the land of the wealthy.

We trade looming buildings for mansions and manicured lawns. It might just be a psychological trick, but it feels brighter here. Even leaving the city to go east toward Olympus, I didn't feel that way. The sun breaks through the last of the clouds and streaks through the window. I tip my head toward it, letting it warm my face, and close my eyes.

This is the distraction I need after the last month—no, strike that. After the last almost *four* months.

Marley snags a parking spot along the boardwalk, near the pier, and we all pile out. Across the street sits the little deli with a hand-painted sign across the top. *Marsha's.*

I follow them over and hoist my bag higher.

"Paula," Janet calls. "Do you have your ID?"

Paula. I make note of the brunette's name. She nods and hangs back, letting the rest of us file into the shop. There's a counter to order sandwiches along the side, and aisles take up most of the space. A row of coolers at the back house the drinks.

We spread out. Marley and Janet go to the deli counter. Erica beelines for the snack aisle. And I feel like a complete idiot, stepping down an aisle filled with canned soups. I just need to kill some time, then I'll make something up about already packing a lunch, or eating a late breakfast...

It doesn't take long, and I let out a sigh of relief when Marley and Janet head outside with their sandwiches. Erica is close behind them. Paula enters and grabs a six-pack of beer, then goes to the counter and pays. The employee barely glances at her ID before handing it back to her.

I join them on the sidewalk before Paula finishes.

"What did you get?" Marley asks me.

"Got it," Paula announces, striding over to us. "Let's party."

Erica whisks Marley away, and I don't get a chance to try out my lie on her. Good thing, too. She'd probably see straight through it.

And if I had to admit my financial truth in front of Janet? No, thanks.

We pick a spot on the beach, which is fairly quiet, and lay out our towels. I grab my romance novel and flop on my stomach, flipping it open. I glance over at the other four out of the corner of my eye. Janet and Erica seem busy scoping out the boys tossing a football farther down the beach, while Paula passes around beers.

"Want one?" she asks me.

I shake my head. "I'm good for now, thanks."

"Suit yourself."

Marley falls down beside me, peering over my shoulder. She wrinkles her nose. "What do you see in romance books, anyway? It's basically just smut."

I roll my eyes. "Guaranteed happy endings, Marley. Nothing beats that."

"And the sex?"

"Well, that's definitely a perk," I allow.

She laughs. "Enjoy your book. I'm going to dip my toes in the water."

In the distance, a cart rolls over the wooden roller coaster. Faint shrieks of joy—or fear—reach us. Janet follows Marley into the water, and after a moment or two, Erica joins them. Paula stretches out on her back a few towels down, sunglasses on and the ties of her bikini undone. Avoiding tan lines, I guess.

A half hour later, I'm restless. I'm not used to just sitting around.

Marley, Janet, and Erica have migrated over to splash in the water directly in front of the boys tossing the ball. They've caught the guys' attention, and it'll probably only be a matter of time before they converge.

Paula might as well be asleep. She hasn't moved since she laid down.

I close my book and stand, brushing sand from my legs. Sliding on my sandals, I head back up to the boardwalk and step into one of the little shops. It's full of touristy Sterling Falls trinkets. Mugs with the town logo, t-shirts, and tie-dyed sweatshirts. I pause at the logo emblazoned on a shirt with *Sterling Falls* under it. It looks like a modernized, simplified column framed by Greek branches. The same that was on the door of Olympus.

I run my fingers over the fabric and mull that over.

Of course they're connected—the town and Olympus. Something like that building doesn't just appear. It must've been around when the town was founded.

A mystery I'll solve another day.

I take my time working toward the back of the store, holding on to the shirt with the logo.

"Is this what Kora Sinclair does in her free time?" The last person I expect to see steps in front of me and tugs the t-shirt from my hands. "Shopping for..." Apollo's nose wrinkles. "Were you going to buy this?"

My face heats. "No. I was just—" I snatch it back and put it on the shelf. "What are you doing here?"

He grins and follows me. "I was in the area."

Apollo wears charcoal board shorts and a light-blue t-shirt. His sunglasses are up on top of his head. Sandals on his feet. Surprisingly, I *can* believe that he was just here for a day at the beach... but just because he fits the imagery doesn't mean I should fall for it. Their whole game is warped around illusion.

"Uh-huh." I need to get out of here.

He catches my wrist and gently pulls me back around. "You didn't buy lunch with your friends."

I narrow my eyes.

"And you drank the soup like it was your first meal in a week," he continues.

"Do you have a point?"

His gaze moves down my body, then back up. "You're thinner than you were before."

I yank my wrist back. "Three months ago, I had a job and money in my account. Thanks to your friend—"

"Jace thought you'd leave." Apollo rubs his eyes, clearly frustrated with something. Me, maybe. "How bad is it?"

I latch on to the name. *Jace*. Another tiny layer of Hades revealed, although I'm not sure I gain any solid information. And then his question: *How bad is it?* Well, I'm not about to admit that some days it's questionable if I'm going to die of starvation. That's a bit dramatic, anyway. If I went more than a few days without food, I could ask Marley for help.

It just hasn't got to that point.

"Come with me," he says.

"Just like that?" I plant my hands on my hips. "I'm here with people."

He grins. My stomach flips. He really has no right to be so handsome. I might not have seen it at first, through the mask, but his smile does something to me. It seems genuine.

And I know exactly how I am when a boy pretends to be *nice*.

"You're with the same people from the fight," he says. "Do they know you stole Hades' mask? That you got caught with it?"

I shake my head once. "Not that they'd care—"

"I'm sure." Sarcasm drips from his voice. "So your bet wasn't with them?"

Don't react. Is that why he's here? To suss out the truth of why I tried to steal it?

"I can't go with you." I shake my head again, firmer. "And it isn't just because I don't trust you. I'm here to try and relax. Something you're not helping with."

He snorts. "Okay. Carry on, then."

I lift my chin and step past him. He lets me walk out the door, and I get the impression that he watches me pick my way all the way back to my towel.

Marley glances up when I return. "There you are." Her gaze moves to something over my shoulder. "Oh..."

"Miss," someone calls.

"He's talking to you, Kore."

I hold my breath and face the voice.

It's not Apollo, though—it's the employee from the deli. He comes over with a package in his hand. "You forgot this!"

"I, um—"

"You decided to get something to eat?" Paula asks.

My stomach chooses that moment to growl. I take the wrapped sandwich from the deli employee.

"I did." I'm surprised my voice comes out even.

On the wrapping is writing. I have to flip it around to read it, and then my throat closes.

I see you. —A

Beneath it, a phone number.

I tear off that part of the wrapping and shove it in my bag. I'll deal with the fact that Apollo just gave me his *phone number* later. Right now, I'm suddenly so hungry I might pass out. I force myself to take small bites of the turkey sub.

To make it last. The other girls pull out their sandwiches, too.

The smart play would be to eat half and save the rest for later. My willpower is a fragile thing, though, and before I know it, I'm pressing my finger into the crumbs and licking them away. I have the feeling Apollo is still lingering out of sight, but I don't know *why*.

Did he follow me?

Was he ordered to keep an eye on me?

Jace. A name to go with his face.

I eye Marley. "Do you know who Hades is?"

She drops her sandwich into the paper on her lap. "No, it's one of Sterling Falls' biggest mysteries. No one knows who the hosts really are."

I hum.

"Got a crush?" Paula asks. "The skull do it for ya?"

"It's the abs," Erica interjects. "His drool-worthy abs."

Marley watches me but says nothing.

It's Janet who sneers. "It's the power. Those at the bottom are always looking for easy ways to climb the ladder."

Ouch.

"That's enough," Marley says to her. "I'm not sure why you have to be such a bitch to her all the damn time."

I stand abruptly, the food turning violently in my stomach. "It's okay, Mar. I'm not really feeling the beach, anyway. Sorry." To soften the blow of my abrupt exit, I lean down and kiss her cheek. And then I just... collect my things and leave.

Because I can't really handle another shitty thing happening.

Once I'm out of sight, farther down the boardwalk, I pull

out my cell and the paper with Apollo's number. I contemplate it for a moment, then send a text.

Me: *Why did you do that?*

I wait a beat, then it vibrates in my hand.

Apollo: *I know what it feels like to be the only one going hungry.*

Apollo: *And you seem too proud to ask for help.*

Well.

Me: *So you just...*

A motorcycle rolls up beside me. The rider has familiar charcoal-gray shorts and blue t-shirt. Apollo flips his visor up and grins at me. "It's easier to ask for forgiveness. You ditching your friends?"

I make a face and start walking. "Only one is my friend. The rest... not so much. It might've been different if I started the year in a better mood, but I..."

But I've been grumpy and isolated, while Marley's friends have probably wondered why the hell she perpetually tries to draw me out of my bad mood. Because we go too far back for either one of us to abandon the other.

The engine hums as he inches along beside me. "What's the plan? Going to walk home?"

"Maybe."

"You know how Sterling Falls got its name?" he asks suddenly.

I pause and face him. Clearly, he's not giving up without... something. "No."

"Want to?" He unclips a second helmet and offers it to me.

I'm... I'm in a dress. And a bikini that never had a chance of getting wet.

He flips the kickstand and hops off smoothly, trading me the helmet for my bag. I stuff my phone under my bikini's strap while he stows my bag in a compartment under the seat. He turns back around and slides the helmet over my head. I meet his gaze through the darkened visor, realizing… well, I didn't agree to this, did I?

But I *am* curious—not really about how Sterling Falls got its name, but *him*.

And I need a way out of here.

That's what I tell myself, anyway, when I lift my chin and let him buckle the strap. His knuckles brush my throat, and my heart takes off.

Maybe my heart is the reason why, when he climbs back on and holds out his arm, I just shake my head at my own foolish choices and swing my leg over. I have to hike my dress up a bit, but no one seems to care. He reaches back and grips both of my thighs. The touch is shocking, and I bite back a gasp. He pulls me flush against him, and one of his hands slip down the outside of my knee. He pats my calf.

I hate that I don't hate it.

Tentatively, I wrap my hands around his waist.

I think boys like him ride bikes like this just for the physical contact. We're touching in too many places. His hand covers mine on his stomach, a quick check, and then we pull away from the curb.

My dad used to ride motorcycles, but I was never interested in them. Just a few quick, daring trips around the neighborhood. I remember clutching his back and swinging between fear and euphoria.

The rush comes back, at least, as we fly through the beachy residential area. There's not a lot of traffic on the road. We head west, away from the coast. We climb a bit, the curving road we're on occasionally giving glimpses through the trees of downtown Sterling Falls in the distance.

We skirt around the town, forest looming on either side of the road.

Eventually, Apollo takes a sharp right onto a dirt road. I yelp, grabbing him tighter. My heart seems to lodge in my throat, and I almost—*almost*—squeeze my eyes shut. But some masochistic part of me needs to know exactly how I'm about to die.

The trail continues up, though, and suddenly there's a wall of rock to our right and a steep drop-off to the left. We come around a curve, and the track opens up. It levels off to a grassy area surrounded by trees. We roll to a stop, and the motor dies into silence.

I yank the helmet off. I don't think my legs will hold me, so I don't bother getting off. My thighs ache from clenching his. In the distance is the roar of water.

"What the hell was that?" My voice is hoarse, like I've been screaming.

He twists around and takes the helmet, setting it on one of the handles. He does the same with his, then meets my gaze.

I'm struck again by his dark eyes and the smirk gracing his lips.

"This is one of the secrets of Sterling Falls." He motions ahead of us.

I can *hear* it, but I don't see it. I stare at him blankly.

"Sterling *Falls*." He grins. "Rumor has it that the sun can hit it just right to make the water seem like polished metal."

"Is that so?" I ask drily.

"You don't seem amused."

"Because I thought we were on a suicide ride."

He swings his leg over the front, then offers both hands. "Come with me."

I quirk my lips. "Is that your catchphrase?"

"Around you, I guess. They only open the gate up from the reservoir once a month. Today's your lucky day."

"Sterling Falls has a reservoir?"

He jerks a nod. "Technically, no. It's just outside city limits, but it supplies water to the town. This waterfall goes down to a river that will empty out near the harbor in South Falls."

I sigh. I mean, we're *here*. I may as well make the best of it—and see if he answers any more questions. He knows things. Obviously. And lest I forget, I'm pretty sure it was him who *stabbed* someone three months ago. As far as I know, he wasn't arrested. He might not have even been questioned.

"You all thought I would leave," I muse.

I take his hands and let him guide me off the bike. My legs do wobble, and he releases one of my hands. He holds my hip, keeping me steady, until I release a shaky breath.

"We did." He leads me to a subtle break in the trees.

A trail appears, winding down a short way. There's a wooden bridge over a stream that leads to a fenced overlook. And there, directly in front of it, is a huge waterfall. We pick our way down, and I rest my forearms on the fence.

"Why did you think I would leave so easily?" A fine mist hits my face.

It really is impressive, though. The water comes shooting over a cluster of flat-topped boulders and crashes down at least eighty feet into a small pool.

He shrugs. His gaze is unreadable. "You seemed like a new—*late*—visitor who was stumbling into something way over her head."

That's exactly what I was.

"But..." I prompt.

He smiles tightly. "But, that didn't happen."

I sigh.

His fingers tighten on mine. “You okay?”

Not at all. I yank my hand back and turn away from him abruptly. I direct my words at the waterfall and try to wrangle my sudden spike of anger. “You’re asking if I’m *okay*? We’re strangers. You wouldn’t know me from a hole in the wall.”

“I think you know that’s a lie.” His voice is almost too low to hear, riding over the crashing water.

I whirl back around. “What were you doing that night? With those other guys?”

Besides Kronos, I haven’t interacted with any other Titan. And I’ve been fortunate to avoid the other gang entirely. Of course, if I was as normal as they assumed, I wouldn’t have met anyone affiliated with the Titans or Hell Hounds at all. I could’ve left Sterling Falls none the wiser to the underbelly of the city and the people who rule it.

Apollo presses his lips together and contemplates me. He’s coming to some sort of decision, maybe about whether to answer me or not. And when he steps forward, I retreat. Habit.

“Are you guys… in one of the gangs?”

At that, he laughs. Tips his head back and lets it all out.

My stomach swoops.

“No, Kora, we’re not in one of the gangs.” He eyes me. “Why do you ask?”

“I’ve heard people talk about them, is all. They seem…”

“You stay away from them.” His tone leaves no room for argument.

It rubs me the wrong way. I narrow my eyes. “You’re really one to give orders.”

He has no problem coming into my space. Boxing me against the fence, with the waterfall at my back. My breath catches, but I'm not suffocatingly afraid of him. I don't know why. My emotions are jumbled, but fear isn't predominant.

Curiosity rides front and center.

It doesn't last. His brown eyes bore into mine, and I can't help but feel like he sees more of me than I want him to. I stifle my questions and curiosity and shove everything into a box in the back of my mind.

"Please take me home."

"Backing away from the fight so soon?" He clicks his tongue.

I ball my hands into fists. "Violence gets us nowhere."

He chuckles and leans in close. He places his hand on the rock wall over my shoulder.

"You'll learn that violence is the only thing that'll get you anywhere in Sterling Falls." He straightens and leaves me standing there.

My heartbeat takes too long to come down from its frantic pace. He doesn't seem to mind, though. When I follow him back to the motorcycle, he puts my helmet back on and clips it with easy efficiency. I climb on behind him.

Another leg pat, and then the motorcycle whines as he spins us around. Loose dirt and grass kick up from the back wheel. My fingers dig into his shirt, my stomach rolling. With a violent lurch, we shoot back down the hill.

I hold on for dear life and close my eyes until we're back on solid—*flat*—ground.

The good thing about the motorcycle?

No talking.

Unlike Wolfe dropping me off at the edge of SFU's campus, Apollo takes me straight back to my apartment.

Without asking for directions.

I should question it, but... I'm not surprised. I'm just

tired. The sun, the exhausting socializing with Marley's bitch friends. The *food*. The adrenaline.

He doesn't say anything when he gets off the bike after me and grabs my bag. I take it from him, but he doesn't leave. He follows me inside and upstairs. I pause at my door and glance back at him, but he just raises his eyebrows. A dare, perhaps.

Letting out a soft exhale, I unlock the door and push it open. He steps past me and hunts around, but his face gives nothing away. I can't seem to release the doorknob, standing just inside the threshold, until he's deep into his perusal. He even peeks in my cabinets in the kitchen, opens the fridge.

His earlier text is burned into the back of my mind. *I know what it's like.*

"Finished?" I finally snap.

He straightens and strides past me. "For now."

I jerk my chin up, but that's the only acknowledgement he's going to get from me.

Once he's gone, I slam the door closed and kick off my sandals. I tip my head back, and an unholy groan escapes me. I don't know how I got here—to this spot in life where I'm always hungry, hiding the truth from everyone, and in way, *way* over my head with a freaking gang leader. And three guys who may or may not want to kill me.

An hour later, I'm still in the same position. I think I've dozed, but the sun is now low enough to blaze in through my western-facing window. And I have homework.

My door opens.

I jerk to my feet, unsure what the hell I'm going to do against an attacker.

I grab my phone. Do I call 9-1-1? Scream?

My neighbors probably wouldn't even do anything, if they're home. My apartment building isn't the best—it's a bunch of college kids who stick to the *mind your own business* rule. While everyone made friends within the first week or so of school, I've stayed locked inside. Out of necessity, but still. I couldn't exactly tell them I didn't want to befriend them because a psychopath might use them against me.

I don't have to worry, though—it's Apollo.

Except…

My eyes narrow at the bags in his hands.

"What are those?" My stomach is in knots again.

He brushes past me, kicking the door shut on his way in, and sets the bags on the counter. He doesn't even acknowledge me, but he unpacks the groceries with methodical movements.

I stare at him—then the food.

"What are you doing?"

He shakes his head once, and it's only then that I realize he's *pissed*. His jaw is tight, the tendons in his neck standing out like he's silently screaming. His movements aren't just methodical—they're jerky.

So I go silent and let him unpack, then tuck food into my pantries and fridge. Even a few frozen dinners and veggies make it into the freezer.

Tears well in my eyes.

"I can't accept this." I dash at my cheek. "Seriously."

"Kora?" He spares me a single glance. "Shut. Up."

"I don't do charity," I explain. "I've never taken a handout. This is too much. Even from you."

Even though you're why I'm in this mess.

He winces.

I should take it. I'm being absolutely ridiculous right now, but what do I have left if I give up my pride? Certainly not my dignity—that burned away with the hourglass seared into my wrist.

Vulnerability washes over me.

He's in my apartment, he's bought me food. He knows my *hunger*.

"I'll pay you back," I promise.

He shakes his head once and stops in front of me. I will my mask back into place as I tip my head back to meet his eyes. Wolfe was right—the masks we wear at Olympus let us be our real selves. It's every other fucking moment of the day that we wear the true masks.

Indifference, Kora.

That's how I survived Kronos, and it's how I'll survive them, too. Apollo and Wolfe and Jace.

But Apollo puts his finger under my chin and lifts it higher, exposing my throat. His gaze flicks down, along the dark strap of my bikini, then back up.

"Don't worry about paying me back. You already owe us." He speaks softly and trails the back of his finger across the edge of my jaw, toward my ear. "Which means... for now? You're an asset. And we protect our assets."

I swallow, reading between the lines.

Once I've paid my dues—I'm no longer their problem. And I'll be back to square one.

CHAPTER 8

My time is up.

Dread races under my skin throughout the morning. As I shower, pull on clothes, get dressed. My phone trills, but I ignore it. I'm jittery in an unproductive way. The cereal I force myself to eat sits heavy in my stomach, each bite another stone.

I dump the sugar-sweetened milk into the sink and rinse my bowl. I have to... I don't know. Pretend today is a normal day?

Go to class.

Do my homework in the library.

Walk home before the sun sets—for my own sanity.

I rush to my closet, a thought occurring to me.

Dad had given me a present, and I thought it was a joke. But it might come in handy today, if I can find it. The little bottle is buried in a box under my shoes. When I unearth it, I let out a victorious cry.

Pepper spray might not save me, but it could give me a chance to escape.

I tuck it in my purse.

And there's nothing else to do. At this rate, I'm going to be late for class.

My senses are on high alert all the way to SFU's campus. If this is truly a neutral ground, I should be safe. Right? I latch on to that as I sit through first one class, then another. Marley and I pass each other in the hallway, and she squints at me like she knows something is wrong.

Fortunately, neither of us have time to stop and chat.

I almost make it to the *walk home* part of my checklist.

"Invisible girl." A man slides into the chair across from mine in the library.

I shove my last notebook into my bag and pause. My fingers linger on the zipper, and the recognition comes swiftly: the guy who usually guards Kronos' office at Descend.

He smirks at me, leaning back and kicking his boots up on the table. "You about done here?"

"Maybe," I hedge. "Or I might stay awhile."

"That would make for an exciting evening." He pulls the front of his shirt up, revealing the gun tucked in his waistband. He covers it again, and his smile widens. "Do you have any attachment to the library? Or the people in it?"

I gulp. "What are you saying? You'd shoot them until I went with you?"

"Boss did say any means necessary. You're an example, you know? Consider yourself a martyr for his cause."

"To not..." I can't get the words out. "What is he going to do?"

"Whatever he wants. Maybe he'll string you up by your ankles outside of Descend. Or put his mark somewhere more visible." His gaze lingers on my throat.

I shudder. "You're not doing a good job convincing me to go with you."

"How about I just shoot everyone in the place?" He plants his forearms on the table. "It would be messy. A bloodbath. The cops would probably look at you as their prime suspect. Girl in such a massive fucking debt, she's driven to homicide."

I stand abruptly, nausea rolling through me. "That's the last thing I want."

"I know, invisible girl." He rises, too, and takes my bag. And purse. He stuffs the latter into my bag and tosses it under the table.

"Hey—"

"No use trying to call for help, or whatever you think you might do to get out of this."

No one pays us any attention as he escorts me out. His hand ghosts along the small of my back, urging me forward faster. We cross the parking lot, and he opens the door behind the driver's seat.

I hesitate, then get in. What else am I going to do, run away? If I had my pepper spray...

Damn it again. The one time I bring it with me, I don't get a chance to use it. Or my phone, also tucked away in the purse now abandoned under the library table.

He slams the door on me. I scoot to the other side of the bench and test the door, but it won't open—even though it's unlocked.

He climbs into the driver's seat and glances back, then laughs. "Childproof."

I scowl and fold my arms over my chest. It hides my trembling hands, at the very least. My leg jigs.

The terrible scenarios go through my mind, worse than Kronos' lackey's examples. He's going to carve what I owe from my flesh. Peel off my fingernails. Break my arm—or cut it off.

I'm going to be sick.

We arrive at the curb in front of Descend. It's approaching six o'clock, and the sun is settling down below the mountains. The sky is twilight-blue. A group of laughing boys pass us—college students who've wandered too far from the safe zone.

Guard-turned-errand boy waits until the guys have passed, then opens my door. He grips my upper arm and practically drags me inside. My heels catch, and I balk against our sudden speed. Inside, the bar is nearly empty. The real crowd won't emerge until later tonight, I suppose. But there are a few men hunkered in booths along the wall.

Titans, probably.

"You don't have to drag me." I try to rip my arm free, but he holds fast.

He chuckles under his breath. "I'll enjoy hearing your screams through the door."

This time, I succeed in yanking out of his hold. "You didn't hear me scream before."

The office door flies open, and Kronos fills the frame. "What took so fucking long? Get her in here." He casts his gaze around, then back to his guard. "Were you followed?"

"No, sir."

"Good, good." He steps aside, and I'm shoved through the opening.

I stumble inside.

There's another man in the room who seems as out of place as I am. With his khaki pants and blue button-up shirt, I'd peg him as an office nerd—not someone who would be *here*. He sits in one of the two chairs in front of the large desk. There are sweat stains under his arms.

He's the least threatening person in the room, so I whirl around to glare at Kronos.

He closes the door behind him. His expression is impassive, but I have to wonder what's going on in his head. He can't be happy that I failed. My time is up, after all. It's been a month since he handcuffed me to his desk and branded me with his hourglass.

I glance to the fireplace, which isn't lit.

He lowers himself into the chair behind his desk, then motions for me to take the last seat. "You've managed to hide my brand. So much so that it seems ineffective. Why repeat something that doesn't work?"

I stay silent and don't move. My heart beats frantically, and I search for... I don't know. A way out of this.

"Do you have the mask?"

I cling on to the indifference that I rely on, but I have a feeling it won't save me anymore. My stomach churns, and I can't answer. I open my mouth, but no words come out.

"No, then." He sighs and twists a ring on his finger. "I feared as much. Henry is here for similar reasons. He borrowed from a shark and forgot about my teeth."

The khakis dude shudders violently in his chair.

Kronos ignores that. "Do you remember our agreement?"

"I do." I have to force my voice to work. My throat is closing, getting tighter by the second.

"Double interest." His eyes light up. "You're looking at a life sentence, invisible girl."

"I—"

"Not so fast." He rises and braces his hands on his metal desk, leaning forward. "You remember. I can't allow anyone to make a fool of me."

I'm the example.

"Sit."

My legs might give out, so I carefully take a chair and

drag it backward. No way am I going to let him take my arm —or worse.

"You had such bravado when you were last here," he muses, sinking back into his own chair. A knife appears in his hand, the blade flashing in the dim light. "Where is *she*? Who are you? A little fear has turned you into a mouse? A little pain chased away your courage?"

I bite the inside of my cheek. *Last* time, I had no idea what was coming. Or the mental anguish the last thirty days have put me through.

So, yeah, she's long gone.

"You borrowed fifty thousand dollars." He pulls out a calculator. "Plus interest—now doubled, for your unreliability. We had *agreed* on monthly payments. On time, no interest. Late, interest. Easy."

Easy. That's the word that got me in trouble with him originally. An easy contract, simple, nothing to worry about. Pages of legal mind-bending that equated to one thing: if you pay, you don't have to worry.

He smiles. "Failure to pay, Kora. Not so easy." He taps out an equation. "This is what you owe me currently." He flashes me the screen, and I try not to pass out. He types another equation and shows me the new figure—easily five times our starting payment. "And this is what you'll owe me if you continue your late payments. Which, of course, is reasonable to assume. You still owe me for last month and this one."

Kronos drops the calculator back into a drawer and slams it shut.

"Now, what is that worth?"

I don't answer him—I can't. I never imagined the amount I owe getting that high. Barely restrained panic sits just behind my ribcage. I'm reminded of Hades asking me the same question—and his answer was *me*.

Kronos better not come up with the same response, or I'm going to lose my mind.

He sighs when I don't answer. "Your ability to pay it back... I don't believe in it anymore, invisible girl. I used to, but now?" He pauses and contemplates me. "A finger. A light punishment for now—but this isn't going away."

The blood drains from my face.

He chuckles. "It's a message to all those who want to do business with me and think they can *cheat* and *lie* their way out of our agreements. A message you can't hide with... *jewelry*." His nose wrinkles, his gaze falling to my wrist.

"I didn't cheat—"

"You failed to get me the mask. And you lied when you said you could pay. What is that if not a liar and a cheat of my system—and my patience? Put your fucking hand on the desk." His face contorts with anger, then smooths out. It seems he's having his own internal battle.

I shake my head. He's going to have to hold me down—or worse—before I touch that desk. My fingers curl, and my nails bite my palms.

"No? This is one alternative." He pulls a gun from under his desk and aims it at the man beside me. "Your life is on the line. What will you do, invisible girl? Will you come work for me? Or perhaps we should come up with another arrangement."

"I—"

"Henry has a gambling problem—but unlike *you*, he's useless to me."

He squeezes the trigger, barely any movement at all, and an ear-splitting *crack* fills the room. Blood sprays my face. I belatedly raise my hand to block it. The gunshot echoes in my head, rattling around, and for a second I can't feel anything. My mouth opens, and I stiffly turn to take in the man's now-lifeless body. He slumps over the edge of the chair, away from me. Blood drips onto the floor from the hole in his face.

He's dead.

Like, *dead* dead.

I touch my face. This is my first up-close encounter with death, and I'm not sure I'm equipped to handle this. My stomach rolls, and I have to tear my eyes away from the slumped man.

"Well?" Kronos taps his gun against the desk.

When I don't move—pretty sure I'm frozen to the spot—Kronos sighs.

"Erik, get in here," he yells.

I twist, trying to keep one eye on the door and Kronos and the body. But when it swings open, no one walks through.

The guard who picked me up from school *falls* through. There's a hole between his eyes, blood down his face. He hits the floor already dead. The noise is muted. Different than the whip-like crack of the gun.

Someone steps over him, and my heart seizes. I grip the arms of my chair tightly as Wolfe's gaze swings around the room. He pauses on me for a second, then stops on Kronos. There's a handgun in his grip, but it's aimed at the floor. A moment later, Jace strides in.

And the room shrinks.

He doesn't look at me. Just fixes an ugly scowl at Kronos until the older man glances away.

"Get her out of here," Jace says.

"We're not done." Kronos leans back, his gun now aimed at me.

Jace blocks my view of the older man. "You're done with her. Got it?"

I flinch when Wolfe hauls me out of the chair.

"Until we meet again, invisible girl," Kronos calls. "Because we will..."

I balk.

Wolfe wraps his arm tightly around my waist and guides me back through the bar, where Apollo sits. The bartender is unconscious at his feet, blood leaking from his ear. The men who had occupied the booth are in similar states, slumped together on the floor.

They could be dead or unconscious. I have no idea.

Wolfe doesn't stop at Apollo, though. The latter just gives us a terse nod, his lips pressed in a thin line, as we pass.

Right outside, past the car I arrived in, is the black Mercedes.

Wolfe puts me in the passenger seat and leans over, quickly buckling the seat belt. I avert my eyes. His arm brushes my chest, and we both stiffen. But I can't seem to form words—nothing comes to mind except inane questions—and he doesn't seem to have anything useful to say, either.

Once I'm secure, he shuts me inside and circles to the driver's side.

He doesn't wait for Apollo and Jace.

The muscle in his jaw keeps jumping. Wolfe is as angry as Apollo was when he saw my mostly empty apartment. The car shoots away from the curb with a squeal of tires, and we fly away from West Falls. Back toward the center of the city and my apartment.

I lick my lips and gag at the metallic, copper taste. That man's *blood* is on my face. I rub at my mouth with the back of my hand and fight hysterics. I spit on my sleeve and scrub at my skin until a patch of my sweatshirt is stained pink.

Wolfe silently hands me a water bottle.

I take it and drink half of it. The cool water eases the burning in my throat. "Wolfe, why—"

"Do not speak. I'm about two seconds away from losing my shit on you." He pushes the car faster. We screech around a corner and stop in front of my apartment. He faces me and lets me see some of the worry in his green eyes, and he reaches out to get something off my cheek.

I imagine my face looks awful with the blood and… maybe even more than blood. Brain matter? My stomach revolts. I'm two seconds away from dry heaving and letting this evening get the better of me.

He gets out of the car and retrieves me on the other side. I don't know if I need it, but he wraps his arm around my waist again. He takes some of my weight and helps me inside, then up to my door.

"I'm locked out. My keys are at the library."

He gives a disgusted grunt. "I fucking hate the Titans. Miserable assholes." He releases me and reveals two long, slender metal picks from his pocket. He inserts them into the lock, and a few seconds later, my door swings inward.

"Wolfe—"

He herds me inside, then goes straight for my bedroom.

My brow furrows. "Wolfe, what—"

"Stop talking," he repeats. "The Titans, Kora? You went to *the fucking Titans*?" He pulls a duffle bag from my closet and tosses it on the mattress. "Pack."

I plant my hands on my hips. "You're going to lecture me then give me convoluted orders? No, thanks."

He stalks closer, stopping inches away.

I flash back to the alcove of Olympus and the electricity

between us. My cheeks heat, and I try to shove away that memory. I can't go from almost having my finger cut off—and watching a man die—to thinking about kissing Wolfe.

Absolutely not.

I blame it on shock. Nothing more than my brain not being able to cope, so I'm redirecting.

"You're packing because you're clearly a danger to yourself." His tone is low and deadly. "You're packing what you need and coming with me, or I take you as is." His gaze flicks up and down my body. "I don't think you want to live in that outfit."

The blood-soaked one, he means.

"I have no choice, is what you're saying."

He lifts one shoulder. "You always have a choice. But the options might not be what you think they are. In this case, it's easy: pack or don't. Come with me or risk Kronos sending someone *else* after you. Maybe they'll break into this apartment like I just did, and they'll put a bullet in your brain while you're sleeping. Or take... whatever he wants from you."

We stare at each other for a moment. This seems to be happening whether or not I want it. The thought of one of Kronos' men coming in here as easily as Wolfe just did terrifies me, and he has to know that. He knows someone hurt me in my past, and that's exactly why he's pushing so hard.

But why the hell he cares about me is a mystery for another day.

I break eye contact first. I retrieve the bag and take it to the closet, quickly shoving in clothes that I'll need. I don't know how long I'll have to stay—until things cool down, I guess? That could take weeks.

Probably not longer than that, though.

I finish in the closet and go to the bathroom, ignoring

the way Wolfe leans against the wall. I lock myself inside and drop the bag. My guard drops, too, but the tears don't come. I saw a man *die*. Kronos shot him like it was nothing.

My eyes burn, but I don't cry. I just take inventory like the person in the mirror isn't me. There's blood on my face, spots I had missed, and my SFU sweatshirt. I grab a towel and wet it, scrubbing at my skin until it's clean. I fight the urge to strip out of my shirt. It won't make the crawling sensation disappear. A scalding-hot shower will probably do the trick, but I can't see that happening with Wolfe on the other side of the door.

I drop the towel and pack my toiletries grudgingly. The essentials. My makeup bag. Face wash.

Am I overthinking this?

The doorknob jiggles, then the door swings inward.

Wolfe appraises me, then the bloody towel in the sink. "You okay?"

"Peachy." I zip the bag and shoulder it. "I'm ready. But don't think I'm happy about this."

He smirks and takes the bag from me. "Trust me, flower. No one will mistake you for *happy*."

I scowl.

I cast one look around my apartment. My laptop and notebooks are in the library where the dead guard left them. Maybe lost and found by now, or taken. A lump forms in my throat, and it doesn't ease when I close my apartment door. Or when I slide back into Wolfe's car.

We glide silently through the dark city and arrive at their giant house. I marvel at the details I had missed. A statue in the center of a fountain on the other side of the house. Flowerbeds framing the front porch, which has columns like Olympus that lends little shade or rain protection.

He backs into the garage, then kills the engine.

I glance at him.

"Don't..." He sucks his lower lip between his teeth for a moment. "Don't take anything he says personally."

My eyebrows hike. "Who? *Jace*?"

"Or Apollo."

"Or you, I suppose."

His eyes narrow. "You were foolish."

"I'm not taking that personally." I raise an eyebrow. "And you were— You know what? Never fucking mind."

I hop out and retrieve my bag. I'll figure out where the hell they expect me to sleep later—right now, I just want to be away from Wolfe. The place is a maze, though, the hallway from the garage leading past open doors, darkened rooms, until I find the huge, open kitchen.

Apollo stands on one side of the wide the island, chopping something green.

Jace sits on the other side, perched on a stool. His gaze is fixed down at something in his lap. And for a moment, from the shadows, I study him.

My stomach lets out an untimely growl.

His gaze flies up, and his expression shutters. "The woman of the hour."

Apollo jerks.

"Did you kill Kronos?"

Jace rises and places my backpack on the butcher block island. The straps fall dangerously close to Apollo's knife. It doesn't stop Jace from unzipping it and pulling out the items slowly.

"Did you want us to kill him?" He lays out the laptop and charging cord, the two notebooks. My slim case of pens. Calculator.

I stick to the shadows as he invades my privacy.

Is he going to do the same to the things in my duffle bag?

"Seen enough?" I finally ask.

He shakes his head and touches each item. "We're just getting started."

"Jace," Apollo says under his breath.

"I didn't realize our invisible girl was a fucking *idiot*." Same anger as Wolfe, but he burns hotter. He clenches his fists and leans on his knuckles, and it's impressive watching him struggle to get a handle on himself.

Impressive and scary.

I drop my duffle bag and inch forward. "Like you gave me any choice in the matter."

He laughs. "Sure I didn't."

"You destroyed my *only* chance of a future." I ball my fists. I do not like violence, but I've never wanted to hit someone more than I want to punch *him*. "What made you do it, huh? Why did you have to take everything from me?"

He glares at me and shakes his head. "You should've never come to Sterling Falls."

I let out a hollow laugh. He's *impossible*. "We don't know each other. What gives you the right—"

"Let's be clear." He steps into my space.

My heartbeat immediately kicks up. He's close enough to touch me, and I'm ill prepared for that to happen. My blood boils.

"This city is mine. The gang you ran to with open arms? Enemy. The university you attend? Run by weak fools who bend to whoever pays them the most. And don't think the cops are any different. Sterling Falls is corrupt, and you stumbled into the wolves' den.

"But instead of chewing you up and spitting you out..." He circles around me. "We let you go. Gave you a chance to leave. Gave you the *choice* to leave."

"A corrupt city," I repeat, turning to keep him in my sights. "That's..."

"An exaggeration? A lie?" He's all predator, but it's clear now that his attention is on me.

I didn't have to see him fight to know that. My instincts are telling me to run as far and as fast as I can away from here. He moves forward, and I go backward, until I bump into the wall. And he still keeps coming.

"It's the truth," he says in my ear. "Because we're the ones who corrupted it."

Lie. It has to be a lie.

"He's not wrong," Wolfe says from the hall behind me. He slips past me and opens the fridge, hunting for something. "The gangs were well on their way to a civil war—until us. We brought everything together."

"And we're the only ones keeping it from falling apart," Apollo adds. "Until we want it to crumble."

I... don't know what to do with that information. They can't be too much older than me, and they want me to believe they have Kronos and whoever else runs gangs in this town—plus the college, government officials, the police—by the balls.

But it seems pretentious. How can three men take on two gangs and a city full of corrupt government officials? If things are as bad as they say, then they don't stand a chance.

Making one girl disappear on paper is one thing.

One small thing.

Destroying the framework of a city is quite another.

"You talk a big game." I shift away from Jace to meet his cold stare. Everything about him seems frozen, right down to the blue of his eyes. Or maybe his chill started there, and it slowly infected everything else. "So why did I make any difference?"

Jace touches my sweatshirt.

The move is so shocking, I freeze for a moment. He pinches the fabric above my breasts and rubs it between his index finger and thumb.

He's touching one of the spots that had soaked in the blood. It's nearly dry after almost an hour. "This could've easily been your blood. And what a shame that would've been, Kora Sinclair."

I shiver.

"As for why you make a difference? That's for us to know. And you..." He lifts one shoulder. "Maybe you'll catch on one day."

CHAPTER 9

"He said he would wipe your debt?" Jace has been quiet while Apollo and Wolfe pry the story out of me, sitting back on his side of the L-shaped couch.

I'm on the other side, hugging a pillow in my lap. Apollo sits in the recliner, closest to me, and Wolfe has claimed the corner of the couch. The latter two have taken turns asking me questions, their tones reserved. And slowly, piece by piece, I told them everything.

Now I feel oddly bare. I've shed my secrets for the first time, and they haven't crucified me for my choices.

I nod once, silently answering Jace's question. I feel stupid now, believing that Kronos would just forgive the debt in exchange for the mask.

"Your friend gave you that mask?" Wolfe looks the most at ease of all of us.

"Yes."

Jace frowns. "Interesting."

"She's been before, presumably." Wolfe glances at Jace.

"Why?" I lean forward. "She's my best friend. She wouldn't do anything to hurt me."

"It just painted a target on your back." Apollo sighs. "Did you see the man who followed you to your apartment again?"

I want to ask him *why* a flower mask would put a target on my back, but his swift follow-up question doesn't give me an opportunity.

"It certainly explains your initial reaction to that fight," Wolfe muses. "You got tense when I told you one of them was a Titan."

I ignore him and answer Apollo. "I don't know. I hadn't seen him before. Maybe he was at Descend, I just..."

"Didn't pay attention." Jace snorts. "Of course. You're worse than a baby."

"And you're worse than a tyrant," I snap. "I didn't ask for your help."

"No, you just wanted Kronos to kill you, too, huh?"

I grit my teeth. "He wasn't going to kill me."

"Just the other guy. And make you a witness." He laughs. "So fucking innocent."

"I managed to do just fine—"

Apollo stands and shoots Jace a look, then back to me. He stops right in front of me. "You're in survival mode. Stealing food or skipping meals. Your mattress was on the *floor*. Your cupboards were bare. Your whole fucking apartment was empty."

I hug the pillow tighter and don't answer.

Quieter, he continues, "I know what that feels like, Kora."

My curiosity reignites. It's been dormant, the need to know these three guys suppressed in the face of all the other shit going on. But for a second, I crave more from Apollo. I want to know his history. What makes him understand this part of me?

"Enough of this." Jace's voice sounds a thousand years old. He grabs the remote and turns on the television, flipping over a movie channel. They don't discuss options—he just picks something, and no one says anything about it.

Apollo disappears, and Wolfe flops into the recliner he vacated.

I count to ten, then put the pillow aside and climb to my feet. I navigate my way from the den to the kitchen, where Apollo stands with his back to me. I open my mouth and close it, struggling with the urge to apologize. Do I owe him that?

"You're almost as quiet as Wolfe."

My lips twitch.

Apollo glances over his shoulder, then tips his head for me to join him. I step up beside him and stare down at the carton of ice cream and the spoon in his hand. He retrieves another spoon and passes it to me.

I lean over, my arm brushing his, and scoop some. It's dark pink, almost purple. Black raspberry, maybe, or black cherry, with chocolate chips. I close my eyes and smile when the raspberry flavor hits my tongue. Black raspberry.

"I haven't had this flavor since I was a kid."

Weird memories try to surface: me as a clumsy four-year-old running around a house with a cone, the melting ice cream dripping down my fingers. Crouching in the closet with my stolen sweets and giggling, ruining my hiding place.

I shake my head. My childhood has always been convoluted in my mind. A tangle of things I never know what to make sense of, or how to differentiate between true memories and figments of my imagination. Even now, with that one? I can't tell who I was hiding from, or whose house I was in. I might've made the whole thing up.

"Why did you go to him?" he finally asks. "You only had to be in Sterling Falls for two seconds to know there are some bad people in this town."

I hop up on the counter beside the ice cream. I lick the spoon clean and drop it in the sink, my appetite vanishing. "I didn't know he was with the Titans. I thought he was just a seedy money lender."

He grunts.

"He tried to warn me against it, but..." I shrug. "I was determined to stay in school."

"Even if you couldn't afford it." He meets my gaze.

"I would've, if my job didn't suddenly forget I existed. I just wanted more for my life than what I was able to get at home. The scholarship wasn't just a partial thing—it was a full ride to my dream school."

Ah, that gets another grimace out of him. At least he feels a bit bad about it, right? Although none of them have said sorry or even offered an explanation for *why* they did it.

I slide off the counter. "I have blood in my hair." Words I never imagined speaking. "Can you show me which room I'm staying in? Unless this was a big joke—"

"It wasn't, Kora. We want you here."

Why, though?

He leads me to the second floor and down the hall, to the last room on the left.

"Here." He pushes open the door and steps aside.

I flick on the light and try to hold back my shock. It's a big room. Bigger than my apartment, I think. There's a stone fireplace framed by two large windows. Two windows on the far right wall, too.

My bag is already on the queen bed, my purse beside it.

The room has a lot of green.

Not my go-to color, really. The walls are mint. The bed has a white duvet stitched with flowers, and the pillows match. There's an open door that goes into a bathroom—my relief about that is immediate—and another open door to a walk-in closet. The four huge windows all have shades pulled down, and dark-green curtains on either side. The rug that the bed sits on is patterned green, white, and gold. Besides that, the only unusual thing is the wall of bookshelves between the windows on the right wall.

They're bare, except for some staged classics.

I have a sudden desire to buy a plant or two. They would go well in the room... perhaps even make it feel more cozy. It feels like someone else's room. A guest's.

And I'm definitely not a guest. More like... unwanted visitor.

"Towels are in your bathroom."

I exhale my nerves. "Thanks."

His expression remains blank. "You're welcome to join us downstairs."

Not going to happen.

Still, I force a smile. "Got it. Um, thanks. Again."

He offers a half smile, then closes the door behind him. I immediately turn the lock on the knob.

Alone at last.

I sag against the white door, and my fingers go to the cuff on my wrist. It still hides the brand, for which I'm grateful. I don't know how they would react, and I don't want to find out.

My phone buzzes from my purse, pulling me from moping too long. I hurry to grab it and swipe to accept the call from Marley. Relief that it isn't a FaceTime video hits me, followed by guilt.

It's for the best, though. She would take one look at me and call the cops. Or ask me a million questions. Not that she's *not* going to ask me a million questions now.

"Hey," I answer.

"I am the worst friend in the history of the world," she declares.

I frown. "No, you're not."

She scoffs. "I'm up there. I let you leave the beach after Janet was a total bitch. I should've gone with you."

I close myself in the bathroom and set the phone, on speaker, on the counter. "No, it's okay. I ran into someone I know, and he gave me a ride back."

"Did you just say *he*? Why is this the first I'm hearing about him?"

Because I'm pretty sure he's a bad guy.

Except I don't say that. How could I?

"I just..." I rub my eyes. "I'm not sure how I feel about him."

"Well, fine. Are you going to be free for dinner tomorrow night? I can bring something over to your place."

I meet my gaze in the mirror. I really do still look like shit. The wide-eyed expression of frozen shock has to go. As does the blood speckled in my hairline. I'm sure it's in my hair, too, but the dark-red color camouflages it.

"Can't," I say absently. "I have a thing."

"A date?"

I pause. At this rate, what's another lie? "Yeah. I'm sorry."

She squeals, and I cringe. Marley is my best friend. *Her* choice in friends aside, I shouldn't be deceiving her. But I can't tell her part of it without telling her all of it.

And I definitely won't do that to her.

She always talked about returning to Sterling Falls in a

positive way. And from her perspective, I can totally see how she'd think it was a great place. She lives in the college district. Her father probably lives in North Falls, in one of the nicer neighborhoods. She didn't have to see the underbelly.

"You need to tell me all about it," Marley continues. Her voice is higher, more excited. "I mean, when you're ready. But... you're going to be ready soon, right?"

Another smack of guilt. She's *happy* for me.

"Okay?" she prompts.

"Okay, okay." I swallow. "Um, I've got to go. I was just about to jump in the shower—"

"No problem. I'm finishing up my homework, then heading back toward campus. But I wanted to check in and apologize. I'm actually heading to a party at one of the frat houses. Want to come?"

I snort. "No."

If I had a nickel, I'd bet she grinned at my quick reply.

"Worth a shot," she says. "Don't forget about me if you fall madly in love, yeah? And if he's cute, see if he has a brother..." Marley snaps her fingers. "Oh! I have condoms. Do you need any?"

I choke. "I'm good, thanks."

"Well, let me know. A girl should always be prepared."

"*Goodbye*, Mar."

"Love ya."

The line drops, and my smile drops with it. I turn the shower on and slowly undress. My body aches, but I put that aside. Catalog and file away to deal with another time.

For now, I just need to keep putting one foot in front of the other.

This isn't the first time I've been thrust into life-altering situations. And, judging from my track record, it won't be my last. But if I've learned anything? I'm a survivor.

I just need to survive today.

And I'll worry about tomorrow when I get there.

CHAPTER 10

APOLLO

I toss the surveillance photo into the fire.

Now that Kora Sinclair has joined us, we're destroying our own damn evidence. She managed to get all the way to the front door of Olympus with Jace's mask—what else is she capable of?

So we're taking no chances.

It's impressive, actually. She had a plan and executed it, and she almost escaped.

Wolfe eyes me, rifling halfheartedly through a box of USB drives. They're labeled in the code the three of us created. He runs his finger over the edge of one, then plugs it into his laptop.

Jace is... Jace.

I don't fucking know.

"What?" Wolfe snaps at me. "You're in a weird fucking mood."

"You didn't go up to her apartment. When you dropped

her off. You left her at SFU?" I raise my eyebrows, not sure if I'm pissed at *his* lack of follow through or all of ours. I wasn't going to say anything, but if he wants to pick this fight... "You barely looked into her at all."

He leans forward and snatches one of the photos from the pile. He stares down at it, his brow crinkling. "I was respecting a boundary."

We've been friends for too long for this bullshit.

"You seem attached," he finally mutters.

I make a noise of disgust.

Kora is safely tucked away in her room. Tucked and locked, although I doubt she'll notice her door also locks from the outside. One of us will unlock it in the morning, before she's had a chance to discover it. There's too much shit lying around the house to let her wander unsupervised. Not until we've got a chance to clean it up or lock it away.

Especially since we now know she has a penchant for getting in trouble.

Jace comes into the den and throws himself on the couch, glowering at the dark screen of the television.

"Well?" Wolfe sets aside the box and stands.

Jace grimaces. "He's being stubborn."

She signed a contract. I can still see her loopy signature on the paper Kronos waved in Jace's face earlier this evening. Smug bastard. I'd never seen the Titans leader so thrilled to have an ace up his sleeve. Not just any sort of contract—a fucking notarized one. A judge, even in our pocket, would be hard-pressed to turn it over.

But all in all, this just underscores something I've known for a while. And judging from the sour look Jace and Wolfe have worn all night, they know it, too.

I crumple the paper in my hand and toss it in the fireplace. "We've strayed from our original mission."

Wolfe's laugh is hollow. "A long time ago."

"And if we hadn't, we probably wouldn't be here." I shrug. "It's our own damn fault."

Our plan was to *destroy* the gangs—not become one. We aren't, exactly, but we are a force to be reckoned with. The only issue is that none of us wanted this reality. We wanted revenge. Retribution. And somehow we got side-tracked.

We wanted to bring the corrupt to their knees, and we ended up becoming part of the corruption.

Kora being here is a huge wake-up call.

Jace shoves his hand through his hair. "You're right. We allowed our greed to get the better of us."

Olympus took off. Our other business adventures took off, too. And suddenly we were too busy to care that the gangs were still doing stupidly illegal shit.

Drugs.

Trafficking.

Stuff we wanted to end with the money from Olympus.

"I vote we get back on target." I meet Jace's gaze. It was his plan, originally. He talked Wolfe and I into this crusade. "We need to stop messing around."

Wolfe sighs. "Dad's going to kill us if he finds out we're back at it."

Another reason we let up: Cerberus James, Wolfe's father and leader of the Hell Hounds, found out about our scheme and threatened to kill everyone Wolfe had ever cared about. Which wasn't a huge list of people, but it was enough.

The Titans found out about the vague details of the threat. They knew it meant that Cerberus wouldn't protect Wolfe anymore, and so my best friend has a huge target on his back. He's safe most places, but if he's caught in West

Falls... Titan territory. They want nothing more than to send his head back to his father.

"We have to do it anyway." Jace stands and grabs another photo. He brushes his finger over her face. Her red hair makes her so fucking obvious. It was dark the first time we met her. The first time we chased her through the woods. The ring in her nose is new, too. Just another thing to make her stand out in a crowd.

Even with the changes, we recognized her as soon as she came into Olympus with the flower mask. *Persephone's mask.*

In the beginning, girls wanted to catch Jace's favor. Wolfe and I are happy to let Jace take the role of ringleader as Hades, but it spiraled out of control. The women who wanted to be Persephone—a goddess who Hades literally kidnapped and dragged to the underworld to marry him—were desperate.

So we banned her.

Persephone, that is.

We threw out anyone who wore a mask that could be perceived as her. We threatened that they didn't know how seriously we could take this, and how far we could go.

The fear did the rest.

Until Kora.

This set of photographs was taken last week on the Sterling Falls University campus. Kora seems bleak in all of them. She's so much thinner than when we first met her, and I hate the guilt that stacks up on my shoulders. She seems stiff in all of them, as if expecting to be attacked at any moment.

We set out to destroy the gangs, and we ended up destroying *her* instead.

That wasn't our mission. That wasn't remotely what we wanted to do.

My thoughts turn to what my sister went through, and I have to fight to remain in the present. Rescuing Artemis from the decisions of my father was one of the worst things I've ever had to do.

She doesn't talk about it any more than I do. And now we've hurt Kora, and the weight presses down on me.

"And Kora?" It's our fault she's here, even if it was her own stubbornness that pushed her over the edge. We just got the ball rolling.

Who knows how many people have seen her with us? After our little display of force at Descend, especially. Word will spread that we have a weakness.

Just because we're corrupt doesn't mean we're infallible.

"She's..." Jace frowns, folding the photo and sliding it into his pocket. "She signed her life away. And until we can figure out leverage to convince Kronos to drop it, she's in danger."

The flash of fury that sweeps through me takes me by surprise. I jump to my feet, angry at myself for letting my emotions get away from me—even for a split second.

"We should've just fucking killed him," I snap at Jace.

"You know we can't touch him."

Rules. Agendas. Kronos has a stranglehold on parts of this city that would be happy to crush us if we acted directly against him. Everything is so tangled, and we've become too worried about everyone else. It can't be as easy as taking out the leaders.

Cut off one head, and two more will grow back.

I rush out of the room and go downstairs, to our home gym. I don't know what's wrong with me. I'm well aware that, in Sterling Falls, people can be bought.

It's the thought of someone else having control over *her* that drives me insane.

Control. It's what I need, how I thrive. Mental and physical.

My heart pounds, and there's a clammy sweat on my skin. This reaction is pure emotion... but it isn't anything a run can't cure.

As for Kronos... he will die for this.

CHAPTER 11

KORA

"You've got to be kidding me." The door rattles in the frame, but it doesn't budge. The knob doesn't even turn.

They locked me in.

I pound on the door, tempted to start yelling. If I didn't feel like a prisoner last night, I certainly do now. I give in to the urge and slap the painted wood with my palms. My sudden shot of adrenaline has my body shaking, and claustrophobia wraps its fingers around my lungs.

"Hey! Let me out!"

I'm so freaking mad, it takes a minute to register the *click* of the deadbolt sliding back. And then the door pushes inward, and I jump back to avoid it.

Wolfe smirks down at me. He has more scruff on his cheeks today than before. It gives him a roguish look. "You good?"

I step forward and shove him back. As soon as my palms connect with his chest, heat floods into my face. He barely moves under my force, but he does snag my wrists before I can retreat. I tug back, but he holds fast.

His dark hair is wet and falls into his green eyes.

And our kiss at Olympus rushes back again, slamming into me with brutal force.

He yanks me forward, and I practically fall into him. He twists my arms behind my back, pinning them against my spine, and his smirk widens into a grin. "Good morning."

I glare at him.

"You've got a set of lungs on you," he comments. "Until I put you in a compromising position? Is that it?"

"Let go of me." I jerk, but his grip only tightens.

He adjusts, holding both my wrists in one hand, and traces my jaw with the other. I go still, unsure what he's going to do. Pinch my jaw until bruises form? Choke me? Or maybe force me down to my knees...

"See?" He speaks softly. "Your mask is firmly in place, mystery girl. You gave me more of yourself looking through holes in flimsy cardboard and glue than you are right now."

I narrow my eyes and move my head away. "Because I thought I was safe with you."

He releases me like I've burned him. "Aren't you?"

"You locked me in my room." I step back and massage my wrists. I make sure the cuff is in place, touching the clasp with my thumb. "I wouldn't have wandered."

"We didn't want to take that chance. You are a thief, after all." His gaze sweeps up and down my body, and his head tilts. "Where do you think you're going?"

I showered—yes, again—and dressed before I tried my door. The last thing I needed was to run into any of them in my sleep clothes. "I have class."

He raises an eyebrow. "Right. And you'd hate to waste that money you sold your soul for."

I flinch. When he puts it like that...

With a sigh, he turns around and motions for me to follow him. "I need breakfast before we go."

I glance at the clock on my phone and shift my weight. "I suppose I have time to watch you eat."

"And eat, yourself, before you wither away."

Ugh.

I hate the idea of taking anything more from them.

My stomach lets out an untimely growl, and Wolfe's laugh floats back to me.

I follow him downstairs and take the seat he points to. He busies himself making coffee, sliding me a mug with a spoon in it, then a bottle of creamer from the fridge. He takes it back once I'm done, dumping some in his own mug and giving it a little swirl before he sets it down.

"Where is everyone?"

He gives me a look. "Everyone? I'm chopped liver?"

"You know what I mean. Apollo and Jace."

"*Everyone* has other things to do. More important things."

I snort. "So, you're babysitting."

He lifts his chin. "Is that so bad?"

"After our last conversation...?" I shrug and pick at my nail. "I didn't think you'd want anything to do with me."

His brow lowers. "Because of a little disagreement."

"Because you said I was foolish, and—"

"You went to a gang leader for money that you couldn't pay back. *Yeah*, you're a fucking dumbass." He rolls his eyes. "And we're doing what we can to get you out of it. Okay? So just leave it for now, Kora, please. Just because we disagreed doesn't mean I hate you."

I pause and watch him. He straightens and glances away, but there's a tightness around his eyes. He might pretend to be uncaring, but I think he actually does give a shit.

Why, though? He can't just be a bleeding heart. Or care. That's ridiculous.

A change of subject is in order, clearly, because I've only taken a few sips of coffee in the silence before he claps his hands and grins.

The good mood, however fake, is back in place. "What are you in the mood for? Eggs? Bacon? Pancakes?"

"Anything." I'm mystified by his behavior. "Can I ask you a question?"

"If you want."

"Who did you guys... stab?"

He doesn't answer for a long moment. He takes the spoon from my mug and stirs his own again, the metal clanging against the ceramic edges. Enough time passes that I wonder if he even heard me.

But then he says, "We are sometimes hired to weed out spies for the Hell Hounds."

I scoff.

"My father is the leader of the Hell Hounds." He watches me carefully, taking a swallow of coffee. "And while we're not on good terms most of the time—in fact, ninety-nine percent of the time we're on terrible terms since leaving the Hounds a few years ago—he doesn't mind throwing us a bone every once in a while."

He smirks at his pun.

I stare at him. "Apollo literally stabbed a guy that night."

"Yeah, and he deserved it. He'd been leaking information to the Titans about Hell Hound business for weeks. If Apollo hadn't stabbed him, my father would've done much worse. He probably brought the man to his on-call doctor and had him stitched up, just to prolong his suffering. If there's anything my father hates more in this world, it's a Titan snitch." He leans on the counter, facing me. "Are you going to tell me about the guy who made you so afraid of men?"

Parker. My ex who left more than one mark on me—both physically and mentally. He's The last person I want to talk about, so I take a page out of his book and keep my mouth shut about it.

He nods slowly, accepting my silence. "We give people what's coming to them."

"And what do I have coming?"

He shakes his head and drains the rest of his coffee, then pushes off the island counter. "I don't think that's my answer to give."

Whose, then?

"Coming?" He disappears down the hall.

Breakfast is clearly forgotten, but it's fine. I can get something at school, maybe.

I groan and follow him. We climb into his car, and he pulls out of the driveway in silence. We get onto the main road, and I risk a glance over at him. His jaw is set, and his grip on the wheel is tight. The muscles in his forearm stand out.

"Are you okay?"

His gaze flicks toward me, then the road. "Perfectly fine."

I grimace.

We fly past the turn for the university, and I whip around to watch the road disappear. "Where are we going?" I demand. "I'm going to be late—"

"You have a Saturday class, little flower?"

I narrow my eyes. "It's Friday."

He chuckles. "It *was* Friday. Yesterday. Now it's Saturday."

Shit. I did go to class yesterday. I was just in such a miserable state, waiting for something to happen, that I forgot. And now it's the weekend, and I'm in a car with Wolfe going... who knows where.

I sigh. "You ever feel like life moves in slow motion?"

He nods. "Sometimes."

Tears fill my eyes.

Crap.

I don't want to *cry*. Not now. Not with Wolfe sitting beside me. But it isn't like I can get out of the car and hide just to let loose a few tears. That's ridiculous.

"Did you sleep?" he asks in a low voice.

I can't get out the *no* past the lump in my throat. I tossed and turned all night, in a bed that was too comfortable, in the unfamiliar room. Every time I let myself relax, Kronos loomed in front of my face with his gun. Or worse, that branding tool.

I settle for shaking my head, and Wolfe's hand suddenly slides into mine. His fingers are calloused and rough, but his touch is gentle. He laces his with mine and squeezes.

"Your business with Kronos is done," he assures me. "We're working on it."

"The big and powerful Hades couldn't save me from that prick, huh?" I use my free hand to swipe under my eyes. I take a deep breath. I just need to change the subject and not think about Kronos. Or my debt. "Okay, so, um... no class. Where are we going?"

Wolfe perks up. "This is the industrial district. We're meeting a business associate, then we'll get breakfast."

I eye him. For some reason, I just assumed that Olympus was their only business. But then again, they grant favors, among other things. Their power can't come from fight nights alone. The way they talk about corrupting the city...

He hits a button, and halfway down a block-wide building, a huge garage door retracts upward. We pull in, and the door grinds closed behind us. I glance around at the stacks of wrapped pallets. There's a forklift against the far wall and an office with a huge glass window off to the side.

"What happens here?"

He hops out and motions for me to do the same. Besides us, the place is empty. Rightly so, with it being a weekend, but the effect is rather eerie. The aisles stretch away from us, into shadows. A chill seeps into my bones, and I hesitate to close my door. Part of me wants to climb back in and lock myself away.

A framework of metal pipes hangs just below the ceiling. A hundred different pipes serving a hundred different uses. I grip the top of the car door and tip my head back farther, taking in everything up there. It seems easier to stare up there than to focus on Wolfe.

But eventually, I need to move. I join him in front of the car, and he takes my hand again. It seems to be a reflex of his to reach for me.

"We control shipping." He glances at me, gauging my reaction to that simple admittance.

"I'm going to need a little more than that."

"Consider what the Titans and Hell Hounds do. They smuggle in drugs. Their bars and clubs require liquor to keep their guests satisfied. They use large-scale shipments to bring in weapons and whatever fucking else they desire. Legal or not."

I nod along to what he's saying.

Sterling Falls is isolated. There's water on two and a half sides—the beaches on the north side are only a small percentage of the land up there. Then the cliffs on the east, and the harbor to the south. Woods surround the rest. And the closest town, Emerald Cove, is over an hour away.

"So..."

"We control the marina and the main road into Sterling Falls." He taps a pallet. "There's a checkpoint station just outside of city limits that prohibits all outside trucking companies. Loads are transferred to our vehicles."

"Is that how you've corrupted Sterling Falls?" I bite my lip. I shouldn't be this bold around him. What happened to my fear? It seems to have dissipated... for now. I tack on a belated, "If I'm allowed to ask that."

He laughs, and something stirs in my chest. I'm surprised at how much I like the sound.

"It was our way in, although we weren't supposed to... You know what? That's a story for another time." He guides me into the office. Behind us, someone pounds on the garage door. He points to a chair behind a giant desk and waits for me to sit. "Stay here."

I swallow and nod.

He goes to the window and pulls the blinds. I'm doused in shadows, the only light coming from the little glass window in the door. And then he steps out, shutting the door firmly behind him.

There's a grinding noise as the garage door rolls upward. I'm curious, above anything else, so I step up to the blinds and part them with my fingers.

Wolfe hits a button next to the door, opening it only enough to duck under it. His legs are visible in the daylight, along with another pair of shoes. They're out there for a minute before Wolfe returns with an envelope in his hand. He closes the door.

I scoot away from the window and sit back down just as my phone rings.

Mom.

My stomach twists, and I hurry to answer it. Maybe I can shoo her off the phone before Wolfe returns.

"Hey, Mom!" Fake cheer.

If she doesn't see right through me...

"Hey, missy. We missed our usual call last night." Her voice is warm and not at all suspicious. But she's right—we usually video chat while she makes dinner at least once a week. It almost always happens when I'm on my way back home from studying in the library. She likes to make sure I'm safe while walking alone.

So, it's a win-win.

Except last night, when the Titan intercepted me before I could get a chance. And when I saw her missed FaceTime call later that night, I didn't have the energy to explain it. Bad Daughter of the Year award.

"Sorry about that. I, um, had a date." I lied to Marley about it—I may as well continue the trend.

"Oh? Well, that's news. You didn't tell me you were talking to anyone."

Wolfe opens the door and meets my gaze. He comes over and leans on the desk, facing me. His leg knocks into mine.

I hold his eyes when I say, "Well, it was a surprise thing. I didn't know I was going until..."

She sighs. "I know things have been rough after everything that happened with Parker. I'm proud of you for putting yourself out there."

Wolfe takes the phone from my hand, hitting the speaker button. I belatedly lunge for it, but he elevates it over our heads.

"Kora?"

I glare at him but keep my voice light when I answer my mother. "Still here, sorry."

"You never did like talking about him."

Parker, she means. The ex who nearly destroyed my life —and one of the reasons I left Emerald Cove in a hurry. I don't like to talk about him. I don't like to think about him.

"It's just in the past, you know? It was traumatic. Every time I hear his name, I relive it." My voice is thick, and I swallow around the lump in my throat. "I'm doing better in Sterling Falls. Away from reminders..."

Wolfe's eyes bore into the top of my head.

I stand, making one last attempt to grab for my phone. But it just puts me directly in Wolfe's space, and he takes advantage. His free arm wraps around my waist, keeping me close to him as he straightens to his full height and backs me to the wall.

Familiar, my body screams. But... not in a bad way. In a way that goes straight to my core. He pushes more of his weight into me, keeping me still. The phone is right over my head, his forearm resting on the wall next to my ear.

I need to figure out what triggers my fear and what triggers *this* response. Because right now, it feels like a crap shoot.

Mom's still going when I zone back in. "...hope this new boy treats you better. And you know if anything makes you uncomfortable, you can tell us. We've got you. We can be in Sterling Falls within the day, if you need us."

Wolfe's gaze softens, and he slowly lowers the phone back between us.

My voice is thick when I answer my mother. "I love you. I've got to go."

"Love you, too. Oh, and call your father! He's anxious to hear how your chemistry test went."

I hit the *end* button and let my head fall back.

He tosses the phone onto the desk behind him and brings his other forearm up, caging my head in. "Mother?"

I suck my lower lip between my teeth.

"Chemistry test?"

"Failed it." My face gets hotter. "Which I blame you for."

He grins. "Is that so?" He ponders me for a moment, and the smile slides off his face. He shakes his head. "I looked into that scholarship we took away from you."

I automatically tense.

Wolfe frowns, easily reading my desire to escape. "Sorry, flower, this isn't one you can run away from. That scholarship... did you lie to get it?"

"What? No." I push at his chest, but he's immobile. "Why would you ask that?"

"Because that scholarship was for little nobodies." He ducks down and runs his nose through the hair just above my temple. "It was supposed to give forgotten foster children a chance."

I close my eyes. "What do you want me to say to that?"

"Just admit that you've been a thief since long before we caught you."

I renew my scowl, meeting his gaze again. He's so close, I'd only need to press up on my toes to kiss him. But unlike the fight night, I have no such desire to do that now.

Okay, that's a lie.

But I don't *want* to have that desire.

There's a small part of me that craves the violence he brings, too. To wrap my hands around his throat and know what it feels like to have him stop breathing.

But that thought jerks me out of my rising anger. If I did *that*, I would be no better than Parker.

"I'm not a thief." I tamp down my scowl. "I got that

scholarship because of my history with an Emerald Cove group home."

"Is that so." He's going with sarcasm. It's laced through his words, sickly sweet with it. "Did you volunteer there with Mommy and Daddy on the weekends? Donate clothes that you grew out of—"

I bring my knee up suddenly, anger making my motion sharp and quick. It connects with his groin dead-on, and I shove him aside in the same breath. He lets out a loud groan, doubling over.

Good. I can't waste any time. I rush out the door and into the warehouse, although my plan dies here. I could go for the human-sized door near the garage one. Wolfe didn't even use it, though, and I have to assume it's locked. Even if it wasn't, I'd be on the street in unfamiliar territory. My throat closes as terror climbs up my spine, and I sprint down the aisle away from the office.

The will to fight had been beaten out of me—but it was my first instinct in this situation. I don't strike back. I tried it exactly once with Parker, and I ended up in the hospital. The first of a collection of trips to the emergency room that didn't set off any alarms with the doctors and nurses. There's nothing quite so defeating as realizing no one sees through the feeble lies.

They want to believe everything is okay. It's easier to believe a girl fell down the stairs or spilled burning coffee on herself than to think that the charming man leaning over her hospital bed pushed her. Or threw that cup of coffee on her. It's a delusion people hold on to so tightly, because the truth will give them nightmares.

Marley was the one who told me about the scholarship. It promised a full ride, plus a meal plan and stipend for books, to help a foster care child. The requirement was easy:

applicants must have gone through the county system. And since Emerald Cove and Sterling Falls are in the same child protective services district, I was eligible. I wrote an essay about my experience, and I was chosen as the recipient.

I was adopted when I was six. The people I call my parents have *been* my parents for the last fourteen years. They are truly my mom and dad. So much so that I don't even remember my old parents. I barely remember the group home, or the kids I lived with while I was there. I *do* remember the hopelessness of it all. How bleak we were to know that our safety died at eighteen.

"Come out, come out, wherever you are..." Wolfe's voice echoes down the warehouse, bouncing off the pallets around me.

It yanks me back into the present.

I choose a row at random and barely manage to fit between two stacks. I don't understand why, if they own the shipping, they have so much shit in this warehouse. A backlog? Seized property from people who refuse to pay?

I crouch and wait.

"Kora..." He's getting closer. "I do love a game of chase."

My muscles tense, but I'm too in my head to decide if this is the good form of adrenaline or fear.

"But what will I do when I capture you?"

I catch a glimpse of the top of his head moving down the center aisle, passing the row I'm in. I crab-walk farther up, toward the door, and pause when my foot catches on a loose piece of metal. It clangs to the floor, and the noise is *loud*.

Shit.

"Not so quiet." He's behind me—close enough to raise the hairs on the back of my neck.

I don't bother checking. I shove myself through into the next aisle and *sprint*. Like my life depends on it. I go back toward the office, thinking—I don't know. I can bar myself inside.

But before I get there, footsteps pound behind me. Arms wrap around my middle, halting my run and lifting me off my feet in a swinging motion.

I scream and thrash, unable to control my wild response. My heel connects with his shin, and his exhale is harsh in my ear.

He sets me down and spins me around to face him, keeping his hands on my upper arms. We're both breathing heavily. I raise my hands and grip his forearms. My grasp on reality fractured for a moment there.

"That was some fear response." His brows pinch together. "Whatever you think, I'm not going to hurt you."

I cringe. Isn't that the standard lie?

Kora baby, it was an accident. Please believe me.

All the shit I had stuffed away comes up again, and bile rises in my throat. My stupid mask of indifference is broken, and I can imagine the horror he can see painted across my expression. It's fire against the backs of my eyes, daring me to show weakness. It's the sting of every injury I've suffered at my ex's hands flaring back to life.

He cups my cheek, and I have to stop myself from flinching away from him. Because for some ungodly reason, I want to believe that Wolfe won't actually raise his hand against me. That he's the same person as Ares, who was so gentle when he realized my issues.

"I'm sorry." His voice is so damn low, rasping against my ears. And then he brightens, a little switch being flipped. "I know how to fix it."

He smiles and releases me. He opens the passenger door, leaving it that way, and climbs into the driver's seat.

The change releases the tension in my body, and I let out a harsh exhale.

It's my choice, I suppose. To get in the car with him, to believe him, to trust him. Or… to pretend. To hold on to the cracking pieces of my guard. Lie to myself that he isn't working his way under my skin.

I nod to myself and get in the damn car.

CHAPTER 12

We pull up to a small, hole-in-the-wall café. It's a blink-and-you'd-miss-it sort of place, the kind that tourists wouldn't think twice about passing. College kids, too, I'm assuming. There isn't even a sign above the door or hours posted.

There's just a picture window with a neon *open* flickering sporadically, the blinds hiding what's inside. The glass and metal door right beside it gives no further clues. There are snapped and broken blinds that clank against the door, in perpetual motion. The glass is dirty, speckled with dried water droplets from overnight rain or splatter from the street.

Wolfe doesn't seem perturbed. He opens the door and motions me through. The light in here is warm and low, and the bustle of movement greets me first. Waitresses behind a counter or at tables. An assortment of patrons spread out across the tiny space, collected in clusters or singles.

The smell of coffee and bacon hits me, and my stomach grumbles. I was hungry before we went on our little trip, but I had forgotten. It all comes roaring back as I glance around, my eyes tripping over the different plates. Eggs and pancakes and fruit-topped waffles, the sweet scent of maple syrup. My eyes might be as big as the plates, themselves.

"Come on." He strides down the aisle, which has a low breakfast bar on one side and booths on the other. The cluster of tables near the windows and most of the breakfast bar are filled. He chooses one of the farther back booths, taking the seat with his back to the wall. No one's down here, but I get the feeling that's exactly why he picked it.

Isolation. Privacy. The same thing with different names.

A waitress appears almost as soon as I've sat.

"What a pleasant surprise," she says to him.

She's older. In her forties, maybe, with silver hair in a ponytail and little wrinkles around the corners of her eyes. She pulls a pad from her apron pocket.

"The usual?"

He grins and reclines, putting his arm up on the back of the seat. "Make it two."

She winks, scribbling it down, and disappears.

I stare at him. He's much more relaxed here, but I can't tell if it's a facade. I feel... tense. Like my muscles can't unclench. I crane around, hyper aware that my back is to the door. I take inventory again. "What did you order us?"

"Are you sure you hate surprises?"

"Depends," I say slowly, rotating back to face him. "Usually, yes. They're the worst."

"They must've been bad surprises, then."

Well, in general? Yes.

"Your friend taking you to Olympus the first time —surprise?"

I nod.

He chuckles. "You didn't seem thrilled to be there."

"And that's what caught your attention? Or the mask I

shouldn't have been wearing?" I still don't understand that. The door creaks open again, and I glance back. An older man with a bowler hat tugged low enters with a slight shuffle.

"The mask drew my attention, but your actions kept it." He sighs. "Sit over here."

"Why?"

"Because you keep looking behind you like you're waiting for an attack." He pats the space beside him. "Plenty of room for two."

Huh.

I get up and take a seat beside him. He doesn't move his arm from the back of the booth, but it isn't the worst thing in the world. Now that I have a view of what's happening, I let out a breath.

"Better?"

"Thank you. I've..."

"Kora, you don't have to explain." His gaze finds mine again.

"I was in the foster system." I have to just... get it out there. As much as he probably doesn't deserve to know that, I want him to think better of me. "My parents adopted me when I was six. I was only in the system for less than a year, but that scholarship didn't say that the kids had to be in until they aged out."

He rubs his hand over his face. "Fuck."

"The only thing I've ever attempted to steal was that mask, and it was because—" I press my lips together.

Wolfe leans into me. "Finish that sentence. We both know it wasn't a bet."

Because the brand fucking hurt. I don't admit that, though.

Luckily, the waitress seems to have great timing. She appears with mugs, placing them in front of us and filling them with coffee. She sets down a glass bowl full of different sugar packets, and a metal cup of cream.

"Food will be out shortly." She taps the table. "Wolfe, are you going to introduce your friend?"

He snorts. "No."

She eyes him for a moment, then leaves.

I stare at her back, stiff once again. "She's old enough to be your—"

"Cousin." He laughs. "On Mom's side. The harmless side."

My curiosity flares. "Do you have a harmful side?"

"Yep." He leans even closer, until his lips are at my ear. "My dad is the leader of the Hell Hounds." His arm that's been covering over my shoulders now slips down, his hand squeezing my upper arm.

"What kind of childhood did you have?"

His gaze shutters. "Not a pleasant one."

We leave it at that until our food arrives. His *usual* is a spinach and tomato omelette, bacon, hash browns, and a small stack of pancakes on the side. With fruit and a dollop of butter on top. My eyes keep getting wider and wider the more plates she unloads.

This could feed five people.

"You get this every time you come here?"

He laughs and slides me a rolled set of silverware. "Yeah, sometimes I mix it up. But generally, we only come here to nurse hangovers. This food has magic in it, I swear."

"I'm that big of a headache?" Am I *teasing* him? Something must've short-circuited in my brain, because that's not my usual behavior. I tease Marley. I joke with my parents. I slip in snide comments around Janet. I don't tease guys who literally look like models.

"Nah, just wanted to spoil you with some good food."

"Anything else?" The waitress-cousin reappears with more napkins and a bottle of maple syrup.

"I think we're good."

My mouth is watering. I don't need much prompting to dive in, and for a few long minutes my mind is blank. The food is *good*. Too good.

I only get through half of it before my stomach cramps. I managed to taste everything, though... A year ago, I probably wouldn't have had a problem putting away most of this. I've been killing myself to eat less, to survive on what I could.

Tears burn the backs of my eyes again, and a lump forms in my throat.

"Hey, hey, don't cry." He drops his fork and twists to face me. "What's this about? I've never heard of anyone crying over pancakes before."

I sniff and swipe under my eyes. "It's nothing."

He nods to himself. His own plates are empty, and he shoves them away in favor of his coffee. He calls our waitress over and asks for a box.

"You don't—"

"Stop it. Apollo's the only one who can cook in our house, and he'll be gone for a few days." He eyes me, then his gaze moves back to his cousin. "And the two slices of pie?"

"Done and done." She collects the plates and leaves us again.

"There, better?" He rubs my arm with the back of his hand.

"What else are we doing today?"

He shrugs. "What do you want to do?"

Wallow in self-pity?

The waitress returns with a box of food I couldn't finish

and a box with two slices of pie, leaving them next to my elbow. "Y'all are all set."

Wolfe grins at her. "Thanks, cuz."

"Don't go getting into trouble," she warns.

He chuckles, and she leaves us alone. The café is filling up around us, but Wolfe doesn't seem in a hurry to leave.

"So, you grew up in the Hell Hounds?"

Maybe it's the wrong thing to ask, because he stiffens. After a second, he forces an exhale. "Born into it. It's where my friendship with Jace and Apollo began. Although friendship seems like too light of a word. What we have is more of a brotherhood."

"Trial by fire?" I guess.

"That's too accurate, flower. Coupled with a severe lack of a mother..." He glances away. "I just don't want to end up like him."

"Your dad?"

He nods once. "He sees the world one way. I see it another."

I bite back my questions and put my hand on his thigh. His gaze immediately drops to my hand, and he covers it with his when I try to pull away.

"Don't retreat. We're having a moment."

"Okay." My voice is breathless. "How does he see it?"

His fingers tighten on mine. "As something to manipulate."

"And you?"

He leans in, his green eyes boring into mine. I'm not afraid of him in this moment, but the two versions of him are eclipsed. And I can see both at the same time: Ares and Wolfe.

"I see it as something beautiful." His lips touch mine.

And I... let it happen. Lean into it, even. I close my eyes

and relish the slide of his lips against mine, the way it seems too innocent. Yet, something stirs deeper inside me. A dark part that questions if he's lying. If seeing the beauty doesn't change what he'd do to it.

We think flowers are beautiful, but we still cut them and stick them in vases to wither and die.

I grip his thigh tighter, bewildered by my own response to him. I shouldn't *want* to kiss him, and yet I can't seem to pull myself away. It isn't an invasion, or overwhelming, or even that hot. It's just...

Good.

It's a balm I didn't know I needed.

My heart thumps harder against my ribs.

His hand inches up my side, but too soon he moves back. He clears his throat and shifts.

"I shouldn't have done that." He gives me measured look. "I've been wanting to, though."

I'm pretty sure my face is redder than a strawberry, on top of the mortification that the first words out of his mouth after kissing me was to express *regret*.

"We should go." I clamber out of the booth and hurry to the exit. I don't know where I want to go, or where he'll take me—as long as it's away from these witnesses.

"Hey." Wolfe catches my hand before I make it to his car. "I didn't take you for a runner."

I scoff. "Do you want to add escape artist to my list of nicknames?"

He tugs me closer. "I can think of a lot of names for you, but that isn't one."

I lift my chin. "What now?"

"What now, indeed?" He pretends to consider it. "Now, we have about two hours before Jace needs us ready to go."

I sigh. "Should I even ask?"

He winks. “Nope.”

My feelings for Jace swing more toward hatred than anything else. Wolfe and Apollo probably had something to do with my scholarship being revoked—but it was Jace who dropped the guillotine’s blade on my neck.

I watch Wolfe on the way home. The muscles on his arms, the tension in his neck. His sharp jaw, and the dark hair that falls over his forehead. It has a little curl in it, but it’s mostly straight. He’s too attractive—the sort of guy who probably had loads of girls in high school and college.

If he went to college.

I ask, and he snorts. “Nope. My education was on the streets.”

Yikes.

“You’re coming with us to the fight on Friday,” he adds. “Just… you seem the type to need to mentally prepare.”

I silently agree with him. But then another, more pressing matter jumps up. “Are you going to lock me in my room every night?”

And the question not spoken: *How much of a prisoner am I?*

His jaw tics. “Best to let Jace answer that.”

“Great. The bully of the group gets to determine my fate for a second time.”

Wolfe doesn’t answer, and soon enough we’re back in the familiar neighborhood, pulling up to the giant mansion gate. He hits a button, and it swings inward.

“What’s the point of a gate if it doesn’t go all the way around?”

“Spotted that, did you?” He follows my finger toward the gap in the wrought iron.

I suppose if someone had planned correctly, it would’ve disappeared into the row of huge privacy hedges that wrap around the back of house. As it is, it stops about two feet short. Enough for someone to slip through if they were determined—or didn't want to use the gate.

"Security hasn't been an issue. No one messes with us and walks away from it."

Why? I want to ask. It's on the tip of my tongue. What did they do to make the gangs... fear them? Is that it?

Wolfe suddenly curses. His gaze flies to the rearview mirror, and the roar of a motorcycle has me craning around, too. Two bikes coast in and stop at the top of the driveway. One revs his engine, drawing attention, then goes silent.

A tendril of fear wraps through me when Wolfe's hand lands on my thigh.

"Kora, it's important that you stay in the car. Call Jace."

I nod once and accept the phone he hands me, already unlocked. He parks in front of the garage door, which remains closed, and removes a gun from the glove compartment. He checks to see if it's loaded, then hops out.

I crack my window. Call me crazy—or just curious. I crane around and hit *dial* next to Jace's name, pressing the phone to my ear.

"To what do we owe this displeasure?" Wolfe calls to the two bikers.

He keeps his weapon at his side, aimed at the ground, but the threat is clear.

And the bikers seem unfazed.

"Wolfe," Jace answers briskly.

"It's Kora." I'm whispering, but... dammit, any louder and my voice would shake.

"What's wrong?" His voice changes to something... more concerned.

It's hard to reconcile that emotion with him, even though I would be concerned, too, if I was calling from his friend's phone out of the blue. "I... we're parked in the driveway and Wolfe is talking to two bikers. They followed us in."

He swears. "I'm two minutes away. Stay in the fucking car."

The line goes dead before I can tell him that Wolfe already ordered the same thing—and I'm not an idiot. But I do lock the doors and hunch down lower.

One of the men has flipped up his visor, but I can't hear what he's saying. He keeps gesturing to the vehicle, though. Wolfe steps subtly in front of it. Still, he doesn't point the gun at them and order them off his property.

Two minutes must've been an exaggeration on Jace's part, because it feels like only thirty seconds has gone by when another motorcycle roars down the street. He boxes them in and hops off smoothly, removing his helmet.

He raises an eyebrow, and I'm not sure how the cocky gesture can become an order. But both of the bikers remove their helmets.

I don't recognize either one. The first, the one who had been talking to Wolfe, has a bald head and tattoos up to his jaw. The other looks vaguely familiar, but I can't place him. He's younger, with short dark hair and much fewer tattoos than his partner.

Jace steps in closer to the older man, listening as he talks. I'm practically twisted in half to see out the back window, but it doesn't help me *hear*. And my lipreading skills are seriously lacking.

Wolfe still seems on edge, only letting out that energy now that Jace is here. Two against two seems like better odds, anyway. Wolfe paces back and forth, then finally settles for a wide stance in front of the car. I wonder where Apollo is. If they were together doing illegal shit. Scaring people into submission. Beating up gangsters. My imagination could keep spiraling like this, on and on with endless possibilities.

But then, Jace points to the road.

The two intruders leave, and I hurry to face forward again. On top of everything, I don't want to appear to have been spying. I hit the unlock button for the doors.

It isn't Wolfe who yanks my door open, though, but Jace. He leans into my space, boxing me in. "What is it about you that always seems to attract trouble?"

I scoff. "Me?"

"Yes, you. You're chaos."

"Seriously? I've done nothing but try to survive." My brows draw together. "And don't get me started on *that*."

He sneers. "It keeps biting you in the ass."

My mouth drops open. "What? How?"

"There's this little thing called *fine print*." He shakes his head. "You're un-fucking-believable. Did you read the contract you signed? Or did he just flip to the last page and point to the bottom line?"

I lean back and cross my arms. My temper is rising—and I've come to the sudden realization that Jace doesn't scare me as much as he probably should. After all, he's gone out of his way to keep me safe. That has to count for something, right?

Maybe not.

This bluster on his part only serves to rile me up. I scowl at him. "Anything that happened after you declared me *invisible* isn't my fault. What the hell did you expect? You ruined my *life*."

Same song, new day.

"You should've left. Ran home to Mommy and Daddy and admitted that Sterling Falls chewed you up and spit you out. Because clearly you're too dumb to stay on the nice side of the city." His expression isn't angry, just annoyed. Definitely not remorseful.

"You should just take that stick out of your ass," I retort, straightening in my seat. "It might make you less of a miserable piece of wet toilet paper."

He pushes off the car and storms away, muttering under his breath.

And I sit there and watch him go, feeling... surprisingly good. Like I won a round against Jace, and it *means* something.

In reality, it probably means I'm definitely getting locked in my room tonight.

"Well, that was fun," Wolfe drawls. "Never heard that insult before."

I jump. The driver's door is open, and he stands in the opening. His gun is gone, his hands empty.

"Fun," I echo.

"Yeah." He grabs the boxed food, plus another white box from the backseat, and motions for me to get out of the car. "Like a boxing match, except you actually sort of held your own."

We go in the front door, and it closes with a heavy *thunk* behind us. He locks it, and his brows furrow when I glance from it to his face.

"So... are you not going to tell me who they are? Except, according to Jace, their arrival is my fault. Because Kronos has..." A contract. That I signed. Like an *idiot*.

My stomach flips. I hate to admit that Jace is right, and I should've read the fine print. It was long, and I was confident that I'd get a job. Pay it back, plus that insane interest. It seemed reasonable. He pointed to the *important* parts—

the timeframe, the interest that would accrue. How to make payments.

Wolfe doesn't say anything.

I stop him just before we reach the kitchen. "Wolfe. Please."

He shrugs and meets my gaze. "You signed a contract that literally put your life on the line, Kora. You've defaulted on the loan—two months without payment, which means he's going to collect in other ways."

"My… flesh." I look down at my arms, struck dumb. It was going that way, anyway, wasn't it? His stupid fucking brand on my skin for the world to see. Except… the way Wolfe is looking at me makes it seem like it's a lot worse than that.

Kronos said this wasn't over, and I didn't believe him.

"Right," he says slowly. "In some cases, it binds people to the Titans for good. They own homes, businesses, *people*. Other times, they sell them off to make the payment back."

What's this worth? Your life?

I shiver.

"Yeah. Think of the businessmen who get into a hole and can't find their way out. The powerful people of Sterling Falls who get caught up in his web. And then he owns them like *that*." Wolfe snaps his fingers to emphasis his point, then turns away. "Kronos has decided you're not worth it."

I gulp and follow after him. He has me hooked, now. I'm greedy to know what doom lies in my future, no matter how horrifying. "What does that mean?"

"He's going to sell you to the highest bidder."

CHAPTER 13

While I have parents, there's always been that pressing *otherness* to me. Strangers used to point out that I looked nothing like them. Teachers were surprised when the dark-haired, tan-skinned couple came to pick up the pale redheaded child. Friends knew, obviously, as did my doctor. But there was always a split second of curiosity around my family.

Rightly so, I suppose.

I love them, but I don't fit.

They're my parents, but I have *biological* parents out in the world somewhere.

Existing without me.

And because of that—maybe to spite it, too—I developed some unhealthy coping methods. Repressing my emotions. Sleeping too little or too much, which usually dissolves into insomnia. Picking at my nails until they bleed.

After the first night of being locked away, my door isn't locked again. I sit on my bed and wait, staring anxiously at it and straining to hear the scrape of a deadbolt. I stay up so late, the sun creeps in through my window.

On the third night, I'm restless. There's only so much pacing a girl can do, and I'm filled with toxic energy. I didn't do much today—Wolfe was the only one here, and he seemed content to let me do nothing. I studied, I stuck to my room. He brought up lunch, and then dinner. Takeout boxes. Both times he seemed distracted, so I let it go.

Tomorrow, I should probably go back to class. I've put it off for too long, and I can't just stay here forever. I finished my homework earlier. And now, the house is silent.

I open my door and step into the dark hallway. My socks lessen the noise of my footsteps as I tiptoe toward the stairs. I haven't ventured up to the third floor, and I'm not sure I want to tackle that in the dead of night.

Instead, I head downstairs. There's apparently a gym somewhere. I know there's more to it than just the rooms I've seen in passing, and it seems safer to explore the first floor.

I feel like a thief, sneaking around and peeking into rooms. I collect them in my mind, making a mental map of the place. There's another office, separate from the one connected to the den. The double doors closed when I find it. Inside, it's empty except a desk shoved in the corner and boxes on the floor. I find a movie room. A game room, with a pool table front and center, is closest to the garage. It might even share a wall with it.

So, I go in the other direction. Past the kitchen and the two-level den with the huge television. There's a door that opens into a staircase leading to the basement, and I'd bet the gym is down there. I peek into the den, contemplating climbing the spiral staircase to see what sort of reading they have upstairs.

Ultimately, I keep moving.

I pause when I come upon a music room. Backlit by

moonlight, a baby grand piano sits in the corner. I flick the light on, and the polished black paint gleams. My chest tightens at the sight of it, and the rest of the room. I check behind me, not sure why I feel guilty, and step inside. There are a few guitars hanging on the wall, a mix of acoustic and electric. A few amps are tucked under them, cords wrapped tightly on top.

There are fabric panels on the walls between the instruments, and square panels on the ceiling, too. Sound absorption.

My instrument is a cello, although I haven't played in months. I almost brought it with me to Sterling Falls, but I'm immensely glad I didn't. I don't know if I would've had the courage to keep it when everything else was falling apart.

Still, I did study piano for a few years. Nothing impressive—just another thing I added to my résumé for college. My high school had free lessons before first period, and I dragged my butt in to learn the basics.

I flip the cover off the keys and drag the bench out, appreciating the ivory. The old piano I learned on had a few cracked and yellowing keys, the edges worn from countless students.

This feels like it hasn't been played much at all.

The keys are smooth and white, the black ones shining under the low lights.

I press the middle C with my index finger, and the tone is crystal clear. I close my eyes and take a deep breath. Then I nod to myself and reopen and place my hands on it. I have a vague recollection of pieces I learned, and one surfaces. I fumble my way through it once, pausing at the end.

Close, but not good enough.

I play it again. Fewer mistakes, but too slow.

Again.

Muscle memory comes back, and tears burn the backs of my eyes. Before I know it, I'm playing this piece from years ago decently well, but I'm silently crying. I couldn't even tell you why—just that there's a heavy grief in my chest that is desperate to come out.

I linger on the last notes, then wipe under my eyes.

"Interesting interpretation."

I nearly jump out of my skin.

Jace stands in the doorway. He has a gun strapped to a visible holster at his hip, one of the few times I've seen them wear it that way, over black canvas pants. A white long-sleeve shirt clings to his muscles. He runs his fingers through his hair, pushing it back, then steps into the music room. The door swings shut silently behind him, and it feels warmer in here from his presence.

"I don't usually play the piano." I have to defend myself against him, although it shouldn't matter.

"What do you usually play?"

"The cello."

He nods once, casting a glance around. "We don't have any cellos lying around, unfortunately."

"Pity."

He eyes me, then comes over and leans on the body of the piano. "Yes, I think it is."

I narrow my eyes.

"Play something else. Don't let me stop you."

A ragged sigh slips past my lips. "I should go to bed."

He shakes his head, then moves and sits beside me on the bench. I scoot over, giving him room, and his body presses into mine. From knee to hip. And our upper arms. He's not just warm, he's burning hot. And I seem frozen by comparison.

"Do you play?" I can't help the surprise that colors my tone.

"Nope." He taps one of the lower black keys, frowning at the sound.

There's a speck of blood on his sleeve, near his wrist. "Did you do something dangerous?"

"Most of the shit we do is dangerous." He pushes his sleeves up, revealing the tattoos on the backs of his hands and racing up his forearms. A compass stands out, but I force my gaze away before I analyze the rest of them. The letters on his knuckles, the black and gray ink on his wrists and forearms. The spot of blood is obscured now, too.

He presses the middle C. It's always struck me as a warm note, and grounding in its own way. I fight the urge to close my eyes and let it resonate in my chest, like I used to do with the cello. A single note could pull me out of the clouds and plant me back in my body.

"Play something." His order is quiet and unyielding.

Tonight, I don't want to argue. Except, there are no other pieces up my sleeve—not for the piano, anyway. So I stumble my way through the same one again. All I can think about is where he's touching me. At some point, I give up. My fingers still.

"I'm better on the cello," I admit softly.

"Do you miss it?" He taps another key at random.

"Sometimes, when I'm alone and feel a hollowness in my chest, I do." I clear my throat, unexpectedly emotional over an instrument... *weird*. But isn't that why I was drawn here in the middle of the night? And especially right now, when I feel exactly as I described: alone. Hollow. "I played in a few recitals in high school. And there's this hush that comes over the audience after they welcome you to the stage, and it's just you and your instrument and your heartbeat. And everyone there is just... behind the spotlight. Until the last note. I miss that. The purposeful quiet before something beautiful."

He doesn't say anything.

And I... I didn't mean to say all of that. Embarrassment rushes through me, and I turn away. I stand and move around the piano, needing to give myself some space to breathe.

He plays another note, then a few in succession.

I tip my head, because it's familiar. But before I can ask, he closes the lid and rises, as well.

"It's late."

I nod once, but I don't feel tired. I'm wired, my eyes like sandpaper. I'll crash soon. Maybe tomorrow. But every time I close my eyes, I see Kronos and his branding iron. Or the man he shot falling over backward.

He watches me for a long moment, then sighs. "I'm not good at this shit, okay?"

I narrow my eyes. "What shit?"

"The whole..." He waves his hand at me. "You seem upset."

I laugh. "Really, Jace? Upset? I feel..." I shake my head and tap my chest. "No feelings in here."

"That's the problem." His gaze turns speculative. "Nightmares?"

"When I sleep."

"Insomnia?"

I nod.

"Jumpy?"

"That's not new."

He grunts. "Fair enough, after that asshole ex of yours. Okay, come on."

"I didn't tell you about him." I stare at him. "How did you find out about Parker?"

He doesn't look back when he strides out of the music room. My curiosity gets the better of me, though, and I follow. Down the hall, back up the stairs. I sort of expected him to give me warm milk and tell me to count sheep.

Instead, he pauses outside my room.

I pause along with him, my abdomen cramping painfully. "You're going to lock me in?"

He shrugs. "Not tonight. Maybe if you're a pain in the ass some other time, I'll reconsider."

My shoulders are stiff when I go into the room in front of him. My bed is pristine, tight sheets and wrinkle-free duvet. I unpacked, grudgingly over the last few days, and everything else tucked away. Out of sight.

It doesn't look like *my* room. It's just a room I happen to sleep in. A closet my clothes *happen* to be hanging in.

"Lie down."

His tone leaves no room for arguments... and I've got to admit, I want to know what he's thinking. So I pull back the covers and climb in, lowering myself until I'm fully horizontal. I don't know what the problem is when I try to sleep, but I just can't do it. My eyes continuously spring open after a few seconds in the darkness, until I give up.

Jace seems out of place in here. In my green room with floral accents. My bookshelves are bare, minus the few notebooks I've set out from classes, and the fireplace remains unlit.

He drags the curtains across the windows, rolls the wand on the blinds to flip them up instead of down, then kicks off his shoes. He takes off the holster, too, and sets it, gun still tucked inside, on my nightstand.

I swallow. "What are you doing?"

He sighs and sits beside me. Not under the blankets. He crosses his ankles and leans back against the headboard, getting situated with a pillow at his back, then leans over and turns off the light.

We're immediately entombed in darkness.

"I'll keep watch," he says a moment later. There's another pause, longer. "It's okay to sleep, Kora. I'll keep the nightmares away."

I roll onto my side, away from him. I don't know if I trust it—or *him*—but I close my eyes. And I don't have the heart to tell him that nothing and no one can stop my nightmares.

I've been trying for years.

"What do you dream about?" The question comes out before I can stop it. It's not the only thing I want to ask him. In fact, it's the last thing I should be asking. I want to know what Wolfe told him about my ex, or my past. I want to know what he was doing that got blood on his sleeve. But instinct tells me he won't answer any of those questions right now.

He doesn't trust me, either.

He's quiet. Just his steady breathing, and the heat of his body behind mine. "My parents, sometimes."

"What about them?"

"They're dead." He sighs. "And when I dream, I see my mother as she was. And I see my father as he is. Rotting in the earth."

I don't know how to respond to that.

His hand lands on my arm, and I freeze. But he doesn't do anything else. His thumb just rubs down my skin, his fingers immobile on my biceps.

"I tried to save you from Kronos, but he refused. For a myriad of reasons, and none of them are important right now. He wants you back in his possession to sell you and get his investment back. With interest, knowing him. His pockets often dictate the decisions he makes." He goes quiet. "But we'll figure it out."

I want to ask *why*. Why me? Why is he helping?

I close my eyes again, squeezing them tighter shut. I don't want to know the answers to the other, darker questions rattling around in my brain. I don't want to think about Kronos, or the two men who came to the mansion, presumably to threaten to take me back to him.

I definitely don't want to think about Kronos selling me to the highest bidder.

"Sleep, Kora."

I've got nothing left in me but to obey.

CHAPTER 14

Jace is gone when I wake up. I stretch, half-expecting to knock into him, but the side of the bed that he laid on is empty. The only sign of him is the upright pillow and the creases in the duvet.

Once I'm showered, I go downstairs. I definitely have class today, although I'm not sure having a bounty on my head changes things. It should, right? But I've spent the last two days cooped up here, and I might go crazy if I stay longer.

Besides, when has hiding worked for anyone?

I march into the kitchen, bookbag slung over my shoulder. I don't know who I'm going to find, but I don't expect *all* of them.

Together.

It's the first time since the night they pulled me out of Kronos' office. I'm not prepared for how overwhelming the three of them are in the same room.

Wolfe is the first to raise his head and grin at me. He sits at the breakfast bar beside Apollo, a bowl of cereal in front of him. Apollo has what looks like an egg sandwich. And Jace stands near the coffee pot, stirring cream into his mug.

It's normal.

And weird.

After the last few days of irregular schedules, and the guys passing each other like… like ships in the night, seeing them all together is an eye-opener. I'm living in this house with all of them. I'm getting to *know* them, but that doesn't mean I'm not a captive.

I have to test that theory. "Will one of you take me to campus?"

Jace's back snaps straighter, but he doesn't turn around. "You think that's a good idea?"

"What's the point of all of this if I don't go?" I counter. It's too early for arguing, though—I need a big dose of caffeine before I can verbally spar with Jace.

I find a mug and step up beside him. He slides me the creamer, watching me out of the corner of his eye. I ignore him until my coffee is the right color, then raise it to my mouth.

Perfection.

Almost too hot, but bearable. And the rush of heat in my belly can be blamed on the coffee, not the three gorgeous men sharing the kitchen with me.

I turn to Jace and lean my hip on the counter. "Okay, go ahead and tell me how terrible an idea it is to go to class, when this whole thing happened because I *wanted* to go to class and you took that away from me?"

His lips press together.

I nod once. "Exactly." Feeling extra bold, I step around him and let my gaze bounce between Apollo and Wolfe. My heart gives a weird sort of lurch. I shouldn't feel attracted to *both* of them, right?

"I'll take you." Apollo leans back in his chair, reaching over and dragging out the third one. "Hungry?"

I beam. "Thank you, Apollo."

Jace scoffs. "This is dangerous."

"They won't expect me on campus."

He snorts and yanks the fridge open. "Sure they fucking won't." He wheels back around and points at Apollo. "You're her shadow. Okay?"

"Yes, sir." He salutes, mostly sarcasm.

I shake my head and find the cereal. One good thing about being left alone—I found my way around the kitchen. I take the offered seat next to Apollo and dig in. His egg sandwich smells amazing, but I don't have the patience to make something like it—or the time.

I nudge him. "Hurry up or we're going to be late."

"You're bossy in the morning."

"Only when the situation calls for it." And then I shut up and finish my breakfast.

Apollo does the same. We clear our plates and head to the garage. He hands me a helmet, and I sigh. "We can't take a car?"

He grins. "Why?"

"Because it's more practical. And won't mess up my hair. And I have a backpack."

"I like you tousled." He leans in and flicks a lock of my hair over my shoulder. "Where's your sense of adventure?"

I roll my eyes. "You want me to be adventurous."

"Okay, maybe not. I wouldn't mind your arms wrapped around me again, though." He winks. "Payment for having to sit through... how many classes today?"

"Just two."

He raises an eyebrow. "Just two."

"Yep." I tie back my hair and slide the helmet on, then

motion for him to get a move on. We're late enough as it is. But he takes a second to strap a gun to a holster in the small of his back. Two knife handles stick out from their sheaths attached to his waistband. He pulls his shirt over them, and he looks semi-normal like that.

When we climb onto the bike, he tugs my arms tighter around him and once again pats my hands. Checking to see if I'm secure or something, but my heart skips a beat. And it isn't from fear of riding this damn bike again. My backpack is heavy, but there isn't an alternative.

We get to campus without trouble, and Apollo coasts to a stop in a parking space. I hop off, and he follows me.

"So, you and Wolfe?"

I glance back. "What?"

"You have a thing with Wolfe," he repeats.

"And?"

He groans. "What do you see in the fucker?"

"Better question: what do I see in *you*?" I roll my eyes and stride away.

Men.

Seriously.

He sits silently behind me through my first class, shadows me across campus and into the library before my second one. He buys us sandwiches on the way, and the librarian shoots us a nasty look when he unwraps them.

He doesn't say a damn word.

The less he says, the more curious I am. I bite my tongue, though, because our silence has become a battle between us. I could be reading into it, but there's a glint of a challenge there. Whoever breaks last is going to have the upper hand. It's one of those things I can feel in my gut.

"Kora!" Marley rushes across the library and falls into the chair beside me. Her blonde hair is braided over one shoulder, but besides that she could've freshly crawled out of bed. Large sweatshirt, leggings. Her face is makeup-free and etched with concern. "I went by your place, but you weren't there. Twice, actually. And is your phone broken?"

Guilt roils my stomach. Our friendship has been off since this whole mess started. I've been dodging her calls left and right—of course she would go to my apartment.

Apollo glances back and forth between the two of us and taps the table. "I'll give you some privacy."

My brows lift.

He stands, taking his loud sandwich wrapper with him, and moves to another table.

"Who is that?" Marley whispers. She fans herself. "My god, he's smokin'. And he has the dangerous vibe going on, too. Is he a student?"

"More like... an overqualified babysitter."

She narrows her eyes. "Why do you need a babysitter?"

Well... shit. She's going to find out anyway, right?

"I took a loan from someone shady when my scholarship fell through." I lean closer to her. I mean, it's the truth. But it's definitely not as truthful as I could be. "He's helping me try to get out of it."

Her eyes widen. "What? Are you serious?"

"I'm sorry, Mar. I kept this stuff from you because I didn't want to burden you, and... It was just a lot when my scholarship fell through."

She grips my hand. "My dad could've—"

"No."

She winces.

Gentler, I repeat, "No, Marley, you and your dad obviously have stuff to work through. Asking you to go to him for help on my behalf wouldn't have done either of us any favors."

She casts a glance back at Apollo. "And you can trust him?"

"I don't know. I think so."

Time will tell.

"Okay, well, you're not allowed to disappear on me again."

"I won't."

She leans in. "Promise me that you're okay? You'd tell me if something was really wrong, right?"

"I... yeah. I would." Another lie. I can't seem to stop. "It was just a raw deal with a loan, and we're getting it sorted."

"Okay. Good." She smiles and stands, brushing invisible lint off her leggings. "I've got to get to class—it was luck that I saw you when I was printing my paper. I miss you."

"I miss you, too."

She leaves, waving, and I gather my own stuff. I have class soon, anyway, and I'm suddenly a lot less hungry than I was a few minutes ago. Apollo notices and meets me near the doors. His dark eyes miss nothing, it seems, because he makes a tutting noise when he opens the door.

He has an opinion—but we're still playing the silent game. This is probably the only time it'll work in my favor, and I savor the quiet. All through my next class, his glare bores into my back. The professors don't act like he's out of place. Their eyes skim right over Apollo as if *he's* invisible. If Marley hadn't seen him, I might be crazy enough to think he really is.

Invisible, that is.

Just like me.

Finally, my second class is done. Conquered. I have a paper to write, but the source material is online. Thankfully, I'll be able to do that on my laptop anywhere, and not chained to one of the library tables with the textbook from the reserves.

Apollo leads the way back to his motorcycle, but we don't make it very far. He grabs my hand, glancing around, and tows me into an empty classroom.

He shuts the door behind me and locks it, then gently guides me back against the wall. I bite my lip. There's a new look in his eye—something restless.

"What are you doing?" I lean on the wall and tip my head back.

Triumph flares in his expression—I broke the silence first. But I'm not entirely mad about the position I find myself in, so I allow it.

"You said earlier that you weren't sure what you see in *me*."

I cock my head. "Correct."

"Which means you were looking. Like you like me or something."

"Ah." I crack a smile. "I suppose it does."

He leans in and brushes his thumb over my lower lip. "I'm going to kiss you, now, Kora." His hand slips down, around my throat. He squeezes just enough for me to feel it.

And I don't dislike that, either. My heart races.

I smirk when he doesn't move, emboldened by his hesitation. "Well, do it already."

He doesn't need more prompting than that. His lips cover mine, immediately taking control. He sucks my lower lip into his mouth, and I gasp when his teeth graze it. I arch into him, grabbing his waist and pulling him closer.

Apollo steps into me. His knee pushes my thighs apart, and he takes advantage of my parted lips. My heart skips, and I dig my fingers into his skin. My whole body buzzes with a rush of adrenaline.

He breaks away, but he doesn't go very far. He stays in my space, breathing heavily. His fingers squeeze on my throat, sliding up until he forces my head to tip back. His gaze beats into mine.

My lips part as my breath is suddenly cut off. My lungs immediately ache.

He releases me a second later, easing back.

I gulp in air and let my head fall back to the wall. "Wow."

He smirks and straightens his shirt.

"Should I even ask what that meant to you?" I tilt my head and try to get my bearings. These... these guys just mess with my mind. Even without meaning to, I'd bet. Did he kiss me to piss off Wolfe? Or because he was jealous?

"That was me throwing my hat in the ring, sweetheart." He leans back in and kisses my cheek, and then his lips graze my ear. "And I look forward to a little healthy competition."

My stomach flips. "Why?"

"You're gorgeous." His gaze runs up and down my body. "And stubborn. And you somehow seem so innocent even though you're not."

I narrow my eyes.

He winks. "It's a good thing. Plus, my sister likes you. You impressed her, and that's not easily done."

"Too many fast flames in her brother's life?" Woof, is that *jealousy*? He's given me no reason to assume there are other women—or *were*, even—but I'm not stupid. I'm not the first to awaken his sexual nature. I need to regain control over myself right freaking now.

He presses his hand to his heart. "Cutting to the heart of the matter. Yes, perhaps you're right about that. And our pasts don't leave much room for trust."

My stomach twists.

He offers me that same hand that was just on his heart. It hovers between us, a silent offer, and I debate for a moment before I take it. I wasn't lying to Jace when I told him I didn't have feelings. Everything has slowly been shutting down in my brain.

Which is good.

I don't want to think about that man Kronos killed. Or Erik, the guard Wolfe or Jace killed to get to me.

I *definitely* don't want to think about how many people have died at their hands, or at the hands of Kronos. Evil bastard. My mind turns over what Jace admitted last night. That Kronos wants me so he can sell me.

Apollo squeezes my hand and leads me back to his bike. We're almost there when, without warning, he yanks me sharply into him. He wraps his arms around me and spins us away, shielding me from the parking lot.

I grasp his shirt, confused for a split second.

Something explodes. The blinding light hits us a split second before the eardrum-shattering *boom*. Apollo drags me to the ground, landing on top of me. He covers every inch of me, his hands protecting the back of his head. Heat sears my skin. I squeeze my eyes shut, pinned to the grass with him on top of me.

He rolls to the side and quickly stands. The gun is out now, and he swings around.

I push myself up slower. My ears ache. There's a loud ringing, but I can't decide if that's my ears or an alarm going off. And Apollo's motorcycle is a pile of burning metal. The two cars on either side of it are toast, too, moved from the force and on fire. Smoke pours from the motorcycle's engine. The tires are twisted, the rubber deformed. The smell of it is appalling.

I just stand there and stare at it.

We… we could've been on the bike when it went off. If he hadn't pulled me into the classroom—

I shudder. Apollo grabs my arm and leads me back farther, just as one of the two cars erupts in flames. The fire rolls upward and out, igniting the other one.

Students pour outside, drawn by the commotion, all the while Apollo leads me farther away. He wraps his arm around my shoulders, cinching me to his side. We slip past a group of students into one of the buildings and we don't stop moving until he's located a women's bathroom. He checks the stalls, then locks the door.

I stop in the middle of the room and look down at myself. The back of my shirt and pants are covered in bits of grass and dirt. The ringing has lessened in the quiet. I can't process anything else. Just the smell of smoke on both of us, filling the room.

"Are you okay?" His voice comes in over the ringing.

I shake my head and touch my ear. "I think so."

He gently grasps my jaw, moving my head to the side to inspect my ear. "It's okay. Ringing?"

"Yeah."

He frowns and pulls out his phone. He shoots off a text, then turns his attention back to me. "Head?"

"Fine."

"We hit the ground hard."

I wince, because it hadn't seemed so hard. It just seemed like he wanted to protect me, and that overrides the pain. "I'm fine. Promise."

The headache might come later. Right now, though, all I feel is… disbelief. Is this what shock feels like?

"Were they targeting us?"

He eyes me, a few lines forming between his eyebrows. "I'd have to assume so."

"What good does it do to blow me up? Don't they want me in one piece?" I cross my arms to stop from fidgeting.

"Great question." He checks his phone again, then lets out a breath. "You might have a concussion. Your head..."

"I probably don't," I counter. I rub my hands down my face and replay it again. The way he saw what was about to happen. His strong grip on my arms, turning me away from the blast. The *big* blast, that probably could've killed both of us if we were any closer. Next to the bike... or on it. "You saved me."

"This is my fault." He paces in front of the sinks. "We shouldn't have come back here. Not when the Titans are looking for you."

"We didn't know." I glance away. What I mean is, *I* didn't know. "But... no one was hurt, right?"

"Just my bike, and whoever was unfortunate enough to park next to me."

I stifle my laugh. It really shouldn't be funny, but—*yeah*. The Titans don't fuck around. Collateral damage, who?

Someone knocks on the door twice, and Apollo tenses. He pushes me into the handicap stall and closes the door. His footsteps take him back to the entrance to the bathroom. I wait in silence, my heart thundering behind the ringing in my ears. It makes it hard to hear what's happening.

And then the door to my stall swings in, and I stare up at Wolfe.

His eyes seem to take in everything at once, from my hair down to my shoes, and then he pulls me into him. His arms band around my back.

Just minutes ago I was kissing his best friend, and now I'm holding on to Wolfe like *he's* my lifeline. My ear presses to his chest, and the sound of his steady, quick heartbeat is... loud.

The ringing is fading.

I adjust my grip, squeezing tighter, and he mirrors my movements. Until I feel like we might be trying to crush each other into us. We stay like that for a while. Too long, really, but I can't help but try to leech the comfort right from his skin. His hands move slowly up and down my back.

I finally take a deep breath and let it out. "I'm okay."

I release him and move back.

He shakes his head. "It was too fucking close. A motorcycle, Apollo, seriously?" He grips my hand, and we meet Apollo in front of the sinks. "They almost got you."

I pull free and grab a paper towel, using this opportunity to clean up my face. We weren't even *that* close, but I suppose it was close enough. We felt it. My skin still feels hot from the blast. It seems weird that, besides some dirt and loose grass on my clothes, I look untouched.

Like we could go through something traumatic and only hold the scars on the inside.

"I didn't spot anyone when we came in. Jace is talking with the sheriff."

The blood drains from my face, and the paper towel falls out of my hands.

They both notice.

"You got an issue with cops?" Wolfe asks.

I wince. "No."

"This will be good," Apollo mutters. "You're a shitty liar."

"You just need to make it until we get home." Wolfe steps up behind me, meeting my eyes in the mirror. "Can you fake being okay until then? Pretend you didn't just hear Apollo tell you that you suck at lying."

I bite my lip.

Indifference. That's what I practiced whenever I walked into Descend. It was the mask I always went for when I had to do something scary. I've been living without that mask... or maybe I never really took it off. In this moment, I can't seem to figure out what happened to it.

I draw in a deep breath and reach for that cold feeling.

Better than numb.

Smarter than it.

Apollo and Wolfe exchange a glance, but I don't bother with that. Whether or not they expected me to stay a shivering, almost-breaking mess? I'm not that girl.

I unlock the door and march outside. Down the hall. I keep my head up and that damn ice mask firmly in place, with Apollo and Wolfe following me. Their footsteps are quiet, but I feel them there.

Invisible support. They went from scary to comforting? I'm *definitely* in shock.

Speaking of invisible... I'm starting to think life was a lot more simple when I was an invisible girl. It hurt more, and I struggled, but it was straightforward. Live to eat and get to class and that was about it.

Now, it's not so easy.

Even though we were inside for maybe ten minutes, if that, outside is completely different. The police and fire department have made quick work of the parking lot, blocking off a perimeter in yellow tape. Officers stand around, keeping students back. And the firefighters seem to have extinguished the flames. The twisted metal and melted rubber that sits between the two ash-covered cars barely resembles a bike anymore. There's some shape left to it. Barely.

Jace stands near the wreck with a man in uniform.

The sheriff, I assume. His uniform is shades of green, a

lighter, tannish-green collared shirt, his name tag on one side and a radio clipped to the breast pocket on the other. Dark-green pants end at the tops of his dark-brown leather boots, and a matching dark-green hat perches on his head. A red-brown beard covers the lower half of his face, although it's been trimmed close to his face.

Overall, I don't immediately spot anything alarming about him.

Jace catches my eye, and his brows draw together. The scowl almost stops me dead in my tracks, but then an officer is lifting the tape for us. After that, well, I can't really turn around and go in the opposite direction, right?

Indifference. It tastes a lot like shock, so maybe I'm halfway there. And the goosebumps have returned, crawling along the backs of my arms. Under the surface, I'm fighting the urge to flee.

Apollo's hand lands on the small of my back, propelling me toward Jace and the sheriff. Without him, I'd have frozen.

The latter lets out a low whistle when he sees me. "Well, well. You're the young woman causing all this trouble?"

Jace bristles. "Don't fucking talk to her."

The sheriff grins and ignores him. He extends his hand toward me. "Sheriff Bradshaw. Pleasure."

I don't bother trying to shake his hand and instead tilt my head to the side. "You think I'm causing trouble?"

He's not the only one. Didn't Jace accuse me of attracting it? Causing, attracting—same result. Chaos.

The sheriff leans in, and his voice drops. "Your face is all over town. According to rumors, anyway."

"All right." Jace glares at him. "You've blown your two minutes to talk to her. We're leaving."

Sheriff Bradshaw's smile never fades. He sticks his hands

in his pockets and rocks back on his heels. "Sure, of course. We know where to find you." His gaze switches back to me. "And I assume if we find *them*, we'll find you?"

"Fuck off, Brad," Wolfe growls. He shoulders past the man and leaves the cordoned-off area.

I follow, eager to be gone. Apollo and Jace hang back, for whatever reason.

Wolfe's black car is half on the grass, over the curb, and completely blocked in by police cruisers. Even on the street side. It's impressive, actually, how they managed to do it while making it seem like Wolfe just had bad luck.

"Fuckers." He kicks one of the cruiser's tires. "Stay here."

My eyebrows hike, and I do not stay put. I trail him back the way we came.

He scowls when he realizes, but I am not going to be the idiotic damsel who's kidnapped when her hero tells her to *stay*. Not that Wolfe is a hero... and I'm definitely not a damsel.

Whatever.

I should probably learn karate or something. That's what the heroes do in the books I read. They learn how to kick ass, and one day it saves them from the villain.

He marches up to one of the officers and waves a hand at the cars. "You assholes mind?"

The officer snickers. "Not at all."

He and Wolfe stride back to the cars, and the officer's keys jingle in his hand. He pauses before he gets in his cruiser and glances at me. His expression turns angry, and his attention flips back to Wolfe.

"You got something to say?" Wolfe snaps.

The officer just shakes his head. "This is supposed to be neutral territory, kid."

"Fuck off. We didn't blow up Apollo's bike."

"No, but your girl here is going to start a war."

An itching sensation creeps up my spine. My shoulders rise, and I do my best to ignore the feeling. I'm not going to start a war.

I'm the most unimportant person in Sterling Falls.

"Titans are hot on your heels," he continues, staring at me. "It's only a matter of time before someone close to you caves and turns you in."

My eyes widen.

Wolfe steps in front of me, raising his hand. Flipping him off, maybe, because the car door slams and the engine rumbles. A moment later, he moves, and we have a clear path out.

"Get in."

I swallow. "You don't want to talk about what just happened?"

He laughs. It isn't the sound I'm used to—it's colder. Hollow. "Not particularly."

"Because—"

"Because he doesn't want you to run off," Jace says behind me.

I spin.

He's *right* behind me. Steam practically blows out of his ears, and his normally ice-blue eyes are burning hot. "You're not coming back here."

Well, right back atcha, buddy. My anger rises to meet him.

I was having a normal day. Nothing bad happened until Apollo's freaking bike exploded. And who's really to blame for that? Not me.

"If anything, you guys should learn to be subtler." I cross my arms. "If they didn't see Apollo's bike, they wouldn't have known I was here. And they didn't target *me*, they hit his bike. Sends a pretty clear message that you three are the problem."

Over Jace's shoulder, I catch Apollo wiping away his smile.

Jace makes a noise in the back of his throat, and that's the only warning I get. He bends down, wrapping his arms around my thighs, and pitches me over his shoulder. I let out a shriek.

"Let's pretend we're normal people." He straightens to his full height.

I grab at his shirt, bunching the flannel in my fists. *Ridiculous*. My face is back to being hotter than the surface of the sun, and probably redder than it's ever been. "You can't just fucking manhandle me. People are watching."

Behind us, Apollo and Wolfe are openly snickering.

Jace jostles me, then strides forward. "Let's pretend I give a shit about *subtle*. Would that have saved you if we let you run around campus on your own? Or would they have just seen the invisible girl, all on her own, and quietly made off with you? Tell me, Kora, who would notice when you went missing?"

I don't have an answer for that. Marley's name is on the tip of my tongue, but then the photograph of her and me flashes behind my closed eyes. Kronos would clean up all the loose ends—and that would include her. My parents, too.

The car door opens, and he deposits me into it. His hand briefly touches the back of my head, shielding it from the top edge of the car, and then I'm closed inside. I sit in the silence for a moment, wrestling with my emotions.

Who would notice? How long would it take?

My parents, who call once a week?

The professors I haven't bothered to develop a rapport with?

Besides my best friend, I have no one in the city.

Fury knocks into me that Jace knows that about me. That he knows—through Wolfe—about my ex. And my lack of friends. My isolation.

They all pile in. Wolfe at the wheel, Jace beside him. Apollo opens the door Jace just closed on me and motions for me to slide over. I roll my eyes and scooch, but I'm not put off by it. Especially when he immediately makes himself comfortable, his knee bumping mine.

I glance around the car, and it dawns on me: I'm not isolated.

I'm not alone. I peek at Apollo, and my smile wobbles.

It's then that I realize I must've dropped my bag.

"Wait, I dropped my backpack—"

"It's apparently evidence." Jace turns his head slightly. "You'll get it back tomorrow, with any luck. The sheriff answers to Kronos when it suits him, and when it comes to you? I have a feeling it will. You won't be coming back here, do you understand?"

I huff. "You can't just... un-enroll me."

"Tried that already," Apollo points out. "Didn't work in our favor."

Jace scowls. "Wolfe, take us to the admin building."

Wolfe's eyebrow quirks up, but he doesn't say anything until we're parked in front of the main steps.

Jace hops out and opens my door.

I scowl. "What, you want me to witness you getting me kicked out of school?"

"I live for your reactions."

Something flutters in my chest. He's joking—and he

means it in a cruel way. But my heart seems to take it differently. And that just makes me more irritated.

We leave Wolfe and Apollo behind, entering the huge marble building. It has a similar style to Olympus, with the huge, ribbed pillars and arched hallways. I hadn't noticed. I don't normally come down this way. Most of my classes are on the other end of campus.

He seems unnaturally calm. His hands are in his pockets, and he saunters slowly down the empty hall. He knows where he's going, too. Up a half-flight of stairs into a shorter hallway, which dead-ends at dark-wood double doors.

He shoves open the doors like he owns the place.

A woman scrambles upright behind a large desk, but he ignores her and strides past.

I hesitate in the doorway, eyeing her. She seems to fit right into the outdated decor of the room, like she's always been there. Curled dark hair, classic red lipstick, and a dark-blue pantsuit. She's probably hiding nude heels behind that desk.

"You can't go in there!"

He ignores her and goes through the second door. Shocked silence spreads from the interior office. The woman glares at me as I step farther in. I do my best to ignore it and edge past her. *Office of the President* is written on a little plaque on her desk.

Well, that explains it.

I step into the university president's office and find him already standing. I glance around the room. The wood-paneled walls are adorned with his accomplishments. Framed newspaper clippings, awards, degrees. It's a pompous office. The giant desk takes up most of the space. A large picture window is at his back, his plush chair shoved aside.

He's locked in a staring match with Jace. He's also sweating, and it doesn't take long for him to break first. He blinks and jerks back like he just went toe to toe with the Devil.

"Sit down, Remus," Jace finally says. "We aren't here for trouble."

Remus Johanssen, the once-imposing president, sits heavily back in his cushioned chair.

Jace tips his head toward me. "Do you know who this is?"

President Johanssen's gaze comes up to me, and he winces. "Kora Sinclair. Yes, I, um—"

"Do not tell me weak excuses." Jace's tone brooks no argument. He drags one of the two chairs away from the desk. "Kora?"

I release a breath and go to it, biting my lip. I'm just waiting for Jace to tell him I'm withdrawing. It wouldn't be anything better than what I was going to tell my academic advisor at the end of this semester—just more abrupt.

More final, too, perhaps.

Jace braces his hands on the back of the second chair. "Here's how it's going to go, Remus. As of today, Kora will be finishing her classes online."

"That's not—"

"Or, you can explain why the school will be shutting down due to threats against students' safety." He cocks his head. "What do you think will cost you more in the long run?"

Remus swipes at his forehead with a white handkerchief. "Please, we don't have an online system. I don't have the capability."

"Then I suggest you figure it out with Kora's professors." Jace's voice is ice—and his expression is thunder.

The perfect storm.

"Okay, yes. I'll do that."

I stand. My skin crawls from being in this office, and I'm not entirely sure why. But Jace straightens, too, and motions for me to leave ahead of him. We walk past the gaping secretary and down the steps onto the main hall. Only then do I let out my breath.

"He's under the thumb of the mayor," he tells me. "Harmless, if annoying."

"Who controls the mayor?"

He glances at me, surprise parting his lips. But then he smirks. He hauls the building door open for us. "You're catching on."

Apollo waits for us, leaning on the car. Wolfe is at the wheel, and sunglasses shield his gaze. They're both vigilant, so I take a second and pause beside Jace.

I meet his eyes. "I'm a quick study."

"One day you're going to wish you weren't," he says softly.

Maybe.

But for now, I have a feeling the more information I have, the better equipped I'll be.

I suppose time will tell.

CHAPTER 15

WOLFE

The parking lot outside the clubhouse in South Falls is filled with rows of motorcycles. The place is out of the way, on the edge of the industrial district. This is the southernmost point of Hell Hounds' control. They've got a long reach, covering most of East Falls, too. Their border stops three miles shy of Olympus—for good reason.

If any of them cross into *our* territory, we don't send them back. They get to swim.

Dogs bark as I walk up, alerting the Hell Hounds of my arrival. I roll my shoulders back and wonder who they have on guard duty tonight. There are a few options, but I'm only worried about one.

The door opens before I get up onto the porch, and a big man blocks the entrance. Neon lights and smoke escape around him, until he takes another step and the door closes behind him. A neat little *snick*, and the bar's music suddenly muffles.

"What you want? You know you ain't allowed here."

I jerk my chin to the side, down a long covered porch. Usually, there will be Hell Hounds out here. Smoking, shooting the shit. Enjoying their women on the backs of their bikes and blowing off steam. But there's an all-hands-on-deck meeting tonight. Which means ninety-nine percent of the Hell Hounds are inside.

And this unfortunate bastard got guard duty.

He steps with me, mirroring my movements away from the door. People think they do it on purpose, but it's more of a subconscious thing. They're paying attention to where I'm going but not how I'm doing it. His shoulders are up, his body stiff.

My knife slides into my palm. I'm the epitome of calm on the outside.

Inside, I'm rioting.

"You got something to say, kid?"

Kid. That's what my father always referred to me as, too. Until I killed his brother in front of him. I would've killed every last one of them if I didn't have Jace and Apollo. They gave me back my sanity piece by piece.

But they're not here, and my sanity is holding on by a thread.

A wild thrill sings through my blood. I've been itching for a fight—but we were hired for a job. And in the midst of everything else happening, this couldn't be set on the back burner. This is the only time my father and I have an understanding.

I told Kora about how we took over the imports and exports, holding the shipping in a stranglehold, but I didn't get into the darker jobs. How Jace, Apollo, and I are good at extracting and uncovering information.

Fortunately, this line of work does well to satiate my restlessness and ease my demons.

I strike out, the side of my open hand hitting him hard in the throat. It's quick enough that he doesn't see it coming. Poor bastard probably expected me to speak, to give an excuse to see my father—or someone else. Like I'd willingly want an audience with any of them.

He stumbles back, choking and gasping, and hits the wall. He keeps moving to the side to get away from me. It would be smart... if I let prey get away so easily.

I shake my head and follow. "No, no, not so fast."

I grab the front of his shirt and yank him into my blade. His shirt, skin—they give way to my blade smoothly. It's the muscle that's harder to push through. And stomach wounds... well, some say they're the slow killers. I resist the urge to twist my blade.

He gags, the sudden pain flaring in his eyes, but he still can't seem to make his windpipe work. Might've hit a bit too hard. Where's the fun when they can't talk? Or beg for their life?

"You know, I've got to hand it to you. You made my job easy." I pat his cheek.

He gurgles now, sinking to his knees as I give in and twist the blade. I could rip it to the side, pull his intestines out and stuff them down his throat. Or just keep twisting. Make that hole bigger. His blood rushes over my hand, dripping off my wrist to the weathered floorboards between us. These wooden planks have seen their fair share of blood.

It just isn't usually Hell Hound blood.

His hands scramble at the blade, cutting his fingers, but his movements are getting weaker. His eyes are wild, so wide. Pupils blown out, although that's probably just the adrenaline. Fear presses in on him, and the knowledge that he's going to die.

I see it the moment it crosses his face.

He's an ugly fucker, too. Big, crooked nose. Dark hair cut too close to his scalp, and a bit uneven. His lips are thin, and there's a thick purple scar down his face, denting his jaw. He's tattooed around it, trying to make it edgy, or scary. Who fucking knows. He's got a face his mother might not even love.

I slide my knife out and swipe the blade clean—clean*ish*—on his shoulder and stow it. I haul him up and propel him ahead of me. He has enough wherewithal to keep his feet under him. Even though he's only got half a foot on me, he probably weighs a hundred pounds more.

I have to reach around him and twist the doorknob, then resume my position hidden mostly behind him.

The door opens, and we step inside.

"You fucking idiot, Robbie," someone yells. "You're supposed to keep watch, not take a fucking smoke—"

It's about then that my victim, Robbie, coughs up blood. It sprays out in front of him, and everyone's attention goes down to the red spot blooming on his shirt.

I kick him forward, and he falls face-first to the floor.

Boom.

Like the bomb that detonated yesterday, nearly killing Kora and Apollo.

I draw my gun and aim it down at Robbie. My jaw sets, and I eye the room. I've got a few extra magazines in my pockets, ready to go in case I need to fire rapidly. Can never be too careful with this crowd... says the man who just made a bloody entrance.

Ah, well.

They shouldn't forget who I am, even when I'm not around.

The large space is full of tables, and each chair has a Hell Hound ass in it. The bartender, one of the novices, slowly sets down the bottle he was pouring from. His mouth is open wide. They don't seem quite sure what to do—whether to pull their guns and shoot, or...

That's probably the part that's stumped them.

The *or*.

These are all familiar faces. I grew up with half of them. Was raised by the other half. Only a few rookies don't *know* me like the rest do. Those unfortunate bastards would've only heard the rumors.

We stay like that for a moment. Them in their seats, me with my gun on their bouncer. The bouncer on the floor with a knife wound in his belly.

Someone claps and rises from the center of the room.

The leader, emerging through the cigar smoke and low lights.

The Hell Hound savior.

And suddenly my past is dragged up out of my memories, presented front and center. Years of running around this place like we owned it. Like we had any semblance of power.

It was a sham, carefully crafted to keep us in place. And it worked for far too long.

Apollo, Jace, and me? We were forged in this clubhouse. By the man who walks toward me.

I clear my throat, recognizing that he could raise his gun and shoot me dead without blinking. He's threatened it before, loudly. To anyone who would listen.

"Hey, Dad."

A hint of a frown touches his lips, covered by the trim goatee. He wears the black leather cut that shows the burning, howling three-headed dog on the back. A white collared shirt. Black jeans. In twenty-five years, I'll probably look like him.

That's a sobering thought.

"What are you doing?" He tilts his head.

I glance around and feign surprise. "Oh, this? I came to give you a present."

His brow lowers, but his voice rises. "Everyone out. *Now*."

They move.

It's impressive how they scramble to comply. Failure to do so often ends with a bullet buried in their skull, or their spine, or their knee. Fear always gets the better of most. Those who aren't motivated by fear have either been through too much or they don't give a shit.

I don't move a muscle, even though instinct screams to obey.

It's a habit I constantly have to break around him.

Silence settles around us—and then the sudden, violent lurch of the man I gutted.

"He'll be dead soon." My father's gaze goes to the gun in my hand, then back to my face. "Want a drink?"

"Not particularly."

He grunts and turns away, headed back to the bar. I stand exactly where I am and watch him walk behind the counter. He ducks down, then resurfaces with a beer and pops the cap off. He'd never fit in as a bartender. He's got too much power, even in the easy way he drinks from his bottle. He seems out of place there, but he doesn't come back around.

He seems content to keep some distance between us.

Or there could be a shotgun within easy reach back there, and he's not entirely sure why I'm here. Even though he should know. It's his fault I'm here.

"Okay, Wolfe. Out with it. You know we don't deal with things like this here."

Here in this clubhouse.

No, he'd rather drag his mess to Olympus. Or worse, our house. And with Kora living there, no fucking way is he getting within a mile of my home.

Besides, this is the easiest way to make sure my father deals with the traitors the proper way.

He and Kronos have power.

The Hell Hounds have everything they smuggle in, their tight grip on the businesses in the southern part of East Falls. They collect rent, deal drugs, funnel a few tourist girls to the harbor year after year. Not enough to raise alarm or stop the flow of spring breakers and families coming up from land-locked cities to the west.

It doesn't help that the police don't give a shit. They care about the money that lines their pockets, not the girls. Those girls? The police know *exactly* where they go.

To a shipping container.

On a boat bound for who the fuck knows.

Sometimes it's Russia. Sometimes it's an Eastern European country. Hell, from Istanbul they could go anywhere in the world.

I grit my teeth. We lost track of the ideology we had when we started.

To shut *that* down.

To save innocent lives.

I hate that we've been distracted. Of all the things, we let this continue—and I'm going to live with that shame forever. Someday soon, the Hell Hounds and Titans will get what they deserve.

My father taps his fingers on the bar. "Well? Are you going to gawk or talk?"

I shake off those memories and force a bland expression. "Robbie recently bought a condo in West Falls under his grandmother's name. She's in a nursing home, so I doubt she's doing much purchasing on her own."

He stares at me, and I can't decide if he's surprised or not. He knows as well as I do that anyone who comes to the clubhouse on the regular, who is known to be a Hell Hound, would never hack it as a spy in Titan territory. It's the simple premise of trustworthiness. If a Titan came to my father, asking to become a Hell Hound, he would be punished to within an inch of his life and dropped on a curb in West Falls.

But there *are* spies. On both sides.

Someone double-crossing my father for the Titans has probably never seen the inside of Descend, the Titan bar. What's the point of being undercover if you're blown before you start? And the easiest way to blow your cover is to be seen somewhere you shouldn't be.

"Fuck," he grunts.

"You use him for anything important lately?"

Buying property in West Falls means he either *was* a snitch, and his duties are coming to an end... or he's planning on turning over everything in exchange for protection.

Either way, it makes Robbie a rat.

Dad rolls his eyes and drains the rest of his bottle. He tosses it into a bin, the clink loud against more glass.

"Your buddy, Wes, is getting in over his head."

He glares at me. "You're telling me this?"

"He has a bounty out on my girl." I bite my tongue. Giving him any more information than is necessary... not good. And that might be the stupidest thing I've done in a while.

My father throws his head back and laughs. Doesn't just laugh. He's practically howling. He thumps his fist against the bar until he can get control over himself, then laughs more. "The girl he's auctioning off is *yours*? How'd you let her strike a deal with him in the first place?"

I narrow my eyes. "Unimportant. What is important is that he's gunning for her."

He waves his hand. "Speaking of guns, where'd you get the one you were waving around a few minutes ago?"

I straighten. I wasn't sure if he'd catch it, but part of me wanted to test it out. See if he could recognize it. I remove the gun from its holster and join him at the bar. I slide onto a stool and set it down. It's almost painful to release it, but I manage. I draw my hand back and rest it on my thigh, forcing stillness through my body.

The firearm is beautiful. One of a kind. It was designed by my mother before she left us.

But back then, it was just a sketch that my father obsessed over.

It was one of the only things he didn't burn after she fled.

The only woman to ever escape Hell Hound territory. In the most ironic of ways, it left me stuck with the miserable, controlling bastard in front of me.

And god, did it hurt to take the brunt of his blame.

He recognizes it immediately, eyeing it with a reverence *only* reserved for impressive weaponry.

"How...?" He reaches for it.

I slide it back to my side of the bar top, then go a step further and stash it back in my holster. "I had it made for myself."

"And?" He's practically salivating, and the hunger in his eyes turns to flint once it's out of sight. He had to know I took that sketch on my way out the door all those years ago.

I take some joy in his anguish. "It's the best gun I've ever owned."

"What do you want for it?" He leans farther forward, bracing on the bar.

"I think Robbie's the last of your spies—for now. I'd keep an eye out for anyone Kronos might win over with an influx of cash from the auction." If the auction happens. "Oh, and this gun? You'll get it over my dead body."

I lean over the bar and use the soda gun to spray water over my hands. I rub away Robbie's sticky blood, partially dried and stuck to my skin. The water drips down onto the rubber mats on the floor and splatters on my father's shoes.

I snatch a rag and dry my hands, then hop down and stride away.

I don't bother saying goodbye, either.

Because fuck him.

CHAPTER 16

KORA

"Get dressed."

I roll my head to the side, but that's the only movement I make.

Of all of them, Jace has been the most... *normal* about the whole situation.

Maybe that's the wrong word, because I'm not sure we even have a normal. But he hasn't treated me any differently. He's found me in the music room a few times since that first night. Each time, I tinkered on the piano until he guided me back upstairs.

The nightmares suck. But they go away when Jace is around. When he sits beside me on the bed, holding my hand.

Yeah, the hand-holding is new.

I don't want to talk about that.

Right now, I'm on the verge of sleep. Jace has been gone for the past two nights, and I've been awake for most of that time.

He steps farther into the room, then pauses and squints at me. Like he can *see* I'm an insomniac, dealing with too much death and change.

I let out a sigh. "For what?"

"We need to go, and I'm not leaving you alone in this house." He doesn't sit on the edge of the bed or make any indication that he's softening. He just sees who I am in this moment, accepts it, and still asks for too much.

"What am I dressing for?"

He smiles, but it's forced. This isn't the relaxed, midnight Jace. This is the man who lives under the Hades mask. Cold, coiled energy. "It's Friday night. You're dressing for Olympus."

I sit up, but he's already making his exit. For the first time this week, my heartbeat picks up with excitement, until it gallops in my chest. I take a deep breath and try to steady myself, then go to the closet.

Wolfe and Apollo have kept their distance. And if I was sleeping through the night, I wouldn't see Jace much, either.

True to his word—and the SFU president—all my professors were in contact about completing my courses online. Someone delivered textbooks to the mansion, brand-new copies wrapped in cellophane. How they discovered I was using library copies, I don't know. I haven't asked.

I haven't got my bookbag yet. The sheriff's secretary called and left a message, asking if I could come down to the station for a few questions.

Apollo deleted the message when I showed him.

The idea of going to Olympus has injected a dose of adrenaline back into my blood. I brush out my hair and braid it, letting it hang down the center of my back. The dress... well, I can't wear that white one again. Twice was a fluke.

This time, I pull out an orange cream skirt and cropped top. It just sort of jumps out at me from the line of clothes, although I can't say I was the one to buy it. Sure enough, there are still tags on each piece.

I gasp, dropping them to my bed. They're *way* too expensive.

Who would've put them here? One of the guys, of course, but which one?

I double-check the sizing, and I'm irritated when it's right. In my underwear drawer, I locate a matching lace bralette and panties.

Okay, someone is fucking with me.

But... it wouldn't be the worst thing in the world to try it on.

So I do.

It's silky smooth and fits like a glove. The skirt flares, fanning out when I twirl, and hangs naturally to my knees. The top has a sweetheart neckline, showing off my breasts, and off-the-shoulder three-quarter sleeves.

Not bad for October.

I think again about how Wolfe and Apollo have acted this week. They've been shifty. They don't actively avoid me, but they haven't made an effort to seek me out. After both of them kissed me, I expected... something more than this.

It hurts. I hate that it hurts, but it does. I've been dodging texts from Marley and calls from my parents. I couldn't bear to talk to them. I'm sick of lying that everything is okay.

"Ready?" Jace stops and stares. "Wow."

"Um..." I nervously trace my hand down the side of the skirt. "Should I thank you for this?"

He tilts his head. "For what?"

"Never mind." So, it didn't come from him. I turn back to the mirror and fix the pink lipstick. "I don't have a mask."

"Taken care of," he murmurs.

He's wearing a black button-up shirt, currently buttoned, and black jeans. There's no trace of the makeup on him tonight, and I have to wonder if they wait until they're in Olympus to transform themselves. They must.

He pushes his hair back, then runs his hand down his neck.

"Well, Jace I-don't-know-your-last-name. Are you nervous?"

He chokes on a laugh. "No. I'm just thinking about how many guys Wolfe and Apollo will have to beat away with sticks once everyone sees you. And it's King."

I snort. "Of course it's fucking King." *Don't think about it.* My stomach knots. "And good—I wouldn't want you getting soft on me."

He rolls his eyes. "On you? Never. Come on. Your chariot awaits."

He extends his hand, and I take it. The familiar warmth spreads through me from our point of contact. It's been getting worse and worse, and all I've done is avoid it.

We join Apollo and Wolfe at the door to the garage, and both give me *much* better reactions than Jace. Wolfe whistles, and Apollo steps forward and takes my hand, spinning me around. I laugh, almost tripping over my own feet.

He pulls me in before I can stop myself, and his lips land on mine.

The shock flickers away like smoke in a hurricane, and I soften against him. Fuck the fact that he's messing up my lipstick, and his hand slides into my hair at the base of my neck. And fuck that he's doing it in front of Wolfe and Jace. It's the kiss I need right now.

But then my wits rejoin my brain, and I break our embrace. I step back quickly, touching my lips.

Apollo looks like the cat that ate the canary.

Wolfe... his jaw is set, but he doesn't seem put off. Intrigued, maybe.

And Jace?

The door into the garage is already swinging shut behind him.

Wolfe rides in the back with me. Apollo drives a bulky, gunmetal-gray SUV across Sterling Falls. Jace is stiff in the front seat, but I really can't focus on him right now.

"You'll call us by our pseudonyms," Wolfe advises. "Apollo's easy to remember. Ares. Hades." He motions to himself, then Jace ahead of him.

I roll my eyes. "I remember."

"Good." He leans toward me, dropping his voice. "Are you ready for this?"

How bad could it be?

THE ANSWER? *Bad.*

"Persephone," I repeat, holding the box containing my new mask.

Jace—*Hades*—grimaces from across the room. "Don't read into it."

"It seems a little fitting, don't you think? Stolen away. Dragged to hell." Minus a wedding, but I don't want to jinx my luck. I glare at the mask in its box. The floral scent is the second thing to hit me after its fragile beauty. "Are these real flowers?"

"Yep." Wolfe-slash-Ares lounges across from me on the couch. Sprawled, really. Apollo is in the bathroom, the last to finish his golden paint. Their masks aren't on yet, and I'm not sure if I'm going to loathe or love the moment that switch happens.

"Why?" I whisper.

"You chose her." Jace stops in front of me and offers his hand. "Whether you realized it or not."

I take it, letting him pull me to my feet. He lifts the mask from its silk bed and holds it up to my face. I support the bottom and turn, and he knots the slim leather ties behind my head.

The eye holes are big enough that I don't feel claustrophobic. The flowers... some are pressed, but others, near my temple and forehead on one side, seem to be sprouting right out of my skin. The effect is eerie. There are a few pearls strung across the bottom, creating a clear separation between mask and girl. It's similar to the mask Marley gave me, but so much more.

He tips my chin up, meeting my eyes. "This is why you were noticed at Olympus, Persephone. This is why our men let you in without taking your money. Old habits die hard."

I don't flinch. Don't think. I just nod along with his words, mesmerized by the way he's staring at me. I don't know what he means by old habits dying hard. It isn't until Apollo loudly clears his throat that I realize I had drifted closer to Jace.

I jerk away and scurry to hide in the bathroom. With the door closed, I can breathe easier. I adjust the straps, finagle the mask. I wiped my lipstick off after Apollo kissed me, so my lips are bare. The orange-cream-colored outfit goes well with the mask of daisies and lilies.

"You're fine," I whisper to myself.

Now it's just a matter of conveying that to the rest of them.

Marley will probably be here.

She might even recognize me.

Apollo knocks on the door, and I crack it open. I peer out through one eye, and he grins.

"Just wanted to tell you that you look beautiful. And I'll see you after."

He's the host, after all.

I open the door farther. I reach out and touch the gold paint on the column of his throat. It comes away on my finger, not yet dry, and I swipe it down my own throat.

He leans his head against the doorframe and makes a pained noise. "One day, I'm going to fuck you after a fight, and you'll be covered in this gold." His eyes are heated, darkening by the second.

A thrill goes through me.

"You'll have to actually fight," I answer softly. I haven't heard of him ever choosing to do it here—not him or Wolfe. "But that scenario? It'll only happen if you win." I imagine myself covered in streaks of gold paint, his body draped over me, and shivers race over my skin. It goes straight to my core, which pulses with need.

I shouldn't be thinking about sex at a time like this.

His smile is quick. "You fucking bet."

I mirror his smile, then close the door again. I lean my shoulder into it, breathing heavily.

What the hell am I doing?

Why am I letting these guys in?

Eventually, I reemerge. Jace—*Hades*—is gone, and Wolfe is the only one to remain. He's on the couch, in much the same position. Plus his mask—so I guess he's transformed into Ares.

His eyes are dark red and unreachable behind his blood-stained, feathered mask, but they still flick to the gold on my throat. He motions for me to come closer.

My breath comes quicker, and I stop in front of him. He reaches out and pulls me down to his lap. I automatically grab his shoulder to steady myself, shifting my weight.

"Do you like him?"

I still and recall his words from when we were still strangers. Masks give us the opportunity to be vulnerable. It's the naked truth. And if I can't be honest in this moment, what sort of person does that make me?

"I like you both," I admit.

He nods slowly, the muscle in his jaw jumping. "When he told me you kissed, I was so fucking mad at you."

A hiss of breath escapes past my teeth.

His fingers tighten on my hip and thigh, as if to keep me in place if I wanted to flee. I don't, necessarily, but now I'm thinking of smacking Apollo the next time I see him. What happened to *don't kiss and tell?*

"And then I realized that it just means I have to work harder," he continues.

I shudder. "You want me to pick you."

He inclines his head. "Not without me proving myself, but..."

"What if I pick neither?" An insane notion, but... An interesting one. "What if I want you both?"

He contemplates that. "I don't know, Kore."

I jolt. "What?"

"I don't know if I can share you." His gaze is steady on me. "Unless you're referring to Kore... in which case, I have to ask: don't you know Persephone was also called Kore?"

"Stop." I push off him. "I mean, yes. I knew that. I'd just forgotten." Because it's too similar to my own name. And my story seems to be inching closer to hers, too. "We're going to be late."

I don't know how I feel about it, actually. That my name

is so close to Persephone's. That I'm wearing her mask. That *Marley* gave me that first flower mask, knowingly or not. Everything has a meaning at Olympus.

He rises. "Lead the way, then."

His presence behind me is comforting on the way to the familiar curtained-off balcony that Ares and Hades occupy. He keeps us on course up a spiral staircase, then down a side hall. The heavy curtain that marks their balcony comes into sight.

Olympus seems different tonight, although I can't put my finger on it. Maybe it's that the halls are already packed with people, but the route we take circumnavigates them. Their presence is distant thunder. The buzz is electric, and it moves through my body in waves. I peek down the hall and spot the Olympus employees manning the black-clothed tables. They're handing out gilded cards in exchange for cash.

They've switched their masks again. Boar the first time I came. Raven the past two times. And tonight, they're...

"Goats," Ares says in my ear.

I turn away. The fur on their masks makes sense now that he says it, and the stubby little horns protruding from the temples. Ares follows me back to their balcony. I hesitate before pushing aside the curtain.

The noise finds me first. At first it's subtle, the buzzing I felt earlier. But then it builds, and keeps building. I step forward, out of the shadows, and realize that Apollo has finished his introduction and people are finding their way inside. Jostling for spots, eager for the violence that awaits us.

Hades is already at his seat, glowering at the growing crowd. His skull mask is firmly in place, and I have to hide my shiver. This is the first time I've been up close to Hades in all his glory. His shirt is gaping open now but tucked into his black pants. It shows off his abs. The tattoo on his chest. The shirt is rolled up to his elbows, exposing more of his tattoos. And the black paint streaked down his throat, his chest...

My heart beats faster. I need to compose myself before he notices. I press my lips together to keep from saying something stupid.

He briefly meets my eyes, then turns his attention back to the empty fighting platform.

Ares takes his seat and drags me down onto his lap.

I place my hands on the arms of the chair and try to propel myself back up. He wraps his arm around my waist and leans in.

His lips touch my ear. "Does this feel familiar?"

I squirm. It does—this happened the first time I came to Olympus. I was more innocent, then. Somehow. Even with the brand on my wrist, and Kronos' threat in my head. Little did I know how much more downhill it would go.

So I ignore Ares.

"Not fighting tonight?" I ask Hades.

"I'm keeping an eye out." He shoots an evil look at Ares, who straightens up.

Well. Consider that problem adjusted.

I don't know why I asked if he would be okay with me picking neither. I've only gone so far as to kiss both of them —and let's not forget that Apollo *told* Wolfe he kissed me. Plus, they're both the reason I'm stuck with them, hiding from a bounty on my head.

The crowd grows, until it seems like everyone who must've come in from the atrium is now either on the main level or crowding the balconies. It's old theater meets fight arena. Elegant and ancient, but gritty and dark. Somehow it pulls both of those worlds together.

Apollo hops up on the platform just as Ares wraps his hand around my throat. He doesn't use any pressure, just guides my weight back against him. His legs bracket mine, and his other hand rests on my hip.

I'm secure against him, but my heart hammers.

His hand slides down my throat, stopping just above my shirt's neckline. I catch his wrist as he pulls away, flipping his palm up. His *red* palm.

His lips touch my ear a second later. "I couldn't let Apollo just claim you like that, flower. If you want both of us, it'll be a work in progress. But let us fight over you—that's half the fun."

I rotate toward him. He's closer than I thought, his nose almost touching mine. I meet his eyes. "And what's the other half?"

"Sex."

My face flames. I'm glad for the damn mask again.

"Fighting and sex." My voice trembles, and I look away quickly. "Interesting."

He chuckles. "And watching you squirm… that, too."

"And my fellow hosts," Apollo booms.

The crowd's attention is suddenly on us. Hades with his human-skull mask, adorned with horns. Ares in blood-red. And me, on Ares' lap with his red handprint on my throat.

A rustling murmur sweeps through the audience, and I wonder if that's because I'm glued to Ares. Neither rise nor acknowledge the crowd. Hades is focused on a balcony across from us, a distant look in his eye. And I wait, and wait, and wait.

Finally, Apollo calls out the first fighters.

The crowd's attention shifts again, and my attention

shifts with it. I focus on Apollo. The deer-skull mask makes him seem otherworldly. Him, Hades, and Ares stand out as the vicious hosts. They're apart from the crowd—but even if their masks were stripped, they would still stand out.

"Saint is here," Hades says under his breath to Ares. He stands and glances down at us. "I'm going to check in with him. Don't do anything stupid. And don't leave her alone."

The implication in *that* is clear enough. He doesn't trust Olympus.

With the number of people around us, I can't blame him —I don't trust it, either.

Ares nods once, then his lips are at my ear again. "What do you want to do, flower? Sit and watch the fight? Or shall we explore an abandoned hall?"

What do I want?

Now that he's mentioned sex, it springs to the front of my mind. That's what *he* wants, I think. And my body has been strung too tight. A little release... well, it wouldn't be the worst thing in the world, would it?

I shift on his lap and pretend to consider it.

But then the fight begins, and one immediately lands a bone-crunching hit on his opponent. I close my eyes.

Ares scoops me up and stands. I throw my arm around his neck, but he doesn't seem like he's going to drop me. One arm under the crooks of my knees, the other at my back. He strides out, shouldering past the thick curtain, and down the hallway. We go away from the other balconies, and he sets me down in a shallow alcove.

"Here?" I glance around, my nerves twisting under my skin.

"No." He grabs one of the sconces and pulls it straight down. It moves easily, clicking into place three inches lower than it was before.

An invisible door swings inward.

I gawk at it. It's perfectly cut in the marble to blend in.

It leads to a staircase that spirals upward.

"Up?" My eyebrow rises. "I thought there were only two floors."

"Top ones are for personal use." He offers his hand.

I mull that over as I lace my fingers with his. He guides me into the staircase, which curves to the right and keeps curving. I'm almost out of breath by the time we reach the top. It's a hallway, with grates on the wall close to the floor. Through them, I can see the fighters far below us.

He leads me down the hall and into one of the rooms. It isn't much—there's a desk and a window, a few chairs. Anticipation thunders through me.

"Are you sure about this? Your history with—"

"Don't mention my fucking ex." I push him back against the door.

His eyes widen, but he lets me do it. I don't know what comes over me, but I want to be in charge for once.

I don't bother with the mask—as he said, our masks only let us be ourselves. I'm starting to disagree with that, but for now? This is as honest as I can be.

I smooth my hands across his bare chest. The red paint is dry and barely smudges. I push his jacket off his shoulders, and it falls to the floor behind him.

"Tell me something." I run my tongue over my lower lip.

"Anything."

I run my fingers down to his waistband, and I slowly undo the belt. Unbutton his pants and drag the zipper down. My knuckles graze his hardening cock, and he inhales sharply.

"Do you want me because Apollo does?" I meet his gaze

and will him to tell me the truth. Like I have the power to force a confession from his lips.

His head falls back to the wall, hard, and then he straightens. He captures my wrists and slowly raises one to his lips. The unbranded one. They haven't said anything about the light-colored bracelet on my wrist that hides my shame.

"Kora Sinclair."

I shiver at the dark tone.

"I want you because of *you*. Not him." He closes his eyes. "We've never fought over a girl before. I didn't think we ever would. Our tastes run different."

Before I can ask what that means, he spins us and backs me against the wall.

"Enough talking."

His lips crash against mine. My hands are caught between us, and I'm sick of waiting—I don't want foreplay. I just want to feel him inside me.

Because, for some insane reason, I trust him more than I ever trusted Parker.

Maybe it isn't so insane.

I shove his pants and boxers down, and he groans into my mouth when I wrap my fingers around his cock. I stroke him, and he matches my frenzy. He lifts me, urging me to hook my legs around his hips, and carries me over to the desk.

My ass hits the surface, and then he's stepping back. He looks devious like this, bare chest except the paint. The room is all shadows and moonlight.

He slowly readjusts his pants and rebuckles the belt. But before I can express my disappointment that he's dressing, he flips my skirt up to my waist and takes in my panties. His lips part, and then he kneels before me. I don't need much prompting to let my legs fall open.

I'm burning up.

He pushes the thin strip of fabric between my legs to the side and leans forward. I stifle my gasp when his lips touch my center. His tongue sweeps across my clit. I moan, resting back on my elbows and trying not to let my head fall back. I want to see what he's doing to me.

"You taste like the sweetest nectar." He kisses my inner thigh, then inserts two fingers inside me.

"Please just fuck me already," I moan.

He makes a tsking noise. "Not until you come, flower."

I squint at the ceiling and don't say anything.

He rises, but his fingers continue to pump in and out of me. His thumb circles my clit. It feels too good. I'm fraying and I don't quite understand it.

"Wolfe."

"Ares." His hand wraps around the back of my neck and pulls me up. He kisses my neck, just under my ear, and I let out another moan.

I hold on to his shoulders, gripping him as a foreign feeling ravages through me. I shudder against him. My eyes shut of their own accord, and every muscle in me tenses. The feeling keeps coming, crashing through me until it finally eases. I let out a breath and relax my grip, but my thoughts are running away from me.

What the hell *was* that?

He pulls out carefully and raises his fingers to his mouth.

I blink rapidly, holding my emotions in check. My knees are weak, and I can't seem to put my mind back together.

He licks them clean, then hesitates. "A penny for your thoughts."

I shrug and look away. I fix my underwear and brush my skirt back down, but Ares still stands between my legs.

"Kora," he says in a softer tone. "I can feel you running away."

Well... yeah. Because I don't think I've ever had a guy pay attention to me like that. To make me come first and only, and not want anything for himself.

I am not going to admit that. Not to him—and maybe not ever.

But my skin crawls, nonetheless.

"Has a guy done that before?" He's staring into my soul.

I push the mask up, off my face. "No. Okay? *No.*"

He carefully removes his mask, too, and sets it aside. He cups my face with both hands, suddenly serious. "You listen to me, flower. You deserve all the orgasms you can handle. And if someone doesn't give you that, they're not worth your time." His eyes narrow. "But no one is fucking touching you again."

I scoff. "Hate to break it to you, Wolfe, but a madman wants to sell me. I don't think that'll come with a no-touching clause."

His gaze shutters. "Don't."

"Let's be realistic."

"Let's be optimistic," he counters. "You're mine. *Fuck.* Ours. I don't know. Either way, just shut up and think positively."

I sigh. "Wolfe..."

"Nope." He steps in closer and tips my head up.

This kiss is slower but no less passionate. I can feel everything he's infusing into me. Heat. Caring. There's desperation there, too. I kiss him back with just as much emotion, because it bubbles out of me like an untapped spring. I want someone to want me. I want someone to care about me.

That loneliness opens up in my chest. It cracks through my ribcage.

He soothes it. His hands on my jaws, thumbs moving carefully across my cheeks.

"Can you believe in happy ever afters?"

I don't want to do this. I don't want my ugliness to infect this moment. So... I lie. "I do."

CHAPTER 17

I avoid the music room. My mood is black, and I don't want to infect that space. Besides, playing the piano over and over has made me realize how much I miss the cello. I should ask my parents if I can pick it up over Thanksgiving break.

Scratch that—I probably won't be going home for Thanksgiving.

And we need to survive the rest of October.

Just beyond the sliding glass doors in the kitchen, and connected to another living area, is a wide patio and pool. Beyond that, the lawn slopes down and away to gardens that seem as otherworldly as Olympus. A stone walkway cuts through the grass, framed by round hedges and flowers. The vine-covered stone entrance to the gardens is the only visible part, and I haven't ventured that way. Giant, wall-like hedges surround the rest of the huge yard, giving complete privacy from the neighbors.

The living area—which always seems untouched—has floor-to-ceiling windows and French doors leading outside. This room, in particular, has an antique feel to it. The walls are cream. The crown molding matches, and mullions break up the large windows. The French doors are off to the side, nearly blending in with the windows. The furniture seems new. A cream-colored couch with an orange-brown throw blanket draped over the back. An argyle rug of the same colors.

I'm bundled in sweatpants and a baggy sweatshirt, courtesy of Wolfe. So I'm not too put off by the chill in the air when I step outside through that side door.

I pick my way across the stones and exhale when my feet touch the cold grass. It's a wake-up call—more than I'm already awake, anyway. It seeps up, instantly numbing my toes.

It's one o'clock in the morning. We've had frost only once or twice overnight, but it even *smells* cold. Frost again tonight, I would bet. I take a deep breath, letting it fill my lungs.

"Enjoying freezing your ass off?"

I smile, although Jace can't see me from here.

This has quickly become our thing.

Although tonight, something weighs on my mind. Maybe I've just been infected by the fights. Like Olympus slipped under my skin and dug in its claws. The violence. The bitterness of people hiding behind their masks.

Ares—*Wolfe*—said people were truer to themselves with the masks. But that's just the issue. People let go of their moralities with the masks, too. Are we really so baseless?

Jace comes over and settles another jacket over my shoulders. I slide my arms into it, then glance at him. He stands on the stone in socks. Gray sweatpants that should be illegal on guys like him. They sit low on his hips, and—*stop it, Kora.*

I'm starting to like him, against my better judgement.

His jacket smells like him. An unidentifiable spice and something sweet. I bundle deeper in it.

"Are you done?"

I frown. My head falls back, and I stare up at the stars. There are a million out tonight. The sky is unsettlingly clear, unlike my head. I just need to spit it out.

"I..." My throat closes.

He touches my shoulder. "You okay?"

The forbidden question.

"I don't want to be bought." I focus on the stars and try not to think about how I could easily be locked in a room for the rest of my short, miserable life. But I think my nightmares have been shifting away from seeing the man Kronos murdered in front of me and toward my future. The uncertainty is enough to drive me crazy, and I feel my sanity slipping away.

"I know."

"No." I turn and face him, and his hand falls away. "I don't want to be bought, Jace. I... If he succeeds..."

His eyes search my face, his brows drawing together. "Why are you talking like we're going to fail? We're not going to let him touch you."

"Because I want to believe in you, but..." I grimace. This is harder to get out than I thought. "But my judgment has failed me before. And every Titan in the city is looking for me. There will come a point where you guys miss something. If Kronos wants the money—"

"Stop." He pulls me back inside and to one of those untouched sofas. Once the door is closed and the lock latched, he returns with the orange-brown blanket. He drapes it over my legs and sits beside me. The next thing I know, he has my ankles and is pulling my feet into his lap.

I lean back against the couch arm and fold my arms over my chest.

His hands land on my bare feet. I jump, but he holds fast. "Easy, Sinclair."

"Don't expect me to last-name you. Your ego doesn't need me to call you *King*."

He laughs. His thumbs dig into the arch of my foot, and my lips involuntarily part. But we're not done talking. I'm not done asking for a favor of my own.

I straighten. "Jace. Please. If he gets his hands on me, I need you to do whatever you can to stop the auction. My parents—"

He presses harder into my foot, and I wince.

"What do you want?" He raises an eyebrow, but his concentration stays on my foot in his lap. "What do you want me to do, Kora? Kill them all? Because, *if* Kronos gets his hands on you, that's what it would take to stop the auction."

"Maybe that's what it'll take." A tear slips down my cheek. "The idea of being owned any more than I already am makes me sick. I have nightmares about permanent handcuffs. And being forced to do things I don't want to do."

"Fuck," he whispers. He pauses, his fingers on the bottom of my foot. "You have a scar here."

"From the forest." I shift and move my legs away. From running in terror and slicing it open, then picking my way out in the pitch-black.

He rises, rubbing the back of his neck. "We took our anger out on you that night."

I curl into myself while he paces. He's clearly thinking things over. My insane, murderous request, for one. Maybe even the probability of Kronos getting his hands on me. I wrap my arms around my legs, resting my chin on my knee.

Then he stops. "Fine."

"Fine, what?"

Jace kneels next to me. "They're not going to get their hands on you. I promise. But if he does, I'll kill every last one of them. Kronos has leverage on us and this whole fucking city, or else he'd already be dead. He's too smart for his own good."

More tears, but I think they're happy. I can't quite tell. I wipe them away and try to smile.

"Rest easy." He touches my hand, then rises again. He disappears into the dark, leaving me to my thoughts.

I lean back and stare at the ceiling for far too long, wondering if I can trust a single word he says. But hope, that damn persistent feeling, is back. I feel her unfurl her wings in my chest and fan them slowly.

I take the cuff off and rub my wrist. The brand still hurts. Aches when I'm only barely aware of it. Stings when I think about it. Feels like fire when I touch it.

Now I dig my nail into it.

I need that pain as a reminder.

Right now, I'm safe.

Right now, I'm alive.

But a week from now? A month?

Something *pops* outside. Floodlights burst on, triggered by movement on the perimeter. In seconds, the whole backyard is illuminated.

I freeze, the light blinding. I can only stare out the windows and grip the blanket, but terror has immobilized me.

Jace reappears a moment later, and he presses me flat. "Stay down."

"No shit," I whisper back.

Fear racks up my chest, and I struggle to take a breath. Panic constricts my lungs in a vise.

He has a gun in his hand.

A second later, I catch a shadow move through the kitchen. My mouth opens, but something stops me. *Recognition*. It's Apollo. He's silent as he goes to the sliding door and inches it open.

Jace steps outside, too, and the two sweep the backyard. I don't know where Wolfe is.

I sit up carefully just as Jace returns. He sees me and scowls, then grabs my arm.

"Why can't you follow instructions?" He drags me farther into the house, into the den where they usually hang out.

I roll my eyes. "I waited until you got back."

I haven't joined them in here for their video games and banter, although I've heard their gatherings a few times through the floor. I've kept myself apart from them—and for good reason. Just because I get along with them one-on-one doesn't mean I should subject myself to all of them together.

"Sit."

"I'm not a fucking dog," I grumble. Still, keeping the ugly blanket in my arms, I take a seat on the couch. I shiver and pull my legs up. I make myself small, sinking into the cushions. My stomach is in knots.

Our easy moment seems to have evaporated.

Jace's face is all hard lines, that gun still in his hand at his side. He waits until Wolfe arrives, similarly armed.

"Front was clear," Wolfe reports.

"So is the back." Apollo arrives. He sets down his firearm on a side table. "Any idea what triggered it? Kora?"

I bristle.

"Easy, Chaos. He wasn't accusing you of anything."

Wolfe comes over and sits beside me, touching my leg. Trying to uncurl me. "You probably wouldn't have been able to set off our alarm and then get back into the house before we noticed."

I narrow my eyes.

"Well, she is a thief, after all." That from Apollo.

They're... laughing.

My mouth opens and closes.

Even Jace seems less stressed than he was a minute ago. He falls into the armchair next to the couch and rubs his face. "Grab the tablet to monitor our cameras. It might've been one of the neighbors' wandering pets, but I don't like to take chances."

"I'll have Daniel over in the morning to upgrade our system." Wolfe takes a seat beside me. "Movie, anyone?"

"Popcorn?" Apollo asks.

My eyebrows might be up in my hairline.

Wolfe nudges me. "You okay, babe?"

Babe? My mind short-circuits.

I burst to my feet and stare at them all. "Really? You're just going to act like nothing crazy just happened? You have —you have an alarm that triggers floodlights in your backyard! What if it was a Titan!" I pull at my hair.

Nope, not okay.

"What if they saw me outside and thought, 'Yeah, here's the perfect chance to snatch her.' No offense, but your reaction time sucks if someone had a plan." A hysterical laugh bubbles out of me. "I could've been gone like *that.*" I snap my fingers.

"What is that?"

I glance over at Wolfe, whose gaze is locked on my wrist.

My bare wrist.

Fuck.

"Um..."

He rises and takes my hand before I can retreat, flipping it up. The brand is an ugly purplish silver color, red around the edges. It's always slightly irritated from the cuff. He turns my wrist so Jace and Apollo can see the hourglass.

They both make noises.

"Kora?" Wolfe's voice is strangled.

I hang my head. "Kronos did that the night he told me to steal the mask."

"Fucker." Jace comes closer and brushes my hair off my neck. "He did this to you?"

"He handcuffed me to his desk." I can barely get that sentence out. I don't understand their reactions. They're upset.

I was afraid that they'd be furious—with me. Not *for* me. And the heavy shame, the burden of my own mistakes. Of course, that was my true motivation for hiding it.

"I'm going to fucking murder him," Wolfe growls. "Fuck any sort of truce. He's dying for this." His fingers tighten on my palm. "Why didn't you tell us?"

"Because I'm embarrassed." I tug the sweatshirt sleeve over my hand. "I wear that bracelet so I don't have to look at it. So I don't have to remember."

"But you remember, anyway." Apollo is on my other side. His chest touches my shoulder. He's that close, but I get the sense that he wants to be closer. They're all crowded around me, and a lump forms in my throat.

I nod.

Apollo kisses my temple. "He'll pay for that."

Wolfe pulls me back down beside him. Then he seems to consider and bundles the blanket around me. He lifts me into his lap, sitting me sideways, and wraps his arms around me.

"To address your earlier concern: we're not worried about the lights that were set off. It happens once a month, at least, and it's always some sort of animal." Wolfe's voice curls in my ear, and his lips touch the shell of it. "And if someone tries to actually get in, he won't walk away. He'll have to be carried out in a body bag."

Apollo watches us for a beat, emotions warring in his eyes. It might be envy. Frustration. His brow lowers, and he still seems tense.

I open my mouth to ask why, but he disappears out the door.

Jace grabs the remote, turning on the television and flipping to the movie channel. "What are we in the mood for?"

"Something with action," Wolfe says.

I nod my agreement. I curl into him, resting my head on his chest. "I might fall asleep."

"Good," he murmurs. "Jace has been taking up too much of your late-night wanderings, anyway. It's about time I had a turn." There's only a touch of bitterness in his tone.

But Jace and I aren't like that. He hasn't made a move—and I'm not sure if I could handle him doing that, anyway. There's always a layer of tension between us, but it's different. He seems aloof.

Something *pops* again, in the distance, and I flinch.

"Apollo is making popcorn." Wolfe's hand moves up and down my back.

"I'm sorry." I bury my face in my hands.

I feel... *weak*. And there's no escaping that. It follows me around, hovering over my shoulder. People tell me I'm strong, or courageous, but I'm not. I have a stubborn streak. An unhealthy amount of fear. A craving for something better.

But that's not bravery. That's... desperation.

Jace and Wolfe don't have words of wisdom, and I breathe in the silence. The buttery smell of the popcorn drifts into the den ahead of Apollo, and then he arrives. He has a tablet tucked under his arm, and three bowls. Wolfe takes one, setting it in my lap, and the guys take the other two. Apollo settles on the other end of the couch.

Jace hits *play* on a movie. Something with Gerard Butler in it.

I manage to watch most of it. An attack on the White House. One man slipping past the defenses and saving the country—and the President. I've seen it before, and the villain isn't always the one waving the gun.

Sometimes it's more subtle than that.

The thought sticks in my head, and I mull it over. But real life and action movies are two very different things. And eventually, my eyes drift closed.

CHAPTER 18

"Kora, I'm worried about you. This is the first time I've seen you in weeks."

I rub my eye and try to seem more awake. Marley stares at me through the phone, her brows lowered in confusion.

"You're not at your apartment. Again. That wall color behind you is hideous. Are you going to tell me, or should I guess?"

"Um..." I glance at the clock. It's past eleven, and I don't think I've ever slept better. Speaking of, I don't remember *going* to bed. I vaguely recall Wolfe's lips pressing into the top of my hair, and him trying to get me to wake up. But I just snuggled harder against him.

"Guessing, it is." She taps her chin. "One-night stand?"

"No." I show her the empty bed on either side of me.

"You moved?"

"Sort of..."

"Does this have to do with that shady loan? Kora. Are you in trouble?"

Nailed it. "The guy from the library. He's been helping me, so I'm staying at his place for now."

She squeals and claps. "Damn, girl. He was smoking hot, so I don't blame you there. And you know what? You deserve to have some fun this year." Her expression sombers. "You've been through a lot, and I know I pushed you to go to Olympus. It really wasn't cool of me, knowing what happened with you and Parker. So I'm glad you're putting yourself out there again. But if he treats you badly—"

"It's not like that." My face feels too hot. "It's been hard to find myself again."

"I know, babe. But I saw the way he looked at you. It's fine, I'm not jealous. I just want to vicariously live through you. And if he happens to have a sibling... Brother or sister, I'm totally not picky."

I lie back. "Well, he has a twin sister..."

Her eyes light up. "Tell me more."

"She's cool. She fights at Olympus."

Marley gasps. Then she gasps again, slapping her hand over her mouth. "You bitch! You were at Olympus last night! Oh my god, I saw you sitting on Ares' lap, but I didn't actually think it was you. You hate fighting."

My face is burning even hotter. "Well, um, we didn't watch most of the fight."

And I don't bother telling her that Apollo, who she briefly met, is actually *Apollo* from the library. I didn't mention his name then, and I'm not going to blow his cover now. How he's managed to stay under the radar without using a different god's name, I'll never know.

Marley's eyes fill with tears. "I'm so proud of you."

I laugh. It's a borderline hysterical one, as I've been prone to lately, but it dissolves into giggles. She's *proud* of me?

"And now I have something to tell *you*."

It's my turn to raise my eyebrows. "What?"

"Janet took home someone from Olympus. She's claiming he's her soulmate." She rolls her eyes. "He wore a Poseidon mask. I'm pretty sure that's the only reason she entertained him."

He must be one vain motherfucker to date someone as shallow as her.

"And I'm having dinner with my father," she announces.

My jaw drops. "Stop it. When?"

"Tonight!" She stands and goes into her closet. "Which is why I need your help..."

We spend the next hour figuring out what she's going to wear. It's surprisingly normal. I laugh more than I have since arriving at Sterling Falls, and before long we're giggling over old memories.

I'm about to hang up with her when someone opens my door—and it isn't Apollo.

Marley freezes, and I wince. She can clearly see him in the camera, so there's no lying my way out of this one. Wolfe stands in the doorway, looking like... well, a sex god, if we're being honest.

He raises an eyebrow. "What are you doing?"

"I've got to go, Mar." I hang up before she can question me—*yes*, coward's way out—and throw my phone down. "Helping my best friend decide what to wear to dinner."

He smirks. "Okay."

"What do you want?"

"To see if you're hungry. We're thinking about ordering pizza for lunch." He steps into the room and shuts the door behind him. "Also..."

Butterflies flutter in my abdomen.

He climbs onto the bed, pushing my phone out of reach and hovering over me.

Thank god you brushed your teeth, Kora.

"I wanted to do this." He kisses me.

I wrap my arms around his neck, pulling him down on top of me. We didn't discuss what happened at Olympus. How I'm pretty sure he could tell I've never had an orgasm... not like that, anyway. Not at the hands of someone else. Not as intense as the one he coaxed out of me.

He nips my lower lip and shifts to the side. His hand slips into the waistband of my sleep shorts, finding its way to my skin. And then lower.

His finger swipes against my clit, and my back arches. He smiles, then kisses me harder. His tongue sweeps into my mouth while his fingers rub me. It takes an embarrassingly short time for tingles to rush through my body. He swallows my moans, keeping our lips sealed together as I come. He thrusts a finger inside me and groans when I clench around him.

He rises, and our eyes connect. "You're so fucking beautiful."

I don't know what to say to that. I feel like a teenager—except, you know, doing it properly this time. Making out. Climaxes. Not worrying about the sex. It's weird and different and kind of nice.

Nah, scratch that.

I can't *wait* for him to fuck me.

I hook my legs around his hips and pull his weight back on top of me.

"What are you waiting for?"

He frowns. "What?"

"I—you—"

"You need to experience the pleasure of receiving." His lips touch my neck first, and then his tongue.

I tip my head to the side when his words register.

"I could just fuck you... but I don't want to rush it."

I huff, my frustration at a tipping point. "What if I just go to Apollo for it, then?"

He goes still, and he draws back. "Is that what you want?"

"I—"

He hops off the bed, leaving me lying there. I'm stuck. My mouth dries, and fear crashes through me that I just ruined it.

But he returns with Apollo close behind him.

"Kora," Apollo greets me, then turns to Wolfe. "What's this about?"

Wolfe's jaw is set. I sit up, but he shoots me a look and I go still.

"She wants sex."

Apollo's brows hike.

"*But*, I'm pretty sure any asshole she was with hasn't treated her the best." Wolfe narrows his eyes. "Truth?"

"Truth." I look away.

"So *I'm* inclined to wait on the sex and focus on her. But *she* threatened to go to you." Wolfe exhales and closes the door.

I think, for a second, that he might've left us alone. But when I glance back over, he's still here. Still in the room, leaning against the door like a gatekeeper.

"What do you want, Kora?" Apollo asks.

I shift. "I don't know."

He nods slowly, coming to stop next to the bed. "Do you want me to touch you?"

My cunt pulses. I don't think I've ever felt desire quite like this, and nerves jangling around with it. My gaze finds Wolfe.

"You want him to touch you, too?" Apollo's question comes out husky.

I squirm and nod. Why not, right? Fuck it.

"Okay," he whispers. He offers his hand. When I take it, he helps me to my feet. His hands skim my hips. "You tell us to stop if you don't want this."

That hits me harder than any of this. That consent is at the forefront of his mind.

"Nod if you agree." He tilts his head. He doesn't miss anything.

I nod.

His hands move up, taking my sweatshirt with it. He takes in my soft stomach, my ribcage that has become increasingly visible these past few months, my breasts. No bra—what can I say? I don't understand people who sleep in bras.

His breath catches, and I raise my arms for him to pull it completely off.

He drops it, and he brushes his knuckles over my nipple. They harden, and I press my thighs together. He repeats the motion. Goosebumps break out down my arms. He cups my other breast, pinching that nipple, and I jolt. I grip his shirt at his waist and fist the material, using it to keep from swaying.

Wolfe circles us, watching my face. He steps up behind me and sweeps my hair off my shoulder. He kisses my neck, moving down to my shoulder. Then back up. He pushes my shorts and panties down. I kick them away. He guides me back, letting me lean my weight on him.

In front of me, Apollo sinks to his knees. I release his shirt and watch the top of his head. He seems transfixed by me. My body. He takes one of my legs and puts it over his shoulder. His head turns, and he kisses my thigh.

I lean back harder on Wolfe, trusting him to keep me balanced. He holds my hip with one hand, and the other flicks my nipple. My lips part.

Apollo reaches the apex of my thighs, and his fingers part my folds. He grins up at me. "You're perfect."

I blow out a breath.

And then he slides a finger inside me, and I groan at the feeling. He curls the finger, but it's not enough. Then his tongue swipes up, from my slit that he's working and over my clit. He sucks, and I swear he's going to pull my soul right out of my body.

One finger inside me becomes two, thrusting slowly. I reach back and wrap my hand around Wolfe's neck, twisting back to kiss him. His erection digs into the small of my back. It's stimulation overload.

He nips my lower lip just as Apollo's teeth scrape my clit, and I shudder.

"She's close," Wolfe says.

Apollo licks and sucks harder, spreading my legs wider to get closer to me. I can't help but move my hips slightly, trying to get more. *And more, and more.* His fingers work some magic inside me, and Wolfe pinches both my nipples.

I come suddenly, jerking against both of them. My back arches, and my eyes roll back.

Wolfe catches me when my knees give out, and he lowers me to sit on the bed. My limbs are jelly. I take a deep breath. But for once, my thoughts aren't crazy. I feel... well, a little like I'm in a dream. But mainly? Not alone. Not with both of them watching me like I just gave them a gift.

And that feels miraculous.

I stare up at both of them, a bit amazed. "That was... Wow."

"We're not done," Apollo declares.

My brows hike. What more is there? Besides actual, penetrative sex—which they've made clear probably won't happen today.

I say probably because both guys are hard, their cocks bulging against their pants. They make no move to relieve themselves, though.

Apollo motions for me to scoot back on the bed. I do, until my back hits the pillows, and he follows. He kisses me sweetly, and I taste... *myself* on his lips. It isn't weird, though. And vaguely I'm aware of Wolfe spreading my legs, murmuring something about having a taste of me himself.

I don't think I can come again.

It feels physically impossible. My muscles tremble.

But then... well. His tongue thrusts inside me. *In me.* I lurch, and Apollo holds me steady. He watches my face. Watches me watch the top of Wolfe's head. And then he wraps his hand around my throat, and I'm sure my heart is going to explode right out of my chest.

"He put his hand around your throat to mark you as his," Apollo says in my ear. "Painted your pretty skin red. I saw your face when he did it. Even behind the mask."

My skin feels bright red *now*, too, but because I'm burning from the inside out.

"I was jealous. I wanted to feel your pulse. Control your breath. I want your eyes on me when I thrust inside you for the first time." His lips are close to my ear, whispering words he has no business saying. Words that make me wetter. His thumb and index finger slide up to my jaw, turning my face to him. That steady pressure is still there, but it isn't enough to make me panic. "When you're used to this, I can't wait to see where we go. How far we can push you."

I shiver.

He tsks. "Not yet, beautiful. Not until you trust us."

My body is on *fire*, the most beautiful agony. I shove against Wolfe's head, but he grips my ass and fucks me with his tongue. And then his fingers slip to my back entrance, and he traces my puckered skin. He pushes it in slowly, and I buck. The new sensation is a whole new level.

"That's it," Apollo says. His other hand moves down and presses on my clit. He's dangerously close to Wolfe's face, but he doesn't seem to care. He pinches it, and I tense. It's all too much.

They continue their assault on my senses until I explode around Wolfe's tongue. My thighs squeeze his head. He keeps going, keeps moving with his tongue, his finger in my ass. Apollo stays right beside me, his hand still keeping my face toward his. His hand on my throat captures my pulse, but he doesn't squeeze. Just observes. Lets me feel the weight of his palm.

The waves keep coming, beating against me. I open my mouth in a wordless scream. I don't know who I'm yelling for, or what. Just that I need some release.

Wolfe slowly lifts his head, kissing my inner thigh one last time. Apollo releases my throat.

I gasp for air and slump back. I think I just ran a freaking marathon.

"She's speechless." Apollo chuckles and kisses my cheek.

"I'm dying," I mutter. "Jesus Christ."

Wolfe laughs. "This is what you were missing."

I eye them and lean into Apollo. "What about you guys?"

He shrugs. "I'll go beat off in the shower."

Wolfe nods. "Yep."

I sigh and sit up. "Okay, well... let me pee, then one of you can use my shower."

Three orgasms.

My stomach growls suddenly, eliciting another laugh

from the guys. Wolfe catches my hand. "I came up here to discuss pizza, and we got sidetracked. I'm so sorry."

I shake my head. "Don't worry about it. That was a worthy distraction."

When I emerge from the bathroom, only Apollo remains. He has a towel folded beside him on the bed. "You mind if I use yours?"

"No." I smirk. "You good?"

He groans. His pants are still tented, belying his agony. "Not in the slightest."

I stand there for a second, then have to shake off my thoughts. *Literally*. I move past him, and he snags my wrist.

"Hey."

"Yeah?" I look down at him.

"You're pretty fucking amazing. Just in case we didn't tell you enough."

I smile. Yeah, I could get used to hearing that. Everyone likes their ego stroked once in a while, right? But my stomach growls again, so I hurry away.

Temptation might kill me—and if I linger, I might do something stupid. Like join Apollo in the shower. *Yeah*, that would require a braveness I don't have.

Downstairs, I check most of the rooms before I end up in the kitchen. Jace's bike isn't in the garage, so I give up. Part of me is glad he didn't hear what just happened. My cheeks burn, and I press the backs of my hands to them.

I pour myself a glass of water and gulp it down. Then I stare into the fridge and contemplate what I want to eat, if pizza is off the menu. Even if they're still ordering it, I need something to take the edge off.

See? Put me in a house with a steady supply of food and I get all soft.

I'm reaching for the deli meat when the doorbell rings. I

pause, glancing down the hall toward the front door. I suppose Apollo ordered while Wolfe was distracted with me... But how did they get past the gate?

I hurry to the front door and yank it open.

No one is there.

A chill comes over me, and I refrain from stepping outside. A lifetime of watching scary movies has prepared me for what the bad guys will do. They snatch the victims when they feel safe. Just checking for the pizza delivery...

The gate is closed.

I stare at it, wondering if I'm seeing things right. How did someone get in to ring the bell? And where *is* that person?

"Kora?" Apollo's voice echoes down the stairs. He joins me a second later, bounding into the foyer wearing nothing but a towel around his hips. His hair is wet, and there are still water droplets on his torso.

I stare at his abs—nothing I haven't seen before, really, since he parades around Olympus like that—but the deep V-cut of his muscles disappearing under the towel... Especially after what we just did, my throat goes dry.

I swallow and jerk away. "Someone rang the doorbell."

He immediately comes closer and pulls me away from the door. "Did you see anyone?"

"No—I thought it was the pizza."

"I didn't order it."

My lips part, but I don't know what to say to that.

He goes to the side table drawer and removes a small firearm. I eye it, then him. I'm not surprised to see it in his hand, but I *am* worried that the situation will warrant it.

I stay exactly where I am while he disappears outside.

A moment later, he returns carrying a large envelope.

"What's that?"

He lifts one shoulder, but his brows are furrowed. "I don't know. It was on the ground."

He locks us in and returns the gun to its drawer, then takes the envelope into the kitchen. I follow, curiosity getting the better of me. When he sets it down, I gasp.

"It has my name on it." I point to the little sticker in the center.

Apollo pauses. "Do you want to open it?"

"Not really."

"Okay." He breaks the tape and tips it, so the paper inside slips out.

It hits the counter, and Apollo hesitates. It only takes a second for the image to be burned into my mind, and I stumble away.

It's a glossy eight-by-ten photo of me. The orange-cream outfit, the flower mask. In the photo, I'm perched on Ares' lap. Except, instead of the red handprint on my skin, it's been edited to look like my throat had been slit. The image is so realistic, I press my fingers to my throat to make sure. They edited blood, too. More blood, anyway, running like a river down my front. And my eyes, behind the flower mask, are completely black.

But that part isn't a photo manipulation—someone *scratched* my eyes out on the printed paper.

"Fuck." Apollo covers the offending photo with the envelope. "Come on."

We go to the den, where his tablet still sits from last night, and I sit beside him on the couch while he opens an app.

"How many cameras?"

"Three on the front of the property. One on the back. They were all clear last night, by the way."

My chest aches. "Who would do that?"

"Hopefully, we're going to find out right now." He rewinds the feed, but there's nothing. No one hops over the gate or opens it. Or closes it, for that matter. He goes back further. He scowls down at the technology, then stands.

"Stay close."

I shiver and do as he commands. We go upstairs, and he pounds on the bathroom door before ducking into his room. *His* room is gray and white. I still don't know whose room I woke up in, but I guess it must be either Jace's or Wolfe's. I can't picture either one of them volunteering. Anyway, I appreciate the flavor of Apollo's room. There are band posters framed and hung on the wall—a classy upgrade to my teenage room, with a bit more finesse—and even though the walls are gray, it's warm.

I step inside just as he drops his towel.

My eyes go down. I mean… I'm mortal, okay? Even in the face of fear. And *damn*. He's huge. We stare at each other—I swear his cock twitches and looks right at me—before I come back to my senses. But now I'm picturing him thrusting into me.

And then I realize what I'm doing, and that Apollo is actively catching me checking him out. I turn abruptly to the door.

He chuckles, then dresses. Wolfe appears in the doorway a moment later, jeans and a white t-shirt that says *Karma, bitch.*

"What's the nine-one-one?"

"Someone gained access and left a threatening photo for Kora." Apollo loads up on weapons.

"Whoa, whoa." I hold up my hands. "Why are you strapping on enough guns to wage a war?"

They both glance at me.

"This wouldn't be close enough to go to war with," Wolfe

laughs. And then his mirth falls away. "Did you clear the house?"

Again?

The unspoken word hangs heavily between us.

Someone got in last night and set off the alarms.

Someone got in *today*, bypassed the cameras, and was able to get that envelope on the front step.

I'm not really safe here, am I?

"You are," Wolfe says.

I didn't mean to ask my question out loud. I cover my mouth and follow Wolfe into his room. It's not the room I woke up in... which means they put me in Jace's room after I stole his mask.

I consider that, then brush off what it implies.

Wolfe slides a handgun into an ankle holster, and another at his hip. He glances at me. "Do you know how to shoot?"

"Not really." I back away to avoid being handed a weapon. "Um, why?"

He grunts. "We'll discuss yes or no questions later. You should learn to shoot."

There are a lot of things I should learn.

"Do you know why I call you a flower?"

I... "No, I don't. I assumed it was the mask."

He lifts one shoulder. "Sort of. But there's another reason."

"And what is it?"

Apollo bangs on the doorframe. "Let's move."

Wolfe winks at me. "Remind me to tell you later."

My stomach flips, and I feel like a lost puppy tagging behind them. They split up at the staircase, Apollo climbing the stairs for the mysterious third level and Wolfe moving silently down. I keep with Apollo. He reaches back and takes my hand, bringing it to the back of his shirt. I understand his message and curl my fingers in the fabric.

We reach the top floor, and my jaw drops. It's not very big up here—probably half the size of the first two floors—but all open. The back wall, overlooking the backyard, is all glass. It lends a beautiful view out beyond the yard.

With a jolt, I realize there isn't another house on the backside of this one. No yard butting up against it.

It's just... trees. A mini-forest stretching away from the house. There are some golden trees, the leaves beginning to change color before they drop. I wouldn't have guessed.

He clears the space carefully, and I don't ask questions. It's almost completely empty up here, just some sheet-covered furniture and an open bathroom door with an adjoining closet. Maybe this would've been a master bedroom, if any of them had chosen to take it.

Apollo's phone buzzes. He hands it to me to read the text.

Clear, Wolfe says.

"It's good down there," I whisper.

Apollo nods. "Go downstairs, then. Wait there."

I don't need to be told twice. This room has a cold chill to it, like something that was long ago abandoned. A place that has so much potential, but they've let it just... sit. I scurry downstairs and find Wolfe as fast as I can.

He's in the kitchen, bent over the photograph. He raises his head when I walk in. "This is fucking creepy."

"I know."

"Who would do this?" He flips it over, hiding the image from sight.

My stomach rolls. Across the back is a single word, written in red.

Leave.

CHAPTER 19

My phone rings.

Terrible timing.

My mother's photo lights up on the screen, her name scrolling across the top. I've already ignored her too much this past week. After everything, I didn't want to risk her sensing something wrong.

I glance at Apollo and Wolfe, who have spent the afternoon meeting with a new security team outside the house. After the head of the security firm left, a new guy showed up. Wolfe and Apollo are outside with the man, who could easily be a model for a tattoo magazine. He's covered, head to toe. The tattoos peek out on his forearms from under the rolled sleeves of his shirt. Climb up his neck and down through the opening in his shirt.

He's intimidating. Maybe because he's a stranger, and I'm not feeling particularly trusting right now.

They introduced him as Saint. The name was familiar—Jace went to speak with him when we were at Olympus. I didn't comment on my recognition and hid myself away for the majority of the day. He seemed nice enough.

But anyway, they still look preoccupied.

I move past the open door and head for the den, then hit *accept* and force cheerfulness into my voice. "Hey, Mom!"

"Kora!" Mom's voice is honey in my ear. "I was getting worried."

I swallow my guilt. "I'm sorry. Things have been crazy around here."

"I talked to Marley," she confesses.

"Oh?" God, what did my best friend say? I step into the den and close myself inside. I love her, but sometimes she acts in what she thinks is in my best interests. Sometimes she's right. Other times? Not so much. If she mentioned a *word* about the trouble I've been in recently, I'm going to kill her.

"She spilled the beans about this boy you're dating."

Shoot. At least Mom says *boy* and not *boys*. I've been dodging her calls—even resorting to leaving my phone off—ever since she saw Wolfe walk into my room. It isn't that I don't trust her, or don't want to tell her stuff... I guess, even just admitting it would make it feel real.

And I'm not sure I want it to be real.

When I do finally get the courage to answer her, I'll have my fair share of explaining. But until then? *Hard no*. I'm still barely surviving and keeping my head buried in the sand.

I sit heavily on the couch and curl my legs up under me.

"Okay, Miss Chatty," Mom teases. "How are classes?"

Totally online. "They're fine. Midterms are coming up in a few weeks."

She might be unloading groceries, the rustling coming through clear from her end. "Midterms already, huh? The semester will be over before you know it. I was thinking your father and I should take a trip up and visit you. Maybe we can come up for Thanksgiving—unless you'd rather come home?"

I stifle my sigh. "I'm not sure. It could be nice to have you up here. But I do miss..." Everything. Normalcy. Our neighborhood. The even, wide streets lined with trees. The kids who often bike around our streets, and the dog walkers. The hum of Emerald Cove is nicer than Sterling Falls, like the town itself has a kinder spirit.

Sterling Falls rejects outsiders.

It makes everyone work for their place.

And I think it has a tendency to break people, too.

"Your father has a friend up there in government. He works in the mayor's office. They were talking about playing golf down here. You could catch a ride with him if you wanted to come down for a weekend."

I perk up. It's unrealistic that I'll be escaping the city anytime soon. But so what? I can dream. "I didn't know Dad had friends up here."

"Just one friend, dear." She chuckles.

Dad's an introvert. He has a small core friend group, and other *friends* are more like acquaintances. For someone from Sterling Falls to make the cut is curious. Especially since I don't recall hearing specifics.

"What else have you been up to?" I fiddle with the fraying rip in my jeans.

"I have some vacation time to use up. We're debating if we should go somewhere or take a little staycation." Something *thunks* in the background. "And other than that? Just some work drama..." She goes into detail about a coworker, and I take the opportunity to zone halfway out of the conversation.

Jace is still gone. He's been out all day, although I'm pretty sure Wolfe and Apollo have both talked to him. It's not particularly worrying—he's the most vexing of the three of them—but I do want to know. Just to satisfy my own curiosity.

Something clinks against the window behind me.

I twist around and come face-to-face with a mask.

I scream and fall backward off the couch. My back hits the floor, legs in the air, and my phone flies away from me.

Someone rushes into the room. I catch a glimpse of shoes, pants, a gun in hand. Then Wolfe is leaning over me, his brow furrowed. "What are you doing?"

"I—"

He helps me stand, and I find a fucking mask propped up on the windowsill. I smack his chest and point to it.

"Did you guys *want* to give me a heart attack?"

It isn't one they've worn before. I don't even know whose it is. But Wolfe grins and leans over, holding the tree-themed mask of bark up to his face.

"Apollo's first mask. We all have originals floating around the house." He shrugs and tosses it on the couch. "Not sure why he brought it down, but it isn't going to bite. You okay?"

"Peachy." I press my hand to my chest. "Oh, shit. My mom!"

Wolfe snatches my phone from the floor.

"Mrs. Sinclair." He grins at me.

My eyes widen, and I shake my head at him.

He ignores it—of course.

I scramble for him, but he holds me off. He nods along to something she says, then laughs. "Yep, that's me! Kora just had a little fright and dropped the phone. She's at my place right now.... That's right."

I groan. "Wolfe," I mouth. "Stop it."

"Marley?" Wolfe's eyes gleam. "We didn't get a formal introduction, no."

My mortification grows when he turns away from me and says something to her too quietly for me to hear.

And then he turns back around, holding the phone back. "Here you go, babe."

I stick my tongue out at him. It's childish, but... so is stealing my phone.

That's what I tell myself, anyway.

I take it and scurry away from him. "I'm so sorry. He—"

Mom's chuckle cuts me off. "I've been waiting for details, honey. No, *dying* for them. He sounds lovely. Can you take a picture and send it to me?" She sighs. She may very well be planning our wedding in her head.

"What did he say to you before I got the phone back?"

"Oh, just that he's lucky to have found you."

I grimace. "Right."

"Don't diminish your self-worth," Mom admonishes. "And listen, I've got to get going. We've got a dinner reservation tonight on the island."

"Oh! Have fun." The alone feeling surges through me again, and I focus on my breathing. Wolfe sneaks up behind me, wrapping his arms around my waist. I tip my head back on his chest. "I'll see about that picture."

"Don't forget. Love you, honey."

"Love you, too."

I thwack Wolfe again, and he throws his head back, unable to hold in his laughter.

"That was fun." He takes my phone and slips it in my back pocket. "Want to get out of here?"

I perk up. "Out? Absolutely."

He releases me. We go to the garage, the big door

already open. I pause at his Mercedes, but he hooks his thumb to the light-blue convertible on the end.

"Really?"

"Jace's prized possession." He snorts. "Asshole never lets us drive it, but since he's not here..."

Annoying Jace is high on my list of priorities. Not sure why, because his anger can be intense. But his *annoyance*? I relish that.

I hop in and quickly pull my hair up. Wolfe slides sunglasses on and hands me a pair.

"There it is." He pauses, facing me.

"There what is?"

"Your smile." He turns the key, and the engine roars to life. "It's been missing since that envelope showed up. Probably even before then."

I roll my eyes, although it's true. I've been feeling... off.

Once we're on the road, I take a deep breath. It isn't as windy as I thought it would be. The windows are rolled up, and it gives me the sense of sitting in a pocket of safety.

"Kora."

I glance over.

"I call you flower because of the mask, yes, but it's more than that."

He readjusts his grip on the wheel and flicks the blinker. We turn onto a narrower road, going east toward Olympus. A back road, though, with forest on either side. I like that about Sterling Falls—there's downtown, but besides the borough-like neighborhoods, it's left wild.

"I'm dying with anticipation, here." I tap his hand on the gear stick.

He shifts, then takes my hand and puts it on his thigh. "You keep surviving. Even when something terrible happens, you keep going. It might feel like winter for you, but you're going to get through this."

Wow. And here I was, equating flowers to pretty things that ultimately wither and die. He has a completely different outlook on them, and I can't formulate a decent reply for a few minutes.

"That's so much deeper than I thought," I finally answer. "Why do you think it's winter?"

He shoots me a look. "Seriously?"

"What?" My eyebrows rise. "I'm fine."

"You're the definition of not fine." He scoffs. "It's okay, though. Because after winter comes a nice long spring."

I grip his thigh and let my head fall back. We turn onto the road that runs parallel to the cliffs, going north to the beaches. I watch the ocean in the distance, then sit up straighter.

There's a person on the cliff. A collection of cars parked off the road.

I lean forward. "What's that?"

He grins. "It's a bit lower than Olympus, so we get some daredevils trying their luck cliff jumping."

I gasp. "Really?"

"Do you want to watch?"

"Yes!"

He leans around me, squinting at the group congregated by the cars. "Oh, Saint and Nyx are here. Perfect."

Saint—the tattooed man. And Nyx... the fighter? It's an unusual name. It can't be a coincidence.

We swing off the road and park at the end of the row of vehicles. Some look over when our engine fades into silence. The small group of eight or nine people are in mixed clothing. Some wear sweatshirts and long pants, others in bathing suits with towels wrapped around them.

"Wolfe." Sure enough, the tattooed girl who fought Artemis separates from the pack and walks toward us. She's tall and thin. Her black sweatshirt hides her upper body, but she wears black bike shorts that expose her legs. She has an impressive tattoo on her thigh, joining with more that go down her calf, and the other leg is bare.

"You jumping?" Wolfe circles around the car and takes my hand.

She grins. "Yeah, probably soon. Who's this?"

"Kora Sinclair, meet Nyx. You might've seen her at Olympus."

"Fighting Tem," I supply. "It looked like a good fight."

Her smile fades into a wince. "Yeah, it was good. I don't like fighting my friends, though."

"Where did you learn?"

"Just watching other people, to start. Taking opportunities I could, when I was able. Then I got in with these guys, and I've been training seriously for the last few years." She's pretty. Black hair so dark it's almost blue, like a raven's wing. Pale skin. Her full lips stretch into a smile again, like she can't help it. "You like Olympus?"

It's my turn to cringe. "It's okay."

"And the flower mask?"

Wolfe chuckles and pats my hand. "You two chat. I'll be right back."

I eye her. "The flower mask they gave me? Were you there last night?"

She nods.

Interesting. "It was beautiful. I'm not sure how they got real flowers on it."

"My fiancé designed it." She comes over beside me and points him out. The tall, tattooed man lounges against one of the cars. Like Nyx, he wears a hoodie and black board shorts. His gaze moves away from the crowd and finds Nyx right away.

"I got lucky with him," she murmurs.

"Yeah?"

"He's a genius with charcoal. And a tattoo machine."

Huh. "Saint, right?"

"Wolfe mentioned him?"

"They introduced us when he was at the house this morning." I shift and hug my stomach. She has an easy energy about her, but maybe it's the setting that has put me on edge. "And Wolfe mentioned your names when he noticed you were here."

"Ah." She motions for me to come with her, and we join the crowd. "Guys, this is Kora. Kora, this is everyone."

They wave and chorus hello. Wolfe leaves Saint and stands beside me. His hand slips into my back pocket, like we're in high school.

And you know what? I blush. *Again*. Because I only got a fake version of a high school romance, and Wolfe feels more like the right version.

"You're up, Nyx," someone calls.

She grins and nudges me. "Best view is on the stairs."

I raise my eyebrows and glance at Wolfe.

"This way."

We approach it as Nyx slips off her hoodie. Her upper body is covered in tattoos. I knew this from seeing her fight, but they're stunning. Most are gray and black. They're all intricate, mixing in with each other. There's a curled dragon that lies just under her collarbone. Its one eye is open and watching.

"That one matches a tattoo Saint has," Wolfe says in my ear.

I jolt. "I wasn't—"

"The dragon draws everyone's eye. It's his best work. Some say there's another one hidden in more intimate spots —*oof.*"

My elbow connects with his stomach. He folds forward slightly and wraps his arms around me. His low laugh resonates in my chest, unbothered.

We reach the cliffside. There's a staircase chiseled out of the rock. On either side are metal poles, and ropes going down in a sort of railing. The steps curve and go down the edge of the cliff, below where Nyx stands.

The waves here don't seem so brutal. Maybe it's the direction, or the elevation, but the water doesn't slam against the cliff face. It just gently rushes up and greets it, then pulls away. The *shush* noise is comforting.

Wolfe goes ahead of me, and he holds his hand out. I take it, grateful for the assistance, and pick my way toward him. The rock steps are shallow, at a slant, and I have the sensation of being a hair's breadth away from slipping off.

I can't imagine climbing up this dripping wet.

"How cold is the water?" I ask him to distract myself from where we stand.

He shrugs. "Probably not too bad. It takes forever to warm up in the summer, but right now it's at its warmest. Just a few steps more. Come on."

We reach where the steps turn from heading out to sea to lying against the cliff face. One side is sheer rock going up to the top, and the other is a straight drop down into the water. The ropes only continue on the rock side, bolted into the wall. The steps themselves are only a foot wide, maybe less.

"Damn." I can see Nyx's face from here, if I lean back. She gives us a thumbs-up, then disappears.

"Ready?" Wolfe asks.

I nod. I like this secondhand adrenaline. It warms me up, and I stand taller when the little group cheers.

Nyx flies over the edge, pushing off at the last second and leaping into the air. She tucks into a ball and flips, then straightens out and plunges feetfirst into the water twenty feet below us.

"Holy crap." I bounce on my toes. It was over so fast, but I could watch a hundred more people do that.

I find Nyx in the water, and she waves up to someone. Saint, on the cliff edge, waves back. A second later, he runs and jumps.

He crashes into the water—a far cry from Nyx's graceful landing—and emerges a few feet away from her. He grabs her and kisses her.

My heart skips, and I wish I had my camera. It seems like a picture-perfect moment. I let the envy wash over me. Both at the courage and the fact that she seems genuinely happy. In this moment, anyway.

They break away with huge grins and swim for the stairs.

Wolfe's lips touch my ear. "Want to try?"

My eyes bug out. "Not on your life."

"I hope you'd think differently if my life was on the line." He bites the shell of my ear.

Heat that has nothing to do with adrenaline bursts through me and goes straight between my legs.

He withdraws. "Okay. Stay here, then."

I clutch the rope. He's *jumping*? He scrambles back to the top, and I lower myself to sit on the step. Saint and Nyx are making their way up carefully. Well, Saint is careful. Nyx doesn't even use the rope. She just walks up like she does this all the time.

"Wolfe decided to take a turn?" She reaches me first.

I hold out my hand and high-five her. "That was awesome. And, yeah, I think so."

"Hope he brought a towel in that fancy car of Jace's." Saint laughs and moves past her. "I'll get ours."

"Thanks, baby." She watches Saint's ass as he finishes climbing, then sighs. "Listen, I don't think I'll have long before Wolfe catches us."

I raise my eyebrows. "Oh?"

"They're good guys. On the inside." She watches me carefully. "Don't feel like you have to pick one."

I frown. "Pick one?"

"I read romance novels." She lifts her chin. "And some of them get quite creative in their dynamic."

"Are you suggesting I create my own little harem?" I shake my head. "That's crazy."

"It's better than picking and breaking their hearts."

I grunt. In truth, I've been loathing the idea of picking between Apollo and Wolfe. The orgasms they gave me together... it was impressive. Intense. But a relationship? With both of them?

And Jace, a voice in my head chimes in.

Fucking hell.

Wolfe lets out a howl, and chills break out all down my spine. It's the same howl they made when hunting me four months ago—and here it is again. But I don't have any time to panic. It's overridden when Wolfe jumps.

I cover my mouth. I can't breathe when he's in the air.

And then he hits the water in a perfect dive, a wave swallowing any trace of him.

We wait, my chest getting tighter and tighter by the second.

He doesn't come up.

CHAPTER 20

Nyx's expression goes from amused to concerned. I barely glance at her, scrambling down the rock stairs. I make it all the way to the water. I'm about to leap in when Wolfe emerges two feet in front of me.

He shakes his head, water droplets flying everywhere, then his gaze locks on mine.

I fall back against the rock and suppress the urge to hit him. My chest loosens, allowing me to take in a breath.

He lifts himself out of the water easily and crouches in front of me. "Kora? What's wrong?"

Fuck suppressing urges.

"You're an asshole." I shove him.

He falls backwards into the water, arms pinwheeling. It's actually a little comical, and his resulting expression is thunderous—then understanding.

He smirks and climbs out of the ocean again, this time not giving me the chance to push him away. He wraps his wet arms around me and swings me up.

I squeal and automatically hold on to his shoulders. We're chest-to-chest, and I squeeze my eyes shut when he rises back to full height. It takes me a moment to reopen my eyes and believe that he's not going to pitch me into the water. But I don't let go of him. We just stay in our tight embrace, my toes barely on the wet rock step.

"You were worried." It seems to delight him.

Jesus, these men. They're going to kill me one of these days.

I dig my nails into his skin. "Shut up."

"I won't." He grips my ass, urging me to wrap my legs around him. "Want to get wet?"

I lock my ankles and wriggle even closer. I face out toward the water, and he faces our climb. Now, it's easier to tell that there's an outcropping of rocks in the distance that breaks the waves before they reach this spot. Still, there are still waves. And one rolls over his ankles now, hitting the wall and spraying my legs.

"I'm already wet." It isn't a total lie... the way our chests are pressed together, the water has soaked through my shirt. My jeans aren't faring much better. And, well, my mind may also be in the gutter.

It's definitely in the gutter.

His laugh vibrates his chest. He ascends, never letting go of me. He makes it seem easy. He's fearless.

"Nice show," Nyx calls when we reach the top.

His hold on me tightens, and I can feel his debate. Whether or not to put me down.

I wish we were back at the mansion, because the impulse to strip and feel him inside me is almost too much to bear. My emotions are a roller coaster I can't control. Up and down. I can actually *sense* my emotions fraying, and I have no idea how to stop it.

"We're going," Wolfe announces suddenly.

Saint follows us to the car and tosses two towels on the hood. "We had a volunteer give those up."

Wolfe hums. "I forgot what it's like hanging out with normal people."

His friend laughs. "Normal? They're my crowd."

And who is that?

Wolfe glances over and appraises them, then nods. His chin briefly touches my shoulder. "All right, then. Tell whoever it was that I appreciate it."

"I'll leave you two to, um..." Saint shuffles backwards. "Whatever the fuck you're doing."

Wolfe stands in silence for a moment.

"You can put me down now," I say in his ear.

"I know I can. I just don't want to."

"The sooner you put me down, the faster we can find a quiet place..."

He cranes his neck back to look me in the eye. Mischief and lust are equal emotions swirling inside him. "Yeah?"

I nod and bite my lip.

He sets me down and hurries to dry off, then winks at me before dropping his boxers. I can't pretend I don't ogle... then realize I've seen *two* cocks in the last twenty-four hours, and they're both superior to any other I've laid eyes on. He pulls his jeans on commando, then shirt. Besides his hair, I'd never have guessed he jumped.

"What does it feel like?" I face the cliff again.

Another boy stands at the top, and I have the feeling he's working up the nerve to do it.

"It's freeing." He comes and stands beside me, also watching the boy. "Our Chosen at Olympus have to do it, too, but worse."

The Chosen—the fighters.

"Worse?"

"Higher. From the cliff *at* Olympus. It's a test of their courage—or insanity. One of the tests, anyway. So many people wanted to fight, we had to limit it somehow."

I contemplate that. Of course not everyone who wants to fight at Olympus can. I'd imagine there continues to be a great demand for it. And choosing fighters may as well be a full-time job on its own. "Is that why they're only twice a month?"

He nods. "That, and we realized we weren't enjoying it when it was every week."

"I see."

My clothes are amiss. I have a wet spot on the denim of my inner thighs and crotch, and the front of my shirt is plastered to my front. The second towel doesn't help me much, but I do lay it down on the tan leather seat to sit on.

"Apollo took you to the waterfall?" he asks suddenly.

"Yeah."

"But not the reservoir?"

"No." I meet his eyes. "Is that where you want to go?"

He looks from me to the towels, then back. "Yes."

"Okay."

So we go. I roll down the window this time, and more air buffs my skin. I let my arm dangle out, floating on the wind. It's nice. We don't speak much, but my hand is back on his thigh. I'm sure he'd be touching me if Jace's vehicle wasn't a manual.

We coast through the main street of North Falls. The boardwalk area. The beach is to our right. Traffic clogs, and at one point he stops to let a mother pushing a stroller cross the street.

He runs his finger over my wrist. "You stopped hiding it."

I nod. "I was afraid that it would be... I don't know. I

think I was just afraid. Of looking at it. Of it being seen. But I'm only going to accept it if I *do* look at it."

He traces my wrist again, the little bump of bone pressing against skin.

Goosebumps break out up my arms.

"Do you fight?" The question just comes out.

"Not at Olympus. I don't like the vulnerability."

I turn to appraise him. He has a strong profile. Good nose, square jaw. His lips quirk under my scrutiny. And then his words replay in my mind.

"Vulnerability. Can you explain that?"

It's fighting, after all. Jace didn't seem so vulnerable when he was on the platform.

"I grew up in the Hell Hounds." He frowns. "Which is more of a motorcycle gang than anything else. If you see their crew riding, it's best to just pull over and let them pass. But anyway—my father is their leader. They establish their ranks by fighting."

I shake my head slowly, not quite understanding.

"If I wanted respect, I was taught at a young age that I had to fight for it." He shifts, then rests his hand on mine for a moment. He seems to take comfort by the fact that I'm not flinching away. "Fighting for me, back then, was about surviving."

"Ah." The understanding dawns.

It isn't pleasure.

It was his *life*.

"That's why you chose Ares," I guess. "Because fighting was his life's purpose. *War* was."

He nods. His throat bobs with his swallow. "Right. I'll fight if I need to—and I'll win because I have to. But for the show of it? No."

"And yet, you founded Olympus."

He cracks a grin, the somberness fading. "Flower, everyone needs a little bloodlust in their life. We started Olympus, but it's the people who return time and again that make it thrive. We're not alone in our needs, however scared of them some of us are."

I shiver, feeling the edge to his words. How *scared* of the violence I am—how much I'm repulsed by it, and the dark needs we don't voice. The ones that live in the shadows.

This is the underworld of Sterling Falls.

I shouldn't have expected different.

WE SEE THE RESERVOIR.

And then we leave as fast as we arrived.

There's a Sterling Falls Academy field trip here today, and teenagers are *everywhere*. The last thing we need is someone spotting Wolfe and I, so he gives a slight shake of his head and turns us back for home.

We stop and get ice cream, and we eat it carefully before piling back in Jace's convertible. Our phones have been too quiet, but he doesn't comment on it. He *does* keep checking his, and my anxiety rises every time he does.

He doesn't say why. And somehow that's worse.

Even though the reservoir is in West Falls—just out of Titan territory—Wolfe doesn't take us the quickest way back. We circle the long way and come down from North Falls. We're two blocks away when Wolfe's phone rings.

He blows out a quick breath and answers it a second later. He listens to whoever called, replies with a quick affirmative, and hangs up.

And then he pulls over.

"What are you doing?"

He frowns. "Sheriff's at the house. And you need to look like you didn't hug a wet man." He hops out and pops the trunk. When he comes back, he has a gym bag in his hands. "Should've searched for this earlier."

I pinch my shirt. It's mostly dry, but my jeans are a different story. And my stomach knots. "Why is the sheriff there?"

"Because he's a prick," Wolfe mumbles. He hands me a pair of shorts, then a t-shirt. "We can tell them we were at the gym."

I snort. Jace's shirt is going to look like I'm wearing a circus tent. But I just unbuckle my seat belt and wriggle out of my jeans.

Wolfe groans and turns away.

I grin. "You okay?"

"Just trying not to get a hard-on."

I laugh and change quickly, managing to do it without flashing the neighborhood. Not that there's anyone to see—he parked beside someone's huge privacy shrubbery, and the house across the street is set far back.

"You can turn around." I knot Jace's white shirt at my hip, trying to make it seem like I'm wearing it on purpose. The shorts are baggy, but I roll the waistband down. It's the best I can do.

Wolfe eyes me. "Okay. Let's go see what Bradshaw wants."

They said he was under Titan control. "Are we safe talking to him?"

He lifts one shoulder. "Let's just assume that we aren't safe talking to anyone."

Great.

When we arrive, there's not just one police cruiser, but three. One on the street, with two of the sheriff's officers sitting inside. Then two cars in the driveway, one with their lights still flashing. They're all the way down the long drive, close to the house.

"Really?" Wolfe mutters.

He hits a button, and the garage door rumbles open. He backs the convertible inside, and the door closes us in again. We watch it go down in silence, until only the yellow-tinted light illuminates the garage. Shadows cut across us, and I slowly withdraw my hand from his leg.

My stomach hasn't stopped twisting. It's full of snakes at the moment. "Is he going to arrest me?"

Wolfe pauses. "For what?"

"Well, I don't know!" My eyes go wide. "Anything. He could make something up and take me to Kronos."

He pauses. "We won't let that happen. Come on."

He opens my car door, then extends his hand to help me out. I take it and grip my phone tightly with my other hand. He releases me just before we go inside. I follow him in, trying not to drag my feet.

I don't like police.

Never have.

I can't quite put my finger on *why*, though.

We head toward the unused front room. Another cold, impersonal staple of the house that I've largely ignored. The furniture seems uncomfortable. It was designed to have unwanted guests here, probably in the hopes that they'd leave faster.

And sure enough, Sheriff Bradshaw is perched on the edge of the couch, looking supremely miserable.

Or maybe it's just the thought of being inside this house with all of us.

He wears the same uniform, but his hat is off. He holds it on his lap. It's his hair, though, that surprises me. I should've guessed from the reddish color in his beard, but his hair is *orange*. It's cropped close on the sides, and the longer top seems to have been severely gelled into place, slicked straight back. The camaraderie I usually feel with fellow redheads is lost on him.

He's just an ass.

Jace leans against the wall, and Apollo lounges on one of the other chairs. If either one of them is bothered by this setup, neither show it. Another officer also stands a few feet behind his boss.

"Sheriff," Wolfe says.

The red-haired man rises, his gaze going straight to me. "Well, still sticking with them?"

My lips twitch. It's sort of obvious, isn't it? I'm here. Walking in with Wolfe.

"Why do the Titans want you?"

Wolfe steps in front of me. "How about you tell us what the hell you're doing here, Brad?"

Jace chuckles. "Tried that already. Seems he wanted all of us as an audience before he spills his secrets."

"And now he has one." Apollo yawns loudly. "Let's get this over with. We have shit to do."

I touch Wolfe's back. It takes him a second, but he moves over and reclaims my hand. I don't answer the sheriff, though. I'm not sure what he wants me to say. If he wants to know what the Titans see in me... he should ask them.

That probably won't happen, though.

I'm the easier target.

"Well, the purpose of our visit was to return this." He lifts my backpack from beside him and sets it on the coffee table.

I resist the urge to lunge for it.

Evidence. Stupid. They had it for too long, did God

knows what to it, and now he's just going to give it back like they did nothing wrong.

"We didn't find anything connecting you to the crime." He raises his eyebrows. "You *seem* like just an ordinary girl."

"Thank you." I pour some false bravado into my words and ignore his implication.

His eyes narrow, and his jaw tics. "Looks can be deceiving, Miss Sinclair. You'll do well to remember that around this bunch."

"Now that you've released Kora's bag, you should leave." Apollo stands and points to the door. "If you have any more questions, you should call."

"Of course, of course." Sheriff Bradshaw doesn't take his eyes off me.

Jace pushes off the wall and gestures to the door. "I'll walk you out."

Wolfe moves me back as they pass, and I'm glad for the barrier. It's just a gut feeling, because the first time we met he seemed fine. A little hostile toward the guys, but...

"Don't worry about him," Wolfe says.

"He's controlled by the Titans?"

He frowns. "Yep."

Apollo watches through the window as the Sheriff and his officer get into their cruisers. It takes them a minute to pull out onto the street, and the third follows.

Jace returns. "Funny how they show up just after we've remodeled our security system."

I stare at him. "Seriously?"

He eyes me. "Could be coincidence."

"We don't believe in those." Wolfe glares at him. "But yes —it *could* be. I don't know why he took her bag to begin with."

"Access to us." Jace goes to my bag and unzips it. He

holds it open. "I need you to tell me if anything is missing. Or added. Or messed with."

Great. No pressure. A sudden blast of nerves hits me, and my hands shake when I remove items. I need to knock it out—it isn't like a bomb is going to explode in my hands.

I pull out my notebooks. A romance novel I had been reading. A handful of pens. A calculator—wait. "Um, this isn't mine."

"You don't own a calculator?"

"I do, but the zero is worn out." I show Jace the keypad, and the perfectly intact number zero. "I've had it forever. It also should have a chip on the corner..."

He puts his finger up to his lips, and I immediately fall silent. I inspect the edges, making sure there isn't a slight little chunk of plastic missing. There is, but it's smaller than the one mine had. It's like someone tried to make a poor imitation.

Why, though?

He takes it from me and pries the back off. Not just the battery part, but the whole thing.

There are a lot of wires, but most of it seems like it would be normal for a mini computer. I have no idea. I try to gauge Jace's reaction, but he's the embodiment of stoic. He closes it back up and takes it with him out of the room.

I glance at Wolfe and Apollo, but they give me nothing, either. Wolfe types something out on his phone, his head bent. Apollo stands near the window.

We wait, but not long.

When he returns, minus the calculator, he sighs. "Let's assume this is the Titans and not the sheriff's office."

My eyebrows shoot up.

"Kronos is getting fucking bold." Apollo comes over and hugs me. "You okay?"

"I'm fine," I say into his chest. I tentatively hug him back. It takes a minute for me to relax against him, and then I don't want to let go. "He just freaks me out."

It's his authority. Who would say no to the sheriff of Sterling Falls? And if Kronos asked him to take me in, no one would question it. The guys would, but who are they against a badge?

I shudder.

"Hey. We've got you." Apollo's lips touch the top of my head.

We.

I consider what I asked of Jace the other night. That I couldn't bear to be sold, and I want them to prevent it however they can. He said he could give me that. He would give me their deaths if I need it.

"Kora."

I clutch tighter to Apollo, unwilling to face Jace.

Jace is my form of a reality check. He probably wouldn't lie to me about my odds. And the Titans using the sheriff has drastically lowered my odds of getting out of this alive. Or at the very least, unharmed.

I know it.

He knows it.

It's the elephant in the room.

"Kora," Jace repeats.

I take a deep breath, inhaling Apollo's pine-and-honey scent, and step away from him.

And when I do? Oh boy.

Jace has his stern face on. His hands plant themselves on his hips. "You do not leave this house without one of us. Don't go outside. You don't answer the door. You don't freaking peek through the blinds."

"So, a real prisoner." I can't say I'm surprised. Not with this new development.

His face softens. "Just until Kronos eases up."

I shake my head. "Yeah, right. He's never going to ease up."

So I go back upstairs as quickly as I can.

Maybe hiding will make this whole situation go away.

CHAPTER 21

APOLLO

Jace glances at me. We secure the plain black masks over our faces and meet at the front of the car. There's no talking—we've done this before. Enough that we can communicate with our body language. Usually Wolfe is with us. This time, he stayed back with Kora.

Protecting her.

There's a particular rule that keeps Wolfe out of West Falls unless the situation is dire—like when we retrieved Kora from Descend. It's a fragile little truce between the gangs. The territories. If a Titan is discovered outside of West Falls, or a Hell Hound outside of their territory in East Falls, it's game over for them.

And that usually means sending the offending member back broken and bloody.

We aren't Hell Hounds anymore. Haven't been in years. But Wolfe carries his father's last name. His looks. Even when Jace and I escaped it, Wolfe can't.

Not completely.

Tonight, there's a greater chance of being caught. This isn't a snatch and grab, or a negotiation with Kronos. Or, as he's known in other circles, Wesley Graves. The name Wesley makes him much more human than fucking *Kronos*, it's no wonder he chose the titan who represents time.

My skin burns at the thought of the hourglass brand on Kora's wrist at his hand.

And how she hid it from us all this time.

She had been wearing that cuff since the first fight night she went to Olympus, when Wolfe picked her out of the crowd. Our employees couldn't stop talking about how bold she was to wear the flower mask. Only recently, since we saw it, has she been leaving the cuff behind. No more bracelets adorn her wrist.

On one hand, I want to applaud her bravery.

On the other, every time I see her healing skin, I have to suppress the urge to drive to West Falls and put a bullet in Wesley Graves' face. It would quiet the ever-present noise in my head. If only for a moment.

I've lived with the rattling in my brain that demands violence since we were kids. That noise is what made Cerberus—Wolfe's father—accept me into his ranks. He heard my anger, tolling clear as a bell, and he harnessed it.

He weaponized me.

"Focus," Jace says through his teeth.

I grunt my affirmation and check my gun.

I'm going in quiet. There's security, but we can bypass it with relative ease. And then it's just a matter of who I find inside. We move together through the shadows, and I point to the fire escape. Wesley owns a building full of apartments. Twelve of them, if our source is right. He lives in the penthouse, but that isn't where we're going.

Descend would've been too easy—and a red herring.

There's no way he's keeping valuables there. Not when he can pack guards into this place, put them on rotating shifts, and never lose any sleep because his family is in danger.

Family.

Wesley Graves.

It's his best-kept secret.

He has a woman and two kids. A teen girl and a six-year-old boy. When we discovered them, we sat on the apartment running surveillance for two weeks and never saw them venture outside.

Just through the windows.

And the woman, she came and went. There wasn't a marriage certificate, and she didn't wear a ring when we did see her. No permanent ties—but they live here. They're cared for by *him*, and therefore something to exploit.

The fire escape is on the south side, which butts up against another apartment building. There's a ten-foot lane of grass that separates the two. The gap is too big to jump or cross roof to roof. And there are two patrolling guards that circle the property every half hour. They take turns from their position inside, so the front is never left vulnerable.

Jace and I make it to the fire escape, crouching to stay hidden. I unclip the smoke bomb from my belt. I also have a few grenades, but those are just in case we get in deep shit. Once the smoke bomb is free, I set it aside and pick the lock on the basement window.

"Two minutes," Jace calls. He strides down to the corner and peers around, then jerks back. "Make that ten seconds."

Fucking hell.

The lock pops, and the window slides open. I spare only a second to see if an alarm is triggered, and when it remains silent, I take the smoke bomb and slip through the opening.

Jace disappears back the way he came.

I close the window and stick close to the wall just as a guard walks past.

Huh. Maybe we *did* trigger some sort of silent alarm when we entered the property.

Either way. The basement is mostly storage. The cleaning service's office is here, too, but the door is shut. It's completely dark, save for the few windows that lend me some moonlight and the glow of an *exit* sign above the door to the stairs. I'm used to low light, and soon, my vision adjusts.

I hit the button for the elevator.

The chime announcing its arrival is loud, and the doors open after a few seconds. I step inside and hit the button for the top floor. I pull the pin on the smoke bomb, dropping it to the ground, and jump out before the doors close.

And then I book it for the stairs.

Going quickly, silently, isn't too difficult once you know how to place your weight. I skip steps on my way up. They don't have guards *in* the stairwells—but they are posted just outside. And once the elevator doors open on the top floor, it'll hopefully distract them.

I hunker down halfway up when the door of the floor above me bursts open.

Two guards rush out and up, not bothering to check below them.

I shake my head. They'll know soon enough that the threat is *below*, not above. But now is my opening. I pull my gun again and creep into the penultimate floor. There's a little foyer and two doors.

Two apartments.

I contemplate both, then go for the far right. The door isn't locked, so I inch in. My training kicks in, and I clear the rooms at the same time I scan for some sort of... filing cabinet. A safe, maybe.

My phone buzzes against my thigh.

I glance at the text from Jace.

I'm in position.

Well, about damn time.

"Who are you?"

I wheel around, my gun rising.

A girl stares at me, a bowl of popcorn in her hand. She seems on the younger side of *teen*. Long dark hair, huge eyes. She's got the gangly appearance of someone who recently went through a growth spurt. And don't girls generally get taller faster? It's boys who take longer to catch up.

Shit.

"Don't scream," I warn.

She rolls her eyes. "There's nothing valuable here."

"Just you."

The girl shrugs. "I'm not particularly important. What are you searching for?"

"A piece of paper."

She laughs. "Oh, well. Good luck with that."

And then she points to one of the doors down the hall. I give her a quizzical look, but she must be completely desensitized. Or a trap. She just turns around and strolls back the way she came. Popcorn in hand.

Damn it, now I want popcorn.

I crack the door, then shove it open. There's...

There's a lot of paper in here.

Stacks and stacks of it. There must be thousands of pages here, piled sloppily on the desk, on the floor. On the chair, even.

No wonder she wished me luck. They might be organized in Wesley's inane system that only makes sense to him. Chunks are separated by huge binder clips. I glance at a few, and my heart sinks.

They're all contracts. Hundreds of binding legal documents.

I have the urge to burn them all.

Shit. I close the door and send a picture to Jace.

He calls a second later. "What the fuck is that?"

"*Contracts*."

Jace swears. "Do you see Kora's?"

"No." And I'm not inclined to shuffle through all of them. We both know hers isn't here.

"I'm going to burn it," I say.

"Apollo—"

"Shut up, J. We both hate his fucking guts. This will make tonight worth the effort, at least."

"And show our hand," he growls.

Well, that, too. But I'm pretty sure Wesley Graves already knows our hand—which is why these are here. The fucker knew we'd come. I think of the girl, and how she looks nothing like how I expected. How she didn't care.

"I think we got played," I say slowly.

Through the line comes the scrape of metal. A rifle's bolt being slid into place.

"We did. You've got incoming. Get to the fire escape."

"How many?" We should invest in Bluetooth headsets or something, because I have to pinch the phone between my ear and shoulder to open the door and keep my gun in hand. The hallway is empty.

My heartbeat is picking up speed. My blood sings.

I live for this side of the life. The danger.

"Twenty. A whole fucking army just appeared."

We did not bring enough ammunition for a war. Didn't

Kora just ogle Wolfe and me the other day when we were strapping weapons on to search our own house? Then, it was worried overkill. Now, double that wouldn't be enough. Our expectations don't meet reality.

"Stairs?" I search the rest of the apartment, then return to the room. If my mental map of the building is accurate, it's on the east side. Which is fine—as long as I can get to the fire escape.

"They're in the stairwell. What—"

"Just keep that fire escape clear." I hang up and stuff my phone in my pocket, then pull the pin in one of my grenades. I rush back to the stairwell and drop it down, then sprint back inside. I toss another into the paper room. I have ten seconds, if I'm lucky. They're temperamental and sometimes hard to gauge.

My first one detonates far below, and the apartment rattles. The floor trembles.

The girl is on the couch, staring at the black screen of the television. She's immobile except for the hand that moves popcorn from the bowl to her mouth.

"You're not Wesley's kid." I haul her up. "Right?"

She laughs, her head falling back. "Nope."

I don't have time for this. "A decoy?"

"An elaborate ruse." Her head rolls forward now, and she pushes up her sleeves. There are dark track marks in the crooks of her elbows. Old scars. And an hourglass brand on her wrist. My heart hurts for her, and I know I'm going to have nightmares about this.

She's Kora. She's my sister. She's every broken girl Kronos has used to further his agenda, and I'm crushed by it.

Her eyes flutter, then focus on me. "It wasn't a bad gig,

you know? Just stay here. Act happy. We were fed. The drugs were nice..."

"We have to go."

Call me a fucking martyr.

And then I pause again. "Brother?"

"Soldier in the making." She giggles and stumbles back. She knocks into the bowl of popcorn. It goes flying, kernels everywhere.

The second grenade goes off, and the wall between that room and this one blows apart from the force. We fall backward. Rubble and smoke fill the room.

I lift my shirt up over my nose and mouth and do the same for her. She coughs and moans, scrambling away from me.

"Stop!"

She screams like a banshee.

"Let me get you out of here." I grab her arm and drag her to the window.

She fights me the whole way, tears and snot running down her face. She lands a good kick to my knee, and I almost go all the way down. My grip loosens, and she runs.

There are more shouts, much closer. The apartment door bursts open.

My time has officially run out.

CHAPTER 22

KORA

I wake up on my stomach, something heavy pressing into me. I shift, but fingers yank my hair and shove my face harder into the mattress. I automatically tense, the sleep fading fast. It takes a second for me to realize what's happening.

He's inside me.

His legs pin mine together, a pillow wedged under my hips. He grips my thigh hard and pounds into me, and his hand wanders to my ass. His touch burns, and trying to move is punished with more pain. Every thrust inside me aches.

I release a muffled cry, trying to get him off.

My eyes are squeezed shut. *I can't do this again.*

He releases my hair to clap his hand over my mouth. My tears are useless, sliding straight into the sheets. He pulls out abruptly and rolls me onto my back.

The weight disappears.

I open my eyes and stare at the dark ceiling. My heart

beats wildly, and I pat myself down quickly. The vulnerable feeling is an itch under my skin I can't get rid of, but my clothes are intact.

It was a dream.

A sick, terrible dream.

I'm fully clothed. My blankets are skewed, but that was probably from me and not the nightmare.

Still, I can't bear to be in bed one second later. The urge to *run* comes over me. I feel like I was doused in sludge. I don't want to be in my own skin anymore. I don't want to *feel.*

I yank my door open and pause in the hallway, unsure of where I'm going. I'm on the verge of hysteria. It bubbles up my throat, holding me hostage.

A soft light comes from under Wolfe's door, and I lock on it.

Before I can stop myself, I knock.

He opens it rather quickly, and his brows draw down.

I walk past him and stand in the middle of the room. There's an open book on his bed, which is still made but... rumpled. A lit-up tablet on his nightstand shows the security feeds around the house.

"Are you busy?" My voice comes out higher than usual.

"Not for you. Couldn't sleep?"

"I had a bad dream," I blurt out.

He closes us in and sits on the edge of the bed. "Do you want to talk about it?"

No. But sometimes these things fester if you don't get them out. I've been holding on to this for too long. My parents couldn't know—I refused to tell them the details. Just that Parker abused me. What parent wants to hear that their child was...

"Sometimes I would wake up and Parker would be

having sex with me." I look away. "He, um, would cover my mouth if I got upset. And he wouldn't stop."

Wolfe's gaze turns thunderous.

"It wasn't the worst thing he did, but that's what my nightmare was. And, um..." I shift, but I need to say it. "If you ever do that to me, I think I'll probably go fucking crazy."

He rises. "I won't. Kora. That's... that wasn't consensual."

"I know."

He eyes me like I *don't* know. And maybe I don't, because it's just now occurring to me that I just told Wolfe if he *raped* me, I would go crazy. Of course I would. But why the fuck would I say that to him?

Guilt hits me a second later, dumping over me. Chills rush down my spine. "I just... I just—"

"Hey, hey. It's okay. Come here."

I sit beside him on the bed. I'm not sure what I'm expecting, but he leans over and kisses my cheek. Quick, then gone.

"I won't hurt you," he says in a low voice.

He knew. Even back then, with the masks on, he *knew* me.

I climb into his lap.

His arms automatically come around me. "What are you doing?"

I press my lips to his throat, and his answering hum vibrates through his chest and into mine. "He was the last one to fuck me." Another kiss on his throat. "He took that. And I want to take it back." The *with you* part is unspoken, but I hope he can feel it. I work my way up, over his jaw, and landing on the corner of his lips. "Please, Wolfe."

He cups my cheek. "Are you sure?"

"Yes."

There's an internal war playing out in Wolfe's mind. The conflict is clear on his face, but he finally nods. "You're in control."

My chest tightens. "What if I don't want to be?"

He watches me for a moment. "What I mean is, you have the final say. You say stop, we stop. You say stay where we are, we stay where we are. Understand?"

I nod and try to rein in the butterflies. I trust him with this. I don't know if I trust him to keep me safe from Kronos. I don't know if I believe that he can stop what's coming for me. But right here? Now? I trust him not to ruin me.

He urges me to stand, then sets the book aside and flips the comforter back. I stare at it. It's different than mine. Different than Parker's. But I still feel my ex on my skin, grunting in my ear like a nightmare looping in my brain.

Wolfe comes around it, pausing just in front of me. "No bed?"

I shake my head.

"Okay," he says simply.

No questions.

He runs his hands up and down my arms, then leans in and kisses me. I'm frozen for a moment before my mind shuts off and my heart takes over. I wind my arms around his neck, pulling myself closer to him. His tongue slips into my mouth, and my thoughts go blank.

He walks us backward, until I bump the wall. His lips tear away from mine, going to my throat. He nips my skin, and I gasp. He does it again, sucking and biting at my neck, while he slips my shorts and panties past my hips. They fall to the floor. I kick them away.

I push his shirt up, and we only separate long enough for me to rip it over his head. He does the same to my shirt, and his gaze drops to my breasts. He sweeps the pad of his thumb over my hardening nipple. I sigh. He cups my breast, rolling the nipple between his fingers.

And then he bends down, taking my other one in his mouth.

I clutch at his shoulders, arcing into him. Little bolts of electricity shoot under my skin, and I'm not sure I can take any more. He releases me and kisses down the center of my chest. Over my stomach, and down lower.

"Wolfe," I whisper. "Please fuck me."

He goes to his knees in front of me and glances up. "We've talked about this, flower." He takes one of my legs and hooks it on his shoulder. "You come first."

My head falls back against the wall when his tongue swipes up my core. He plays with my clit, just brushing over it while he pays attention to everything else. I'm panting by the time his mouth finally lands on it.

He takes my hands and puts them on his head.

My eyes flutter shut, and I run my nails against his scalp. When he does something with his tongue that makes me squirm—in the best way possible—I tighten my fingers in his hair. And he stays there. And stays there. Until I'm trembling, my nerves building and building.

"I'm going to come," I pant. "Wolfe."

He hums. The slight vibration is the last thing to push me over the edge. I hold on to his face and move my hips, trying to get more as my orgasm sweeps through me. He catches me, gripping my upper thighs, before my knees give out. Well, knee. One leg is still on his shoulder.

He sets my foot down with a quick kiss, then shucks his shorts off. His cock springs free, and I swallow.

"Condom," he mutters.

I grab his hand. "If you're clean, I trust you."

He pauses. "Are you on birth control?"

"IUD." I don't bother to say Parker made me get it. That would be a mood killer.

His eyes darken. "If you're sure."

"I am. Please."

He kisses me hungrily, giving me all the emotions I thought I had lost. They flood through me. His hope and anger and lust and joy. My chest swells. But it's over too soon, and he turns me around. He takes my hands and puts them on the wall, then nudges my legs wider.

And then I feel him at my entrance.

"Ready?" He kisses my shoulder.

"Fuck me senseless," I order. And softer, "I'm ready."

He thrusts into me, and my lips part. He's *big*. I knew that from ogling him... but still. It's one thing to see it and another to feel him inside me. My back arches, and he groans in my ear.

"You feel perfect. Too fucking perfect." He pulls out slightly, then back in. Deeper.

"God," I choke out.

"I'll allow that."

I push against him, moving to meet his excruciatingly slow thrusts. He's going to kill me like this, but then I notice the slight tremor in his muscles. The pain he's taking to go inch by inch.

I twist my upper body back to kiss him. Our open mouths crash together. I suck on his tongue, and his hips jerk harder. My moan mixes with his, and his restraint breaks.

He pounds into me, so hard I might just shatter. My hands on the wall are the only things keeping me from face-planting.

His hands slide up and down my front. He pinches my nipple with one hand, and his other goes to my clit. The stimulation is almost too much, and we stop kissing. Our mouths are still touching, sliding against each other with every move, but we're just sharing space.

And I come apart in his hands. On his cock.

I face forward again, my head bowed as I climax. It crashes through me, stronger than the first, and I clench around him.

"Fuck," he growls. He moves faster, harder, and then stills all the way inside me.

His cock pulses, and his forehead hits my shoulder until his body relaxes.

Holy shit.

He pulls out and spins me around so I'm facing him. There's worry and amazement in his expression. "Kora?"

I smile up at him, tired and buzzing. "That was fantastic."

"Can I please have you in my bed, now?" He nuzzles my cheek.

This... this surprises me, too. I try not to let it show, but I can't remember the last time someone wanted me to stick around after they blew their load. Even now, his cum seeps out of my cunt.

"I need to use the bathroom," I whisper.

He eyes me, then nods. "But you're coming back."

"Yeah." Mainly because the idea of going back to my bed alone seems terrible. Not with Wolfe looking at me like he wants to do that again.

I hurriedly brush my teeth—again—and pee, then cross the hall back into Wolfe's room. He's in bed, his black boxer briefs back on. He has an arm behind his head, and in the other the book.

I watch him from the doorway until he glances up at me.

"Get your ass over here, flower." He tosses the book on

the floor.

I grin and close the door, then climb in with him. He immediately reels me closer. He stretches to turn off the light, and we face each other on our sides.

"Do you want to talk about it?" It's a repeat of his earlier question.

An open invitation to talk about Parker, I guess.

"No." I snuggle closer. He's still shirtless, and I am, too. All I put on were my panties. The skin-to-skin contact warms me from the inside. "But thank you."

"Anytime, flower." He sounds on the verge of sleep. "I hope he got what he deserved."

I moved in with Parker after I graduated high school. It wasn't supposed to be a long-term thing. My parents were taking a trip, and they didn't want me to stay alone. I had the job, was trying to save up for college, and their vacation was to celebrate a milestone anniversary. Twenty-five years. Who wants to take their adopted daughter on what was essentially going to be a second honeymoon?

They were going to be gone for a month.

Things with Parker were already rocky. I walked on eggshells around him. Living with him just made everything worse. He started off charming, and I didn't see through my eagerness for affection when things changed.

I finally realized enough was enough. He pushed me just a little too far. Did a little too much damage. So I broke it off… but it wasn't enough. I still saw him. So I left. I gave up my home because I couldn't face Parker.

"He didn't," I whisper. It's easier to admit in the dark.

Parker is why I don't trust my judgment.

"He will," Wolfe answers.

Wolfe's phone ringing wakes us. He's flat on his back, and I'm curled into him. Our legs are tangled. I don't remember quite how we got in this position, but his arm is around my back, and it tightens when he becomes more alert.

Like he knows I'm going to try and withdraw.

He stretches and reaches for it. I catch Jace's name on his screen before he accepts the call.

"What happened?" Wolfe asks immediately.

Jace's voice is low. I can't hear the words, just the baritone timbre.

Wolfe sits up straighter and turns on the lamp. He hops out of bed and finds his shirt, keeping the phone against his ear.

I stay where I am, terror freezing me solid. Jace and Apollo went out on some sort of errand. That's what they called it—an *errand*. Most errands that happen in the middle of the night aren't the good sort. I know that, and I didn't ask. What can I say? I didn't want to know.

But now, I can feel it. Something bad happened.

"Kora."

Wolfe's voice snaps me out of my panic.

"Get dressed."

He's already putting on his jeans.

"Are they okay?" I force myself out of bed to hunt for my forgotten clothes. They're gone. I can't find them. I stare at the floor, because clothes can't just disappear.

His hands land on my shoulders, and I jerk.

"Go get fresh clothes, babe." He looks worried and sounds soft.

The two don't make sense.

And he didn't answer my question.

But the underlying urgency has me moving faster, so I rush across the hall into my room and find jeans, socks, boots. A bra. *God*, a bra. I was having a panic attack freaking shirtless. I throw on a sweatshirt, then yank my phone off the charger.

Wolfe meets me in the hall. His hand on the small of my back propels me downstairs, straight to the garage.

"Are they okay?" I ask again.

We get into a black Jeep, and it rumbles to life under us.

He glances at me. "This car is bulletproof. Reinforced steel body. It's military-grade stuff. Jace got it for emergencies."

I swallow. He didn't answer the question. *Again*. He peels out, and I cast a glance backward. The garage door shuts, and the gate slides closed. We fly down the street. I find the door handle and squeeze it, worry and fear warring for the primary emotion.

"Wolfe, please tell me."

His grip tightens. "Pretty sure it was a trap."

"*What* was a trap?"

"They were trying to steal the contract."

My jaw drops. "The one Kronos made me sign?"

"We thought we were being clever. Jace and Apollo were blindsided."

"But Jace called you." I sit up straighter and will him to drive faster. "Jace called you, so Apollo—?"

"Injured." He glances at me. "Jace didn't make it sound so bad."

"Then why—"

"Kora, please. Just stop. He didn't tell me everything."

I nod. He got to stay home with me while his friends ran off to play... thief. And it didn't work. My concern has to be only a tenth of what Wolfe is feeling right now.

We rocket past Sterling Falls University. The streets are

silent, and it helps our speed. The green clock on the dash tells me it's four o'clock in the morning.

The sun will be rising soon.

Wolfe tosses me his phone. "Read that."

My hand is shaking almost too badly for me to make out the words. "It's Jace. He sent an address."

I tell him what it is, and he slams his hand on the steering wheel.

I jump.

"It's West Falls," Wolfe grits out. "If I'm seen there, I'll be shot on sight. Or worse."

Well, that's not good.

"Normally, I wouldn't give a fuck. But if I'm shot, who's going to stop them from taking you?" He shakes his head and presses the gas harder. The engine whines, then we shoot forward. "Open the glove box."

Now's not the time for hesitation, so I practically dive for it.

There's a little handgun there, three magazines beside it.

"Have you handled a gun before?"

Apollo asked me the same thing—and my answer was *not really*. But I opt to go for the more truthful answer this time.

I swallow. "Um, a few times. Yeah."

"Load it. Show me."

I insert the magazine and pull the slide back. The top cartridge loads into the gun, and I show him.

He glances at me and nods. "Okay, good. This one doesn't have a safety, so don't touch that trigger unless you want to shoot someone."

"You're... you want me to hold on to it?"

"Yes. Just don't shoot Jace or Apollo. Or me."

"I'm just going to try not to shoot anyone." I keep my

hand on it, my index finger safely away from the trigger. Accidentally setting it off could be really bad.

His lips quirk, but he doesn't refute that. And I don't bother to tell him that my only experience shooting was at a seminar at the community college. We did a week on gun safety and handling, and we also got to practice. But my aim was terrible.

The instructors all said I was tensing in anticipation of the kickback. How could I not? At that point, I was already dealing with Parker's temper tantrums. Flinching and tensing was becoming second nature.

There's a noticeable difference when we enter Titan territory.

It isn't that it looks different, really. Just the feel. This side of town has a hostile energy to it—or maybe that's just because we're outsiders. We automatically slow to a more acceptable speed. There are people on the street here, too, even at this hour. Not a ton, but enough that I have a hard time focusing on anything other than straight in front of me.

A car turns onto the street ahead of us, coming our way.

Wolfe swears and makes a quick turn onto a side street, then pulls over in front of a house. He kills the lights.

I crane around and watch the car follow onto this street. Its headlights bounce over our Jeep, and Wolfe tenses. He moves quickly, grabbing the back of my neck and guiding me toward him. His lips touch mine just as the car passes.

Someone from that vehicle stares in at us. I catch it out of the corner of my eye. But they make a disgusted face, and it keeps moving. It inches down the road.

Wolfe sits back, touching my lower lip. "Patrol."

My eyes widen.

"They're hunting for Apollo and Jace."

"Why?"

He shakes his head. "I would've left you at home if I could've, Kora. But I don't trust that, either."

I reach over and touch his arm. "I know. It's okay."

"It isn't. But we'll deal with that when we get home."

"Uh-huh." I narrow my eyes, but he clams up. Truth is, I don't trust being alone in the house, either. And the guys are growing on me.

We crawl through Titan territory, avoiding oncoming vehicles. We stay in the downtown area. Tall apartment buildings stand close together amidst houses and businesses. There's one on the block ahead that is all lit up, and it's crawling with Titans.

"What the hell happened in there?" I lean forward, but I can't see more than the front side of the building that the headlights illuminate. Their cars block the road. "They're not still in there, are they?"

"No. They're close, though."

He takes a turn, and two blocks later, we pull into small parking garage. The first two levels are packed with cars. They all have stickers that say *West Falls Resident* on them. We're going to stick out like a sore thumb if we have to leave the Jeep here—or if a Titan decides to patrol it.

Wolfe takes us up to the third level and backs the Jeep in between two other vehicles. It's more sparse up here, but Wolfe doesn't seem bothered. He hops out, drawing his weapon.

Since he didn't tell me to stay, I follow.

I'm afraid to make any sort of noise. We both carefully shut our doors, and then the lights flash as the locks engage. I keep the gun in my grip. We take the stairs down to the ground level, and Wolfe halts me in the shadows. A truck passes, and I can see two men in the cab. Once it's rounded a corner, Wolfe offers his free hand.

I switch the gun to my left and take it, and we hurry across the street, down a narrow alley between two houses. It continues down to the next parallel street, but we don't make it that far. He stops at a gate in the fence and slowly opens it.

We enter an overgrown backyard, tall grass brushing my ankles. Wolfe goes ahead of me and cuts a path to the dark house. It faces the parallel street, not the one we came from. There's a wooden porch with a covered grill on it. A round glass table with some dirty plastic chairs. The steps sag under our weight. The sliding glass door has blinds blocking our view in, and Wolfe taps on the glass three times. He holds up his hand, telling me to wait where I am.

I stop on the stairs.

All sorts of terrible scenarios come to mind. Like the fact that that Apollo is probably hurt, or worse. And we need to somehow make it back to the parking garage undetected, then out of West Falls. The patrols are searching for them.

This is a suicide mission.

The glass door slides open, and Jace emerges.

His gaze cuts from Wolfe straight to me, and my stomach flips.

"Get in." Jace's voice is low.

I scurry over and move past him, but he grips my upper arm.

"Whatever you do, just keep calm and quiet. Okay?"

I nod once and tug free. Wolfe and him hang back. I make my way through the small, outdated kitchen and set the gun down on the counter. My footsteps are absorbed on a thick carpet when I reach the hallway. There isn't much light in here, but I fumble my way into the front room.

There's an unmoving shape on the couch, and the stench of blood.

CHAPTER 23

I cover my nose and mouth.

Is he dead?

And then he inhales. The noise is sudden and awful, like he wasn't breathing before I came in. My heart lurches. I force myself to take a wooden step forward, although my fear isn't that he's dead—it's that he's living in agony.

"Hey."

I jump at Apollo's rasping voice.

"Hey, yourself." My eyes are adjusting to the darkness. His white shirt is ruined, but I can't tell if it's blood or something else. It's lifted, and there's a stark white bandage around his abdomen.

"Nothing to worry about," he whispers. "What are you doing here?"

I kneel next to him and take his hand. Of course he's trying to minimize it for me, when it's clear he's been injured. I can't speak for a moment, eyeing the bandage and his shirt. Up close, I can tell it *is* blood.

"Wolfe didn't want to leave me alone at the house." I squeeze his hand.

"Smart."

"He's in the other room with Jace. What happened?"

He struggles to sit up and leans against the cushions. His face is a mask of pain just from that movement, and he takes a few ragged breaths before he can speak. "We were played. Kronos spun a lie for us, and we didn't see the deception."

"You tried to get the contract?"

He coughs. The cough turns into a fit of them, and he hunches over. "Goddamn, that hurts. We tried, Kora. I'm so sorry."

"And how...?"

He laughs. "It turned into a shit show pretty fast."

"And he left a trail of bodies." Jace hands Apollo a cup of water with a straw in it. "Kronos will want to retaliate."

I look up at him. "This is my fault."

Apollo immediately makes a noise of disagreement.

Jace just holds my gaze for a moment, then turns and leaves the room. I watch him go, and my heart leaps into my throat. I don't know how I'm supposed to navigate this. The rug has been whipped out from under my feet, but I don't know where I'm going to land.

"Hey." Apollo touches my cheek, turning me back toward him. "It's *not* your fault. At all. We all make choices, and we all live with them."

We automatically go still when another vehicle's headlights swing through the curtains of the front window. There are voices, too, yelling at residents to open their doors.

It's Titan territory. Their word is law.

I peek out the window and watch as lights flicker on in the homes around us. People open their doors.

It's just a matter of time before they end up at this one.

"Whose house is this?"

Apollo frowns and stands. He keeps a hand on his side,

and his expression is pained. "A friend's parents' house. They left a few years ago, so we use it when we need a place in West Falls."

Which can't be too often... right?

"We need to move." Jace returns, taking my arm and guiding me away from the window. "You're with me."

"Me?" I squeak. "But Apollo—"

"Is going with Wolfe." He scowls down at me. "I don't have time to argue with you."

My gaze finds Wolfe, who has stuck to the kitchen. He takes my hand and wraps my fingers around the gun. He nods, and it could be meant to be encouraging. But all I feel is a bundle of nerves writhing under my skin. Jace and I are leaving Wolfe—who, by his own admission, would be *shot* if found by the Titans—and *injured Apollo* on their own.

But before I can do anything, protest, or ask why, Jace has me hurtling out the back door and across the grass.

He keeps a tight grip on my arm, just above my elbow. We stick to the fence going down the alley, staying hidden in the shadows. He stops us just before it ends. I strain to hear anything.

I peer back the way we came. Flashlights bob at the alley's entrance.

I tug at my arm, getting Jace's attention, and point.

He doesn't react, but he releases me. I switch my gun back to my right hand. My palms are slick with sweat. The Titans pound on another door, and I can't tell if it's the one Wolfe and Apollo are in or a neighbor's.

Jace takes the gun from me and tucks it in the waistband of my pants. He pulls my sweatshirt down over it. Then he does the same with his and offers his hand.

"Act normal."

I scoff. "Seriously?"

But I take his hand anyway, because I'd rather have that as a lifeline than nothing at all. We step onto the sidewalk, glance both ways, and cross the street. He keeps our pace intentionally even. Not in a hurry.

There's no one on this street—not yet. But they're working their way in this direction.

"You think this is new for anyone in West Falls? The Titans have conditioned them for it. Our act is for anyone watching, not just the gang members banging on doors," Jace says under his breath. "The Titans will be asking if they see anything unusual. And since most people were sleeping when you arrived, they might've missed you and Wolfe. But now they'll just see a couple walking toward their cars for an early work shift."

It... it does make sense.

But my neck pricks with awareness, and I fight the urge to turn around.

"Is Apollo going to be okay?" I whisper.

He nods and squeezes my hand. "Of course. We've all taken a few bullets before. It wasn't as bad as it could've been."

That doesn't make me feel better. He was *shot*.

He holds open the door to the parking garage. We climb up to the third level, and I'm breathing heavily by the time we get there. I need to work out.

There's a lot of things on the *I need to* list. Work out, learn how to actually shoot, to fight. Go home. That last one probably won't happen.

The Jeep's lights blink, and Jace grins. I can practically hear him silently thanking Wolfe in his head for the armored vehicle—or maybe he just really likes the Jeep.

I don't know.

I climb in and take the gun out, keeping it on my lap

again. He pulls out of the parking space at a much more docile speed than Wolfe would've.

He gestures to the firearm. "If you want it easier to grab, at least put it in your hoodie pocket. So if we're stopped..."

"Do you think they'll recognize me?"

"They might be too focused on looking for two men. And they only got a look at Apollo, although they probably suspect I'm the second one."

Great.

We pull onto the street and head farther west, taking detours to avoid the Titans out on the street and the cops in front of the big, burning apartment building. The cops are new, probably arriving shortly after we saw it.

I don't question our route—I'm sure Jace has a plan in play. That's my hope, anyway.

Sure enough, the houses get bigger. More spread out. Nothing compared to North Falls, but it's clear there's a little more money in this area. We turn south after that, and his speed increases once we hit the industrial district.

Here, there are a lot of people out. It's almost five by now, and the sky is lightening. I suppress my yawn. Warehouses are bustling. There's a fish market near us, judging by the sudden smell. Trucks are being loaded, workers arriving to their shifts.

I relax a little.

We're out of Titan territory.

Jace turns onto the main road that'll take us to Sterling Falls University. We'll take it past the campus, then angle northeast, to where the mansion is.

"Thank you for trying," I say quietly. "It was a nice..."

"Please don't say it was a nice try." He grimaces. "It was a fucking waste of resources."

And now Apollo is injured.

"Well, I appreciate—"

Bright headlights come out of nowhere.

Then the squeal of tires.

Jace jerks the wheel, but it's too late.

I turn my head. The oncoming semi truck's grill fills my window. Its lights sear my eyes. I barely have a chance to brace before it smashes into the back half of the Jeep. The impact is too much for our vehicle, no matter how tricked out it is, and we skid sideways.

I scream, but the noise is lost in the screech of metal on metal.

We're airborne for a second, then upside down.

I cover my head. My seat belt locks and keeps me from hitting the ceiling. The ground rises to meet my window. I squeeze my eyes shut and brace for the hit, holding on to anything I can find.

My head bounces off something, and my vision goes white.

I don't know if I lose consciousness, but I come back into full awareness with a blast of pain to my head. I struggle against my seat belt. My stomach rolls as the white spots flicker in my periphery.

"Jace?"

We must've kept rolling, because my seat belt is the only thing that keeps me from falling into him. My chest aches, a deep bruise in the making where the straps dig into my skin.

I raise my arms, fighting gravity, and brace one on the dash. Some of the pressure on my chest eases. I touch my temple, and my fingers come away slick with blood. There's a rushing noise in my ears, and I try to figure out how badly I'm injured. The blood is all I can focus on for a moment.

My head kills. The pain slams behind my eyes.

I take a shaky breath.

And then my attention drops to Jace. He's motionless below me, lying against the cracked driver's-side window. Grass presses up on the other side of the glass. He's so fucking still, for a moment I can only stare at him. There's bits of broken glass around him, in his hair. His eyes are shut.

Dread slides like mud through my veins.

He's not moving.

"Jace," I repeat. My voice is hoarse. "Jace, wake up."

I release my hold on the dash and reach for him, gasping at the renewed pain across my ribs. My fingertips graze his sleeve, but I can't reach any more than that. Can't get a good grasp on him.

I tug at my seat belt, then hit the button to release it. Nothing happens. I press it again, but it's jammed. *I'm stuck.* I yank at it. My breath comes in short spurts, and time has slowed down. The Jeep's battery is still on, and I squint at the green glow of the clock on the dash.

My hands tremble in front of me, and I squeeze my eyes shut. This is just a dream. A terrible nightmare. But when I open my eyes again, I'm in the exact same position.

Frustrated tears burn the backs of my eyes, and I reach for him again. "Wake up."

I can't tell if he's dead or unconscious. There's blood on the glass below him. I blink hard, trying to focus. The puddle of blood spreads. *He's bleeding a lot.*

The clock hasn't moved. We seem to be frozen in this moment. My stomach churns, and I touch my face again. My skin is ice, but my cheeks burn. A cold sweat breaks out across my back, and a violent shiver racks through me.

"Please be alive," I whisper to him.

"Here," someone yells outside the car.

There's a thunk, and then a groaning noise.

My door is ripped open, and a man appears above me.

"There you are." He kneels in the opening with a knife in his hand.

I cringe, but he only reaches down and slices my seat belt away. He grabs my hoodie before I can fall into Jace. His fist bunches the fabric at my throat, and he one-handedly hauls me out of the Jeep. I stare at him, trying to comprehend what's happening. He might be in his thirties. Tan skin. He wears black gear and a logoless black ball cap on his head. There's a gun at his hip, and another empty sheath for the long blade in his hand.

He puts it away and grips me properly, hands on my sides, and passes me to someone else on the ground. More hands grab me, and I exhale sharply when my feet touch the ground. I stumble to the side and catch myself on the tire.

They don't seem like firefighters—the sort who would be involved in a rescue like this. But there are a lot of them on the scene already. *The scene*. The wind shifts, blowing smoke from the Jeep's hood over us. I cough, and the man pulls me away.

The world spins, and I squeeze my eyes shut.

He pats me down roughly, and his hand's still on my stomach. "Look what we have here?" He removes the gun and tucks it in his pocket. "Finders keepers?"

Oh god.

Not an accident. The headlights coming out of nowhere. The sick crunch of the semi truck's grill into the body of the Jeep.

My stomach churns. I push at his hands and swing around, trying to get a better idea of *where*. The dizziness hits me next, and I blink rapidly to try and clear my vision. To stop the ground from slanting under me.

We're between the industrial district and downtown. There's a field on either side of the road that acts as a clear separation between the two. Squat warehouses on one side, and taller, leaner buildings on the other.

The huge truck that hit us idles on the road, looking no worse for the wear. And the Jeep is mutilated. The man drags me across the field, back to the road, and broken glass crunches under our shoes.

We're leaving him. I twist around just as the man who pulled me out hops down empty-handed. The Jeep is mutilated. The back half is completely crushed, and the gray smoke billows out of the hood.

I tear at the hands holding me, but my movements are sloppy.

"Jace!" I scream. I need to get back there. Where there's smoke, there's fire.

The guy grabs at me, easily regaining control. "Hey, quit it."

And my mind... just... shuts down. My gaze drops to my shoes and sticks there.

"How do we know she's the right one?" A second male voice.

Someone yanks my wrist away from my body. They shove my sleeve down, revealing the brand. "This. Plus, they don't fuck with any girls. Just this one."

They. Apollo, Jace, Wolfe.

"Kill him." A cold voice. "If he isn't already dead."

I want to scream, but it only echoes in my head. The noise seems to ricochet until I can't hear anything else.

Two men head toward the Jeep, where the smoke is taking over the sky. One climbs up, using the undercarriage to leverage himself.

I twist my wrist and break free again, stumbling after them. I only make it two steps.

They catch me again, stopping me from charging back to get Jace. One lifts me off my feet and turns, heading for the truck. I kick out. Behind the truck are two more SUVs waiting. Another man in black leather climbs up to the back of the semi-truck and opens the door. It rolls up, revealing an empty container.

My disillusioned bubble *pops*, and sound rushes into me. I open my mouth and scream as loud as I can, begging for help. It's useless—there's no one on the street who shouldn't be. Just the men who are actively kidnapping me.

I kick, but I can't seem to get my limbs to connect.

I can't get in the truck. If I do, I'll be gone before anyone can figure it out. I give in to the feral instinct. My movements get sharper, harder, and finally my elbow hits.

The person holding me yells and drops me, and then something cracks against my spine. My legs buckle, and my knees slam into the ground. I barely manage to catch myself on my forearms before my head hits the pavement, too. The impact clacks my teeth together.

The gun. *The gun.* If only I hadn't taken it out of my waistband.

They still would've found it.

Another one captures my wrists. He torques my arm up behind my back, and pain explodes into my shoulder. I fold with the pain, until my cheek touches the ground. The rough asphalt scratches my skin. The cold seeps in.

"She's a feisty one." Something presses into the small of my back, keeping me in place.

It doesn't matter—I'm not going anywhere with my shoulder about to pop out of its socket. I whimper, but it's lost in the laugher that answers him.

I don't know how long he keeps me there, with what I imagine is his knee on my spine, before he relents and pulls me up. Bits of gravel stick to my face. He keeps me ahead of him, and I choke back my nausea when I see where we're headed.

He lifts me into the truck, and more hands grasp my arms. My feet leave the ground. I don't have the energy to kick out or fight—until a gunshot goes off outside the truck.

Jace.

Before I can react, a hand wraps around my nose and mouth.

My air supply vanishes. The lack of oxygen renews my struggle, but I can't break their grip.

I'm going to die.

Jace is dead.

And Apollo might be, too.

Wolfe will be next, if they didn't already find him.

Black spots take over, and my struggling gets clumsier. My hands slide off the wrist. I'm lowered to the floor.

"That's it," my captor says. His face swims over mine, dark eyes beating into me. His hatred is palpable. A black mask covers his whole face, the tight fabric painted with a leering skull. Not quite like Hades—more jarring.

He still has hold of my nose and mouth. I shake my head violently, willing myself to stay conscious. My lungs burn, and tears leak down into my hair.

The mask. *Death*. It's fitting to go out like this.

CHAPTER 24

WOLFE

A fist pounds on the front door.

I hoist Apollo up, ignoring his grunt of pain. His eyes flutter.

"Stay with me, asshole. I'm not carrying you the whole way out of here." I adjust my grip and check to make sure he's still conscious. "Heavy motherfucker."

"I heard that." He keeps one hand on his side, and he stumbles with me.

"Good." I smile through my nerves.

This isn't the first time one of us has been shot, but it isn't ideal timing. Or placement.

We go out the back door, and Apollo motions to the floorboards of the porch.

"You want to hide under the porch?"

He shrugs.

"You're out of your damn mind." I help him down the stairs. "I don't suppose the Titans know Nyx's parents are long gone. What do you think? Want to gamble on it?"

"Fuck off."

I change my grip, taking more weight, and we move quickly to the gate. I leave him against the fence and peek into the alley.

Two men are coming toward us. And any gunshots will draw more attention.

I shove my weapon back in its holster and pull my knife instead. The trusted blade hasn't let me down, and I send a quick prayer up to the god I pretend to be.

Part of me doesn't believe they exist. But another part knows Olympus has magic in its veins. It isn't just our illusion that guides it. It's everything. The atmosphere, the people. The grandeur. We took it and made it something new, but Olympus wouldn't be *Olympus* without the building.

"What are you doing?" Apollo asks, his voice pitched low.

I roll my eyes. "What I have to."

We need to get out of here in one piece. So I step out into the alley and wait.

It doesn't take long for them to notice me. One is familiar. A fighter at Olympus, I'd guess. Not one of the better ones. I'm pretty sure he fought the college kid the first night I met Kora. We know who they are before they step foot inside Olympus... but it's dark. So who the fuck knows.

"What do we have here?" the fighter crows. He nudges his buddy. "A dog in Titan territory."

"That's a punishable offense," the other says.

I raise my arms. "You want me? Come and take me."

My knife catches their eye, and they exchange a glance.

Here's the thing: searching is exhausting. That initial adrenaline gives them wings at first. Every Titan wants to be the one to find Apollo and Jace, but there are a whole lot of spaces to check. A whole section of the city. And after their tenth house, or twentieth, the annoyance will begin to burn. It creeps up, until they'll just want to *hit* something.

And I just gave them a silent invitation to do it the bloody way.

They seem to agree, because their guns don't come out. The unknown one charges forward.

The dance ends quicker than it began. He gets a few swings in, but then the tip of my blade catches his throat. He stumbles back into his friend, his hands clamped around his neck. Blood runs through his fingers.

"You're going to pay for that," the fighter growls.

I shrug.

He's smarter about it. He tries to sweep my legs out from under me. Constantly shifts. It's taking too long. I stow my knife and grin at him. The smile is what throws him off.

When he next comes at me, I catch his arm in my hands and twist, slamming it down to meet my rising knee. The sickly *crunch* of bone is audible through his gasps.

I use his pain to reel him in. My blade is suddenly back in my hand, like a natural extension, and I plunge it into his neck.

I rip it forward, slicing through his windpipe and arteries.

He's dead in seconds.

"All clear." I rap my knuckles on the gate.

I've got a fair amount of blood on me—Apollo's, these two Titans'—and my friend's lips quirk when he limps into the alley.

"What?"

He laughs. "So subtle. Fucking help me."

I shake my head and grab his arm again, putting it around my shoulders. We step over the bodies. If Apollo wasn't injured, I'm sure he would've been happy to help me with the Titans. He has a way with a knife that's unrivaled—even by me. He makes it look like art.

Ahead, a car slows to a halt at the mouth of the alley.

Apollo tenses, but I keep towing him forward.

"It's fine, you big baby." I snicker. "It's Nyx."

"Fuck you," he groans. "You brought her into this?"

"Who did you want us to call? Tem?"

He lets out a pained noise that I ignore. He's the idiot who got shot, so he can pay for a little bit of agony along the way.

The car doors audibly unlock when we get close, and I open the back door. I shove Apollo inside, narrowly avoiding smashing his head on the top, and then slide in after him. My friend inches to the opposite side.

"Sorry, Nyx." I close us in.

She cranes around. "You good?"

"Me?" I chuckle. "Yeah, I'm fine."

"You're covered in blood."

I shrug. "Yeah."

"And you?" Her eyes narrow on Apollo.

"Can you question us on the drive? We need to get home. Jace and Kora got a head start." I lean forward. "We appreciate it, though. And your questions. And the fact that you care."

Only a bit sarcastic. I *do* appreciate that she cares. I don't want her asking things she has no right to know, though. That will only lead to trouble for her down the road.

She shakes her head, facing forward and pulling out onto the street. Her back windows are tinted dark enough that we don't have too much to worry about. She still avoids a majority of the angry mob hunting for us, though. And we drive slowly past the police and fire trucks parked in front of the apartment building.

There's a crater missing from one side.

"What the fuck did you do?" She leans forward, trying to see better.

"Great question. A few grenades. A smoke bomb or two. Um... went through a good amount of ammunition." Apollo is fading. His eyes flutter shut, and his body relaxes.

That's not good.

I scoot over and pry his hand away from his side, then swear.

"What is it?" Nyx tries to look back, but I glare at her.

"Get us to the hospital. Right now."

"COME ON, BUDDY." I have most of Apollo's weight on me, half-carrying him like I earlier threatened *not* to do, and we shuffle sideways into the local hospital's emergency department.

They get their fair share of gang violence—usually from the scum who don't warrant the use of the private doctors. The staff knows not to ask too many questions. It's how they survive. It's how we survive, too.

Apollo's bandage is soaked through, and blood pulses over our fingers. It splatters on the linoleum, leaving a trail in our wake. He keeps going in and out, so I hold his hand over the wound. He's lost a lot of blood.

A nurse at the desk looks up, and her face goes pale.

She hits a button that calls an alert, then rushes for a wheelchair.

Soon after that, they're pushing Apollo through the doors. She tries to stop me from following her, but I show her the gun in my waistband. I don't point it at her—I'm not a complete heathen—but she backs away like I tossed her a loaded grenade.

I hurry after Apollo. They transfer him to a stretcher, and someone *else* stops me. I let out a frustrated huff, but the guy stands firm.

"We're taking him to surgery. You cannot be there for that."

"Fine," I snap. I flex my fingers and ignore the urge to reach for my gun. "How long will it take?"

He lifts a shoulder. "Depends on what we find, and how much damage there is. We'll work fast, but I'm not going to guarantee you a time."

Great.

He directs me to a waiting room. After a few minutes of pacing, however, I go to the nurses' station and leave them my number. On second thought, I call his sister, too. Tem is a force to be reckoned with, especially when it comes to her brother.

I don't give her the detail she wants. I can't.

One thing Apollo was very clear on: Artemis stays *out* of this life.

She screams at me over the phone, until I pull it back from my ear and stare at the floor. Do I feel guilty? Fuck yes. I was having sex with Kora while they were on a mission. I should've been there. When the phone goes quiet, I put it back to my ear and apologize.

I can't remember the last time I said those words to someone other than Kora.

Tem stops blaming me and says she'll come soon. Except, I can't be here. I'm already halfway gone by the time I hang up with her.

Fucking Apollo.

At least Kora is safe with Jace. I hold on to that thought as I jog back outside.

The look in her eye when she realized we were separating guts me again. But if she saw me kill those Titans, what would she think?

Her ex controlled her with violence. She might not have completely spelled it out, but it's clear to see from the flinchiness, from her fear. From the scars that have almost completely faded from her skin. Her body remembers, and so does her mind.

So what would me killing two Titans have done to her?

Outside, Nyx is long gone. There can be a lot of questions surrounding a gunshot victim, and I didn't want anyone talking to her. Not tonight, and not ever.

We protect our own.

I dial Jace's number, but it goes straight to voicemail. He might've lost it escaping from the Titans. So I call Kora instead. Her phone rings and rings, and her chipper voice finally says, "You've reached Kora! I'm not here right now..."

I growl and hang up without leaving a message. What a time for them to not answer their phones. Instead, I walk through the parking lot until I find an older car. It's pretty easy to pop the lock. Once I'm in, I bend over and touch the wires. It purrs like a kitten.

My phone rings, and I fumble for it. It isn't the nurse. It isn't Kora or Jace, either.

"Dad?" I can't recall the last time my father and I had a conversation over the phone. I'd just assumed he had lost—or deleted—my number. When he needs something, he usually talks to Jace. Then again, Jace's phone is going to voicemail. So, I guess that's the reason for the call. Business. Still, the caution in my voice shines through. "Did you need something?"

"Where are you?"

"I'm at the hospital. Leaving the hospital." I clear my throat. "Again, did you need—"

"Your vehicle is on the news." His voice is clipped.

My brow furrows. "What?"

"Your Jeep. The armored one you were always so fond of. It's on the news."

Fucking hell. "I'm not in front of a television, Dad. Can you be any more specific?"

He sighs. The exasperation is familiar. "It looks like it was smashed up pretty badly. It rolled into the fields in South Falls."

"What?" My Jeep is *smashed up*? I pull my phone away from my face and stare at the screen. Nothing from Jace since he called hours ago. Nothing from Kora. "How the hell did it roll?"

"Looks like it was hit," he says evenly.

Frustration floods my system, and I grip my phone hard. "I need to call you back."

"They've got it surrounded," he adds. "The sheriff's department. They found—"

"I'll call you back." I hang up on him and dial Jace's cell.

It goes to voicemail again.

I call Kora. Again.

This time, hers doesn't ring. "You've reached Kora! I'm not—"

I hang up.

I haven't had a panic attack since I was a kid, suffering from frequent bouts after my mother left us. Dad instilled into us that *panic* is for weak, pathetic underlings—not leaders.

But it's visceral as it claws up my throat, and I work to swallow for a few long seconds. I can't seem to get enough air in my lungs. I press my hand to my chest and screw my eyes shut. White flashes burst behind my eyelids.

I'm losing it.

I force my breaths to slow. In and out. My lungs scream, but I keep my eyes shut, hands gripping the steering wheel, and keep breathing to counts. It only takes a minute or two for the pain in my chest to ease, and I open my eyes.

Okay.

I'm back under control.

And then I unlock my phone and try them again.

Jace.

Then Kora.

I call my father back, and he doesn't answer.

Fuck.

As a last resort, I call Saint. He's not someone I would usually call—he stays on the legal side of our operation, whereas Nyx can be a little in the gray area—but he answers before the phone's even fully rung.

"Are you okay?" he immediately asks.

"I—yes, I'm fine. What the fuck is going on?"

"There's a news chopper circling your Jeep in South Falls. The police aren't saying anything, but the news is reporting that the DEA is on scene." He pauses. "It doesn't look good, man. I don't know if whoever was driving was injured, or—"

"Stop." Why the hell would the Drug Enforcement Agency be at a car accident scene? And an even better question—what the *fuck* happened to Jace and Kora?

"You need help on this?"

Do I need help? I need a fucking lifeline.

But I can't bring him into this without knowing what *this* even is. A move from the Hell Hounds? An attack from the Titans? Or maybe someone who just wanted to see us fall.

"Not yet. But stay by the phone. And... thanks." I wince. *Thanks, Wolfe? Really?*

He clears his throat. "I'm here if you need me."

I hang up and toss my phone into the passenger seat. This car is clean, so I guess there's a bright side. Only a few crumpled straw wrappers in the empty cup holder, and a folded receipt on the seat.

I sit for a moment, then pull out of the hospital parking lot. I'm going numb as I drive, on autopilot straight to Olympus.

The police, bless their idiot little hearts, haven't connected us to it. So if they're hunting for us, thinking that they can bring us in on a bogus arrest warrant for planted drugs, there's a chance it can act as a safe house.

I park in front of the main doors and jump out, sprinting inside. It's always had its own sort of presence, like how I imagine a pantheon felt in ancient Greece. The careful, reverent way people must've acted—and the bold things they would do to gain a god's favor.

We didn't even have to change much to suit our needs. Most of the hallways are traps. Besides the training rooms, which lead into the main fighting area, there are vanishing hallways and staircases. Things that appear one moment then close off the next, unless you know how to reopen them. It's to keep our guests out and show us who's trying to peek behind the veil of our operation.

They're dealt with separately.

I love every inch of the huge space.

I go into Hades' room, straight to the far back wall. I pull out one of the books, and a door in the bookcase cracks open. I step inside our weapons room and stock up.

This could very well be war, after all.

My phone rings.

Saint.

"They took her," he says without preamble.

My chest tightens. "How do you know?"

"Because a countdown to the auction just went live on the dark web." He lets out a breath. "She doesn't look so good."

An auction—that answers the *who*. The Titans. Kronos.

Anger surges through me. "Send it to me."

"Done. We're trying to see if we can track it, but this shit is almost impossible. And we know the Titans have at least one tech-savvy person who could mask something like this."

"Thanks." I hang up and click on my messages. The link Saint sent is a weird one, but I trust him enough to click it. My phone goes blank, then suddenly reloads with a video. It's a dash cam of an SUV following the Jeep, keeping its distance. The Jeep suddenly lights up from the side.

I grit my teeth as a semi-truck smashes into my vehicle. It flips it, but the truck keeps coming. It turns at the last second, avoiding going off the road, too. The Jeep rolls. It takes seconds, but it plays again in slow motion. It rolls into the field and comes to a rest on its side. From this view, I can only see the undercarriage of the Jeep off the road and the truck idling off to the side.

My screen blacks out again, and it seems like time has jumped. Men move in formation toward the Jeep, guns drawn. One man, all in black, climbs up and uses a tool to pry the door off. He reaches in and lifts Kora out.

He hands her off, and they pat her down. Even from here, I can see the blood on her head. Someone finds the gun in her sweatshirt pocket and tucks it in the small of their back.

I cover my mouth and try to keep breathing. She puts up a hell of a fight against all of them. Even though there's no audio, I can *feel* her scream. Her gaze stays off camera, to where the Jeep must be.

She's screaming for Jace.

She breaks loose for a split second, but they kick her down. She falls to her knees. My teeth clench hard when someone comes up behind her and grabs her wrist. They yank it back and up, until she folds with the pain. She goes down hard, and the sick fuck shoves his knee in her back. I can't see her face from this angle—just the spread of her dark-red hair on the pavement.

I'm going to be sick.

The fury rattles my bones, demanding escape. Demanding me to let my demons take over and exact my revenge.

They keep her like that for a handful of seconds, then get her up and maneuver her into the back of the truck.

Then the camera jerks and points to the sky.

The video cuts out again, replaced with a digital timer ticking down.

Five days.

I watch it again, absorbing every detail. I breathe through my nausea. After Kora is pulled out, they don't show the Jeep again. Jace never makes an appearance.

They shouldn't have been vulnerable like that. They shouldn't have even fucking *been* there.

I stalk through the room, to the boxing bag hanging from a chain, and slam my fist into it. I pummel the shit out of it, over and over until I'm a sweating mess. I need to funnel my anger into something more productive, but my mind is splintered.

This was planned to take Kora.

Kronos knew that we'd eventually hit that apartment to

destroy the contract. He set the trap perfectly for us, and we walked right into it.

I yell. My knuckles split. The pain is welcome, though, as the video plays on repeat in my mind. The way they dragged her away from the Jeep. It was silent, but that doesn't stop me from imagining her agony.

But where the *fuck* is Jace?

CHAPTER 25

KORA

The room they keep me in is small and dark. There's one window, but it's been painted white. There's a metal cage over it, too. When the sun rises, the glow from that window is the only thing that gives me any light.

I've been here for five days.

Kronos checked on me the first day. He pinched my chin and turned my head this way and that, hissing through his teeth at the marks on my neck and the scratches on my cheek. If I wasn't so afraid, I might've made a comment about lacking virginity. Because in the back of my mind, I know that's the sort of thing these sick fucks like.

He pressed his thumb into the cut on my head, too.

A short while later, someone came in and cleaned me up. They stitched my head and bandaged it, all without a word. I was given two over-the-counter painkillers, which did a great job of barely dulling the throbbing for a few hours.

But I haven't seen anyone since. The door has a little slot

on the bottom that locks from the outside, and twice a day a tray is slid through.

I have a toilet in the room, and a tiny metal sink.

It reminds me of prison cells for solitary confinement. And then I have to wonder if I'm going to go insane from it. How long can a person go without speaking to another?

But today... Today is already different.

Morning came, but breakfast did not.

I don't have to wait long for footsteps to approach and halt outside my door.

I feel funny. Like I'm not altogether here.

Part of me is somewhere else. My muscles don't ache anymore, and tears don't fill my eyes when I think about what happened to us. Jace is gone, and I can't even cry for him.

He was supposed to figure out a way to stop this.

And I keep imagining them bursting in with their guns blazing, mowing down all the Titans who had a hand in this. But that's hard to do if they're dead.

I open my eyes—I don't know when they closed—and I can hear the echo of the gunshot in the car. A scream gets stuck in my throat, but I keep it down. Barely. I've been in this twilight state for too long. My skin crawls.

The deadbolt scrapes back, and the door swings inward.

A man stands in the hall, a young woman in front of him. She has long blonde hair, and her dress is black with daisies on it. She could be my age, maybe a little younger, and seems too innocent to be facing me.

"You going to cooperate?"

I jerk at the man's words, but my tongue won't work. My mouth seems full of cotton. My head rises and lowers in some form of a nod, and that seems good enough for him. He has a tray of food in his hand, and I take a step forward.

"Come with me." The girl has an ethereal vibe. Like she could float away, too.

So I follow her, and I know this is how fairies lured their human prey into the forests. By being too much. The hallway is bright, and I raise my hand to block my eyes. I stumble along behind her down a short, narrow hallway. The floor is concrete, and the walls are plain drywall. The concrete is cold under my bare feet, and I wrap my arms around myself.

New construction—or at least, unfinished construction.

Or renovation.

I giggle to myself. There are too many options—I shouldn't have tried to guess. It could be any number of reasons why the walls wouldn't be finished.

"Shut it." The man uses the tray to jab my back.

I fall silent.

She leads me into a room that has a real bathroom attached. I spot the shower through the open door. The man puts the tray on the dresser, then backs away from us. Another lock grinds, shutting the girl and I in.

"Are you okay?" I have to ask. It comes out scratchy, though, because I haven't used my voice in five days. And I have to ask because I'm certainly not, which means she might be in danger, too.

She nods once and points to the bathroom. "Shower. Wash your hair. And the rest of you."

Today... today feels big. And not in a good way.

I close the door, but she opens it again. She gives me an apologetic look, and I carefully nod. I strip, setting my clothes on the toilet, and turn the water on as hot as it'll go. I don't bother checking myself out in the mirror. A quick glance shows me that the skin around the stitches has bruised a mottled deep purple and yellow. The rest of me is fine, to an extent. I'm in limbo between seeming healthy—minus my face—and sick.

The lack of food and exercise is one thing, but a few weeks of living with the guys had done wonders before that. I'm back to square one.

Once I'm clean and dry, I emerge to find an outfit laid out on a chair. The girl leans against the wall, eyes fastened on the painted window. She has makeup spread across the dresser.

The food is gone.

My stomach clenches, and I stare at the empty tray. "Why did you do that?"

She just shakes her head. "Get dressed. And then I need to make you seem..."

"Sellable?"

She winces. But it's true.

That's what today is. Auction day.

They gave me white panties and a white shift dress. I slide it over my head and sigh. The straps are tiny. The top doesn't do much to cover my chest. I adjust it, but there isn't much to be done.

She motions for me to take the chair, and I close my eyes while she does... whatever she plans on doing. A bit of foundation, concealer for under my eyes. Mascara. She taps a tinted gloss on my lips. She brushes out my hair and pins it so it covers the stitches on my temple.

If Jace was alive, he would've gotten me out of this by now. Apollo was injured when we left him and Wolfe in Titan territory.

What if Kronos captured them, too?

My heart gives a painful thump, and I try to rein in the sudden blast of grief. My lips tremble before I press them together.

"Please don't cry." She ducks down until we're face-to-face. "If you ruin this makeup, they'll take it out on me. So please, just pull yourself together for a while. You can break again when you're alone."

I sniff. Her eyes are wide. Full of fear. That floating sensation has disappeared, replaced with the surety of my reality.

I just want to survive.

So I nod and swipe under my nose. Clear my throat.

She nods, too, and then goes back to her job.

I'm left barefoot when she finishes, but there aren't shoes for me to put on. No sandals, or the boots I wore when they took me.

She knocks on the door. The man unlocks it and steps back, tipping his head. I stride out. The pain in my head is returning a little at a time, and every step I take grounds me more in reality. I follow a snaking hallway into a large, open room.

It's brighter still in here. It has potential to be a venue space, with high ceilings and white shiplap walls. A few chandeliers are mounted above our heads. There's a camera set up on a tripod, facing a shallow white platform with a white canvas erected behind it. It looks like a photographer's setup.

Kronos stands off to the side, talking with a man in a charcoal-gray suit.

I jolt.

Sheriff Bradshaw.

He's out of uniform, of course, but the red hair and beard are as much of a giveaway as my hair is.

My arrival catches their attention. Kronos strides toward me, leaving the sheriff behind. He stops a few feet away and grins at me. Today, he's in a suit, as well. He rocks on his heels, his hands finding their pockets.

"Excellent. Tell your wife she did an impressive job."

The man behind me grunts his acknowledgement, and my heart stops. She's his *wife*? Definitely not by choice. He's... scary-looking. She didn't exactly seem thrilled to be here, either.

"You're in the business of marrying people off?" I press my lips together. I shouldn't have spoken at all—shouldn't have drawn more attention to myself. But... what's the point? I have their focus no matter what I do.

Kronos smirks. "Such cheek. But, yes. Shall we revisit *your* contract?"

There's something in his gaze, and it grows bigger when I wince. Apollo said it was a trap. *We were played*. His words bounce around in my head.

He pulls out a tablet and clicks a button. An electronic version of my contract loads on the screen, and he swipes through several pages before pausing. There's a highlighted portion there, and my stomach churns. I signed the document having skipped right over this part.

In the case that the Lendee is unable to pay back the loan, defaults, or misses payments, he/she agrees to submit to an indentured servitude until such time that the loan is forgiven. This servitude may be transferable at the Lender's discretion.

God. I'm going to be sick.

He knows it, too. He steps back quickly as I double over. I heave, vomiting on the floor and barely missing his shoes. When my stomach has stopped churning, I straighten and wipe my mouth with the back of my hand.

He steps around it and grabs my shoulder, yanking me closer. "I would backhand you if I didn't care about your pretty little face. The disrespect." He shoves me back, and I narrowly avoid the liquid.

Someone rushes forward—the girl who did my makeup—with a roll of paper towels. She falls to her knees in front of it.

"See, Kora? We'll train you to behave. Like this one." He snaps his fingers. "Here's how this is going to work. You're going to sit quietly. If you make a fuss or try to signal for help, I'll make sure your worst fucking nightmare purchases you. Nod if you understand."

I stare at him, seething, and slowly nod. In my head, I picture his death. I picture Jace, Wolfe, and Apollo storming in and killing every fucking one of them.

It's a delusion I hold on to tightly.

One of his Titans leads me to the platform. He's tall and lean, with light-blond hair. I purposefully meet his gaze, biting the inside of my cheek to keep from turning away. His eyes are blue, but not nearly as crystal clear as Jace's. His lip curls. Then he shoves me into a chair and goes to the camera.

A red blinking light comes on.

I brush my hair away from my face and stare down the lens.

Something flickers behind me, and Kronos calls out, "Yep, just like that."

He might be talking to me... or someone else. I wish that floating feeling would come back. But the longer I go, the clearer my head becomes.

They were drugging me.

My gaze drops to my hands, in my lap, and I struggle not to change my expression. Of course they were drugging me—if not, I *would* have gone crazy. Especially with thoughts of what happened to the guys pressing in the back of my mind.

And that's why she got rid of my food.

The lights in the room dim. I eye Kronos again, and he smiles. He's *giddy*—unsurprising. He's about to make his money back. My palms are cold and clammy.

A spotlight suddenly illuminates me, and my first instinct is to shield my eyes.

Kronos comes forward and yanks my wrists out in front of me, zip tying them together. He brushes his finger over the hourglass brand. If my stomach had anything in it, I'd be in danger of puking again. The plastic pinches into my wrists, and then he releases me. My hands fall uselessly back into my lap again.

"You, unlike some others, didn't flinch. I admire that." He pivots and hops back down off the platform and going to the other side of the camera. "If you had more to offer me, I might've been tempted to keep you. Chin up, girl. Let them see your face. And your tits."

I do lift my chin—to scowl at him.

Fucking bastard.

"Is Jace dead?"

He pauses. "Did you think he survived my man's bullet?"

My mind goes blank. There was a part of me that didn't believe he was actually gone. I should've let myself believe in that—but I opened my big mouth. The hope I was harboring for rescue shreds. The backs of my eyes burn, but I still can't cry.

Pity fills Kronos' expression. "Hold on to any fantasies of them coming to save you. Because that's all it'll be—a fantasy. There are no such things as knights in shining armor. No one is coming. Just your buyer."

I bite my tongue and focus on not letting my emotion show. My chest aches with the devastation, like someone just cut out my lungs and stomped on them. I take shallow breaths and keep my eyes on my feet.

The Titan goes to a computer set up at a table behind the camera. Cords stretch from one to the other. He types quickly, then hits a button and gives his boss a thumbs-up. I stare at him, but he ignores me and rechecks the camera.

"Live feed," Kronos tells me. "There's no audio, though, so don't bother crying for help."

The Titan angles the laptop for his boss to see, and Kronos watches over his shoulder.

"We've been hyping this up all week. Took some work, masking our location. But it's all virtual nowadays. No need to host people in this big space of mine, although we could've easily done it that way." Kronos leers. "Stand up and spin around. Nice and slow."

My body is tight, but I follow his directions. I rotate carefully. The plastic ties on my wrists dig into my skin.

"People are placing bids online already," he adds. "The dark web is a fascinating place. It draws all the people hiding their nature in public..."

My eyes go to the sheriff. He doesn't seem uncomfortable. The opposite, in fact. He lounges back and watches me through narrowed eyes.

He's on my shit list.

And Kronos.

And every fucking Titan who manhandled me to get me here.

And the stupid blond man behind the computer.

I lose track of how long I stand under the lights. Kronos stares at me, watching me sway. He occasionally barks an order at me, telling me how to move or where to turn.

"I'm curious who will come out on top," Kronos tells me at one point.

It's hard to keep my eyes open, but I blink at him. My legs tremble.

"They'll pay, and we'll send you wherever they fucking want." He grins, and his attention shifts to the sheriff. "I do love it when a plan comes together. And to think, this all started when a little scrap of a girl begged me for a loan. If she had told me then that we'd end up here, well. I don't think I would've believed her."

The sheriff scoffs. "You mean you didn't see dollar signs when you saw her?"

Kronos laughs. It scratches my ears and sends a slithering feeling down my spine, and I shudder.

"You're not so invisible now, are you?"

I recall the way he threatened my parents. Marley. The tone of his voice that dared me to leave Sterling Falls. He made this town feel like a cage—and it was Jace, Apollo, and Wolfe who opened the doors. Even as they tried to form their own walls around me.

"Okay, Brody, I'm tired of this. Loop the feed and put her away until it's over."

The camera shuts off, and the Titan with the computer leaves it there to get me off stage. He forces me forward, past his boss. His hand grips my arm. I bite my tongue to keep from saying something I'll regret.

But in my head, I add Brody's name to my list.

Kronos takes his seat at the computer, staring at the screen. "See you soon, girl."

CHAPTER 26

I used to think a lot about my future. Where I would end up and who I would know. What I would be doing.

I don't have many memories pre-adoption. The group home I was in is hazy at best. There were a lot of other kids there, packed into big rooms with bunkbeds and separated by gender. It was loud. The couple who ran the place were nice enough, doing what they could. They tried when other people didn't.

My parents and me in a courthouse, though. That's my first real memory. I gripped my new mother's hand as the judge granted the adoption, and I was officially theirs.

Happy tears all around.

Six years old, and I had a new family.

My old family faded away like they never existed. And, truthfully, they didn't. No one could tell me anything concrete. Just that my mom dropped me off on the steps of a church in Emerald Cove in the early morning. But when I try to recall her face, or the church, or the person who found me, there's nothing.

I wasn't a baby to be abandoned—I was five years old. I

could talk. I could wander. It's a miracle that I was still sitting there hours later when someone showed up for service. The clergyman who found me took me in, called a social worker, and I was delivered promptly to St. Theresa's.

A few months later, I was placed with my now-parents, and the rest is history.

But my future… that was always abstract. Even after the adoption, I couldn't figure out who I was. I went to school and got a job when I turned sixteen. Dad taught me how to drive and sat in the backseat when I took the test for my license. I collected freedoms like they could give me wings.

A high school diploma.

A license.

Community college.

Everything derailed when I met Parker. My future shrank to the day ahead, not the decade. I was charmed by him, like everyone else. And fooled by him… like everyone else. Until he showed me what was behind *his* mask.

Then… the accident that made me realize I needed to get away from him.

I won the scholarship to SFU.

More freedoms I pinned to my shoulders, and suddenly I had somewhere to go. An escape from Parker and Emerald Cove and feeling *stuck*.

Funnily enough, I went from one version of trapped to another.

My thoughts wind back to the kids I shared a space with at St. Theresa's. If they made it out and decided what to do with themselves. If, once I figure out where *I'm* going, I'll see them again.

Futures are tricky. Hard to predict, and harder still to keep on track.

And now… now, I don't have a future.

I'm so afraid that I've wasted my life. I've suffocated my own soul for some idea in my head. I should've left Sterling Falls after what happened at Olympus. I should've come clean to my parents about the money and asked them to take me home. But once Kronos got his hooks in me, I was never going to leave. Not when he threatened to find them and take my debt from them.

I've kept all these freedoms like badges of honor, but I really should've been forging them into armor.

My door unlocks, and Sheriff Bradshaw steps into my room. He glances around the small space, and then his gaze hits mine. Crashes into it, really. I'm not expecting such a vitriol response.

He comes and kneels next to my thin mattress. "You don't know what's at stake here."

I draw my legs in, wrapping my arms around them. I've been in this dress for the past few hours, and I'm so cold my bones feel frozen.

"I think I do." My throat aches, and my mouth is dry. "I'm at stake."

"You need to see the big picture."

I narrow my eyes. My stomach growls—a painful reminder of how long I've gone without food. The tray they brought sits untouched in the corner. I dumped the orange juice they gave me and filled the cup with water from the little sink. It's the only thing I've had since... I don't know.

I can't remember.

He slides a folding knife out of his pocket.

I automatically jerk back, but he tosses it onto the mattress without opening it.

"What's that for?"

He shrugs. "What do you want to do with it?"

"I can't escape. This place is a fortress." I stare at it, then pick it up. I flip it open, and it takes me another few seconds to get it to close. I set it back down beside me and try to make sense of him. Not just the visit, or his anger when he first came in, or the knife. But... all of it together. "So, the buyer?"

He inclines his chin.

"Who is it?"

"He hasn't said." The sheriff rises. "But you're better off if you leave Sterling Falls, don't you think? Get away from here before it gets worse."

With blood on my hands, or as a captive?

I lose my chance to ask him.

He walks out, and the door locks again.

I can't have that much time. Kronos didn't say how long the auction would go—I suspect he has some ulterior motive with that.

My brain has been shut off for weeks—maybe months—and now I'm *awake*.

It was Wolfe. Being with him opened the floodgates, and now my meticulous walls are broken. I can't keep everything out. The drugs Kronos fed me helped. Whatever sort of sedative... I'm guessing it was a sedative. Not a hallucinogenic. Not an upper. Not injected or smoked.

It was in my food, or maybe the drink.

I don't know.

I pick up the knife and flick it open.

Shut.

Open.

I practice until I can do it one-handed. And then I try to hide it on my body, somewhere this thin shift will cover, because I don't have another choice. I replay the crash in my mind, trying to sharpen the faces of the Titans who were there. And the ones who went toward the Jeep while I was dragged away. Which of them pulled the trigger on Jace?

Grief is strange.

I can't really feel it, but I know it's there. And one day, it might burst. But today it's an uncracked egg behind my ribcage, tender and fragile and separate.

Eventually, the sun sets. Right on cue, the door opens again, and the original Titan comes to retrieve me. The one with the wife. He zip ties my wrists again, this time behind my back.

We walk down the hallway, and my future shrinks again. Every step narrows it down further. We skip the large room, however, and go outside. I squint, and the cold air buffs my skin. Goosebumps raise on the backs of my arms. If my hands were free, I'd cover my chest. I need more layers of protection against what's coming.

He leads me to an SUV and opens the back door. Kronos sits inside, in the farther seat. The Titan prods my spine, and I step up. Climb in. My movements are robotic.

Kronos smiles at me. "Good news, girl. Your owner is local."

I shiver.

"They paid more than your debt, which was my main goal. Truth be told, we surpassed that relatively quickly. The deal is done, digital contracts signed. If you escape, I won't come after you—but they will."

I eye him.

"If you're good, I'll even tell you who it is."

Great. So I can have a name for the monster coming for me.

"I think this worked out quite well for us." He nods to the driver, and we pull away from the curb. "You don't have to leave Sterling Falls, and I don't have to pay to transport you across the country."

I can't sit back with my wrists bound behind my back. I perch awkwardly while he lounges beside me. We go down a winding, tree-lined road, and turn onto another. And another. We are deep in the forest, and it takes almost fifteen minutes to reach a paved road.

"Where are we going?" My voice is so low, I can barely hear myself.

But Kronos catches it. He glances at me, then back to the window and the racing scenery. Like I'm inconsequential. "Here's how these things work. I deliver you to a neutral third party location and leave you there. Your new owner will pick you up at their leisure. They'll get the address when the funds clear."

I lick my lips. "And when is that?"

He whips back around, renewed interest in his gaze.

"Oh, I like your fear." He leans into me and brushes my dark-red hair off my shoulder. "I forgot that about you. How delicious it is. I wonder if your new owner will let you keep this, though. It's a little childish, don't you think?" He flicks my nose ring.

I cringe away from him, but I can't get far.

His fingers tangle in my hair, yanking me closer. My scalp burns. His face is right there, his nose against my temple. And when he inhales, I do my best not to shudder. He doesn't release my hair for another moment. He watches me up close instead.

Then he lets go.

I fall back against my window, scooting away.

He laughs.

We head toward downtown. Past Descend, which seems

quiet at this time of night. Not quite late enough for patrons to want to get lost in their drinks.

"Campus?" I straighten. We're not quite at SFU, but close. Definitely in the college district. The car stops in front of a row of houses, and I'd be willing to bet students live in them.

Kronos puts his phone in his breast pocket and faces me. He frowns, his gaze dropping to my chest. "You're going to draw attention like that."

I glance down at my outfit. The dress. My bare feet. "If you wanted me in something else..."

He waves a hand. "No. Stay."

He disappears outside, the door slamming into place. I meet the driver's gaze in the rearview mirror, and he quickly looks away. I've been so raw, I'm now numb to it. I've given up on hoping that someone will save me.

Kronos returns. He opens my door and cuts the ties on my wrists, then throws clothes at me. *My* clothes. The hoodie I was wearing, the jeans. I have to shake out remnants of glass, and there's a bloodstain on the hem of my pants. I put everything on quickly, leaving the dress in place under the sweatshirt. There's no way I'm going to take that off in front of them.

I tuck it up into the sweatshirt, knotting the fabric so it doesn't hang down. I glance for my boots, but he didn't give them to me. I stay barefoot.

"Take her," Kronos orders.

He steps aside, and his lackey hauls me out. I open my mouth to scream, but something hard and cold touches my side, slipping under my hoodie.

"You know what that is," the Titan says. "I don't mind pulling the trigger. Try it."

I swallow and press my lips together. I debate fighting

them—making a run for it—but this car isn't the only one Kronos took. There's another two behind us, with Titans climbing out of the vehicles. They spread out, relaxed. Like nothing is wrong.

I memorize their faces. As many as I can see.

He leads me like that, with the gun against my ribs and a hand on my shoulder, into one of the houses. Kronos follows. We go past the stairs that lead up, down the front hall, and stop at the basement door. I resist for a split second, but my will to live wins out.

I descend.

It's not quite empty in here, although the rest of the house looked it. There are boxes against the walls, furniture shoved aside. The Titan releases me and grabs a folding metal chair. He drags it into the center of the basement.

"Sit," Kronos says.

I don't like basements. But I follow his order, because I want to know if he's going to give me a name. The buyer.

My skin crawls. He referred to them as my *owner*.

The Titan secures each wrist separately to the chair with new zip ties. I bite back a wince as the cold metal pole of the chair presses into my skin. He does my ankles, too, then steps aside. Kronos checks them, yanking at my wrists, and nods to himself. My skin is already raw, and they keep stinging after he backs away.

"You can go." Kronos jerks his head to the stairs. "Wait for me outside."

The Titan doesn't waste time abandoning us.

"Smile." Kronos raises his phone and takes a picture. He tsks and sends a message, then stows it. "You were purchased by a corporation that has been operating in Sterling Falls for the last five years."

My brow furrows. "Okay?"

"A corporation run by another corporation, which seems to only exist on paper." He scowls. "Unfortunately, they submitted a last-second bid that was much higher than expected, and my team wasn't able to block them in time."

My stomach swoops.

"We got to the bottom of it, though." Kronos' expression turns dark. "While Jace King's associates *were* successfully blocked... Cerberus James was not."

He's livid.

But the name... that name is familiar. "The Hell Hounds leader?"

If you escape, I won't come after you—but they will.

Why would they put in a bid? Wolfe wouldn't go back to them. He said as much in the diner—that his relationship with his father was absolutely shit. And he implied that his father was one scary motherfucker.

So *why?* To spite Kronos? To parade me in front of Wolfe and Apollo? But not Jace. There must have been no more strings to pull. No last-ditch efforts to get me out of this. No guns-blazing scenarios that I kept dreaming about.

The awful burning feeling behind my eyes comes back, stronger than ever.

Kronos makes a show of glancing around, that anger still radiating off him. He's contemplating something. Coming to a decision.

"I've never known hatred quite as potent as the hate I feel toward Cerberus." He stops in front of me and forces my head up, his fingers gripping my chin. "Jace, Wolfe, Apollo... they were a different ball game, and they're inconsequential now. But *him*. He doesn't understand the order of things. The Hell Hounds push and push, and I'm fucking sick of it. And they don't get to have you, too."

What happened to the guys? He's talking like they were all taken out.

I swallow down my fear. Shove it down, down, down.

He's losing control, and I wish I had the faintest idea how to help him rein it back in.

"Let me go, then. Get me out of town."

"No!" He screams in my face, spit flying. His cheeks redden. "No, no. Why do the Hell Hounds want you? What value do you bring to them?"

A tear slips down my cheek. Finally, a tear. *Now*, when I should have gone back to my indifference. But that mask shattered long ago. "I don't know. I'm no one."

"Yes, *cry*." He shakes his head and crosses the room. In the far corner are red gas cans.

No. True terror spikes through me, and I pull at the ties.

He picks up one of the cans and shakes it. The liquid sloshes inside, and my nausea returns.

"Fitting," he mutters to himself.

He dumps gasoline on the floor. Splashes it on the boxes, the furniture. "I wonder. Do you think they care enough to arrive quickly? Do you think they'll *hurry* if they know you're in danger?" He glances at me over his shoulder. "They might even rush in here to save you—or maybe not. If you take one thing with you to the grave, let it be this: you can't trust a dog."

"Please." The single word escapes with more tears.

The stench of gasoline fills my nose.

"Please? *Please* won't save you, girl." He comes closer, but he doesn't douse *me* in the accelerant. Just the walls. The boxes. The floor is concrete, but the rest of the house will go up like a matchstick. "I would love nothing more than to see all of them suffer. And what better way than to deny them of something they'd pay a million dollars for?"

Kronos lights a match and goes to the stairs. The single, small flame burns in his fingers, and the Titans' leader blows me a kiss.

Then he tosses the match.

It arcs through the air, almost extinguishing in its flight. It hits one of the boxes, and the gasoline catches instantly. In a matter of seconds, the whole line of boxes against the wall is on fire.

I jerk at the zip ties as Kronos ascends the steps. The door to the basement slams closed. My struggle intensifies, and I open my mouth in a silent yell. Fear has closed my throat. I jerk too hard, and my chair tips backward.

My head cracks into the concrete, and pain bursts through the back of my skull. The last thing I know is the heat of flames racing toward me.

TO BE CONTINUED...

Fighter (Sterling Falls, #2) is available now!

ACKNOWLEDGMENTS

I KNOW. I left you on not one, but technically three cliffhangers there, didn't I? I do hope you'll stick with Kora and the guys (and me). Their story is just getting started.

First, I have a massive thank you to give to the readers who stuck with me from previous stories. My RH adventures are just beginning, but your support means the world to me.

Second, a big hello to new readers! Thank you so much for joining me. If you want to commiserate, come join the SMassery Squad on Facebook.

To my alpha readers, Rebecca and Ari: I love you both. Jasmin, thanks for coming along with me on this insane journey!

To my beta readers: Jolie, Erica R., Erica G., Amber, Tara – you all know I value your feedback. And special thanks to my new beta readers, Brandy, Clarissa, Anelise, and Shawna. You guys rock!

And last big thank you to my team of editors, designers, and support. You all helped me bring this book to life and I couldn't be more grateful!

ALSO BY S. MASSERY

Dark Bully Romance

Fallen Royals

#1 Wicked Dreams

#2 Wicked Games

#3 Wicked Promises

#4 Vicious Desire

#5 Cruel Abandon

#6 Wild Fury

Crown Point University

Brutal Obsession

Mafia Romance

DeSantis Mafia Series

#1 Ruthless Saint

#2 Savage Prince

#3 Stolen Crown

Romantic Suspense

Broken Mercenaries Series

#1 Blood Sky

#2 Angel of Death

#3 Morning Star

ABOUT THE AUTHOR

S. Massery is a dark romance author who loves injecting a good dose of suspense into her stories. She lives in Western Massachusetts with her dog, Alice.

Before adventuring into the world of writing, she went to college in Boston and held a wide variety of jobs—including working on a dude ranch in Wyoming (a personal highlight). She has a love affair with coffee and chocolate. When S. Massery isn't writing, she can be found devouring books, playing outside with her dog, or trying to make people smile.

Join her newsletter to stay up to date on new releases: http://smassery.com/newsletter

Made in United States
Troutdale, OR
01/10/2024